BALLISTIC

PAUL LEVINE

ISBN: 978-0-9828113-6-8

CONTENTS

ILLUSTRATIONS

BOOK ONE

The Prophet, the Sergeant, and the Shrink

-1-
Are You Ready for the Apocalypse?

Times Square, New York City–September 1994

The young man who calls himself Zachariah blinks against the neon of a megawatt Manhattan night. Cocks his head and hears dueling symphonies in his brain. A thunderstorm of Wagner on the port side, a cannonade of Tchaikovsky to starboard. Schizophrenia in stereo.

Zachariah steps off the curb and pulls up the collar of his trench coat. Rain pelts him. Cleanses him, he thinks, as clueless tourists and scummy gutter rats surge by on both sides. Yokels and locals. Sinners all.

Hookers in halter tops, goosebumpy in the wet chill. Gangbangers in leather, pimp-rolling, toe-walking, trash-talking skull crackers. Corn-fed, name-tagged conventioneers, heehawing across the big city, checking out the bars, Singapore slinging watery drinks at nine bucks a throw.

Lifting his face to the rain, eyeglasses steaming, he splashes through a puddle. Stops at a kiosk filled with filthy magazines. The devil's own diaries. Creamy breasts and pouty lips. Who will save them?

Splashing through a puddle, wagging his finger at Bernie behind the counter, telling him, "All the animals come out at night."

Bernie looks at the young man through rheumy eyes. "You're telling me."

Zachariah sweeps his arm across a panorama of lustful sinners. "Some day a real rain will come and wash this scum off the street."

"How many times you seen *Taxi Driver*? 'Cause I gotta tell you, Zack, it's making you even weirder, if that's possible."

A radiant light amps Zachariah's mind, a divine glow inspired by the Truth and heavenly doses of mescaline. He reaches into his trench coat and hands Bernie a pamphlet. On the cover, a drawing of an ornate temple exploding, pillars shooting into the air like flaming spears. Zachariah levels his gaze. "Pilgrim, are you ready for the Apocalypse?"

"Hell yes." Bernie tosses the pamphlet aside. "But to tell the truth, I thought it already happened."

⁊

Outside the store, the neon flashes "Adult XXX." Inside, the pot-bellied clerk with the retro sideburns hacks up a wad of phlegm, cursing the weather and his own clogged sinuses. He empties an ashtray, counting the butts, and curses himself for his three-pack a night-shift habit. He switches channels on his seven-inch black-and-white, then looks up to see a clean-cut young man stroll into the shop, trench coat spotted with rain. Wiping raindrops from his wire-rim glasses with his tie, another accountant or salesman copping a cheap thrill.

The clerk glances at the bland, nothing face. Always check them out, watch for a thug with an attitude and a Saturday night special. Trench Coat tries to flip through "Salt and Pepper Studs," but it's stapled shut. Peeper doesn't even know the rules. He loops around a free-standing display of dildos and cockstraps and approaches the counter.

"If you're looking for the video booths, they're in the back," the clerk says.

"My visions need no video," Zachariah answers.

2

"So whadaya want, buddy?"

"Salvation for all eternity."

The clerk shrugs. "Eternity's expensive. We charge a quarter a minute for video. Fifty cents for live peeps. Ten bucks for the live sex theater."

"Sodom and Gomorrah are upon us, and you, sir, are the gatekeeper of hell."

Ah, one of those. The clerk hacks again, then spits into the trash can. For minimum wage and no health plan, why put up with this shit? "Hey, buddy, if you wanna buy...buy. If you wanna look... look. If you wanna preach, haul your ass out to the street corner."

Zachariah pulls two quarters from a pocket. "I shall buy. But, as it is written in Revelations, 'I know where you live. It is the place where Satan has his throne.'"

"You got that right, fella. I live in the Bronx."

ℰℴ

A whorish red sign with a flashing arrow points to "Live Peeps." Hallucinating now, Zachariah feels as if his feet are slogging through a wet slime, the vomit of hell. He enters a dark booth the size of a toilet stall. Latching the door, his senses hypertuned, he inhales the tang of disinfectant barely masking the ocean saltiness of semen. Through tinny speakers, he hears the Red Hot Chili Peppers urging, "Give it away now!"

He slips the quarters into a slot. A shutter slides up and light streams through a window from the miniature interior stage where a bored stripper bumps and grinds, her backside facing a booth directly across from him. She chews her gum and pastes on a smile of slutty sincerity, smacking the other guy's window with her mushy ass. Naked except for her red spiked heels, she dances across the stage toward Zachariah.

Come to me, Jezebel. The angels screech her name in his ear.

He steeples his fingers under his chin, studying her. A scar, fibrous and purple, jags across her belly. She is pale under the glare

3

of the lights. Her hair is dyed a coppery red, top and bottom. Shaved into a design down below, what is it? *A cross!* Blasphemous bitch. She will pay. They will all pay.

She wiggles and pouts. Then, boom! The music stops, and so does she. Stands there a moment, hip shot, then points to the tray in the window, waiting for her tip. He folds a pamphlet over twice and places it in the tray.

On the other side of the glass, she picks up the pamphlet and unfolds it, her eyes going hard as she read aloud in a Southern twang. "'Are you ready for the Aypo-ca-lipsee?' You think I can pay the rent with this shit?"

She looks up, ready to shame a couple of bucks out of him, but he is gone.

Zachariah climbs the stairs to the second floor. Two middle-aged men pass him on their way down, averting their eyes. *Confront your sins, heathens!*

He hands a ten-dollar bill to a burly Hispanic man with a ponytail and the tattoo of a snake wending across his knuckles, then enters the small theater. Four geezers are spread out, one to a row, hands disappearing into their laps, watching the stage where a naked punk is slipping it to a skinny woman on a soiled mattress.

The woman's bare, dirty feet are wrapped around the punk's pimply back as he listlessly pumps away. Neither makes a sound, though the mattress is wheezing, and one of the scuzzbags up front is breathing so hard, he might go into cardiac arrest.

Zachariah heads down several steps and hops onto the stage. The heavy breather in the front row huffs out a "Hey!" The couple untangles, the punk's pecker hanging forlornly at half-mast. "It ain't amateur night! Get outta here."

Zachariah turns to the audience of disgruntled whackers and lets his voice slip into the sing-song of his beloved Brother David. "Babylon, mother of prostitutes, abomination of the earth, hear the Word!"

"Aw, shut up!"

"*Chingate!*"

"What a *meshuggeneh!*"

Forgiving the fools who know not what they do. "Behold a pale horse!"

The door bursts open and Snake Knuckles hauls ass toward him.

"And his rider's name was Death!" Zachariah unbuttons his suit coat and extends his arms. Jesus on the Cross. A battery pack hangs from his belt, and packets of Semtex are taped to his waist.

Snake Knuckles leaps onto the stage but Zachariah sidesteps and calls out, "And Hell followed him!"

He pushes a switch on the battery pack...

&

At his kiosk, Bernie sees the orange flash before he hears the thunderclap. An explosion that spews glass and plaster across the street, barely missing him. Pedestrians duck and run as the shrapnel rains down, and where there had been a tawdry little porn shop, now there is a gaping crater of flame. A hot wind sucks piles of magazines from Bernie's counter, tumbling them down the street, plastering them against windshields, and inhaling them into the inferno.

And still no one has answered the question, "Are you ready for the Apocalypse?"

-2-
In the Belly of the Beast

Chugwater Mountain, Wyoming

Deep inside the missile silo, Sergeant Jack Jericho dangles at the end of a rope and pulley, a harness buckled around his waist. Above him, the sky is crystalline blue. He is a shade under six feet, broad of shoulders and shaggy of hair that has not been regulation length since basic training. He has slate-gray eyes and a nose that has been broken twice, once by a slag bucket that slipped its winch in the

5

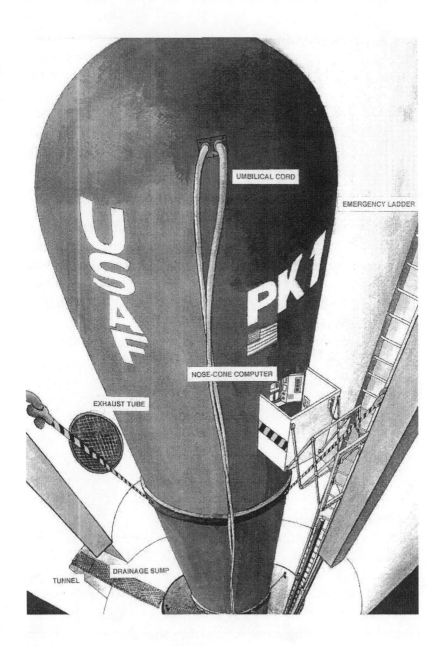

coal mine and once by a fist that found its mark.

Jericho pulls in rope, hand-over-hand. Closes his eyes and imagines himself scaling a lodgepole pine in a shaded forest. Climbing up the hard, scaly bark, grabbing a sturdy limb overhead. Catching the crisp scent of the high timberland. White aspens, Douglas firs, and a thicket of snowberry and juniper. Bluebells, too, sprouting out of the rocky soil of an upland clearing.

Mind over matter, it works for a moment. What had the doc called it? Creative visualization. *"The mind's eye can see whatever the brain wishes."*

Yeah, and a lot the brain doesn't wish. Try *not* thinking of a brick wall. Or of a mine shaft filling with water, men screaming to the Father, the Son and the Holy Ghost.

Jericho opens his eyes, reaches up and grasps the handle of the exhaust tube cover. He catches a whiff of the oily slickness of metal and hears the *thumpa* of the generators far below him in the sump. Damn. Tries to bring back the forest, tries to summon the sound of rippling water in a rocky stream. *Thumpa-thumpa.* Like the heartbeat of a leviathan.

He looks up. The bluest of skies is still there, visible only because the six-foot thick concrete cap is open. He looks down toward the drainage sump and the polished steel floor of the silo.

Jericho uses his legs to kick away from the silo wall, and the rope spins out of the pulley, giving him slack. He propels himself several yards, extends a soapy brush to a grimy spot on the wall, then begins scrubbing. Sweating now, though it's a consistent fifty-eight degrees inside Chugwater Mountain. Sweating not from the heat, but the confinement, the sense that the encircling wall is closing in.

In the belly of the beast.

He breathes heavily, wiping his forehead on the sleeve of his shirt just above the three stripes. Again, he unwillingly conjures up the mine. The creak of the timbers, the explosion, the rushing water and the darkness. Then the screams, and finally the silence. The doc knew all about the dreams. Had his own from Vietnam. He was a clinical psychologist, on retainer for the union. Wore a ring in his ear, tied his hair in a ponytail. Some of the older miners called him a pansy, until they got close enough look him in the eyes. Glacial ice. Jericho didn't want to know what those eyes had seen. He visited the doc in his office, a trailer at a job site, and asked a question.

"Will the dreams go away?"

"Scars fade but never vanish. Create your own dreams, sing your own songs."

"I can't go back in the ground. I need to get out of here, go somewhere far away."

"There is nowhere far away."

The doc had been right. Sleep came hard. Jericho bedded down with a bottle and a dreamscape of ghosts. Joined the Air Force, re-upped, and re-upped again. Now, two thousand miles from the West Virginia coal mines, he finds simple joys in the outdoors. An eagle soaring over the vast prairie, the haunting lunar landscape of a rocky basin, the startling quickness of a deer bounding through the grasslands.

Jericho finishes scrubbing the acidic residue near the exhaust tube and spins around in his harness. His job is to clean up after a test firing of the LEGG, the launch eject gas generator. Unlike other intercontinental ballistic missiles, the one with the Orwellian name of "Peacekeeper" is cold launched, propelled out of the silo by a burst of compressed gas. The solid fuel of the first stage ignites only after the missile is in the air.

Jericho drops his soapy brush into a pail built into his harness. He bristles when other airmen call him the base janitor, but even Jericho figures he is little more than the clown who follows the elephants with broom and pan. He looks up again at the brilliant sky, imagines himself in waders standing in the shallow water of a cool stream, whipping a fly toward a whirling pool where the big trout lurk. For a moment, he is out of the silo, out of the mine.

He kicks off the wall again, a little too hard, and...*clang!* He bangs into the nose cone of the missile that is suspended from cables, the Longitudinal Support Assembly in Air Force jargon.

The cables are attached to the walls of the hardened silo, and in the event of an enemy's nuclear strike above ground, the missile will sway, then steady itself, and be ready for launching. In theory. As with so much in the missile program, no one knows what really will happen in the event of thermonuclear war.

Seventy-one feet tall, a little less than eight feet in diameter, the Peacekeeper, or PK, is topped by a nose cone containing ten nuclear warheads. Each warhead is seventeen times more powerful than the bomb that leveled Hiroshima and ushered in the nuclear age. At this precise moment, the seat of Jack Jericho's olive green coveralls are polishing the nose cone. With a layer of dark rubber covering the missile's four stages, the PK is sleek, breathtaking and black as death.

Jericho winces as the metallic echo reverberates through the silo.

"Yo, Jack! You turn this place into Chernobyl, the captain's gonna be steamed."

Jericho looks up to see Sayers, a senior airman standing at the edge of the elevated gantry one hundred feet above the floor of the silo. Sayers wears camouflage green and loam battle dress and polished combat boots. Compared to Jericho, he looks like an ad for GQ, a muscular African-American all spit and polished.

"Captain's already steamed," Jericho says.

"No shit, look where he put you. Hey, if I had your detail, you know what I'd do?"

"What?"

"Kill myself," Sayers laughs.

Then he jumps.

Jericho watches a perfect swan dive off the gantry, Sayers sailing into space, his body arcing down the side of the missile toward the steel floor below. Lower, lower, a millisecond from crushing his skull, then...BOING! A bungee cord catches and springs him back up toward the gantry. He bounces twice on the cord, swinging between the missile and the wall.

"You're next, my man," Sayers cackles.

Jericho continues scrubbing the wall. "Only if you put a gun to my head."

"C'mon Jack. You need some excitement in your life."

-3-
Freudian Flim-Flam

Washington, D.C.
Warren Cabot, the Secretary of the Air Force, spears a slice of
rare tenderloin and turns to Christopher Harrington, the California
congressman with the telegenic smile and a constituency of Orange
County right wingers. Outside the windows, a light rain is falling,
peppering the calm waters of the Potomac. A shell glides by, worked
by six women wearing Georgetown University t-shirts.

"I'm not admitting weakness, Chris," the Air Force Secretary
says. "I'm recognizing the realities of the new world order. We're
dismantling more than half our missiles under START II. Blowing
up the silos and filling them with concrete."

"I didn't vote for the damn treaty," the Congressman says, as if
to clear the record.

"Fine, but it's a done deal, Chris. Question now, what's the
effect on the readiness of the remaining missile crews? That's why
Dr. Burns is with us."

Secretary Cabot gestures with a fork full of filet mignon in the
direction of Dr. Susan Burns, who gives her business smile and
nods, then slices her poached salmon. At thirty-four, having earned
a Ph.D. in psychology with a thesis on soldiers' response to stress
in warfare and an M.D. in general psychiatry, she will let the two
stags bloody each other for a while. She wears her long, dark hair
up, and today she omitted the makeup and dressed in the most
conservative of her blue suits. Still, she had turned the heads of the
brass – their medals clinking, ribbons rustling – when she entered
the Joint Chiefs Dining room.

The Congressman gives Dr. Burns a grudging nod and motions
toward the uniformed steward for a second Scotch on the rocks. "I

just don't believe in sticking pins and needles in our boys to find out if they've ever seen their mommies naked."

"Boys and *girls,*" Dr. Burns adds with a pleasant smile. "Women command launch capsules, too."

"Not if I had anything to say about it," the Congressman fires back. "No offense, Dr. Burns, but I don't put much faith in all that Freudian flim-flam."

Dr. Burns stays quiet, admiring the American eagle on the fine china, arrows in one claw, boughs of peace in the other. No use further antagonizing the man who holds the purse strings on her project to test all soldiers with access to nuclear weapons.

"For the love of mercy, Chris," the Secretary says, "why are you such a Neanderthal?"

"Once a Marine, always a Marine."

The Congressman is still a Colonel in the Reserves, but so what? Susan is acquainted with plenty of Marine officers who accept women as equals...or close to it.

"The Corps was fighting the British before the Declaration of Independence was signed," the Congressman continues. "We've made more than three hundred landings on foreign shores."

Not that the Congressman has landed on any foreign shores himself, Susan Burns knows, unless you counted congressional junkets to Hong Kong, Singapore and Bangkok. Now what's he saying?

"We didn't need women then, and we sure as hell don't need them now, except for political expediency, and you know I don't play those games."

No? What about stirring the pork barrel for a California defense contractor that makes guidance systems for missiles that are being mothballed? Susan Burns could tell from the Air Force Secretary's look that he was probably thinking the same thing.

"Our women pilots have excellent records," Secretary Cabot says. "So do the women in support units."

"If you ask me, we're just appeasing the left-wing, fem-Nazi contingent."

"Damn it, Chris! You've been in office so long, you're starting to believe your own flack. It's a new world out there, and we've got to make use of all the expertise we've got."

"Including lady shrinks, I suppose?"

"I vouch for Dr. Burns, and that ought to be good enough for you."

Susan Burns stifles a smile. The old Air Force eagle still has some arrows in his quiver. "Gentlemen," she says, "this isn't about me and it isn't about women. It's about the readiness of the missile squadrons. The enemies are monotony, boredom, and a sense of futility. Not one missileer in fifty believes he – or *she* – will ever turn the key. If the President ordered a strike, there's significant doubt the missileers would fire. They'd get the launch code and think it was a computer malfunction."

"Even if that's true," the Congressman says, "I fail to see how a shrink is going to help."

"Our preliminary studies show a marked decline in alertness and discipline. We need to construct psychological profiles of the men and women in the launch capsules, compile hard statistical data, then treat the problem."

The Congressman sips at his Scotch, then to the Secretary and waves his napkin, surrendering. "Okay, Warren. It's your call, but if *60 Minutes* comes calling about this boondoggle, I'll refer them to you."

The two men exchange smiles, and Susan Burns finally understands. It had all been a charade. The Congressman never intended to block the project. He merely wanted artillery cover if the news media likened the project to price supports for bull semen or thousand-dollar balpeen hammers. If that happened, Susan Burns could go back to treating bed-wetting teenagers in suburban Virginia. I've got a lot to learn about politics, she thinks.

A steward appears and silently slips a silver tray holding a small envelope in front of Secretary Cabot. Opening the envelope, the Secretary examines a note, his brow furrowing. "Isn't that the damndest?"

"What?" the Congressman asks.

"You remember that break-in at the Denver Armory?"

"Yeah, the Army lost some ordnance."

"Automatic weapons, ammunition and some obsolete land mines," the Secretary says, looking around, then lowering his voice. "Plus enough plastiques to make the Beirut bombing look like a fraternity prank."

"That wasn't in the reports."

"No, and neither will this. There was an explosion at a porn shop in New York last night. Traces of Semtex were found in the rubble. Based on the chemical composition, it's special Army issue."

"So why rob an armory to blow up a porn shop?" the Congressman asks.

"Excellent question," Dr. Susan Burns says, patting her lips with a napkin, "and I'll bet the answer can be found with a little Freudian flim-flam."

-4-

Hell's Half Acre

The broad plains north of Rattlesnake Hills are broken by mountains and buttes rising unexpectedly from the flat earth. Wyoming is a land of contrasts. Towering mountains of granite that boiled up from inside the earth over three billion years ago. Flat prairies of wheatgrass and junegrass. Steppes covered with sweetly pungent sagebrush, the scent carried by the strong, continuous winds. On the arid badlands, eroded boulders form exotic sculptures in demonic shapes. Not far to the south, traces of wagon wheels carved into the rocks are still visible on the old Oregon Trail.

Near the south fork of the Powder River, in an area of dry buttes and rocky gullies, is Hell's Half Acre, a canyon of eroded pink rock, forming pinnacles that could be the frozen flames of Satan himself. Three miles to the west, near a stream, is rolling ranch land. Some is fenced, and cattle graze serenely on the grasslands that are also the home to jackrabbits, cottontails and rattlesnakes. Mule deer and pronghorn antelope feed in the nearby woods.

Over a rise from the grazing cattle, farther from the stream, a man in commando fatigues uses wire cutters to snip through the bottom two strands of a barbed-wire fence. As he spreads the opening with gloved hands, eleven similarly dressed men wriggle through, belly-up, using their rifles to keep the wire from catching on their fatigues. In their wake, clouds of dust rise from the parched earth. In a moment the men are gone, and with the top wires still intact, the fence does not appear to have been breached.

The commandos flatten themselves to the ground and creep ahead through the scrubby brush, holding their M-16A2's, official U.S. Army issue, in front of them. They move slowly in what marine rifle squads call the "low crawl." The morning sun is in their faces, which are painted loam and light green to blend in with the surroundings. They wear Kevlar body armor and carry extra magazines of 5.56 mm. ammunition in pouches on their cartridge belts. Their helmets are covered in brown burlap.

As they move higher on the ridge, the brush becomes heavier, and the leader, Gabriel, a rock-jawed man of thirty with squinting blue eyes, cautiously stands and extends both arms away from his body at a forty-five degree angle. At the signal, the men get to their feet and move into wedge formations, a point man with three riflemen behind him. The two side units break away diagonally as Gabriel's middle wedge moves straight up the ridge. A dozen men in all.

Gabriel raises his right hand, and his unit stops. He reaches down, brushes some leaves away from the ground, exposing a trip wire, then leads his men around a buried land mine. At the top of the ridge, he signals again, and his men halt. Gabriel crawls to a vantage point where he can see into the hollow. Using binoculars, he scans the scrubby landscape. Four hundred meters away, halfway up the slope of the next ridge, is a bunker reinforced with sandbags, mounds of dirt, and logs. Twenty meters behind the bunker is a century-old miner's cabin of blackened logs, its walls sagging into the ground.

The target.

To get there, his men will have to work their way down the ridge, cross the dry coulee in the hollow, then work their way back up the far ridge, in direct view of the bunker.

Suicide.

Gabriel knows the lesson taught every soldier since Gettysburg: one dug-in infantry man on high ground can stop three equally armed men advancing from low ground. He signals his RTO to crawl forward and uses the radio to call the point men of the other two wedges. "We'll lay down some hellfire from here. You'll flank them. Thirty seconds."

His men take positions at the top of the ridge, stretching out into the prone firing position. Two prop their rifles on bipods. "Ten seconds," Gabriel says, then counts it down. On his command, they erupt with a blistering barrage, their weapons set on three-round bursts.

But they must have been expected, for the return fire is immediate and overwhelming. His men flatten, grinding their faces into the ground, and for a moment, their guns are stilled. Gabriel, still standing, winces. He is a man with no fear of death. "Keep it steady!" he shouts, and his men resume firing. Good men, pious men. He prays for them to succeed, to overcome their fears.

Gabriel extends his right arm straight down, then moves it horizontally in the infantryman's signal to fire faster. His men empty their magazines, clip in new ones and spray the hollow with shells, seldom hitting the bunker or its fortifications. They do, however, kill a lot of rocks.

So different here than on the firing range, Gabriel thinks ruefully, as the return fire zips over their heads. But his troops will learn. The firing slows as the men catch their breaths. Combat drains the adrenaline, exhausts the soldier who hasn't learned to pace himself. "Keep it up!" he implores them. "Fire."

At something, at anything, he wants to say. Gabriel is a

generation too young to have served in Vietnam, but he has studied its history and knows the woeful inaccuracy of the infantry with the M-16A1. In many fire fights, it took an astonishing one hundred thousand rounds to inflict a single casualty. Lack of fire discipline and malfunctions. He knows that, at this moment, his men are firing wildly, perhaps blindly. He would have liked another month of training.

Gabriel peers into the hollow and a flash of movement catches his eye in the sagebrush. His riflemen see it, too. They turn and fire, finally hitting something. He watches as the brown hide of a large animal, a deer or elk tumbles into the underbrush.

Enough. If the distraction hasn't worked already, laying down a few hundred more rounds won't help. "Unit two, go!" he shouts into the radio. To his right, four commandos work their way down the ridge, but oblique fire from the bunker stops them just short of the coulee. They take cover behind dusty rocks in the dry riverbed. Unit two's leader scans the left flank with his binoculars but cannot see any movement except for a jackrabbit that runs a zig-zag route away from the shooting.

"Unit three, where are you?" Gabriel demands. "Matthew, go now!"

"We're halfway there. Relax, brother." The voice is calm and reassuring. Halfway down the ridge, Matthew clicks off the radio as he leads his men through dense underbrush. He is tall with a thick neck and arms cabled with veins, his hands work-hardened. His men move quickly, breaking twigs, kicking over rocks, their movements masked by the blazing gunfire to their right. Speed, not stealth, is their ally now.

As they cross the coulee, the four men slide into the rectangular "echelon left" formation with Matthew at the point. They have flanked the bunker and have a clear shot up the ridge to the miner's cabin. Moving at double-time now, with rifles at port arms, they break into the clearing twenty meters from the cabin.

Just outside the cabin door, a soldier has his back to them. He is peering down toward the bunker on the far side, his hand resting on an M-9 service pistol in a holster. They storm him, the soldier turning just in time to catch sight of Matthew slashing at his chest with a fixed bayonet. The soldier instinctively leaps backward, and the blade catches in his flak jacket. Matthew pivots and swings the rifle butt in a horizontal arc, belting the soldier across the jaw and toppling him to the ground. Two other commandos stand over him with rifle muzzles pointed to his chest as Matthew and a fourth commando burst through the flimsy cabin door.

They tuck and roll and come up in the firing position. Their rifles are pointed directly at the head of a long-haired, handsome man of thirty who sits at a redwood table reading the Bible. The man, who calls himself Brother David, calmly presses the button on a stopwatch, closes his Bible and looks at Matthew with dark, piercing eyes. "Your best time, to date, my brother. Sliced a minute thirty-five off last week's maneuver." His serene smile is that of a king pleased with a loyal subject. "I believe we are ready."

Matthew takes off his helmet. His long hair is tied into a ponytail. "Perhaps two more weeks would be better."

"God waits for no man."

Matthew nods. His leader has spoken. "Thy will be done, Brother David."

The soldier from outside staggers into the cabin, his chin in his hand. Blood seeps from his mouth as he approaches Matthew. "You broke my jaw," he whimpers through swollen lips.

Brother David stands and clasps an arm around the wounded man's shoulder. "That is nothing compared to the pain you will inflict on the army of Satan."

-5-
Graveyard Shift

The sun blinks through the tree tops on a crisp Wyoming morning. Towering blue spruce and Ponderosa pines form an umbrella over the two-lane road. It is September, and the Aspens are turning gold, their round leaves fluttering, whistling their songs in the wind. A red-headed woodpecker beats out a staccato beat against a fir tree, and somewhere in the underbrush, rabbit-like pikas are squeaking their distinctive sounds.

The Air Force Jeep emerges from the forest and begins climbing through the Rattlesnake Hills. Road signs warn of moose crossings. Whitecapped mountains are visible on the horizon.

Senior Airman Sayers is at the wheel of the Jeep, Airman Reynolds next to him. Jack Jericho is sprawled across the back seat, his helmet pulled over his eyes. "Sarge asleep?" Sayers asks.

"Asleep, hungover, dead, or all of the above." Reynolds runs a hand over his crew-cut. A freckled redhead with a southern accent, he wore his hair in a pony tail before joining the Air Force, and even now, cannot believe the stubbly bristle he finds under his hand.

"Yo, Jack! You awake?" Sayers asks.

From the back seat, an unintelligible grunt.

"C'mon Jack. Get up."

"Leave me the hell alone."

Sayers jerks his thumb in Jericho's direction. "That's what two weeks on the captain's graveyard shift does to a man."

"Not to mention ten years of hard drinking," Reynolds adds.

Sayers downshifts as the grade becomes steeper. A stream runs alongside the road, clear water tumbling over rocks as old as the earth itself. Above the bank of the stream, a porcupine gnaws at the trunk of a pine tree. Across the road is a seemingly endless chain-link fence topped by razor wire. "No Trespassing" signs emblazoned with the Air Force insignia dot the fence every several hundred yards.

"Uh-oh," Sayers says, looking toward the sky and slowing down.

"What is it, Spike?" Reynolds asks.

Sayers' first name is Timothy, but with his round glasses and narrow face, his buddies back in Brooklyn thought he looked like Spike Lee. Before he joined the Air Force, Sayers sometimes cadged free drinks and impressed aspiring models and actresses by claiming he was scouting the neighborhood for a movie location. He still tries the scam occasionally while on leave, but less successfully. At a bar in Laramie, he discovered, the locals didn't know Spike Lee from Robert E. Lee.

"Buzzards dead ahead," Sayers says.

Jericho stirs and sits up, sliding back his helmet, squinting into the morning sun. He's unshaven and his eyes are puffy. He pulls a warm can of beer from a rucksack, pops the top and puts it to his lips. He gargles noisily, spits into the road, then opens the wrapper on a Twinkie and gobbles it in two bites.

"Disgusting," Reynolds says. "Breakfast is the most important meal of the day. Back home, I'd have hominy grits, black coffee and molasses bread every morning."

"Hey Reynolds," Jericho says, his voice thick from a case of the dry tongue. "If I gotta hear one more time about your momma's eggs still warm from the chicken's ass, I'm gonna puke."

Sayers laughs. "Hell, Jack. You're liable to puke, anyway."

"I was just being friendly," Reynolds says, pouting. "Besides, eggs don't come out a chicken's ass."

Jericho ignores both of them and watches half-a-dozen turkey vultures drift in slow circles overhead. A year of perimeter maintenance duty with these two, and he still marvels at the weirdness of their conversations. Within a few minutes, they start up again.

"Hey Sayers, how many folks are there in Wyoming like you?"

"You mean handsome and manly?"

"I mean black."

"Not many, man. Three thousand or so, not counting me."

"That's why there's no graffiti."

"There's no graffiti 'cause there's nothing in this hayseed heaven to put it on 'cept trees and rocks. Graffiti goes on underpasses and buildings in the projects, and if you got the balls, the po-lice station."

"Yeah, well it ain't so bad out here," Reynolds says. "Even Jericho likes it when he's sober."

Now, Sayers stops the Jeep alongside the fence, then shoots a concerned look into the backseat. "More nightmares last night, Jack?"

Jericho's grunt could be a yes, could be a no.

The buzzards are directly overhead, circling lazily in the wind currents, waiting. Now, the men see what the birds are after. A large elk with a full crown of antlers is caught in the fence, its hide bloodied from the struggle to get free.

"Never told me this Wild Kingdom shit in the recruitment office," Reynolds complains.

"All I ever heard," Sayers says, "was that wild blue yonder jive." He jams on the hand brake, and the three men get out and cautiously approach the elk.

When they are ten feet away, Sayers pulls a .45 from a side holster, but Jericho seizes his wrist. "No need for that, Spike."

Reynolds lets out a low whistle in Jericho's direction. "It lives! It talks, it walks, it brushes its teeth with Budweiser."

Jericho grabs a saw-toothed survival knife from a sheath on his leg. "You two cowboys back off. I'll handle this."

Amused, Reynolds slouches against a wooden fence post and lights a cigarette. "Here we go again. Daniel Friggin' Boone."

Three feet from the trapped elk, Jericho stops, the frightened animal watching him through eyes the size of half-dollars. "Hoo boy," Jericho coos. "You are a beauty."

Blood oozing from its wounds, the animal bucks and stomps, lifting its head until it can no longer see Jericho. With startling quickness, Jericho leaps forward, grasps its antlers, and raises his knife to the elk's neck.

"Jeez, Jack, we coulda shot him!" Sayers calls out.

But Jericho doesn't cut the animal. Instead, he swiftly slices away the fence wire, then gently pulls it from the elk's hide. He reaches into his pocket and brings out a handful of tiny red berries.

"Yo, Jack!" Sayers sounds alarmed. "That ain't Bambi."

"Mountain ash," Jericho says. "For pain and healing." He crushes the berries in his fist and lets the red syrup flow into the animal's wound. The elk stiffens but doesn't bolt, and Jericho gently strokes the tufted hide behind its ear.

"You learn that Tarzan shit back in Stinkhole, West Virginny?" Sayers asks.

"*Sinkhole*. Asshole."

The elk, which had been paralyzed with fear, seems to relax as Jericho strokes its back.

"Hey Sayers," Reynolds calls out. "You know what a West Virginian calls a deer caught in a fence?"

"What, man?"

"His first fuck."

The two airmen laugh.

"He's an elk," Jericho says.

Reynolds shrugs. "Elk, moose, Rotarian, whatever."

"Yo, Jack," Sayers says. "How come you didn't stay home and marry a coal miner's daughter?"

Jericho steps back, and the elk bounds away, heading for the woods.

"Or your sister?" Reynolds chimes in.

It happens with electric speed.

Jericho whirls, and the knife flies from his hand toward Reynolds' head. With a solid *thwomp,* it sticks in the fence post just inches above Reynolds' crew cut.

Speechless, Reynolds reaches up to feel his scalp as the knife, buried deep in the wood, vibrates like a tuning fork.

"Shit man!" Sayers yells. "You're crazier than the boys in the 'hood."

Jericho walks to the fence post and pulls out the knife. "My sister's the only family I've got left."

Then he walks away, watching the elk disappear into the woods, admiring its majesty, envying its freedom.

Sayers and Reynolds exchange baffled looks. From their hours of endless banter, they know Jericho is a loner. Until now, he had never said a word about his family or his life before the Air Force. Then the same thought occurs to each of them. They really don't know Jack Jericho at all.

-6-
Baptism of Beer

A few miles from the ranch where Brother David's warriors of God live and train is the town of Coyote Creek. A tavern, a general store, a gas station, a rod and gun shop, a few dozen weathered wooden houses. Little to do, other than the annual rodeo.

Inside the Old Wrangler Tavern, an elk's head is mounted on the knotty pine wall above a scarred mahogany bar, the antlers serving as a rack for cowboy hats, hunting caps, and even a jock strap. A bartender with a walrus mustache and an enormous stomach draws beer from a tap whose handle is the plastic form of a naked woman.

Half a dozen ranch hands and loggers stand at the bar, hands wrapped around mugs of beer. They are a scruffy, bearded lot, in soiled jeans and red plaid shirts, a few of the younger guys with bandannas on their heads instead of cowboy hats.

Above the bar, a TV is tuned to CNN where a blond female reporter stands in front of a gutted building breathlessly jabbering into a microphone. "The FBI reports no leads in the latest porn shop bombing. Tuesday's explosion in New York killed five and injured thirteen. Like the earlier blasts, no group has claimed credit for the attacks."

The bartender wipes the bar with a wet towel and shakes his head. "Why blow up a jerk-off joint?"

"A political statement," says one of the bandanna guys. "A protest."

The bartender barks a laugh. "Protesting pussy? You want a political statement, blow up the I.R.S."

The others murmur their agreement. "The I.R.S. can listen to your phone calls," says one of the grizzled men.

"Not only that," another says. "Every car manufactured after 1979 has a computer chip built in. A bureaucrat in Washington hits a switch, and your engine will stop dead."

"That why you still drive a '78 Chevy pickup, Will?" another guy says, laughing.

"Yeah, and it's why I keep my thirty-ought-six in the gun rack with five thousand rounds of ammo and provisions for six months under the barn. When the revolution comes, I'll be ready."

"Me too," the bartender says. "I got two dozen kegs of Coors in the shed out back."

Which sets the others to laughing. Will turns toward a long-haired man standing alone at the end of the bar. The man is lean and muscular and wears a blue chambray shirt and khaki pants. "What about you, fellow? You think there's going to be a second revolution?"

"A Second Coming," Brother David says. "The angel poured out his bowl on the sun, which scorched people with fire. They cursed the name of God and refused to repent."

"What the hell?"

"Revelations, chapter sixteen, verse eight. It is the Word."

Will studies the man, decides there's no use going down that road. His ex-wife was a Bible-thumper, used to drive him crazy. "Well, the Word's making me thirsty." He motions to the bartender for a refill.

No one moves to join Brother David at the end of the bar. He sips a cup of coffee and resumes watching television. On the screen, an anchorman with gray hair and a somber tone begins to speak, and the screen goes to a videotape of the President shaking hands with several men in the Rose Garden. "At the White House," the anchorman says, "the President welcomed the United Nations Nuclear Non-Proliferation Commission, which today begins a tour of U.S. missile bases scheduled to be shut down under the START II Treaty."

The bartender tosses his towel in the direction of the sink. "What bullshit! Business ain't bad enough, they gotta pull out the Air Force."

"See, I told you so!" Will puts down his freshly poured beer. "First the missiles, then our rifles. The U.N. and the Trilateral

Commission are gonna confiscate our guns and give them to the Zulus and the Zionists."

Brother David walks to a nearby table and sits, joining a younger man who nurses a bottle of beer and a woman who holds a cup of coffee, gone cold. There is an air of peacefulness, of knowing calm, about Brother David, who smiles placidly. "Hello, Billy. Rachel. May the glory of God be with you."

"Thank you for coming, Brother David," Billy says. Neatly dressed in jeans and an open-collar shirt, he is a baby-faced, twenty-four year-old with rimless glasses and pale blond hair. "I've looked to the Lord for answers, just like you said. But..." Tears form in his eyes. "There aren't any answers. Not for me, anyway. Kathy said she'd wait for me, and now she's going to marry my best friend, and..." His voice takes on a pathetic whine. "I'm stuck out here in the woods for another six months. What can I do?"

Rachel leans across the table and gathers Billy's hands in her own. In her late twenties, she wears no makeup and hides her figure under a shapeless granny dress. "Brother David understands, Billy. He loves you. He'll take care of you. And so will I."

Brother David stares hard at Billy, then squeezes his eyes shut, beads of sweat forming on his forehead. When he speaks, his voice is a whisper, "I see a quiet house. In the Midwest, I believe. There is a child, just one, a little boy, but no man there. Still, the house has the feel of a man. In the closet, there is a uniform, as if he might come back." He pauses a moment, takes several deep breaths, and continues, "There is the sense of loss. Was your father killed in the service?"

Billy's lower lip trembles. "No, but he was in the Army. He left my mother. And me. He never came back."

David's gaze seems to trace an outline around Billy. "Your auric fields are weak. There is purple and gold, and that's good, but the colors are muddy, not vibrant. You are unsure, misunderstood, still in the process of awakening, and are not appreciated for what you have to offer."

"Yes," Billy says excitedly. "Yes, it's all true, but can you help me?"

Suddenly, Brother David grabs Billy's beer bottle and slams it on the table. Foam erupts and streams down the long neck. David dips an index finger into the pool of suds that surrounds the bottle. He reaches across the table and draws the sign of the cross on Billy's forehead, then touches the tip of his finger to Billy's lips. "Drink of my blood."

Billy takes Brother David's finger into his mouth as an infant would his mother's nipple. He stares, wide-eyed at the man he considers the Savior. David rewards him with a beatific smile, then withdraws his finger. He grabs Billy's head, cupping his hands around the base of his skull. "Do you seek everlasting life?"

It isn't a question so much as a demand. Billy can't say a word, but he nods against the pressure of David's hands.

"Good, William, good. Because you, Lieutenant William Riordan of the United States Air Force. You hold the key. And only I can turn it."

-7-
Blood of our Ancestors

Two hundred fifty thousand years ago, the weather cooled, and the polar ice sheets spread southward. Mountainous ice caps flowed down over the plains, carving out canyons, depositing giant rocks in improbable geometric formations. Glaciers sliced semicircular bowls called cirques out of canyons and shaved opposite sides of ridges into narrow, jagged crests. Left behind were blue lakes, deep gorges and spectacular rock formations, at once inviting and otherworldly.

The Air Force Jeep pulls to a stop alongside a craggy wall streaked with mineral deposits. Water trickles down the rocks like rivulets of tears. It is a spot of enduring beauty in the wilderness, a place marred only by the scar of the government fence topped with razor wire that lines the road.

The three airmen – Sayers, Reynolds and Jericho – get out of the Jeep and walk toward a Native-American man in buckskin who is kneeling at the fence.

"Hello, Kenosha," Jericho says, going down onto his haunches, showing respect by neither towering over the man nor asking him to stand.

Kenosha's face is creased by the sun, his black hair pulled back into a ponytail. He could be fifty or seventy. Judging from his barrel chest and clear dark eyes, he is closer to fifty. He points to the smooth tears in the bottom strand of wire.

"Hunters?" Jericho asks.

"Hunters kill for food, not sport. Come."

Kenosha scrambles under the fence, and Jericho follows.

"Yo, Jack!" Sayers calls after him. "We're supposed to report the security breaks and keep moving. We're already behind schedule, and Captain Pukowlski will have your ass if—"

"Puke can wait."

"C'mon, Jack!" Now it's Reynolds. "We got no time to pow-wow with the last of the friggin' Mohicans."

Jack stops and turns. Silently, he draws the saw-toothed knife from its sheath and gestures toward Reynolds. Turning to Kenosha, he says, "Should I scalp him or do you want to?"

Kenosha suppresses a smile and seems to weigh the question judiciously. Then he goes into his routine. "Red hair will bring plenty wampum. And I need ornament for rear-view mirror of pickup. Maybe his balls would do."

"No. Too small."

Reynolds turns to Sayers. Disgusted. "I told you Jericho had flipped out. What do we do now?"

"We wait," Sayers tells him.

Jericho puts the knife away and follows Kenosha several yards along a path of fine, reddish-brown soil. Again, they squat on their haunches, and Kenosha points to footprints in the dirt. "Combat boots."

Jericho nods and picks up several spent cartridges. "Five-point-five-six millimeter. Military issue."

"I know. That is why I want you to see this."

They walk up a rocky slope. Neither man speaks for several minutes as Kenosha leads them higher up the incline, the rocks yielding to a grassy ridge. Below them in the hollow is a dry coulee and on the far ridge is a sandbagged bunker and an old cabin of blackened logs. They work their way down the ridge, walking through waist-high, pungent sagebrush. A rustling in the bushes, and a jackrabbit bounds away. As they slow on the flat ground of the hollow, Kenosha gestures toward the underbrush. Jericho pushes his way through tumbleweed and grama grass, and half-a-dozen vultures beat their wings and take off, cawing out angry cries. Deep in the brush is the carcass of a moose, its hide peppered with bullet holes.

"Who would do this?" Kenosha asks.

Jericho shakes his head. "I know how you must feel. Just as your ancestors did when white men slaughtered the buffalo."

"What are you talking about, Jack?"

"When the white man shoots animals for sport, he kills your brother."

"My brother went to Utah State and sells tax-free bonds in Salt Lake City."

Undeterred, Jericho goes on, "I understand your oneness with nature. The sap that flows through the trees is the blood of your veins. The earth does not belong to man. Man belongs to the earth."

"Jack, my friend, are you drunk?"

"Hell, no. I'm in touch with your spirituality."

"You sound like some bullshit special on PBS"

"But I've read all about the Indian tribes of the West," Jericho says, "your identification with nature, your pantheism."

"Sorry, Jack, but I'm a Lutheran."

"Oh."

Kenosha motions him to follow, and they begin walking up the slope of the ridge beyond the old cabin, bracing themselves on rocks for the steep climb. With a wry smile, Kenosha says, "In case you're suffering from any illusions, Jack, I've also got a satellite dish on the double wide, and I order imitation pearls from the Home Shopping Network. Every morning, I get the Chicago Tribune on the Internet, and I got a little money put away in an Individual Retirement Account, too."

"I see."

"None of us talk about that river and sky shit anymore Jack, except when someone sticks a microphone in our face. Maybe Tatanka Yotanka, who you would call Sitting Bull, talked that way. Maybe Chief Seattle really wrote that letter to the Great White Father in Washington, and maybe he didn't. 'What will happen when the secret corners of the forest are heavy with the scent of many men and the view of the ripe hills is blotted by talking wires?' If you ask me, Jack, a Hollywood screenwriter had a hand in that."

"You're a cynic, Kenosha. You're not one with the land."

At the top of the ridge, they pause. Kenosha turns to face Jericho. "Don't get me wrong. I love nature. I get a calendar every year from the Sierra Club. Fine pictures of eagles and pumas." He gestures down the slope toward the carcass of the elk. "I hate this as much as any decent man – red, white, brown or black – because I can't stand to see needless death or needless waste. Animals are creatures of beauty, and I treasure them. But no more than you do, my friend."

"I'll write a report and try to find out who did this," Jericho says, "but I can't believe that anyone in the 318th would have—"

Kenosha silences him with a wave of an arm. He points into the next valley, a lush, irrigated landscape. Strands of trees, rocky cliffs, a tumbling stream, then open fields with grazing cattle...and finally, incongruously, a semi-circle of ten ugly concrete silo caps, blemishing the land like poisonous mushrooms. "The 318th did this, did they not?"

No use denying the obvious. "Guilty as charged. What do you suppose the old chief's screenwriter would have said about our so-called Peacekeepers?"

"He would have said they rape our mother, the Earth."

"We're taking them out, filling in the holes."

"I knew it would happen. Sooner or later, either you would do it, or the earth would do it for you. In the end, my friend, the earth will prevail."

"You didn't learn that on the Home Shopping Network," Jericho says.

Kenosha locks Jericho with a level gaze. "No. Maybe a little of that tree sap still flows through my veins."

-8-
The Brass Are Coming

A battered VW Beetle with a roof placard, "Old Wrangler Tavern," grinds its gears and chugs up the incline of a road made of crushed rock. Inside, Jimmy Westoff, a pimply seventeen-year old in jeans, denim vest and cowboy boots, stomps the accelerator to the floor and talks to himself. "Fuck me, this thing's gonna die. Next time, I'll take a mule."

The car travels along a perimeter fence topped with razor wire. Jimmy laughs as he passes a rusted sign – "Rattlesnake Hills Sewage Plant - No Trespassing" – and drives through an open gate.

"Sewage plant," he says, and spits out the open window. "Air Force is full of shit, that's no lie."

Another half mile up an incline, he pulls to a stop in front of a Quonset hut with a metal roof and no markings. At the sound of his squealing brakes, two Air Security policemen wearing berets and sidearms emerge from the hut.

The first one out, an E-3 with the name tag, "Dempsey, R." slips a flask of bourbon into his back pocket. "Jeez, Jimmy, what took you so long? Those burgers are gonna be colder than Captain Puke's heart."

"Ain't my fault Uncle Sam dropped you in West Jesus," Jimmy says.

"Duty, honor, country," the second airman, Carson, says

without conviction.

"Yeah, well next time, you oughta ask for duty at a so-called sewage plant closer to town."

Dempsey counts out some bills and gives Jimmy the money. "Ain't no more next times. When they close this baby down, we got nowhere to go but back to the world."

Jimmy hands Dempsey several bags of burgers and fries and starts to make change. "Keep it," Dempsey says.

"Wow. Thanks, general. Two bucks. I'm gonna head to Las Vegas for the weekend." Jimmy gets back in the VW and coasts back down the hill before popping the clutch to fire up the puny engine.

Carrying the burgers and fries, Dempsey hops into a Jeep just inside the perimeter fence. "Man the fort," he tells Carson.

"Hey, you forgetting something?" Carson asks, tipping an imaginary bottle to his lips.

Dempsey shrugs, pulls out the flask and tosses it to his buddy. He hits the Jeep's ignition and kicks up gravel pulling away. It's less than a mile up the road to a windowless Security Building on the lower slopes of the mountain. A steel bridge with a barred door runs like an above-ground tunnel through the building and beyond it to a cone-shaped steel elevator housing cut into a rocky cliff. Several hundred feet beyond the Security Building is the silo cap, a circular pad of concrete six-feet thick and fifty feet in diameter.

The Jeep passes a small wooden barracks and a mess hall built in the shade of a strand of pine trees. A dam and a lake stocked with trout sit at the top of the mountain, and an aqueduct winds down the slope from the dam.

Inside the Security Building, half-a-dozen bored non-coms slouch at their desks shoving paper from the in-box to the out-box and maybe back again, too. Teletypes clack and security monitors scan the perimeter of the missile silo, both above and below ground. Lights show green on motion detectors, though they'll blink red if either an Iraqi Mukhabarat squad or a field mouse crosses breaks the beam.

Captain Pete Pukowlski, a stocky 40-year-old with a brush cut and a menacing glare, walks through Security Command looking over shoulders, occasionally shooting glances at a bank of video monitors. Airman Dempsey's face appears on the screen of one monitor, winking into the camera. A non-com buzzes Dempsey through the security door.

"Chow's here," Dempsey announces, handing out burgers. Captain Pukowlski grabs two and continues making his rounds.

An airman with loosened tie and grease-stained cuff picks up a ringing phone. "Three hundred eighteenth Strategic Missile Squadron, Airman Cooper speaking."

※

In a grimy tee-shirt, Jack Jericho stands at a communications shed, somewhere in the wilderness, speaking into the phone. "Sixty-ninth bucket brigade, swab jockey second class Jericho reporting from behind enemy lines."

Through the phone, he hears Cooper's frantic whispers. "Jeez, Jericho, Captain Pukowlski's shitting razor blades. You better get—"

From somewhere in the room, the captain's voice drowns out Cooper. "Is that Jericho? Gimme that!"

Jack waits a moment, then there he is. "Sergeant, get your ass back by 1500 tomorrow, and be in uniform for once."

"Why, you got a war planned?"

"V.I.P.'s are coming from D.C., so try to pretend you're an airman. And don't be bringing back any more road-kill raccoons."

"Yes sir," Jack says, "but those were possums, and last time you liked them...medium rare."

"Jericho, you're a friggin' disgrace."

"Captain, are you eating one of those Wrangler burgers, all the way?"

"Yeah, how'd you know?"

"I can smell the onions, sir."

With the captain still puzzling over that one, Jericho hangs up the phone. Thinking about the brass from Washington coming tomorrow. Knowing the captain will put on a dog-and-pony show and not wanting to be either one.

-9-

Jeremiah Was a Bullfrog

Midafternoon in Coyote Creek, and Brother David drives an old pickup truck with Rachel sitting next to him. David wears a ten-pocket bush jacket favored by Hemingway wannabees and newspaper photographers. Rachel wears a beige dress that comes to her ankles. A stenciled sign on the door of the pickup reads, "Eden Ranch." Matthew is in the truck bed with a man who calls himself Jeremiah. Matthew's shoulder-length brown hair is out of its ponytail, and his beard has the unkempt look of an ancient prophet. Jeremiah is an African-American man of 30 with chiseled features and an untamed Afro. A red bandanna is tied around his neck. Both men wear loose fitting pants and sandals.

The truck travels down Main Street, past the Old Wrangler Tavern and the gas station, pulling to a stop in front of a general store.

"Walk with me," David says to Rachel, and the two of them get out and head down the sidewalk. Matthew and Jeremiah hop out of the truck bed and enter the general store.

Few pedestrians are about in this tumbleweed town. David smiles placidly at a couple of passing ranch wives. "Afternoon, ma'am," he croons, tipping an imaginary hat, and the women's pace quickens going by him.

"Your charms don't seem to work here," Rachel says.

"They fear what they cannot know." David clasps a hand around her shoulder, and they stop in front of a rod and gun shop, David admiring a shotgun in the window. "On the other hand, *your* charm seems to have woven its spell over Billy."

"He wants to believe. He may even think he believes. But he does not. He is weak and afraid."

Brother David kisses her on the cheek. "Then we must make him strong and fearless."

∽

Matthew loads cans of beans and boxes of rice into the bed of the pickup truck. Sensing movement behind him, he turns to see three local toughs surrounding him. All three wear low-slung jeans and cowboy boots. A wiry ranch hand called D.D. because he spends every Saturday night in jail for Drunk and Disorderly, chews on a piece of straw. "Hey Jesus, get a haircut!" he calls out.

Matthew ignores him and continues loading the truck.

"Yeah, and while you're at it, get a shave," says D.D.'s husky buddy, a guy they call Hoss because he's the size of a horse and just as smart. "And take a bath, for Christ's sake."

"Everything I do is for the sake of Christ," Matthew says calmly.

"Yeah, we know," says the third one, Cletis. "You Jesus freaks think the world's gonna end."

"Oh, it shall," Matthew says, "precisely when it is prophesied."

"Maybe we should put your lights out ahead of schedule," Hoss says, and his buddies laugh.

Jeremiah comes out of the general store carrying a fifty-pound sack of flour. As he steps off the curb, Cletis trips him, and Jeremiah tumbles to the pavement. The bag tears, and flour spills. Jeremiah gets up, dark eyes blazing. Matthew lays a calming hand on his shoulder. "Let it go, Jeremiah."

This sets Hoss to giggling. "Jeremiah? I thought it was Aunt Jemima."

"Naw," D.D. says. "It's like the song." Which he tries to sing, "Jer-e-miah was a bull-frog."

Just as tuneless, Cletis joins in, "Was a good friend of *thine*."

Hoss bends over and scoops up a handful of flour from the torn bag. Slowly, he approaches Jeremiah, who stands motionless, waiting. "We don't like hippies, coloreds, or queers around here," Hoss taunts him, "and you look like all three."

"Yeah," D.D. adds. "We know what you choir boys do out at that ranch. Pray all day and bugger all night."

This sets Hoss to giggling in a high-pitched squeal.

Jeremiah is silent. Matthew doesn't make a move.

Slowly, deliberately, Hoss extends his hand – palm up and filled with flour – toward Jeremiah. For a long second, neither man moves. Then, Hoss blows a cloud of flour into Jeremiah's face. Cletis bursts out laughing. "Hey, Jeremiah, you got your wish. You're a white boy now."

Still, no movement from Matthew or Jeremiah.

"What's the matter, waiting for the Lord to help you?" D.D. mocks them. Then he sees that Jeremiah is looking past him. D.D. turns to find Brother David and Rachel on the sidewalk behind him.

"The Bible tells us to turn the other cheek," David says with equanimity. "But the Book also instructs that we must teach the children so that they will know. Therefore, we must show you the light." He nods to Jeremiah.

It happens so quickly that Hoss never moves, never raises his hands, never even cries out. Jeremiah's hip pivots and he throws a lightning *age-zuki*, the knuckles of his right fist striking Hoss squarely on the Adam's apple. The big man topples to the street, gagging.

Matthew snaps out a *mae-geri* front kick, catching D.D. in the groin, then spins into a *ushiro-kekomi*, a thrust kick to the rear, which lands directly in Cletis' solar plexus. Cletis drops to a knee, sucking wind. Matthew locks his hands together and drops Cletis to the pavement with a thunderous downward punch to the back of the neck.

Hoss gets to his feet and reaches under his pantleg for a knife sheathed to his leg. But he is too slow, Jeremiah peppering him with a flurry of jabs to the face. Hoss brings up his hands to protect himself, but he's already spouting blood from gashes above the eyes and his nose is a leaky faucet. With Hoss warding off head blows with his arms, Jeremiah backs up and lands a kick squarely on his sternum, cracking it, and the big man goes down, clutching his chest, coughing up blood-stained mucus.

D.D. tries crawling toward the general store, but Matthew grabs him by a foot, drags him back, his nose banging on the sidewalk, letting loose a flow of blood. Matthew gives a hard twist, breaking D.D.'s ankle with a sickening snap. D.D. rolls over, clutching his leg, screaming in agony.

It had taken only a few dizzying seconds, and now it was over, the three locals moaning, begging for peace. With Rachel clutching his arm, David walks into the circle of destruction. Suddenly, the whimpering D.D. reaches into his boot and comes out with a short-barreled .38. Blood dripping from his nose, face twisted in pain, he points the stainless steel gun directly at David's heart.

David's response is a tranquil smile. He lifts his left palm to show that it is empty. He runs his right hand behind his back, slips it beneath the flap of his bush jacket and removes a hand grenade from a metal loop. He continues to smile as he holds the grenade toward D.D., then pulls the pin.

D.D. licks his lips and says in a shaky voice, "That thing ain't real."

"In twelve seconds we'll find out," David replies, holding the grenade in one hand and the pin in the other. "Nine, eight..."

"Shoot him!" Hoss yells.

"Six, five..."

Cletis scrambles to his feet. "Don't do it, D.D.!"

"Three, two..."

Looking into the bottomless depth of David's penetrating stare, D.D. drops the gun. David swiftly inserts the pin in the grenade.

"Son-of-a-bitch," Hoss whines.

"Was it real?" D.D. asks, like the poker player who folds but still insists on seeing the winner's hand.

"Oh, most assuredly," David tells him. "Standard Army issue."

"Then what's the trick?"

"Ah, the trick," David says, letting them see the warmth and wisdom of his holy countenance. Enjoying it now. He is the rabbi, which he knows from his studies of the ancient Hebrews, means *teacher*. "The trick, as you call it, is the essential message of life. The trick, my simple lost child, is having no fear of death."

"Crazy fucker," D.D. says under his breath, but David hears him, and approaches. D.D. staggers back a step, afraid of being hit. David stops, his face a few inches from the cowardly heathen, who cringes in fear.

"On your knees, sinner."

"What?"

"On your knees before He who would save you."

D.D. drops to his knees, his head level with his teacher's groin. David feels the power now. Lording it over the fallen man, a King among peasants. David leans over and lifts D.D.'s head by the chin. "Now, what lesson have you learned today?"

"Lesson?" Even when he is not in excruciating pain, D.D. is not the quickest mind in Wyoming. Now, he is completely befuddled.

"Again, my child, what have you learned?"

"I don't know," D.D. says, fighting off tears. "I skipped a lot of Sunday school."

"Then I must tell you." David releases his grip, letting the infidel sink to the pavement. "The lesson, you woeful sinner, is this. Never fuck with the Lord."

-10-

The Trout Are Calling

Airman Sayers drives the Air Force Jeep, Reynolds next to him, Jericho sprawled in the back. The sun sizzles just below the mountains on the horizon, and the clouds shimmer with a lustrous glow over the valley. Folded beds of black and purple shale slope down toward a rock-strewn river.

A rancher in a dusty pickup pulls out and passes the Jeep on the two-lane road. The pickup coughs a burst of oily smoke. The Wyoming license, with its cowboy and bucking bronco, is personalized, "BEEF."

Sayers flicks on the headlights as the Jeep approaches a bridge. "Captain's got no cause to bust your chops, Sarge."

Slouched with his helmet over his eyes, Jericho is silent.

"Only weapon the Captain's ever held," Sayers continues, "is the little one between his legs."

"Which he only fires on solo missions," Reynolds adds.

The Jeep rumbles across the bride. Jericho stirs and looks out at the water tumbling over small rapids in the moonlight. "Stop the Jeep!" he yells.

Sayers hits the brakes and the Jeep squeals to a stop. "What?"

Jericho's head is cocked toward the river. "I can hear them."

"Who?" Sayers says.

"The trout. They're calling to me."

"Nothing doing, Jack," Sayers says.

"Spike's right," Reynolds says. "We'll never make it back in time if—"

"Go on without me. I'll meet you at the sentry post at 1500 hours tomorrow. Puke'll never know."

Sayers pounds the steering wheel in frustration. "You crazy? How you gonna get back? Call a cab, rustle up a buffalo? We're a hundred miles from base."

"Not as the crow flies," Jericho says. "Fifty bucks says I beat the two of you there."

Sayers and Reynolds swap startled looks. Then they exchange high-fives and, in unison, yell, "You're on!"

-11-
A Great Star Will Fall from the Sky

The setting sun slants through a stained glass window and across the altar in the Eden Ranch chapel. A beacon from heaven.

The chapel is a converted horse barn that still smells of straw, sweet molasses feed, and creosote. About eighty worshipers sit, ramrod straight, on wooden benches. Women without makeup in long, flowing dresses, men in baggy pants and sandals and a pack of children, many barefoot, digging their toes into the wood chips that cover the floor. Matthew and Jeremiah are in the back row, flanking the door.

At the altar, Brother David looks out over his flock. "I see your auras, and they are strong and vibrant," he proclaims. "You are healthy in body and spirit, and your halos reflect your holiness."

He goes on for a while about his parishioners' energy fields and the body's seven major chakras points. Finally, he slips from his New Age mumbo jumbo into fundamentalist Biblical preaching. Dropping his voice into a seductive sing-song, he calls out, "Our cities are sewers of pornography and sin!"

The congregation murmurs its righteous ire. In the front row, Lieutenant Billy Riordan, in jeans and a pressed blue oxford cloth shirt, stares in rapt attention. Next to him, Rachel laces her fingers through his and squeezes. He blushes. On the other side of Billy is a ten-year-old girl in pigtails who prays silently, but moves her lips.

"In Isaiah, it is written, 'I will punish the world for its evil, and the wicked for their iniquity,'" David chants.

"Amen!" they cry.

"In Revelations, it is written, 'I have the keys of Hades and of death.' It is our Savior's proclamation that He alone has authority over hell and the grave.'"

"Amen!" the faithful chorus.

"And how, my brethren, do we achieve everlasting life?"

"From the Word!" they shout back.

David nods. "In chapter two, verse ten, it is written, 'Be faithful, even to the point of death, and I will give you the crown of life.'"

More prayerful "amens" are sung to the heavens.

David beseeches them, his voice thundering across the chapel. "Do you believe!"

A unanimous chorus of "hosanna" and "praise the Lord."

"As is prophesied in Revelations, 'The angel shall sound his trumpet and a great star, blazing like a torch, shall fall from the sky. The waters shall turn bitter, and the wicked shall die.'"

"Let the torch fall!" Billy screams from the front row.

"Amen!" the others roar.

"The Day of Reckoning beckons!" David cries out. "Are you ready for the Apocalypse?"

In the front row, Billy rises from the bench. "Yes! Praise the Lord, I am ready!"

From the back, bellows of affirmation, the crowd frothing with devout fervor.

"Are you ready to do the Lord's work, no matter the price to be paid?"

"Yes!" screams Billy. Around him, the others join in.

David beams. His army of the righteous would follow him anywhere. Of course, they will have to. He closes his eyes. He has been listening to his own voice. Detached, floating above them. Tasting his words, believing them one moment, doubting the next. Am I the vessel of the Lord, he wonders, or the false Messiah? Not a charlatan, surely not that. For *he* believes. The voices he hears are real. But do they come from Him or from the fallen angel, Satan? What bitter irony there. Lucifer with his ventriloquist's voice, leading the shepherd astray.

A final thought, too. Could the voices simply be his own? David pictures a second brain inside his skull, wrinkled gray matter festering with disease, polluting his thoughts. Didn't his father send him to the shrink when he first saw the visions? Then later, the judge ordered him treated. But that year was a jumble. The shooting, the carefully constructed plea, the hospital with the sloping green lawn. An active imagination, his mother used to say about him. The shrink used a different word. Delusional.

David opens his eyes and lets his voice rise to the rafters of the old barn, maybe even to heaven itself. "The fools all around us will not listen! We cannot convince them with either reason or faith. Will you join me?"

The roar is deafening.

His eyes sparkling, David looks directly at Billy. "Then, my brothers and sisters, come and accept Paradise."

David steps down from the altar and the worshipers drop to their knees, closing their eyes, and opening their mouths as he approaches. He places a pill, much smaller than a Communion wafer, on the tongue of each of his followers. Billy swallows the pill, his eyes closed in rapture.

"Bless you, my brother," David says, lingering just a moment, before moving down the row.

✑

The bunkhouse was once a tack room, and even now, old saddles, their dry leather cracked, hang over wooden rails. Rachel escorts Billy into the bunkhouse and gives him a sisterly kiss. By design, Matthew and Jeremiah have bunks on either side of Billy. Faithful lieutenants, they will report everything to David.

Rachel walks up the path to the main house past a target range where enemy soldiers made of aluminum pop up from the ground. The main house is a sturdy affair of flagstone and pine with gabled windows and a green-shingled, pitched roof. The ranch had been owned by four generations of Carsons, the first, Colonel Nathaniel Carson, a nephew of Kit Carson, the famed guide.

They were Wyoming cattlemen to the core, but the fifth generation – two brothers – wanted nothing to do with the freezing winters and blazing summers, the endless work and the isolation. The brothers put the ranch on the market, and Brother David bought it in the name of the Holy Church of Revelations. To come up with the cash, his followers sold their own homes and cars and maxed out their credit cards with no intention of repaying.

Brother David renamed the place Eden Ranch, and his followers still grazed some cattle and planted vegetable gardens. Now David lives on the second floor of the main house in what had been Colonel Carson's bedroom. Walls of knotty pine, the mounted heads of a bighorn sheep and an antelope, and rifle brackets above a brick fireplace.

David holds an antique rifle, missing from the brackets. He embraces it, a look of distant sadness in his eyes as Rachel enters the bedroom.

"Billy is ready," she says.

"Let us hope."

David lifts the old rifle, aiming at an imaginary enemy outside the window where the sun has set over distant, purple mountains.

"You are distracted tonight, David."

"I have seen the launch in a vision."

Rachel catches her breath and does not even try to hide her excitement. "Is it beautiful?"

"It is heaven."

"What else did you see?"

There is something else he remembers, a sheet of grayish white, billowing in the wind, flowing toward him. When he saw it, a chill swept over him, and even now, he feels its cold breath. "Nothing else," he says. "I saw nothing else."

He opens the breech on the rifle and holds it out to her. "This is a Springfield-Allin breechloader, a repeating rifle."

"I am not interested in such things."

"No, but you love parables." He runs his hand across the smooth barrel. "At one time, this was the deadliest weapon known to man. In the Big Horn foothills, not far from here, thirty-five cavalry men were surrounded by fifteen hundred Sioux, their best warriors, led by Red Cloud and Crazy Horse. The soldiers were in the open but quickly circled their wagons and brought out these new rifles, the likes of which had never been seen before. The Sioux were fearless, the greatest fighters the world has ever seen, but they were cut down in charge after charge and finally retreated to the hills."

"It's strange," she says, "but I always thought you would identify with the Sioux, not the cavalry."

"It's the weapon. The weapon makes all the difference. I must get it."

"You will, David. You can do anything."

He doesn't answer but instead replaces the rifle in its brackets.

"You're the Messiah," she says.

"Am I?"

"If you don't believe in your own power, we cannot succeed."

He shows her a mysterious smile and sits on the bed. "We'll die. You must know that success means death."

"Death is the path to everlasting life."

He sighs. "So it is written."

They have been down this path before. She knows her role. Build him into the God he is. "David, they all believe in you."

"*They* are sheep."

"And you are their shepherd. That is how it is meant to be. But you must never show doubt. They draw their strength from you."

"I dreamt of my father again," he says abruptly.

Her face shows concern. "Tell me."

"He called me the name. I had a gun and shot him twenty, thirty times. Like the cavalry with the Springfield, I just kept shooting. He was dead, but he kept taunting me."

"Was your mother in the dream?"

"He was hitting her, calling her names, too."

Rachel sits on the bed and wraps her arms around him. He lays his head between her breasts and she unbuttons her dress, exposing herself to him. With one hand, she guides a breast toward his mouth. His eyes closed, David sucks at her. She gently rocks him and hums a lullaby. Outside the window, it has grown dark and windy. The branch of a tree is driven against the wall of the house, the sound of a giant bird's fluttering wings. Inside, as David drifts off to sleep, his last conscious thought is of his mother.

ↄ〇

Billy lies in the bunkhouse on a cot, fully clothed, somewhere between sleep and hallucinatory semi-consciousness. He tosses from side to side, vaguely aware of a dryness in his mouth. Floating,

floating ever higher, looking down on it all, seeing the Truth in brilliant colors, listening to Brother David's voice echo in his brain, feeling the effects of the pill, a potent mixture of mescaline and peyote.

"As it is written in the Revelation of St. John the Divine..."

On a hillside of the greenest green, two giant stags paw the earth, snorting sulfurous fire from their flared nostrils. They viciously lock horns and battle, powerful legs kicking up clods of dirt, then with a powerful jerk of its head, one stag breaks the other's neck.

"I am Alpha and Omega, the beginning and the end..."

Billy is in an elevator that plummets madly into a bottomless, rocky cave, the arrow above the door spinning wildly counter-clockwise as the elevator plunges, lower and lower.

"Who is and who was..."

A combination lock *clicks* as the dial spins furiously. A computer screen flashes with six-digit numbers whirling by in a blur. Billy struggles with a key as large as he is, trying to lift it into a giant lock.

"And who shall give you the Morning Star."

In a brilliant blue sky, the sun explodes, and Billy watches it, reflected in Brother David's dark eyes. David smiles, but his face dissolves, melts in the heat of the sun, and now Billy sees only a mushroom cloud rising to the heavens, a joyous firestorm vaporizing everyone and everything on earth.

-12-
Little Brown Jug

A bleak Air Force utility shed of corrugated metal stands in a dry basin alongside a darkened road in the Wyoming countryside. The two airmen will spend the night and return to base in the morning. Reynolds unrolls his sleeping bag on the concrete floor. Sayers opens a rucksack and pulls out plastic food pouches containing their M.R.E.'s, meals-ready-to-eat in military jargon, the source of endless complaints among the soldiers. He tosses one to Reynolds, who opens the pouch and pulls out what looks like a popsicle stick with a malignant tumor.

Reynolds examines his dinner in the light of a forty-watt overhead bulb. "What do they call this mystery meat, shit on a stick?"

Sayers reads the label, squinting through his glasses. "Mock shiskebab."

"When I offered to die for my country," Reynolds says, "I didn't mean ptomaine poisoning."

Sayers digs through the rucksack. "Jericho didn't take his. Maybe we got another choice." He comes up with a third pouch and reads the label, "Chipped beef on toast with brown gravy."

Reynolds takes a look. "If we had truth-in-labeling, that'd be called, 'diarrhea on shoe leather.'"

Sayers lights a match to a heating tablet, which begins to glow. He sticks the two M.R.E. pouches in a canteen cup, pours in some water, and holds the cup over the burning tablet. "It's moving."

"What is?"

"The shiskebab. Or maybe it's the chipped beef. I think it's alive."

Reynolds crawls into his sleeping bag. "I'm not too hungry, anyway."

Sayers turns off the light and douses the heating tablet. "Me neither. Let's get some shut-eye, finish up tomorrow and go collect our bread from Jericho."

In the darkness, both men try to get comfortable on the rock-hard floor. "Damn, Spike, what I wouldn't give for one of those vibrating mattresses at the Shangri-la Motel in Casper."

"Yeah, well this ain't so bad. Think about poor Jericho. At least we got a roof over our heads."

After a moment, Reynolds sniffs at the air. "You squeezed the cheese!"

"Did not!"

"Did so!"

"No way!" Sayers says. "The one who smelled it dealt it."

Still in his sleeping bag, Reynolds tries to roll away from Sayers but only succeeds in banging into a steel post that supports the roof of the shed. "Damn! This is like being in jail."

"We're still better off than Jericho," Sayers says.

～

The nighttime air is cool and scented with sagebrush. The moon casts a creamy glow over a stunning pylon of volcanic rock more than twelve hundred feet high. Twenty million years ago, this wedge of phonolite with its edged prisms was the core of an erupting volcano. Wind and rain over the millennia have erased the surrounding walls, but the hard rock core remains. Now, it catches the moonlight and reflects it over the valley and the small, tumbling stream.

Jack Jericho first saw Devil's Tower in a movie. The extraterrestrials landed there in *Close Encounters of the Third Kind.* Years later, stationed at Malmstrom Air Force Base in Montana, he had driven here on leave. He camped out in the shadow of the Tower, fished in the stream, and like the little aliens, was transported somewhere else, at least in the spiritual sense. When a maintenance position opened in the 318th Missile Squadron in Wyoming, less than 100 miles away, Jericho jumped at it.

Jericho would lie on his back and look up at the Tower. He knew all the Indian legends, the seven little girls who were attacked by bears while playing on the giant rock, then soared into the sky and became the constellation Pleiades, or Seven Sisters.

Tonight, in the moonlight, Jack Jericho plucks a mushroom from the embankment and tosses it into his helmet, which is filled with parsnip and acorns. He stirs the mixture, then pours it over a trout, which is sizzling on a rock in an open fire. He pokes at the fish with a twig to keep it from sticking.

"And now *monsieur,*" he says aloud, doing his best imitation of a stiff-lipped sommelier, "would you care for a fine Chardonnay to go with your *terrine des poissons a la creme de caviar?"*

Jericho grabs a small jug from his rucksack, pulls out the cork with his teeth, and sniffs. "Ah, robust, not subtle, with just a hint of Aunt Emmy's corn and Granny Jericho's barley." With his eyes closed, he takes a long pull, swallows, then coughs and sputters like an old Ford pickup. "No," he says, his eyes moist, "not subtle at all."

Jericho takes the fish from the fire with a flat stone he uses as a spatula an begins eating with his fingers. Another pull on the bottle, and he breaks into song.

"Ha! Ha! Ha! You and me,
Little brown jug don't I love thee,
Ha! Ha! Ha! You and me,
Little brown jug don't I love thee."

He takes a drink, licks his fingers. Another pull, and the jug is empty. Jericho staggers to his feet, grabs his saw-toothed knife, and cuts several low-hanging branches from a fir tree. When he has enough, he begins building a small lean-to. He pulls up several handfuls of long grass from the embankment for a bed, then cuts a cat-tail stalk. Crushing the bark of a spicebrush twig under a rock, he makes a paste which he squeezes onto the cat-tail. Then he kneels at the water's edge and begins brushing his teeth.

A movement catches his eye and Jericho lifts his head. A white-tailed fawn, no more than three feet tall, stands on the opposite bank of the river watching him. Jericho salutes the animal with his cat-tail toothbrush. "Ha! Ha! Ha!," he sings softly. "Little brown deer don't I love thee."

Then Jericho resumes brushing his teeth, and the fawn lowers its head to drink from the river. They face each other across the water in peaceful harmony. Finally, the fawn turns and prances up the bank and into the woods.

ఇ

The tumbling rapids echo along the riverbank, carrying Jericho into a deep sleep, but still the nightmare comes. The ground beneath him shudders. Above him, Devil's Tower erupts in volcanic flames and lava spews from the earth. He wants to run, but there is nowhere to go, for now he is deep underground. The earth moves, slipping out from under his feet. Timbers crack, lights go dark, men scream. Somewhere he hears his father's voice but cannot see him. His father, who took him into the mine when he was just a boy and gave him a helmet that sank over his ears. His father, who needs his help now. But which way? The foreman yelling for the men to follow him. And Jericho tries to move, crawling through the darkness, but in the dream, he's slogging through quicksand. He can't move. The screams grow louder. He is sinking. Deeper and deeper until...

A horse whinnies. A horse riding into his nightmare? And Jericho is half awake now, thinking it through, when the horse whinnies again.

He opens his eyes and rolls out of the lean-to onto the bank of the stream. A rider on a white horse looms over him. The morning sun is a fiery ball behind the rider's head, masking his features in a halo of flaming spears.

"Are you with Jesus?" the rider asks.

"No, I'm with the 318th," Jericho says, squinting, trying to clear the cobwebs from his brain.

"Then you are a blasphemer," the man says.

"Blasphemer, boozer, brawler, and a few other words that start with 'b,' though brave and brilliant are not among them. Now, who the hell are you?"

Jericho squints but cannot make out the face of Brother David, who is dressed all in black, from his boots to his cowboy hat. "I am a servant of God."

"I'll bet the pay's lousy, but a great retirement plan."

"Do you mock me, pilgrim?"

"No, I don't," Jericho says, becoming serious. "I don't mock anyone's beliefs. I just go through life minding my own business. But if you were to ask me, I'd say God doesn't want servants. He wants us to get on with our lives without hurting each other or doing too much damage to this good, green Earth."

"That is not enough, pilgrim. Some of us are destined to carry out His will."

"And how would you know just what He – or She – had in mind?"

"The aura of your chakras is a muddy brown, reflecting your confusion."

"Yeah, I've been meaning to take the old chakras into the shop for an aura change."

The white horse gambols sideways, and the rider pulls tight on its reins. "The fool makes light of what he does not understand. As it is written, 'They shall run to and fro to seek the Word of the Lord, and shall not find it.' Amos, chapter eight, verse twelve.'"

"Amos said that? Does Andy agree?"

"Your soul is damned. It is all in the Book. It is all prophesied."

"I never thought you could find answers in books."

"Not *books*! The Book, for there is only one."

"I didn't learn a lot in school, but I do remember a teacher saying something like, 'Beware the man of one book.'"

David seems to appraise him. "You are not quite the bumpkin you try to be, are you?"

Jericho's eyes are nearly closed, the effects of a hangover accentuated by the glare of the morning sun. He puts some country twang in his voice. "I don't hardly know what you mean."

"Oh, but I think you do. The expression is, *Timeo hominem unius libri*. 'I fear the man of one book.' It is attributed to Thomas Aquinas."

"Never met the fellow."

"I suppose not. He probably didn't make it to Possum Hollow, Arkansas or wherever you perfected this down-home persona which doubtless serves you well amongst the cretins you must deal with on a daily basis."

"Sinkhole. I'm from Sinkhole, West Virginia."

"How nice for you. How utterly perfect."

"It surely is. Maybe you've been to the Club Med there."

"Judging from your boots and fatigues, you're in the Air Force. An enlisted man, I suppose."

"Jack Jericho, E-5. You can call me Sergeant." He shields his eyes from the sun with a hand. "Now, what's your name, and why do you keep the sun behind you like a Sioux war party?"

"Why do you think, sergeant?"

"Well, you're either hiding something or you just like to make other people uncomfortable."

"What is it *you* are hiding, Sergeant Jack Jericho, under that mask of insouciance?"

"Damned if I know, but if you told me what *in-soo-city-ants* means, I'd take a stab at it."

"You're an interesting specimen, sergeant, but I don't have time to show you the way."

For the first time, Jericho notices the butt of a dark metal rifle protruding from a saddle holster. "Say, you haven't been hunting moose with an M-16, have you, Reverend?"

David tugs the reins, and the horse angles a few steps to the side.

"Hear the word, pilgrim. 'The angel shall sound his trumpet and a blazing torch shall fall from the sky.'"

"What is that, Bob Dylan? No, the Beatles, right? 'Lucy in the Sky with Diamonds'?"

"The Bible teaches us to suffer fools gladly if we ourselves are wise," David says.

"Must have missed that sermon."

"You should join my congregation. Are you a believer?"

"Unless I was drunk as a skunk, I went to church every Sunday, up 'til the time we lost our preacher 'cause he was caught diddling one of the choir boys. I guess you could say my beliefs have been tested."

"Do you know the Day of Reckoning beckons?"

"Funny, that's what the preacher said when he was sober. When he was drunk, he said, 'the day of Beckoning reckons.'"

"You are lost and wicked." David yanks the reins to one side and roughly digs his heels into the horse's ribs. The animal splashes across the river and bolts toward the woods, and in a moment, horse and rider are gone.

"I ain't wicked," Jack Jericho says to himself, blinking against the glare of the sun. "I'm just like most everyone else."

BOOK TWO

In the Hole

-13-
The Valley of the Shadow of Death

The second lieutenant approaches the steel door of the Security Building, his combat boots crunching along a gravel path. He wears a blue flightsuit with zippered pockets and a black scarf, signifying the Black Pirates of the 318th Missile Squadron. Pinned to his chest is a medal depicting a missile blasting toward four stars. A missileer's heaven. A sleeve patch shows a metallic fist gripping three lightning bolts, all sheathed by an olive branch. The iron fist in the velvet glove.

His nametag reads "Riordan, W." He has pale blond hair and wears wire-rimmed glasses. He slides a coded card through a slot in the steel door, and a red light blinks above a recessed combination mike/speaker. "Lieutenant William Riordan, reporting," he says crisply.

"No shit," comes a scratchy voice through the speaker. "Hey, Billy, you're damn near late. That ain't like you. And Owens was early. That ain't like him."

"I have three minutes, sir."

"Don't 'sir' me, Billy Riordan. Call me Valoppi or just plain 'V.' Call me any damn thing you want. I'm a second louie, just like you, and if I hadn't taken that ROTC money, I'd be wearing a pin-striped suit and pulling down forty k a year in a major accounting firm."

"It's against regulations for Owens to proceed into the hole without me," Billy says. "It's a no lone zone."

"Yeah, so what? In another week, Billy boy, there'll be no more regs, no more Technical Orders, no more missile, no more nothing."

The latch buzzes, and Billy opens the door and enters the security bridge, an enclosed tunnel which runs through the building and beyond it to the silo elevator housing. Twenty paces along the metal bridge, Billy comes to a grated steel door with an electronic lock that can be opened only from Security Command inside the building.

Billy looks through the bulletproof window into Security Command, the nerve center of the building. A sign under the window reads, "Controlled Area. It is unlawful to enter this area without permission of the installation commander. Use of deadly force is authorized. Section 21, Internal Security Act of 1950."

Billy slides an ID card through a tray, and Lieutenant Valoppi pushes it back without looking at it. He is a handsome, dark-haired 22-year-old with an open collar and loosened tie on his Class A blue uniform. "Billy, you don't have to show me your ID. You don't have to give me a voiceprint, fingerprint, or urine sample. You don't have to thank me, kiss me, or blow me. Just get the hell down the hole."

"It's in the T.O. I show you my ID. You visually confirm, and if there's a question as to either my identity or authorization to proceed, you secondarily confirm by asking me the password of the day."

"Look, Billy, I haven't had my morning coffee, but I've seen your pathetic face every day for the last fourteen months, except when you're on leave and disappear to God knows where, so I don't have to visually confirm, secondarily confirm or otherwise confirm. Besides, you don't *know* the password."

"I must disagree, Lieutenant Valoppi. This is my duty shift, and I have lawful access to the password, which I memorized yesterday." Billy takes back his ID card and carefully places it into a sleeve pocket which he zippers shut.

Valoppi shakes his head, tired of dealing with the little dweeb, but bored enough to want to have some fun. Behind him, two airmen at desks have stopped shuffling their papers to listen. "Oh yeah? All right, Riordan, if that's really your name, I challenge! What's the password of the day?"

"Sky King," Billy answers.

"Wrong. Is your name Ivan? Are you some filthy Russian spy."

"Nah," says one of the airmen behind Valoppi. "The Russians are our pals."

"Okay, smart guy, then who the hell's the enemy?" Valoppi asks.

"How should I know?" the airman says. "I only work here."

Billy is tapping on the window. "The password *is* Sky King. I'm never mistaken about—"

"Wrong!" Valoppi shouts, "because I just changed it. From now on, until they close this sucker down, the password is 'bite me.'"

Annoyed, Billy stands silently at the window, waiting.

"Say it, Riordan."

Still no response.

"You're going to be late. Captain Puke won't let you lead chapel services on Sunday, Billy boy."

Billy shoots a nervous glance at his watch.

Valoppi smirks at him. "C'mon, say it."

"Bite me," Billy whispers.

"Can't hear you," Valoppi sings out.

"Bite me!"

Laughing, Valoppi hits a button, and the electronic latch opens on the steel door.

Billy pushes through the door and chugs at double time across the security bridge toward the elevator housing, an enclosed steel hood that shields the entrance to the elevator. Once there, he quickly punches the day code into the Permissive Action Link pad, and a reinforced steel door rumbles open. Billy steps inside, and the door closes.

The elevator is built to withstand earthquakes, direct hits by conventional weapons, and indirect hits by nuclear warheads, so it is a slow but solid ride down through the hard rock of Chugwater Mountain. "The Lord is my shepherd, I shall not want," Billy recites, looking into the lens of the TV camera overhead. "He causes me to lie down in green pastures. He leads me beside still waters. He restores my soul. He guides me in the path of righteousness for His name's sake."

The elevator comes to a smooth stop, the door opens, and Billy heads across the underground catwalk, his boots clacking across the steel steps. A sign warns, "No Lone Zone."

Along the catwalk to the capsule, another sign is posted: "Safety first. There is no substitute for safety." He can see the light from the launch control capsule fifty yards away. The blast door, required under Technical Order A-17 to be closed at all times, is open. As usual. "Yea, though I walk through the valley of the shadow of death, I will fear no evil, for thou art with me. Thy rod and thy staff, they comfort me."

Billy wordlessly enters the launch control capsule and nods to his crewmate, Owens, who stands drinking coffee behind the two missileers about to go off duty. Owens' sandy hair is cut close on the sides, but he's let it grow on top. A cowlick in front gives him a Huckleberry Finn look. He yawns and watches the two missileers make entries in their log books. Sanders, the crew commander, is nicknamed Curly. He is a black 1st lieutenant with a shaved head. His teammate, Lauretta, is a female missileer, a 2nd lieutenant just overweight enough to be considered voluptuous by the men in the hole. Both are strapped into B-52 flight chairs, which are attached by rollers to a metal railing.

Lauretta, the deputy, sits directly in front of a series of olive green communications racks seven feet high. If the United States were under attack, she would have received the Emergency Action Message from the President or the National Command Authority by any of a variety of communications gear, some high tech, some still with a utilitarian, pre-computer age feel. Messages are received in code. The decoding manual, the Sealed Authentication System in Air Force lingo, is located in a simple red metal box above her head. Sanders has a matching box and manual. Each box is secured with a combination padlock that would cost less than ten dollars at the local hardware store. The missile crew is unarmed, the .38 caliber revolvers of yesteryear having been mothballed. Contrary to popular myth, the guns were not intended to force a recalcitrant crewmate to turn the key. Rather, in the unlikely event that security was breached in the launch control capsule, they were to be used against trespassers, protesters or terrorists.

But it never happened.

Not once since the beginning of the ICBM program.

So now, the basic security at launch facilities is intended to protect airmen and equipment from deep penetrating enemy warheads, not from homegrown terrorists, though at this point, no one really believes that either danger is real.

The missile crews of the 1970's and 1980's had another explanation for the sidearms, one never found in the four hundred page launch manual called the T.O., or Technical Order. In the event of thermonuclear war, each U.S. launch facility would be targeted by one or more Russian ICBM's. The launch control capsules are steel cylinders fifty feet long and twenty feet wide, their interior ceilings curved like old-fashioned lunch diners. They are buried deep in the rock and attached to the roof of underground caverns by four hydraulic jacks intended to act as shock absorbers. In the event of anything but a direct hit from a Russian SS-18, the capsule and the PK missile should still be operational for a counter-strike if one has not already been launched.

In theory.

As with nearly all evidence related to nuclear war, everything is theory, conjecture and supposition. The crew members could be injured or trapped inside a damaged capsule. A deep penetration ICBM would surely destroy the elevator shaft and seal the emergency Personnel Access Hatch, turning its insulation of sand into fused glass. The missileers who survived a direct hit would be trapped in their capsule. The sidearms, the missile crews concluded long ago, were to be used on themselves.

Now, Billy Riordan, the deputy on the next twenty-four hour duty, stands behind Lauretta. In front of her, the vintage 1965 teletype clacks out a message that will need to be decoded. It is surely one of an endless stream of tests. That is life in the hole, interminable preparation and repetition of routine procedures. Nothing, it seems, is ever real.

Lauretta tears off the teletype message and lays it to one side. It's not an EAM, so there's no possibility that the country will be at war in fifteen minutes. If it had been, she would be opening the padlock, grabbing the SAS manual, and decoding the message. Then, if it turned out to be a launch command, she would enter the six-digit Enable Code and the four-digit Preparatory Launch Command. In addition to the one PK just down the tunnel, they control another nine located in separate silos several miles away.

To launch, they would each take a key from the red boxes. After entering the Enable Code and the Prepatory Launch Command on their consoles, they would remove a plastic strip covering two keyholes, one in each console approximately twelve feet apart.

No Lone Zone. Even Shaq doesn't have the wingspan to launch by himself.

They must turn, hold and release their keys simultaneously, or the launch command will not be accepted by the computer in the fourth stage of the PK. There is another safeguard, too, against a mistaken or renegade launch. Another capsule must enter the identical codes, a second "launch vote," making the procedure double fail-safed.

"Hey, Owens," Lauretta says. "They don't pay overtime, so you can figure this one out." She makes a paper airplane out of the teletype message and sails it to him. He catches it but makes no effort to unfold or read it.

"You sure you want me to? It's probably a love letter from that major at Malmstrom."

Lauretta ignores him and runs a quick check on the other communications gear, AFSAT, the link to the Air Force satellite system, SLFCS, the survivable low frequency system with underground wiring intended to withstand a nuclear blast, and SACDIN, a more modern digital network run by computer. There's also the telephone with direct links to NORAD in Cheyenne Mountain, STRATCOM at Offut Air Force Base in Omaha, the National Military Command Center in the Pentagon, and the Alternate Command Center buried inside Raven Rock Mountain in Maryland, just in case the Pentagon has been obliterated by an enemy attack. The phone itself is something of a relic, a black, rotary dial model the likes of which are not seen on TV commercials extolling the virtues of AT&T versus MCI.

The launch facilities are like that. While the Minuteman III's have computers and fancy monitors with on-screen commands, the Peacekeeper capsules still have the old lighted boards descended from the Titan project in the sixties. The irony is that the PK is the newer missile with greater range, accuracy and punch. In front of Sanders in the commander's chair is a console festooned with multi-colored lights. Each light is emblazoned with its own descriptive term, the jargon, too, reaching back to the beginning of the missile program. "Strategic Alert," "Standby," "Missile Shutdown," "Fault," "LF Down," "LF No Go," "Enabled," "Launch Command," "Launch Inhibit," "Launch in Progress," "Missile Away,"

Beams sweep endlessly across Doppler radar screens, and security monitors attached to the capsule's ceiling show live shots of the base above them as well as the PK missile three hundred yards down a tunnel from where they now sit.

Owens, who would have been a decent running back at Oklahoma if he hadn't torn up a knee, leans on the back of Sanders' chair. "Get your rocks off today Curly?"

"Day ain't over yet," Sanders says.

Owens watches the digital clock on the console change from 0759 to 0800. "Now it is."

Sanders and Lauretta unbuckle their harnesses, and Owens finishes his coffee. "Ain't fair, Curly. How come I'm stuck with Bible Billy while you get Miss Intercontinental Ballistic Boobs?"

Lauretta kicks her flight chair down the railing and bangs into Owens' leg. "Hey!" he cries out.

Lauretta jabs a finger into his chest. "Because spending twenty-four hours with you, Owens, would be cruel and unusual punishment."

"Okay, okay," Owens says, raising his hands in surrender. "Jeez, a guy can't even joke around anymore. Right Billy?"

"Not in the hole," Billy answers. "'Missileers shall maintain a constant state of readiness. Space Command frowns upon non-service related activities such as playing cards, personal conversation, and horseplay.'"

"Not to mention farting when the vent fan's down," Owens adds.

Sanders and Lauretta remove their combination locks from the red boxes, then Owens and Billy fasten on their own. "See you guys," Owens says. "And be careful, it's hell up there." In a moment, Sanders and Lauretta are gone, heading across the catwalk toward the elevator.

Billy and Owens buckle themselves into the flight seats, and Billy hits a button. With a pneumatic *whoosh,* the blast door begins to close. The door weighs eight tons and is solid steel, four feet thick. Five steel pins, the size of fireplace logs, are recessed into the door and extend into ports in the wall to seal off the capsule. A separate latch on the door locks the pins into place. Until recently, the door opened and closed with a hand air pump, it taking nearly a full minute to operate. In recent renovations, a button on the deputy's console operates the pump, but it still takes nearly thirty seconds for the pins to insert or retract and the giant door to move.

"I knew you were going to do that," Owens says.

"What?"

"Seal the blast door."

"It's in the T.O. You're supposed—"

"I know what's in the regs, Billy. But if we ever got an order to launch, or if incoming were headed this way, don't you think we'd have time to punch that button and close the damn door?"

"That's not the point. We're trained to do exactly as we're taught. If we foul up the little things, then the—"

"*My* point is, I hate feeling like a sardine in here."

"I'm sorry, but I feel strongly about this."

"That's what I love about you, Billy," Owens says. "You are so damn predictable."

-14-
The Race

Stripped to his boxer shorts, Jack Jericho swats at a mosquito that has targeted his neck as ground zero. "Skeeters biting better than the trout," he says to himself. Behind him, Devil's Tower radiates a prism of colors from the morning sun.

Bending over the stream, Jericho fills his helmet with water, then props it upside down between two rocks in the blazing fire. He cuts long, thin slices of tannic tree bark with his survival knife and drops them into the helmet. As the concoction boils, he cuts sturdy four-foot long branches from a pine tree, then lashes them together with twine. Along the embankment, he finds a half-buried Styrofoam cooler, its bottom punched out.

"Tourists," he says derisively.

He takes the cooler and ties it to the cross-section of branches, then carefully lifts his helmet from the rocks and cools it in the stream. Finally, he dips his fingers into the helmet and streaks the orange liquid across his face and body.

Digging into his rucksack, Jericho grabs the jug of moonshine and works out the cork with his thumb. He puts the jug to his lips but it's dry. Staring in disbelief at the empty jug, he sighs, "Was it good for you, too?"

❧

Ten miles downstream from Jack's campsite, Sayers and

Reynolds stand on a bridge, urinating into the tumbling water fifteen feet below.

"Ow, that river's cold," Reynolds says with a laugh.

"Yep, and deep, too," Sayers boasts.

They zip up and lean on the bridge railing, looking upstream. Reynolds lights a cigarette. Sayers pops the top on a beer and slaps at a mosquito on his neck, squashing it in a tiny pool of blood.

"The sarge'll never make it," Reynolds says, exhaling a puff. "Never."

Sayers looks at his watch and takes a pull on the beer. "I feel sorry for the him. Puke'll have his ass."

"It's his own damn fault. His job's to maintain the machinery in the sump, but you can't hardly get him down there."

"That's because of his claustrophobia."

Reynolds tosses his cigarette into the stream. "His what?"

"You heard me. He's been treated for claustrophobia and depression."

"The hell do you know?"

"When I pulled two weeks of clerical duty," Sayers goes on, "Puke had me photocopy all the personnel and medical files in the 318th. Made better reading than the Perimeter Fence Maintenance Manual."

"Bet you picked up some real dirt."

"Sure did," Sayers says. "Say, did that penicillin knock out the clap you picked up on a three-day leave to Laramie?"

"You prick! You read my file."

Sayers drains his beer. "Don't worry. I ain't gonna sell it to Oprah."

"I don't get it. Why'd the captain have you—"

"Space Command's sending out a shrink who's gonna separate the men from the bedwetters. 'Course they already know Jericho goes into a panic in tight spaces."

"So they assign him to the sump," Reynolds says in wonderment.

"Ain't that just like the Air Force?"

Reynolds tosses his cigarette butt into the river. "What do you think they'll do with him?"

"Probably make him an astronaut." Sayers looks at his watch again. "C'mon, let's get back and collect our money from the sarge."

Just as they start to leave, something catches Sayers' eye. Upstream, a raft made of tree branches and an old Styrofoam cooler bounces over a dizzying set of rapids. A man hangs on as the raft disappears in a gully and washes out the other side.

"Look at that fool," Sayers says, shaking his head. The raft bounces off a rock, spins in a whirlpool, and heads toward them. "Who the hell would ride this river on that—"

"Say, that looks like..."

"It can't be," Sayers says, but at the same time knowing it is. Who else would it be?

The wild water carries the raft closer. It's rocking and rolling over the rapids.

"The bastard!" Sayers yells, tossing his beer can at Jack who passes under the bridge, waving and laughing.

As the two airmen race for their Jeep, the raft sideswipes a boulder and capsizes. Jericho is tossed into the drink but hangs onto the raft, his legs trailing behind him as he is carried down river.

-15-
The Missileer from Mars

Brother David walks along a path of wood chips past the firing range, Rachel is at his side, a husky commando named Gabriel trails behind, carrying a Mossberg 500 shotgun. On the range, Matthew supervises as the commandos, spread out in prone and kneeling positions, fire at pop-up targets of enemy soldiers, the shells *pinging* from direct hits. Nearby, other commandos use rope ladders to scale a ten-foot high wooden fence, then drop to the other side and dance through an obstacle course of old tires. In a shaded area near a strand of birch trees, another group practices hand-to-hand combat and bayonet fighting.

As they approach a gravel driveway, Brother David stops next to a ten-ton truck where a man in a face shield is welding a snowplow to the front bumper. At the rear, other commandos load boxes of ammunition and weapons into the bed of the truck, then fasten a tarpaulin over the load.

"We are ready, Brother David," Gabriel says.

David looks to Rachel, who nods her agreement.

"Then, let it be Judgment Day," David proclaims.

❧

The speedy OH-58 Kiowa helicopter settles down inside a circle of rocks on a ridge near Chugwater dam. Captain Pete Pukowlski sits at the wheel of a Humvee, watching as a young woman duck out the door, a shapely leg visible as her skirt hikes up. Dr. Susan Burns hurries toward him, her dark hair blowing in the rotors' backwash. If she's a shrink, the captain mutters to himself, give me some therapy.

The helicopter is airborne again by the time Dr. Burns settles into the passenger seat of the Humvee and gives Pukowlski a firm handshake and a businesslike smile. He introduces himself, then says, "There's something I want you to see before we go back to the base."

He drives along a gravel path down the backside of the mountain into the next valley. Overhead, a lone eagle soars in the clear blue sky. They pass the dry river bed where once a stream flowed, before the dam was built to accommodate the missile base. They drive past fenced fields with grazing cattle and a pond with a whirling hot spring. From somewhere on a wooded rise, an elk bugles, challenging other bulls to fight.

"Not much like D.C. out here, eh Doctor?" he says as he slows the Humvee to negotiate a turn.

"Thankfully not," she says.

"Not to pry or anything, but your regular patients, would they include anybody I might have seen on television?"

"Maybe. I've treated lobbyists, TV reporters, congressmen."

"Congressmen," the captain repeats. "Doesn't seem to have done much good, does it?"

"Special Forces, too," she says.

He shoots her a disbelieving look.

"I developed the battery of psychological tests for Delta Force. They take the best soldiers from the Rangers and the Green Berets, and I test them at Ft. Bragg. We try to weed out the lone wolves, the borderline personalities. We separate the men who can be trained as killers from those who just yearn to kill."

"Jeez, Special Ops." Impressed now. Pukowlski would have loved to have been an Air Force commando, but he washed out of training with the 20th Special Operations Squadron in Florida. The Cowboys, they call themselves, after the Bon Jovi song, "Dead or Alive." Guys in nifty flightsuits and red scarves who can fly attack helicopters blindfolded. Shit, Pukowlski thinks, not my fault I get airsick, remembering throwing up on an instructor's boots in a Pave Low chopper.

"The ones who get through the preliminary testing go to Camp Dawson in West Virginia," she continues. "I observe them in the field and construct psychological profiles. The Army tests their physical capabilities with grueling field maneuvers. I test their mental capabilities with carefully chosen questions."

The Humvee is nearly halfway down the mountain now and the road straightens out a bit. "Yeah, like what?" Still thinking he should have been a commando. Remembering, too, that loud noises make him incontinent.

"Let's say you're behind enemy lines and an eight-year-old girl picking tulips spots you, compromising your mission. Are you willing to cut her throat?"

"Jeez," the captain says.

"Nobody said it would be easy," Susan Burns says. "Or try this one. A foreign national will give you intelligence that will save the lives of your entire platoon, but only if you perform fellatio on him. Will you do it?"

The captain thinks a moment. "Would he settle for a handjob?"

Dr. Burns shakes her head. "Sorry."

"What are the right answers?" the captain asks.

"There aren't any. Just as in life, the questions pose unsolvable dilemmas."

"You can say that again." Pukowlski pulls the Humvee to a stop on a plateau just above a worksite. They sit quietly a moment before he says, "It's quite a day for the 318th." Below them is an open missile silo surrounded by workers and heavy equipment. Two camouflaged deuce-and-a-half trucks pull away from a missile silo loaded with dismantled machinery – pumps and electronics gear peeking out from under the tarpaulins. A HEMMT ten-ton tactical truck with a hoist lifts a launch generator from the open silo and drops it into a flatbed truck. "You should have been here yesterday, doc. We pulled out the warheads, then sent them off to Texas to dilute the uranium and plutonium. To me, it was like a funeral."

"I didn't realize the dismantling was this far along," she says.

"Dismantling's not the right word. We're blowing the damn things up."

"That's required under START II, isn't it?"

"Yeah, all fifty PK silos will be history. Plus about 300 Minutemen II's, and a helluva lot more. 'Course nobody asked my opinion of the whole disarmament deal. Not that they asked me in '91 when they took all ICBMs off alert or when they reprogrammed the Command Data Buffers so the missiles are no longer targeted. And not that they asked me when they folded up SAC in '92, and don't you think General Curtis LeMay was turning over in his grave when they pulled that one?"

"I'm sure you're right. 'Bombs Away' LeMay wouldn't have approved."

The captain's eyes narrow into slits. "That's what you east coast, left-wing intellectuals might have called him, but in the Air Force, he was known as 'Old Iron Pants,' and if you don't know why, you've never flown a bombing mission."

"Have you?"

"What's that got to do with it?" the captain asks, sharply. He turns his attention back to the silo, and after a moment, says, "Yeah, the bureaucrats changed everything. Closed down SAC, moved the missile program into Air Combat Command, and when that didn't work, they shoved it into Space Command with the satellite folks. Didn't ask my opinion of that, either. Hell's bells, does anyone know what's going on?"

"What is your opinion about dismantling the silos?"

"Same as my opinion about having to babysit a lady shrink. Both are about as welcome as a carbuncle on my butt."

"Sort of a double whammy for you today."

"Triple. A delegation of Nu-clear Non-pro-lif-er-ationists from the U-nited Nations are here, and they're so tickled they're wetting their pants." He shoots a look at her. "Don't get me wrong. It's nothing personal. I just wish the Congressional committee that sent you out here would get tested, too."

A thirty-two wheel flatbed truck called a transport erector pulls across an intersecting road, headed down valley. Lashed to the truck, like Gulliver in the land of Lilliputians, is an impotent LGM-118A Peacekeeper missile. Pukowlski gestures toward a Humvee on the ridge just below them where five men in suits watch the truck leave. "There the U.N. boys now. I would have asked them to join us, but I'd hate 'em to see a grown man cry."

Susan Burns studies Pukowlski, who appears truly anguished. "If it's so painful, why insist on being here? Why punish yourself?"

"You asking that in your professional capacity?"

"Would the answer be different if I were?" she asks.

"Nah, I just wanted to lie down on a couch, that's all. 'Course if I raise hell about destroying the Peacekeepers, you'll write me up for being a warmongering psycho."

"We're still deploying Minutemen III's and Polaris missiles, and we'll still have thirty-five hundred nuclear warheads even after START II is fully implemented, so what's the problem?"

He doesn't answer, but instead points toward the silo where workers in hard hats are stringing cable around the perimeter of the open hole. "I hate to see anything destroyed, much less anything this beautiful. We're talking about man's greatest achievement, the ability to launch a hundred ninety-five thousand pound vehicle straight out of the ground and send a tin can filled with ten independently targetable warheads halfway around the world at eight times the speed of sound and then hit a bullseye on the Kremlin."

"And *that's* our greatest achievement?" Dr. Burns asks, astonished.

"Do you have any idea the technology that's gone into this? The autonetics, the aerodynamics, the ballistics, the nuclear weaponry?"

"I think I have a rough idea."

He raises his voice. "Then what is there to compare with it? Run-proof panty hose?"

Susan Burns bristles. "That is completely uncalled for, captain, and makes me doubt your ability to fairly command a unit of both men and women."

"I'm sorry, Doctor. It's hard to teach an old dog like me. I remember the first time I saw one of these big cocks – pardon me again, Doc – shooting out of the ground at Vandenberg in a night launch. Jesus, it was like God himself pulled the trigger and lit up the sky. So, I'm serious when I say, what is there to compare with our nuclear technology?"

"Many things. The discovery of antibiotics, the U.S. Constitution, Mozart's Requiem Mass – anything but this." She motions toward the hole where the men have finished laying the cable.

"This," Pukowlski says, "has kept us strong and free."

"We're losing focus here, captain. It's not the technology that I deal with. I'm concerned about the combat readiness of the men and women who will work in the remaining missile squadrons. What's their attitude now that the Cold War is over? Are they alert? Are they disciplined?"

They watch as the men in hard hats head away from the silo

at double time. The last of the trucks has pulled onto the road. A siren wails from a Quonset hut several hundred yards away. Then... KA-BOOM! The sound echoes off the ridges as the silo implodes. Concrete crumbles, and steel rods break. A cloud of dust drifts skyward.

Susan is distracted by something on a distant ridge. Squinting into the sun, she strains to make it out. "Who's that?" she asks, turning to the captain.

"Where?"

She turns back, but no one is there.

"I could have sworn I saw a man wearing buckskins on a horse, right up there," she says, pointing.

The captain barks out a laugh. "Little Big Horn's due north of here just over the Montana line, and a lot of folks report seeing old General Custer wandering around, looking for his men. 'Course, most of those folks have spent their afternoons on a stool at the Old Wrangler Tavern. So if you're seeing cowboys or Indians on horses, doctor, I'm gonna have to write you up."

Below them, there is activity once again. Like grave diggers covering a coffin, bulldozers begin pushing mounds of earth into the hole.

Captain Pukowlski starts up the Humvee and pulls away. "Those questions of yours aren't hard to answer. I can't speak for the whole missile group, but my squadron's bright-eyed, bushy-tailed, and combat ready twenty-four hours a day, three hundred sixty-five days a year. In the 318th, we do it by the book, doctor. I guaran-goddamn-tee it."

❧

Deep in the hole, Airmen Owens and Riordan have their heads buried in blue loose-leaf binders emblazoned with the Air Force insignia and the words, "Technical Order." Owens turns a page and unfolds a color photograph. It's Miss September, nude from her red toenails to her cascading blond hair.

"Tawny's favorite book is 'Bridges of Madison County,'" he says. "Ain't read it myself, but it's okay with me. I do great with intellectual girls." He resumes reading. "Uh-oh. She likes men who work outdoors, have great tans, and drive convertibles. That leaves us out, Billy."

Billy Riordan turns a page in his thumb-worn Bible, tucked inside his binder. "Fallen!" Billy nearly shouts. "Fallen is Babylon the Great, which made all the nations drink the maddening wine of her adulteries."

"Good, Billy. That's very good," Owens says, not even disguising his contempt. "You are the fucking missileer from Mars. Now, I'm gonna read the Playboy Advisor to see what brand of condoms are the silkiest and slipperiest, and you're gonna shut the fuck up or you're gonna have to be reborn again, 'cause Billy, I swear, I'm gonna kill you!"

They both return to their studies, every few minutes looking up at the bank of video monitors. One shows the missile in its silo, steam rising from the idling launch generator; another displays the perimeter of the above-ground facility. A third monitor, aimed at the sentry post, suddenly goes a hazy white, and they both stare at it, uncomprehending.

Owens adjusts the focus, and the picture clears. It's a pair of bare buttocks, close-up, which disappear only to replaced by another set. Their radio receiver crackles. "Launch control, this is sentry post one. Can you confirm reports of excessive lunar activity?"

"The Air Police are really assholes," Owens says.

"God forgives them," Billy says, and Owens grits his teeth and goes back to his magazine, wondering if the captain would let them put a tanning bed in the Launch Equipment Room.

-16-
A Trout in the Milk

Captain Pete Pukowlski slows his Humvee at a bend in the

road just a mile from the missile squadron's sentry post. The river, which tumbles over rocks farther upstream, flows gently alongside the road here. "I'm afraid you're going to find my squadron pretty boring," the captain says to Dr. Susan Burns.

"Boring?"

He turns to face her. "Yeah, compared to the fruitcakes you see back in D.C., my men are boringly normal, run-of-the-mill guys."

"Look out!" she screams.

He wheels back, sees a figure darting across the road, then slams on the brakes. The Humvee swerves and screeches to a stop, barely missing a man who dives into a ditch at the side of the road. "Shit buckets!" Pukowlski shouts. "What damn fool...!"

They get out of the Humvee and approach the ditch. Pulling himself up the embankment is a man wearing only dog tags and boxer shorts. A knife is strapped to his leg. He is sopping wet, muddy, and his skin is streaked orange.

"Jericho!" Pukowlski thunders. "What the hell!"

Jack Jericho snaps a crisp salute, mud dripping from his hand. "Sir." He turns toward Dr. Burns. "Ma'am."

"Sergeant, you're out of uniform," Pukowlski says, not knowing what else to say. Getting angrier, turning red.

"But on time, sir."

"And you look like a goddamn Apache."

"Insect repellent, sir."

Susan Burns suppresses a smile. "Captain, I assume this 'boringly normal run-of-the-mill-guy' does not turn the key."

"Jericho a missileer? Hardly. When he's not AWOL, he mops up the sump."

Jericho clears his throat. "Begging the captain's pardon, I maintain the launch eject gas generators, sir."

"You pathetic excuse for an airman," Pukowlski fumes. "Sergeant, you just earned yourself a job so deep in the hole you can apply for Chinese citizenship!"

"So this sergeant's duties are underground?" Susan asks, the shadow of a thought crossing her face.

Pukowlski is puzzled. "Yeah, why? Can you think of a way we can leave him there when we implode the silo?"

"I think I've found my first guinea pig."

"Jericho ain't crazy, doc. Lazy and stupid maybe, but not crazy."

"Thank you, sir," Jericho says.

Susan Burns studies him. "I think there's more to Sergeant Jack Jericho than meets the eye." She looks him up and down, and at that moment, the tail of a fish emerges from his boxers. "Sergeant, is that a trout in your shorts, or are you just happy to see me?"

Jericho is too embarrassed to answer.

Pukowlski is apoplectic. "Dammit, Jericho! You were under strict orders to complete your perimeter duties and return immediately to the base, not go fishing."

"Fishing, sir?"

"Yeah, fishing. You expect me to believe that rainbow just jumped into your shorts."

"No, sir. But fish have been known to leap into my boat just to save time."

Dr. Burns clears her throat and says, almost apologetically. "I'm afraid I have to agree with the captain's conclusion that you've been fishing, sergeant. Even Henry David Thoreau would find the evidence compelling."

"Who?" Pukowlski demands.

"A writer fellow," Jericho helps out. "He said that sometimes circumstantial evidence is very strong, 'as when you find a trout in the milk.'"

Dr. Burns arches her eyebrows and gives a little smile. "You're a man of surprises, Sergeant Jericho."

"*The Maine Woods* is my favorite book," Jericho explains, "other than the *Launch Generator Maintenance Manual*, of course."

"What the hell does milk have to do with this?" Pukowlski growls. "If you're thinking about getting the cook to try a new recipe, forget it. That trout is history, and so are you. Drop the fish, sergeant."

"Respectfully, sir—"

"Now! That's an order."

"But if—"

"No if's, and's, or but's! Now! Cut it loose."

Jericho takes his knife and slices the drawstring of his boxers. Three trout drop to the ground along with the boxer shorts. Dr. Burns's eyes flick to Jack's groin.

"Well, sergeant," she says, smiling, "I'm happy to see you, too."

-17-
Tunnel Rat

Cool and damp deep inside the mountain, a steady fifty-eight degrees. Beneath the silo floor, the launch generator beats its steady *thumpa-thumpa*. The missile hangs in its cables, waiting. Always waiting.

The gantry, a metal work cage, sits halfway up the silo wall, just below the level of a mesh grating. The grating hangs open, and inside, an exhaust tube runs upward at a slight angle from the silo to the dry river bed one hundred feet above. Acidic residue from tests of the launch generator coats the inside of the exhaust tube. Spiders spin webs across its three foot diameter, and field mice scamper along its length, claws scratching against the metal.

Jack Jericho crawls upward, scouring the tube with a soapy brush. It is a task as useful as scrubbing the inside of a car's tailpipe... three days before junking the car.

"Hey, tunnel rat!" The voice echoes through the tube from the silo. A touch of Georgia. Reynolds' voice. "Gotta borrow your elevator. Have a nice crawl."

Shit. Jericho hears the electrical whir of the gantry riding its rails down toward the silo floor. Reynolds enjoying it, getting even with him for the knife trick, he knows. Now, Jericho either has to squirm all the way to the top and pry off the screen on the exhaust pipe in the river bed, or go back into the silo and leap onto the ladder that runs up the wall. It's only four feet from the exhaust tube opening to the ladder, but if you miss, it's eighty feet straight down.

Jericho keeps scrubbing, knowing that when the tube bends and he loses the light from the silo, the sweats will begin. Not that he won't be able to see. He's wearing the Air Force's version of a miner's helmet. But when he flicks the lamp on, when the shadows begin dancing up the wall, when the distant sound of the launch generator becomes the rumble of the pumps in the mine, the visions will start.

Jonah may have been stuck in the gut of the whale, he thinks, but I'm jammed up its rectum.

Jericho hauls himself around the first bend in the tube and reaches up to turn on the helmet lamp. As he does, an exposed bolt catches his sleeve. His arm is bent at an awkward angle above his head, and for a moment, he is stuck. He tries to wriggle backward, but the curvature of the tube stops him. Sweat streams down his face. From somewhere above him, he hears the *pinging* of groundwater dripping into the tube.

He squeezes his eyes shut, trying to shut it out, but he cannot. He tries reciting Thoreau. "'Talk of mysteries. Think of our life in nature – rocks, trees, wind on our cheeks, the solid earth!'"

But the earth is not solid here. It spins around him. He is dizzy, nauseous. The *pinging* grows louder, becomes the roar of rushing water, and now there's no stopping the ghostly shapes that form in the darkness. The roar of the water becomes deafening, and a thousand noises mingle, then echo from inside the cavern. The crashing timbers, the crackling wires and the screams. Always, the screams.

Feeling the water rising around him, the visions come, too. He sees men crushed under tons of rock and wood, hears the life squeezed out of them. Their bodies become skeletons, crawling toward him, bones *clacking*, grasping for him, reaching, reaching...

To drown it out, to hide from the hideous din, to run from the blood-soaked bony hands, he bellows into the darkness, the wail of a wounded animal. Time and again, he shrieks at the night, at his own fear and shame.

-18-
Rye Whiskey I Cry

"Would you describe yourself as a leader or a follower?" Dr. Susan Burns asks, looking up from a notepad.

Jack Jericho stretches his neck. Sitting in straight-backed chairs always seemed unnatural. "Don't your fancy books have any other choices?"

"Like what?"

"Like loner. I just want to be left the hell alone."

"Would you rather be rich or famous?" she asks.

"Neither one interests me. But if I was rich, I'd buy an Orvis graphite fishing rod."

"Feared or respected?"

"I just want to go through life without hurting anybody else. Isn't that enough?"

"I don't know," Dr. Burns says, "is it?"

Jericho scowls and doesn't answer.

"Perhaps we can place these questions in the context of your life. Tell me what you remember about the mountains," Dr. Burns gently orders.

"The flowers in the spring. Mountain laurel, azaleas, a bunch of others, I'm not sure of their names. And the birds, hoot owls and whippoorwills, and quail in the pine forests. When they whistle, it sounds like they're calling out, 'Bob White.' You can hunt them in season, but I never did. I laid out seed in the back yard and made friends with a couple of them every year. They were darn near tame."

The sounds around them are not the calls of birds in the forest but the constant *thumpa-thumpa* of the launch generator below them in the sump. They are sitting in metal chairs in the Launch Equipment Room, halfway down the tunnel that runs from the launch control capsule to the missile silo. Around them are metal shelves stacked with huge batteries, cables, electrical gear and spare parts. A bare 75-watt bulb illuminates the room, casting shadows across the floor.

Jericho has cleaned up. He's in the utility uniform of olive coveralls, three stripes on his sleeve, no medals on his chest. Dr. Susan Burns, in her blue business suit, looks at him with the practiced demeanor of detached professionalism. "What first comes to mind when you think of home?"

"Home baked bread slathered with molasses."

"How did you and your friends spend your time?"

He pulls a package of Zig-Zag cigarette papers from his pocket. "When we weren't reading Dostoevski, you mean?"

"Sergeant, this is serious."

Jericho slips into a down-home Appalachian accent. "Hell, doc, us hillbillies kept busy shuckin' corn, raisin' barns, and duelin' banjos. Once we got the cable, everythin' changed. Movin' pitchers all the way from New York City."

"Your use of self-deprecating humor to change the subject is an obvious ploy," Dr. Burns says, drumming her pencil on a note pad.

"Is it, doctor? Or is it a manifestation of primary anxiety, a response of the ego to increases in instinctual tension?"

Her drumming stops in mid-beat. She opens Jericho's personnel file and thumbs through it. "You had three years of college."

"Guilty as charged. All that book learnin' and look where it got me."

"Why'd you drop out? Your grades were exemplary." She looks up from the file and shoots him a quizzical look. "You majored in English, and..." She smiles at him. "You minored in psychology."

Jericho doesn't answer, just tamps some tobacco into a cigarette paper. She resumes reading, then says, "After your junior year at W.V.U., you took a summer job in the coal mines. Your father was a miner, wasn't he?"

Jericho licks the paper closed and slips the cigarette into the corner of his mouth but doesn't light it. "My daddy used to take seventy five pounds of corn meal and mix it with three hundred pounds of sugar, a little yeast, some bran and about three hundred gallons of water. In four days, *voila,* or as we say in the mountains, 'Holy shit.' Fifty gallons of mountain dew, or if you prefer, whiskey."

"Your father was a bootlegger."

"No, Al Capone was a bootlegger. My daddy was a moonshiner who didn't give up his day job. 'Course, in the mines, it's always night, isn't it?"

"Tell me about your father."

"What's to tell?"

"Were you embarrassed by his illegal activities?"

Jericho laughs. "No, was Richard Nixon's family? Look, there's nothing wrong with moonshining. The government lets you bake bread and sell it to your neighbors, but not cook up some rye whiskey. Mountain folk are independent and don't necessarily listen to the government, which never did much for them anyway. My daddy's daddy made corn liquor and drove it to his customers down valley. I don't know what he enjoyed more, sipping the whiskey or driving like a bat out of hell, avoiding the revenuers."

"So you admired your grandfather?"

"He was his own man, didn't take orders from anyone."

"And you do?"

"I take orders from everyone from an E-6 to the President. Hell, I even take orders from a lady shrink."

"Did your grandfather work in the mines, too?"

"He was a farmer, forty acres of rocks and sandy topsoil. In the winter, he made whiskey. You know why they call them moonshiners?"

"Why?"

"'They work at night so the revenuers can't see the smoke from the stills." Jericho breaks into a song:

"Rye whiskey, rye whiskey,
Rye whiskey I cry.
If I can't get rye whiskey,

I surely will die."
Susan Burns looks at him sternly.
"What'd you expect?" he asks. "John Denver?"
"Your father," Dr. Burns says.
"What about him?"
"When I asked about him, you changed the subject to your grandfather, then to the etymology of moonshining, and finally to a mountain song."
"I don't follow you."
"Oh, but you do. You purposely avoid talking about your father."
"If I did talk, would it bring him back?"
"No. But it might bring *you* back."
Jericho shakes his head. "I've done this before."
"Do it again. Tell me about your father."
"My daddy drove a '60 Dodge with the heaviest springs you ever saw. Forty cases in the car, and it wouldn't sink an inch. No one ever caught him either."
"What are you leaving out?"
He avoids her gaze. "Leaving out?"
"The day job," she says, sternly. "Tell me about the mine."
His eyes harden. "You've read my file. You know all about it."
"If you don't cooperate, I'm required to report you to the captain."
"The captain can kiss me where the sun don't shine."
"Very colorful. You play the role convincingly."
The unlit cigarette in the corner of his mouth wags at her. "It's not a role. It's who I am."
Her voice is harsh and reproachful. "It's who you *were*. But you left the mountains ten years ago. You've been stationed on six different bases around the world. You read books, which believe me, sets you apart. Yet you cling to your earlier identity."
"Can any of us escape our identities?"
"Do you want to?"
He smiles ruefully. "I forgot. You shrinks don't answer questions.

You just scoop 'em up and toss 'em back like a quick-fingered shortstop." He sighs and says, "What do you want to know?"

"Your feelings after the accident in the mine."

He looks into the darkness. The *thumpa* of the generators is not unlike the pumps in the mine. He closes his eyes and feels the cold, black water filling the shaft, knee-deep now. He reaches out, trying to catch onto a wet, rocky wall, but his hand slips off. A powerful shearing sound from above, the earth ripping itself apart. He has lost his helmet and covers his head with his hands. Rocks pelt him, and a roar thunders from above. A falling beam glances off him, slashing his shoulder and back. Even now, he winces with pain and opens his eyes to see Dr. Susan Burns looking at him with compassion. He has seen the look before and hates it. Hates his own weakness that attracts the sympathy of others.

"My feelings," he says, bitterly, "were real simple. My father and brother were dead, and I wanted to be."

"Why do you blame yourself? Could you have saved them?"

"I could have tried. Instead, I ran."

"According to the reports, you followed procedure. You went to the emergency shaft and the evacuation route."

"Right, I followed orders," he says sarcastically.

"You did what you were supposed to do."

"I did what I was *told* to do." He lets it hang there, remembering. He can hear the gantry inside the silo running up its track. Beneath them, the mixture of a dozen mechanical and hydraulic sounds. "For a long time, I thought about killing myself, but the closest I got was nearly drinking myself to death."

Neither speaks for a long moment until she says, "Is that why your wife left you?"

Jericho's laugh is little more than a rasp. "Cleaning up my puke at three in the morning sorely tested her patience."

"I understand your running from your past, but why do you hide your intelligence?"

"Why do you hide your sexuality?" he shoots back.

For a moment, they both listen to the pumps and the thumping generator below them. "What's that supposed to mean?" she asks.

"Somewhere, someplace, someone told you that your good looks were a hindrance in your profession. So you don't wear makeup. Your blue suit with its Little Bo Peep white silk blouse and bow is right out of a Dress for Success guide in some woman's magazine that probably also gives advice for orgasms in five minutes or less without the nuisance of a companion. You're not married or engaged, at least, you're not wearing any rings. In fact, you're not wearing any jewelry, unless we count that sports watch that's waterproof to forty feet. I figure you use the built-in stopwatch to get your twenty-five minutes on the treadmill at a trendy gym in Georgetown where the TV's are tuned to C-Span instead of ESPN."

"Actually, I use it to time those five-minute orgasms."

Jericho laughs. "But you do have a sense of humor, Dr. Burns, and that makes up for a lot."

She turns away, her cheeks coloring. "I can't believe I said that, Sergeant. Forgive me. It was very unprofessional of me."

Now, Jericho studies her. After a moment, he smiles broadly. "No, it wasn't. It was very professional. Nicely done, but the shy blush was a little over the top. It was your effort to break through to me, to show you're human. Or maybe it's even more complicated. Maybe, you're encouraging some transference. Maybe you want me to relate to you as if you're my long lost wife."

"Sergeant Jack Jericho," she says, a touch wistfully, "you are a man full of surprises, and you are so much smarter than you look."

"Thanks, doc," Jericho replies, slouching in his chair and flicking the unlit cigarette through a grating into the black water of the sump. "And you're purtier than a trussed-up hog on Christmas Eve."

She exhales a sigh and closes his file, then clicks her pen closed and slides it into a pouch in her notebook. "All right, Jericho. Let's make a deal. You stop playing hayseed and I'll stop playing doctor."

"Then what do we do?"

"We talk. Has it ever occurred to you that you may not be the only one to have suffered a loss?"

He gauges the seriousness of her look and says, "I'm listening."

"I'll tell you a story about a father who was a psychiatrist and also taught at the university, a mother who was active in the P.T.A., and a nine-year-old tomboy with freckles who could skip rope blindfolded and hit a baseball farther than any of the boys."

"The American ideal," he says, tentatively.

"So what question should you ask, Jericho?"

"What are you leaving out, Dr. Burns?"

"Did I mention that my mother slept with every man who smiled at her, and there were a lot of big sloppy grins in my hometown? Did I mention that my father drank, and that the former probably contributed to the latter?"

"I'm sorry," Jericho says, embarrassed. "If you don't want to tell me this—"

"Of course I do! That's the point, Jericho."

He looks into her dark eyes. "All right, tell me about your loss."

She looks away and cocks her head, as if listening to a far off voice. "My father committed suicide, hung himself in the foyer of our home. He slung one of mother's belts over an exposed beam. It was a red leather belt that she wore with a matching skirt. Why do you suppose he didn't go down to Home Depot and buy a stout rope?"

He thinks about it a moment. "Because your mother wore the red leather outfit when she stepped out and your father knew it. He wanted her to suffer."

"You missed your calling, sergeant. You have a natural talent for discerning psychological symbolism. Now tell me, why did my father hang himself in the foyer of his own home? Why not park the car on some deserted road and run a hose from the tail pipe? Why not dive off a bridge?"

"Same reason. He wanted your mother to find him. He wanted her to wake at night and see him hanging there."

"Then what a pity that she didn't find him."

"Who did?" Jericho asks, but even as the words come out, he knows. He grasps both of Susan's hands between his own. "Oh dear

God, I'm sorry."

She looks away and does not see the tear tracking down Jericho's cheek. "My mother had an appointment at the beauty parlor and then should have gone home to put the roast in the oven. Does anyone cook roasts anymore, Jericho? Anyway, I guess she didn't want to waste that new permanent, because she headed straight to a Holiday Inn just off U.S. 1 where they had a back elevator and the assistant principal of the elementary school – my school – could get a room cheap for a couple of hours. This was a man who would pat me on the head and say I'd be even prettier than my mother."

"If this is too painful for you, why not just—"

"Shut up, Jericho! This is healthy. You really ought to try it." She runs a hand through her hair and looks at Jericho straight on. "My mother didn't show up, so I walked home from school. The key was under the mat, just like always, and as I was opening the door, I was thinking about Oreo cookies and a big glass of cold milk. I opened the door and at that precise instant, the three of us are forever frozen in time. My mother was no more than a mile away, her red-tinted hair spread across a motel pillow. Just inside the door was the lifeless shell that had once been my father, swinging gently in the breeze of the air-conditioning, his face twisted into a mask of pain and horror. And there I was, in the last seconds of my childhood."

"I am so very sorry," Jericho says, squeezing her hands.

She looks up at him. "No more milk and cookies, Jericho."

They are both silent a moment. Then Jericho says, "What can I do to help?"

"Don't you understand you just did?"

He shakes his head.

"Just listening," she says, "letting me work it out is therapeutic. And if I can, I'll help you."

Jericho gnaws at his lower lip. She waits, letting him summon it up. Finally, he says, "Tell me about the pain. Does it ever go away?"

"No."

"What do you feel now?"

"Anger at the utter unfairness of it all. A searing, red-hot hatred for father, for mother, for the whole damn world."

He lets go of her hands, giving them a final pat. "Then you're in worse shape than I am."

"What does that mean?" she asks.

"I only hate me," Jack Jericho says.

-19-
The Power and the Glory

Until today, Captain Pete Pukowlski always loved giving The Tour.

In the past, he had escorted Congressmen, VIP's from aerospace companies, and delegations of our so-called Allies from Western Europe. Hell, he even showed the place to two Russian Air Force generals after the fall of Communism, though only because he was ordered to, and even then, he carried his .45, loaded with the safety off, just in case they tried any sneaky commie tricks. He also refused to answer their questions about the inertial guidance system and the megatonnage of the Multiple Independently Targetable Reentry Vehicles – ten Avco Mk 21 RV's to be exact – that sit atop the big cock of the Peacekeeper.

The third time General Itchykov – or whatever the hell his name was – asked about the missile's accuracy and throw weight, Pukowlski told him, "We can drop twenty megatons right down the chimney of Boris Yeltstin's *dacha*. Does that answer your question, Ivan?"

Not that Ivan was the general's name, but Pukowlski, who was damn proud the chairman of the joint chiefs was as Polish as kielbasa, would no more call this Rusky "General" than he would paste a "Make Love, Not War" sticker on his Jeep. Anyway, old Ivan didn't need a translator to figure it out, and he damn sure stopped asking questions.

Today, as always, Pukowlski starts The Tour in the Security

Command Center, then moves across the bridge to the elevator
housing, then brings them down into the launch control capsule.
Owens and Riordan are on-duty in the hole, and he's advised them
to have their shoes shined and their chins shaved. "Spit-and-polish
today, men. Let's not give the bastards an excuse to go after the
missiles we still have left."

Strapped into their flight chairs, Owens and Riordan make
a show of studying the gauges on the console in front of them.
For once, they're following orders, and Pukowlski is thankful.
He knows it's stultifyingly boring work. Twenty-four shifts, one
missileer allowed to catnap while the other stays on duty. And
he knows the whole shebang is almost over. Which makes today
bittersweet. Pukowlski stands behind the two missileers, the U.N.
Committee members at his side, casting suspicious glances at the
old console, the drab green communications racks, the sweeping
radar beams, the multi-colored lights. There is a 1960's feel to the
place, Pukowlski knows, and he considers himself a dinosaur, too.
Pukowlski shows them the thumbwheels under the yellow metal
flaps where the two launch codes are entered and then the slots
where the keys are inserted. That's when the questions come up,
and his answers are always the same.

"Of course it's completely fail safe," he tells the U.N. delegation,
a committee of thousand-dollar suits from England, Japan, Israel,
Russia, and Germany. "First, you've got to enter the Enable Code.
That's like pulling the hammer back on a gun. Then you need to
enter the target info, the Preparatory Launch Command, which is
also coded. That's like pointing the gun. Finally, you've got to turn
the keys. That's pulling the trigger. And the same commands must
come from a second capsule, guarding against having a couple of
lunatics under my command."

He shoots a look at Owens and Riordan, who are both poker-
faced recruiting posters. "There's also a safety measure that's so
classified, even I don't know it, and if I did, I wouldn't tell you."
The delegation chuckles a little. "So, in short, gentlemen," he
continues, looking at the Israeli, who coincidentally is indeed quite

short, "there's no way on earth there could ever be an unauthorized launch."

The Englishman, a gent in a grey suit, silk polka dot tie with matching pocket handkerchief, watches Billy Riordan, who stares intently at the console, not even appearing to blink. "And these lads with the keys," the Englishman says, "who are they and how do you assure their competence?"

"The missileers are the elite, the cream of the crop," Pukowlski says, watching Owens suppress a smile. "They have rigorous training and complete psychological testing prior to be assigned to a launch capsule. We're constantly alert for any hint of trouble in their personal lives. Drunk driving charge, they're out of the hole. Divorce, out of the hole. Hell, if they get a prescription for codeine from a dentist, they're out of the hole for a week." Pukowlski clears his throat and points to a monitor, which shows the Peacekeeper in the silo. "Now, gentlemen, if you don't have any further questions, shall we proceed to the highlight of the tour?"

The Englishman nods, gives Billy Riordan one last look, then follows Pukowlski out the blast door. The captain escorts the delegation down the tunnel from the launch control capsule toward the silo. He makes a mental note that Owens and Riordan didn't close the blast door behind them. A year ago, hell, six weeks ago, he would have written them up. Now? What difference does it make anyway? They pass the Sleeping Quarters/Galley on the right and the Launch Equipment Room on the left, then enter the silo, passing over the grates of the drainage sump. More spacious than the newer underground facilities, this one is the last of the old Titan silos, now converted for the Peacekeeper.

They enter the silo where the PK, a "damage limitation weapon," in Air Force parlance, is suspended by steel cables from the walls. Heavy propulsion hoses run from generators under the silo to the base of the missile. "Here's why we've got strategic stability in the world," Pukowlski tells them.

"Strategic stability," the English ambassador repeats in an accent laced with the House of Lords.

"The absence of overt conflict," Pukowlski says. "What you might call 'peace.'"

"Then why don't you?" the Englishman asks. Pukowlski doesn't like the snotty tone of voice, and besides, he considers the English a bunch of fairies, so he ignores the question.

They walk in a circle beneath the suspended missile, ducking under a suspended umbilical cord that hangs from near the top of the missile. He pauses to let them look up into the burners. "A four-stage power plant," he says, "the first three fueled by solid propellant, the fourth hypergolic liquid. This baby is cold-launched from the canister by a launch eject gas generator. *Whoosh!*" Pukowlski makes a gliding motion with his hand, and for a moment, the crew-cut, husky forty-year-old is a kid again. "When it's cleared the silo, the computer in the deployment module sends a signal to fire up the rockets, and the first stage ignites. Lordy, what a sight that is. And fast? This baby hits apogee at an altitude of four million feet in fifteen minutes, two thousand miles down range."

"Who builds this rocket?" the Israeli ambassador asks.

Pukowlski gives him the fish eye. "Why, you want to buy stock or maybe get some preemptive deterrence insurance against the A-rabs?"

"We are at peace with our neighbors," the Israeli says brusquely.

"Yeah, aren't we all? Anyway, the first stage was built by Thiokol, second by Aerojet, third by Hercules, and fourth by Rocketdyne. The guidance is by Rockwell, I.M.U. by Northrop, assembly and testing by Martin Marietta and Denver Aerospace. First string, All-American know-how, top to bottom." He winks at the Japanese ambassador. "You fellows do a helluva job with Toyotas and TV sets, but if you want a four-stage ICBM, there's only one place to shop."

"We do not want such a thing," the Japanese ambassador says. "Our memories of Hiroshima and Nagasaki are still alive."

"Little Boy and Fat Man," Pukowlski says, almost wistfully. "Before my time, and obsolete as a buggy whip by today's technology. You know Little Boy hit Hiroshima with only twenty kilotons, a lousy fifth of a megaton of U-235 in a gun-assembly bomb. Nothing like the fission-fusion-fission thermonuclear warheads today. Can you imagine the damage that ten warheads, each with two megaton lithium deuteride cores, could do?"

"Yes," says the Japanese ambassador. "I can."

"'Course you fellows are our friends now, and we let bygones be bygones. We had our Pearl Harbor, you had your Hiroshima."

The Japanese ambassador's look is not as forgiving. "And Nagasaki."

"Yeah, war is hell."

There is mumbling in foreign languages that Pukowlski neither understands nor cares to. Leading the visitors toward the gantry, he says, "Let's take a ride."

They squeeze aboard, Pukowlski hits a switch, and the gantry runs up the track in the wall of the silo. As they ascend along the shaft of the missile, nearly close enough to touch its dull black surface, Pukowlski launches into his statistical routine. He could be a tour guide telling visitors how many steps there are inside the Statute of Liberty. "The PK is seventy-one feet long and eight feet, seven inches in diameter. Fully loaded with fuel, it weighs one hundred ninety-five thousand pounds. What you're looking at is a coating of black rubber that covers the Kevlar skin. Up at the top, what looks like a silver bullet, is the titanium shroud covering the nose cone. The shroud ejects when the PK's still on the way up, just two minutes into flight. 'Course, it's already at four hundred thousand feet altitude. From there on out, the MIRV's are exposed. They're made of carbon-carbon, about four feet high, kind of look like black ice cream cones coming at you, pointy-end first, but they're flying at six thousand miles an hour, and instead of filled with strawberry or chocolate, they've got the power of God inside."

"I don't believe I've ever heard nuclear weaponry described as divine," the Israeli ambassador says.

"You don't hang out in the right church." The ambassador is a chubby little guy with curly hair who reminds Pukowlski of a comedian he saw on the cable. What the hell was that guy's name?

BALLISTIC

The gantry stops at the level of the nose cone. The captain hits a switch, and the cage extends horizontally toward the missile.

"Now, you're gonna get an experience only a few human beings have been privileged to partake," he says with excessive formality. The cage stops just inches from the nose cone. Pukowlski reaches out and touches the tip. Then he strokes it, his hand caressing the shiny, smooth titanium shroud. "Put your hand on the greatest power the world has ever known," he tells the group. "You can even feel the computer clicking away, and if you close your eyes and use your imagination, you can feel the might of the dragon."

The ambassadors whisper among themselves, but none reaches out to pet the missile. Embarrassed, Pukowlski clears his throat and hits the switch to retract the gantry to the wall. "You fellows gotta forgive me. When I'm this close to the power and the glory, I get downright poetic."

⁊

Dr. Susan Burns has joined lieutenants Owens and Riordan in the launch control capsule. On a monitor above their heads, Captain Pukowlski is visible on the gantry, stroking the shroud, the ambassadors watching him.

"Puke's copping a feel again," Owens says. He has run his flight chair all the way to the far end of the console, and he sits there, alternating his attention between the monitor and the multiple choice questions on the Minnesota Multiphasic Personality Inventory answer sheet. "'Would you rather be rich or respected?'" he reads aloud. "Shit, that's easy, Dr. Burns. If you're rich, you can buy respect."

He fills in a blank, then continues reading, moving his lips slightly. "'Did you ever cheat in school?' Jeez, who didn't?"

"Lieutenant Owens," Dr. Burns says. "Would it be possible for you to complete the test silently?"

"Sure thing. Almost done." He gives her a smile that even tip-hungry barmaids have found resistible.

86

While Owens finishes revealing the innermost depths of his skin-deep personality, Susan Burns moves to Billy Riordan. First she attaches a blood-pressure cuff on his right arm. Then she hands him a Rorschach ink blot card.

"Tell me what you see," she instructs him.

"Chaos," Billy says without hesitation.

"Of course, but what do you make of it? What images or emotions are evoked by the drawing?"

"You don't understand, Doctor. What I see really *is* chaos. Anarchy, carnage, bloodshed, lambs led to the slaughter."

Susan Burns watches the digital readout on the blood-pressure gauge as the numbers soar higher. She pauses to make a notation on a pad. Just then, a *rumble* as Owens rolls his chair down the track toward them. He shoots a look over Billy's shoulder and says, "I'll tell you what I see, doc."

"Lieutenant Owens! Let your deputy do—"

"A woman with massive warheads, real first-strike hooters," he goes on, unperturbed.

"Owens, please!" she pleads with him. "I'm required to test both of you while you're on duty, but you're making it impossible."

"Sorry, but whadaya think? Am I normal?"

"Owens, you're a certified, card-carrying American male."

"Thanks, doc," he says, then rolls down the rail to the other end of the console.

Susan Burns turns back to Billy Riordan and flips to the next ink blot.

"Now, Lieutenant Riordan, what do you see?"

Billy takes his time with this one. Beads of sweat form on his forehead. Susan Burns watches as the blood pressure hits a way-too-high 210 over 135. "What is it, lieutenant? What comes to mind?"

Softly. "The fires of hell."

"I see."

"Do you, doctor?" Louder now. "Do you see the pestilence, war, famine, and death?"

"Why don't you explain it to me?"

"It is written in the Book. It is sung by angels in the heavens."

"Do you mean that literally, Riordan? Do the angels really sing?"

"Everything in the Book means just what it says. The angels are real, and so are their songs."

"Are there times you can hear them?"

"Now," Billy says. "I can hear them now."

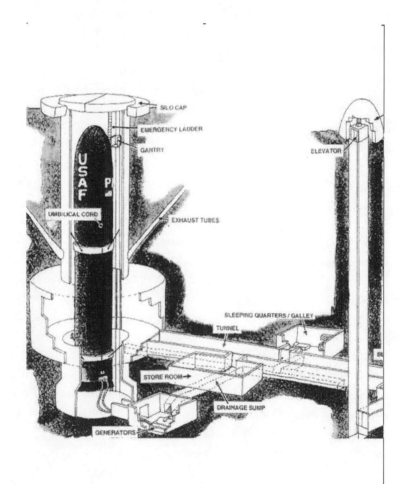

BOOK THREE

Soldiers of the Apocalypse

-20-
Kill Them All

An old VW van shifts gears and heads slowly up the road of crushed rock, winding around the mountain. Inside, Rachel drives and Brother David sits next to her, holding a Bible. He is in his country preacher's garb, black suit, white shirt, and thin, dark tie. A blonde ten-year-old girl with pigtails sits on his lap.

The van passes the sign, "Rattlesnake Hills Sewage Plant - No Trespassing" and approaches the sentry post of the 318th Missile Squadron. David picks up a microphone. "We shall throw Satan into the abyss and seal it for a thousand years," he proclaims, his voice tinny and shrill though the speaker on the van's roof.

Inside the Quonset hut, Air Security Policeman Carson has just discarded a useless nine of clubs and picked up a king of hearts. Three kings. "Damn. Never fails. I'm one card away from gin, and look who shows up."

"Your whole life is one card away from gin," Air Policeman Dempsey says, taking a short pull on a silver flask of bourbon. "Keep playing. If we ignore them, maybe they'll go away."

The amplified voice of Brother David grows louder, "Judgment day is at hand!"

"Damn right it is," Carson says, tossing down a stray queen of clubs. "I knock with seven. Whadaya got?"

"Shit. I can't count that high."

"Loser plays cop," Carson says, laughing.

Dempsey puts on his beret, just a bit crooked, hitches up his pants, and heads outside.

☙

Deep underground in the launch control capsule, 1st Lieutenant Owens skims his seven-month old copy of *Playboy.* He looks up at a security monitor and sees Air Policeman Dempsey approach the van in front of the sentry post. Brother David gets out, carrying his Bible. The little girl in pigtails gets out, too, carrying a bouquet of long-stemmed Indian paintbrush flowers. "Hey Billy, look. The God Squad is back."

But Billy is huddled over the answer sheet of his personality test, using a Number 2 pencil to shade in the blanks. Dr. Susan Burns watches him, occasionally making notes on her pad, trying to classify the young 2nd lieutenant. Schizophrenic is a word that comes to her mind. She makes a note to expedite the results on the urine drug screen.

Nothing in Riordan's file reveals any prior incidents of mental instability. Born in Cleveland, an only child of average intelligence, he was one of those kids who went through high school without gaining fame or infamy. No extracurricular activities, no detentions or arrests. His parents were divorced when he was six. His father, a career Army non-com, was transferred to South Korea when Billy was twelve, and then to a number of other posts during his teenage years. Though he always paid his child support, Sgt. Wendell Riordan hadn't seen his son since moving away. Billy enrolled at Ohio State, sleepwalked through Air Force ROTC and liberal arts, and after graduation, was commissioned as a second louie. He did his missile training at Vandenberg Air Force Base in California where he adequately performed the routine, repetitive tasks assigned to him. His personality tests placed him in the vast, gray dull mass of men who lead lives of neither fame nor infamy.

"Captain's gonna throw a hissy fit," Owens says, looking at the monitor. He shoots a look at Billy, who is chewing his pencil as he studies the questions on the printed form. "Hey, doc," Owens says, "can a multiple choice test show multiple personalities, 'cause if it does, Billy boy's gonna be off the Richter."

Susan Burns ignores him, and Owens goes back to his magazine.

❧

Air Policeman Dempsey has his thumbs hooked in his belt. "Like I told you before, Reverend, this ain't Yellowstone. It's off limits to—"

"No place on earth is off limits to those seeking the Word," David says. He nods to the little girl, who wears a yellow sun dress with blue polka dots. She giggles and hands Dempsey the bouquet of blood-red flowers. "These are for you, mister," she says, "a present from heaven."

Dempsey takes the flowers, feeling a little foolish. "Thank you. Security Command could use a little decorating."

"And perhaps I can leave something for your brothers-in-arms to remember me by," David says. He hands his Bible to Dempsey, who now has a bouquet of flowers in one hand and the good Book in the other. Something in the movement of David's hand catches Dempsey's eye.

The glint of the sun off shiny metal.

A blade.

If Dempsey had the reflexes of a great athlete, or if he had been primed for trouble, or if he had not consumed half a flask of bourbon before lunch, or if his hands hadn't been full, perhaps he could have leapt back, unsnapped his holster, and pulled his Colt Government Model .45. But all he does is stand there, dumbly disbelieving, as the blade of a stiletto sweeps a graceful arc toward his neck.

The blade catches Dempsey's carotid artery and severs it cleanly. As blood spurts into the air, he clutches his throat and staggers, falling into David's arms.

"Help!" David yells. "Your friend fainted. Help us here!"

Air Policeman Carson stumbles out of the Quonset hut to see David propping up Dempsey. Carson rushes in that direction, then stops. A fountain of blood shoots from Dempsey's neck and cascades over a bouquet of flowers scattered on the ground. Even with his training, there is a moment of utter paralysis, a frozen second of hesitation.

❧

In the launch control capsule, Owens looks at the monitor, where David seems to be helping Dempsey stand up. "Get a load of this," Owens says. "Dempsey's drunk again."

On the screen, David waltzes Dempsey three paces to the left and out of camera range.

"Dempsey's lucky the captain's still in the silo," Owens says, looking around, but neither the psychiatrist nor Billy pay any attention to him. He turns his attention back to a *Playboy* pictorial on women fire fighters, wondering if they hold the hoses so lovingly when they're really on duty.

❧

The rear door of the van bursts open, and the broad-shouldered Gabriel leaps out, followed by six men in commando garb – camouflage uniforms, combat boots, helmets, cheeks smeared with eye-black, assault rifles at port arms. Gabriel raises his rifle, a ribbed-silenced MP-5.

Airman Carson backs up toward the Quonset hut. "Oh, shit! Oh, holy shit!" He turns and scrambles through the open door of the security post, his knees rubbery. He's reaching for the phone when five slugs *thump* through the metal skin of the Quonset hut and cut him down.

The next sixty seconds proceed with deadly synchronization.

One of Gabriel's men uses wire cutters to snip the lines on the security cameras.

A five-ton truck with a snowplow pulls out from behind the bend on the gravel road and plows through the security gate.

Commandos pour out of the truck and spread into an infantry attack formation. Leapfrogging each other along the access road, ducking behind trees and bushes, they work their way toward the security building. Except for the crunch of boots on gravel, and the distant song of an Audubon warbler, no sounds disturb the tranquil setting.

At the head of the formation, Matthew leads two commandos to the outer steel door of the security building. At the same time, James, a slight bespectacled commando with pale, wispy hair and acne scars, pries open an electrical box adjacent to the building. He pulls out a handful of wires and begins cutting.

At that moment, an airman in shorts and running shoes jogs around the corner of the building from the direction of the barracks. He's wearing earphones, listening to music. He sees the commandos and stops short.

A burst of automatic weapons fire drops him. He tries to stand, holding his abdomen where his intestines protrude from a gaping wound. A second burst punctures his throat, and he falls to the ground, drowning in his own blood. The earphones have come off, and for a moment, there is the faint, ironic voice of Jimmy Buffet, praising the wonders of cheeseburgers in paradise.

⌘

In the launch control capsule, the monitors go blank, the sweeping beams on the radar screen fade to black, and the teletype stops clacking.

Owens bangs on the console. "Not again. Billy, you want to crank up the generator?"

Billy is still huddled over his multiple choice test, Susan Burns watching him.

"Never mind," Owens says, "I'll do it myself." He hits a switch, and a whirring noise emanates from the sump.

❦

Gabriel leads a second group of commandos through the stand of Ponderosa pine trees beyond the security building. There, in the shadow of the aqueduct that runs down the mountain from Chugwater Dam, two wooden buildings – the barracks and mess hall – sit peacefully next to a baseball diamond cut into the weedy soil.

The soldiers of the Apocalypse take up positions behind trees, peering toward the buildings through scoped —16's. In front of the mess hall, close to the baseball field, two soldiers play catch, their voices carrying toward the woods. Gabriel hears them debating the relative merits of the New York Mets and the Atlanta Braves. Even from this distance, he can detect the southern accent of the Braves' fan. Gabriel gives a silent signal by pointing to the commando nearest him. *You take the one the left. On three.*

Gabriel sights the ballplayer, who faces him. Aims at the center of his chest. *Two to the chest, one to the head. Makes the perp good and dead.* Gabriel's father was a cop in Houston, and that's what he always said. But a quick burst here, three 5.56 millimeter slugs, all aimed at the chest would likely blow out Atlanta's sternum, lung, and maybe his heart.

Pop, pop, pop. The riflemen fire simultaneously, and the ballplayers crumple to the ground. At the sound of the gunshots, a barechested airman, his face covered with shaving cream, emerges from the barracks. He sees the fallen airmen, whirls around, looking into the woods, but does not see the attackers. A gunshot from the trees creases his temple, and his shaving cream beard turns red. A second later, a fusillade peppers his body, and he falls. The commandos emerge from the trees and fire on full automatic, shredding the wooden walls on the barracks.

Attached to the rear of the barracks is a small concrete block building, the latrine and showers. Standing under a roaring shower head, lathered with soap, oblivious to the danger, Airman Reynolds sings "Do It To Me" in a voice never mistaken for Lionel Ritchie.

☙

Inside Security Command, five airmen play poker at a desk littered with donuts, Styrofoam coffee cups and poker chips. From outside, the muffled crackle of small arms fire. Lieutenant Cooper spills his coffee. "What the fuck was that?"

"Probably one of the Air Police taking target practice," an airman says.

"Bet we get venison for dinner," says a third.

Suddenly, the room goes dark, and the humming equipment goes silent.

"Generator!" Cooper yells.

Someone hits a switch and the lights come up to half power.

☙

The door to the barracks is in splinters. The remaining airmen, wounded and bleeding, are in hand-to-hand combat with the commandos. Pistol fire echoes through the close quarters. Gabriel uses a knife to eviscerate a young airman and leads his men through the barracks. "Kill them all!" he orders.

Using his bunk for cover, Airman Sayers empties his sidearm into the advancing commandos, then ducks for cover behind a footlocker. A noise from behind, and Sayers whirls around. A commando bursts through the back door and surprises him, the M-16A2 just inches from his face. Instinctively, Sayers reaches for the barrel and they wrestle for the gun. Sayers get leverage and dumps the commando to the floor as gunshots shatter the window above his head. The commando is on his knees when Sayers gets him in a headlock and twists, breaking the man's neck.

Sayers gets to his feet and sees another commando with an Uzi turning toward him. Just as a volley of slugs rips into the wall, Sayers dives out the open window.

∽

"Where the hell's the captain?" someone shouts in the semi-darkness of Security Command.

"In the silo playing tour guide," someone else answers.

Lieutenant Cooper tries to take control. "All right, everybody pipe down. We probably just blew a fuse. Anybody reach Dempsey at the sentry post?"

"He doesn't answer."

"Shit! What the hell's going on?"

Before anyone can answer, the dull thud of an explosion flattens the outer door of the security building and rattles the wall of the command center.

"Jumping Jesus!" Cooper is on his feet. "Get on the horn to STRATCOM! Raise Space Command! Now!"

The Radio Operator grabs a headset and punches buttons on his transmitter.

"Satellite hookup, now!" Cooper shouts. "Weapons, now!"

Another airman fumbles with a set of keys. A second explosion, this one on the security bridge. The pass-through window is shattered. Dust sifts down from the ceiling. The airman finds the right key and opens the weapons locker. Three other airman jostle each other, tugging at rifles that are bound together by nylon straps. Boxes of bullets and loaded magazines fall from the locker and clatter to the floor. A few shells roll crazily across the tile.

Cooper stands at the communications desk, screaming into a microphone. "Come in, STRATCOM! Answer, goddamit!"

Another blast, and the reinforced door implodes. Four commandos burst in with military precision, two to a side, one high, one low. A pink laser dot finds Cooper's forehead in the dim light. With a soft *whap*, he takes a shot between the eyes and topples over backward. An Airman raises a rifle, but a staccato beat from a commando's Uzi tattoos his chest with three slugs. Another airman draws a bead with a handgun, but Matthew splatters him with a blast from a twelve-gauge pistol-grip shotgun.

It is over in seconds.

The airmen are all dead. Security Command is in the hands of the Holy Church of Revelations.

-21-
Figs Shaken from a Dying Tree

In the launch control capsule, Owens angrily bangs switches on the console. He picks up a phone and listens to a dead line. Slams down the phone. A look of frustration. "Where the hell is everybody?"

"Probably just a short in the number two generator," Billy Riordan says. "Let's not start World War III."

"Oh, look who's got an opinion," Owens says, frazzled. "Thank you very much, Billy boy. Thank you very goddamn much."

"Is there a problem?" Dr. Susan Burns asks.

Owens doesn't know what to say. It's never happened before. Buried underground and out of communication. A woodchuck could have eaten through their electrical lines or a missile fired by some crazy Russians could have nuked them. Suddenly, the phone rings, and Owens jumps. "Whoa! There they are." His body relaxes just a bit. "No problem, ma'am. Now, let's see who's home." He picks up the phone and barks, "Capsule Command, Lieutenant Owens. Please identify."

"Security Alpha," the voice says. "Everything all right down there?"

Firmly now, "Day code, Security Alpha."

"Day code, Sky King. Now what's going on in the hole?"

"Jesus, what's going on up there?" Owens asks. "Where the hell you been?"

"Sorry 'bout that, Capsule Command. Electrical crew fouled

up, must have sliced some wires."

"Yeah, what about the backup?"

While Owens waits for an answer, at the other end of the line, Brother David looks around the Security Command Center, which is a shambles. Dead airmen are sprawled over desks and chairs, the walls have been shot up, the window to the security bridge shattered. "Backup shorted out," David says. "We'll report it."

Behind him, Matthew surveys the damage. Rachel, carrying an Uzi, is at his side. A commotion, and David turns. Airman Reynolds bursts into the room, soaking wet, a towel around his waist. "Quick, call STRATCOM! Call NORAD! Call the President! We've been..."

He sees the massacre, stops short, knows in that instant he's a dead man.

The *thwomp* from Matthew's silenced MP-5 drops Reynolds who was going to say, "overrun" but simply says "fucked" as his dying word.

David grimaces and hangs up the phone. "Let's move!" he commands Gabriel.

A sudden look of worry crosses Matthew's face. "The PAL code for the elevator!"

Rachel hands David a brown envelope with a tie seal. "Billy has done his job so very well."

In the launch control capsule, Owens yells into the dead line. "Security Alpha, do you read me? Come in, Security Alpha!"

At the far end of the console, Susan studies Billy, who is oddly serene. "What's happening, Lieutenant Riordan?"

Owens wheels around. "Why ask him? Billy's been out to lunch for the last six months."

"Riordan!" Susan implores him.

Billy recites the answer as if memorized from his catechism. "Stars in the sky will fall to earth like figs shaken from a dying tree."

"What does that mean?" she demands.

"Just what it says. The Bible is not allegory. It is the Word. Are you ready for the Apocalypse?"

-22-
Name that Neurosis

Captain Pete Pukowlski leads the U.N. delegation down a ladder into the generator room beneath the missile silo. The *thumpa-thumpa* of the launch generator is as soothing to the captain as a mother's heartbeat to an infant. "You've seen the brains and the balls of the missile," he says. "These are its legs."

Pukowlski steps over a taut hose that runs from the generator to the canister sheathing the missile. He waits a moment, surveying his domain, as the ambassadors gather around him. "The missile's shot out of the tube by a blast of heated gases that are pressurized to three hundred twenty pounds a square inch. *Whoosh*!" The captain makes a plunging motion with his arm. "It's pretty much like the Polaris on the subs, or one of those toy rockets where the kids pump it up with air pressure."

"A toy?" the Israeli ambassador asks. "That is a rather casual reference to a weapon of mass destruction."

Jackie Mason! The name comes to Pukowlski. The ambassador reminds him of Jackie Mason.

"Well, of course, this baby's not a toy," Pukowlski says, retreating. "Not with ten MIRV's on the top. And of course, the rocket's not the weapon at all, just the delivery system, but my point is, the initial propulsion is the same as..."

Oh the hell with it, the captain thinks, just letting it go. Why try to justify anything to these bozos? He catches sight of Sergeant Jericho mopping the floor of the generator room, a furry brown animal crawling around his neck. A couple of the ambassadors have noticed the goof-off, too, and Pukowlski clears his throat to get their attention, then plows ahead. "Anyway, gentlemen, when the missile is clear of the silo, the computer in the fourth stage sends a message to fire up the rocket engines. And, my friends, when those burners ignite, it's Mardi Gras, the Fourth of July, and

Christmas..." He shoots a look at the Israeli, trying to recall the name of that Jew Christmas before giving it up. "All rolled into one."

But the ambassadors do not seem to be in the holiday spirit. At the moment, they are watching Jack Jericho go about the mundane task of swabbing the floor while a rodent perches on his shoulder. Pukowlski shoots Jericho a murderous look which goes unacknowledged. As usual, Jericho's mind is elsewhere. "Sergeant!" Pukowlski shouts. "Get rid of that rat."

Startled, Jericho snaps to attention, or the best he can while holding a mop. "Sir!"

"Did you hear me, Jericho?"

"Yes, sir. But it's a ferret. It kills rats."

"And I kill sergeants. Do you follow me, Jericho?"

"Like a duck behind its mother...sir."

Jericho stuffs the ferret in the large front pocket of his fatigues, grabs his mop, and heads down the ladder into the drainage sump.

❧

David and Rachel lead a contingent of commandos across the security bridge. In his dark suit and tie and carrying a leather briefcase, David looks like a lawyer rushing to court, albeit a lawyer splattered with the blood of a deceased Air Security Policeman. The barracks having been secured, Gabriel joins the procession, while Matthew remains with his men in Security Command. At the elevator housing, David types out an alpha-numeric code on a PAL keypad. The computer screen flashes, "Access Granted," and the massive steel doom rumbles open.

Suddenly, from behind them, "Halt!"

Carrying an M-16A2 service rifle, Sayers runs toward them across the security bridge. A commando drops to his knees and swings up his assault rifle, but Sayers dives to the floor of the bridge, shoulder rolls, then flattens himself into the prone firing position. Sayers has never before fired a gun in anger, unless you count a perfunctory shot with a .38 at a black BMW filled with drug dealers that was cruising his Brooklyn neighborhood. Now, in the fraction of a second that will spell his life or death, his training comes back to him, just as they said it would:

"Describe the M-16A2, airman."

"A lightweight, magazine-fed, gas-operated, air-cooled, and shoulder-fired weapon, sir."

"State the maximum range and maximum effective range."

"Maximum range, three thousand five hundred thirty four meters, sir. Maximum effective range five hundred fifty meters, sir."

Sayers is only twenty-five meters away when he lets the first burst go, and two commandos fall. "Take him!" David shouts. "Blast him to hell."

Another commando fires wildly, spraying the security bridge with his Uzi but missing Sayers, who squeezes off another burst and takes out the shooter. Then he swings his rifle toward the long-haired man in the blood-spattered suit, the one shouting orders to the others. Odd, Sayers thinks, how he stands there squarely in the middle of the elevator housing, giving me a full target, unafraid. *I'll cut him in two.* Sayers has him in the front sight, aiming for the middle of his chest, is ready to add polka dots to his tie. Squeezing the trigger now, and...

Nothing.

Jammed.

Damned.

And the rest of it comes back, too.

Swab out the bore and chamber with a patch moistened with CLP. Clean upper receiver of powder fouling, corrosion, dirt, and rust. Clean bolt carrier group.

Who the hell ever thought we'd really need these things? Which is Sayers' last thought as he futilely tries to clear his weapon and Gabriel puts one bullet through his left eye with an MP-5.

"Providence truly smiles on us today," David says, leading his faithful into the elevator.

ᘓ

"What's the T.O. say when security doesn't answer?" Owens asks, banging down the phone in the launch control capsule.

"But security answered," Billy Riordan says.

"Yeah, then hung up."

"The power probably went down again."

Their flight chairs are centered on the command console. Dr. Susan Burns sits behind them, watching and listening.

"Something's screwy," Owens says. He hits a switch on the console and a tape rewinds. He hits the "play" button and his own voice comes from a speaker mounted on the wall.

"Yeah, what about the backup?"

A pause, then, "Backup shorted out. We'll report it."

The sound of chairs scraping the floor, then a muffled voice. Owens stops the tape, hand cranks the reel backward, then hits a button that enhances background sound and suppresses sound closest to the mike. The voice is still muffled, and because of the slow play time, the tone is a deep bass, but the words are audible. "Qu-ick. ca-ll STRAT-COM. Ca-ll NO-RAD. Ca-al the Pres-I-dent. We've be-en..."

Another pause and then a rich *plumping* sound, a hammer smacking a ripe melon. And then slowly, a deep baritone, "fu-cked."

"Without having been kissed," Owens says. "Jesus H. Christ, what's going on up there!" He quickly slides down the console toward the communications racks. Ordinarily, the deputy is in charge of communications, but Owens wouldn't trust Billy Riordan to call for home delivery pizza. Owens has his choice of an array of communications gear, but he chooses the most reliable, the old black rotary telephone. He dials the number for the duty officer at STRATCOM and gets a busy signal. Damn! He flicks on the AF-SAT up-link transmitter to bring in a satellite. When he's made the connection, Owens struggles to keep the fear out of his voice, "STRATCOM-1, this is Launch Facility 47-Q. Do you read me?"

❧

The headquarters of U.S. Strategic Command, called STRATCOM, is buried deep in a blast-proof bunker at Offut Air Force Base outside Omaha, Nebraska. The cavernous War Room is lined with computer consoles and high-tech communications gear. On the front wall, the Command Center Processing and Display system, commonly called the "Big Board," shows North America, Europe and Asia overlaid with colorful tracking symbols representing movement of aircraft and naval fleets.

Colonel Frank Farris leans over a communications technician and speaks into a microphone. He has finished his fourth cup of coffee and third donut in the last hour and is pleased to have something to do besides the crossword puzzle. "We read you, 47-Q. We've lost the link with your security officer."

"No kidding," Owens says. "That's why I'm on the horn. If this is a drill, no one told us about it. What the heck's—"

"Stay cool, 47-Q. We have no record of a security drill, and no other capsules report any irregularities, but go to Condition Yellow. Secure the capsule, terminate elevator access, scramble communications."

"Affirmative, STRATCOM."

Owens clicks off the phone and takes a look at the open blast door. "Hey Billy, you heard the man. Now, how the hell do we scramble communications?" He opens the T.O. and leafs through the pages.

"I'll shut down the elevator," Billy says.

Dr. Susan Burns watches as he punches several buttons on the console. Leaning close to him, she says, "Billy, I know you've been under great stress, and I want to help, but you've got to tell me—"

"There's nothing you can do. Nothing." He fiddles with a switch, then turns to Owens. "It won't lock down."

"What!"

A buzzer sounds, and a woman's soothing mechanical voice comes over the speaker above their heads, "Elevator access granted.

Elevator in motion."

Owens stares are a digital display showing the elevator's steady descent into the hole. "Now, who—"

"Probably Security coming down to find out why the lines are dead," Billy says. "Hope they're not as spooked as you are."

"Yeah, well they're not trapped like sardines in a..." Owens notices the blast door is still open. "Billy, are you fucking deaf? Close the door! Do I have to come down there and do everything myself?"

"The door is open for saints and sinners alike."

Owens' eyes go wide. "What the fuck are you—"

"We welcome the righteous and the wicked. Salvation is open to all."

"Are you out of your cotton-picking mind?" Owens swivels toward the blast door. From outside comes the *clacking* of boots on the catwalk connecting the launch control capsule to the elevator. Owens kicks his flight chair down the railing toward Billy, then reaches out to punch the red button that will close the blast door. Billy grabs Owens' arm with both hands and yanks him away.

Owens is heavier and stronger, and he shakes Billy off and reaches out again. This time, Billy pulls a snub-nosed .38 from a zippered pocket in his flightsuit. "Freeze!"

Owens stops short. His hand is a six inches – a million miles – from the button. "You are fucking crazy!" He grabs the gun, twisting it away while he pounds at Billy's face with his free hand. They struggle awkwardly, still seated in their flight chairs.

Susan Burns leaps from her chair and dives for the console, hitting the red button. With a soft hydraulic *whoosh*, the pressure begins building to close the eight-ton door. The door is reinforced with steel pins and coated with space-age polymers. Closed and locked, it secures the capsule against a nuclear blast above. Now, it begins its painfully slow closing.

A jumble of sounds, Owens and Billy grappling with each other, their breaths coming in short, harsh exhalations. The door is halfway closed. The pounding of the boots growing louder. A shout from outside, "Go for it!"

A commando dives for the entrance and lands across the doorway. As the door closes, cracking his ribs, three other commandos use the man's back as a springboard to vault inside. Owens, one hand around Billy's neck, tries to wrestle away his gun. Gabriel swings his rifle butt and smashes Owens across the forehead. Billy holds his throat and coughs. Terrified, Susan watches helplessly as a woman in an ankle-length dress and a man in a blood-spattered dark suit enter the capsule. The scene is so beyond belief as to be utterly surreal.

Brother David surveys the console, a look of self-satisfaction on his face. Then he heads straight for the blast door control panel and hits a green button. He does this, Susan notes, as naturally as a driver flicking on the wipers. Knew what he was looking for, a cocky smirk on his face. A chill runs through Susan with the realization that this man, whoever he is, knows what he is doing. And that look in his eyes. So strange. A burning intensity but at the same time, an icy remoteness.

The blast door slowly opens wide enough for two commandos to drag their injured cohort inside. David hits a red button and waits as the door slowly closes with a liquid *pflump* of its seals. He pulls out a walkie-talkie. "Matthew, the angel has landed. Maintain the perimeter."

He turns to the others, seeming to take inventory. He spreads his arms over the glowing lights and sweeping radar beams of the console. "Ah, the splendors that I behold. Home, sweet home. Wouldn't Daddy be proud?"

-23-
The Unstable Boy

Jack Jericho listens to the rhythm of water dripping from the drain into the sump. He is hunched over the Launch Eject Gas Generator, up to his knees in grimy water, tending to a pump beneath the floor of the tunnel that connects the missile silo to the launch control capsule. Twisting a monkey wrench against a stubborn valve, his hand slips and the wrench *clangs* off the tubing and slams into his knee.

"Dammit and little chickens!" He rubs the knee and hops on one foot, splashing through the sump. When the pain eases, he returns to the valve, tightens the wrench, and uses two hands to lever it open. In a moment, the pump is primed, and water begins flushing down the pipes and out of the sump. Bent at the waist in the low channel, Jericho heads toward the silo. "Now, Susan," he says to himself, "I mean, Dr. Burns. Don't judge a book by its cover." He stops, takes the measure of his own words. "No. Stupid and defensive. A total cliché."

He resumes walking, splashing through the draining water. "I've got potential, Susan. Yessir, I was named 'best fly fisherman' in the Sinkhole Senior class. He keeps moving but shakes his head. "No. Sounds like I'm bragging."

Unseen by Jack Jericho, three of Brother David's commandos head through the tunnel connecting the launch control capsule to the silo. They are unaware that beneath the steel flooring under their feet, the sergeant walks through the drainage sump. Instead of proceeding down the tunnel to the silo, the commandos turn right and enter the cramped Sleeping Quarters/Galley. In the event of nuclear attack, the underground facility can house a dozen men as long as they don't all need to sleep at the same time. Six bunks are crammed into the small space along with a small galley and canned provisions.

The commandos enter with rifles ready. They scan the room, find it empty, then head back into the tunnel.

In the drainage sump, Jack Jericho turns left and heads toward a ladder just beneath the Launch Equipment Room. "So doc," he says to himself, "maybe we could grab a buffalo burger at the Old Wrangler Tavern sometime. When? Oh, anytime you want. As Thoreau wrote, 'time is but the stream I go a-fishing in.'" Again he shakes his head, "No. Don't put on airs. Besides, she's probably a vegetarian."

The commandos cross the tunnel and enter the Launch Equipment Room. Guns at the ready, one man to a row, they search between the floor-to-ceiling shelves stacked with electrical equipment, tubing, and spare parts. The youngest commando, Daniel, a round-faced nineteen-year-old towhead, walks down a row of shelves filled with radio gear, passing over a grate in the floor. Beneath him in the drainage sump, Jack Jericho does not notice the shadow pass over his head. Jericho squeezes between two floor-mounted pumps as he climbs onto an orange steel ladder set into the wall. As he climbs onto the first rung, his tool belt swings loose, and a stud driver *clinks* against a pipe.

Above him, Daniel hears the noise and whirls around. Nothing.

Daniel turns back and slowly in front of him, a steel grate is lifting from the floor. Keeping quiet now, nervously moistening his lips, letting the man get out of the grate, his back turned.

Jack Jericho hoists himself from the opening, turns and stares into the barrel of an assault rifle. "What the hell!"

Daniel pulls the trigger, but the gun doesn't fire. He fumbles with the safety, which had been left engaged.

Jericho leaps down through the open grate, bangs into the ladder and plunges roughly into the black water of the sump. He gets to his feet and scrambles crab-like down the sump as a burst of automatic weapons fire comes through the open grate and ricochets behind him.

In the Equipment Room, the other two commandos race into the row where Daniel stands, firing into the darkness below. "Down there!" he yells. "I think I winged him."

The older commandos look at him skeptically, then climb down the ladder into the sump.

Jack Jericho stomps wildly through the knee-deep water as if he were pulverizing grapes. Arms flailing, heart pumping, adrenaline in overdrive. That dreaded feeling, running away. The only difference is that here, there is no one to save but himself. He ducks under low-hanging pipes, wades out of the drainage area, then stops to listen. Splashes and shouts behind him.

Jericho moves again, scuttling along in the channel. He stops and crawls into a nest of tubing. He waits a moment, listens to a scratching sound, looks up and sees a brown rat scurrying across some PVC piping. He reaches into his pocket, pulls out the ferret, and points toward the rat. "Go fetch, Ike." The ferret scampers up the pipe and disappears.

Jericho goes deeper into the recess of the channel behind the tubing. He comes to a bank of electrical boxes, opens one and tears out a handful of wires. The yellow bulbs of the channel go dark.

In the overwhelming blackness, the sound of the pumps seems louder. He hears something, cocks his head to listen like a deer in the woods, but the commandos behind him have stopped, at least for the moment. Again, the sound, what is it? A wail, and then a scream. He is back in the mine, the men calling to him, their hands groping for him, bloody with desperation to drag him down. He shakes off the vision as well as the urge to simply curl up in the web of piping and hide.

He starts up again. His eyes do not become adjusted to the darkness because it is total blackness, just as it was in the mine. Still, he knows the way, knows when to duck under low-hanging pipes, knows where the channel forks into two paths. He keeps moving, trying not to splash.

Behind him, flashlights click on, shooting beams down the narrow channel. Damn. Jericho takes the right-hand fork and disappears into the shroud of darkness.

∽

In the launch control capsule, Brother David settles his gaze on Susan. "Who, pray tell, are you?"

"Susan Burns. Dr. Burns. I'm a psychiatrist."

David's eyes light up. "Oh, how fitting. Perhaps later we can play some games."

Rachel turns to him. "David, there is no time for self indulgence."

He ignores her and says to Susan Burns, "I'm particularly fond of 'Name that Neurosis.'"

"Neurosis? Just a preliminary diagnosis, but if I had to guess, I'd say we're into major psychosis here."

David tosses back his head and laughs. "That's good. Humor is so unexpected coming from a shrink."

"David!" Rachel insists.

"Fine." He turns to Billy Riordan and simply says, "The key."

Wordlessly, Billy gets up, walks to the red metallic box set into the wall, and enters the combination on the padlock. Back in his flight chair, a woozy Owens stirs. "Billy, don't do it!"

But Billy is on a mission. He opens the box, takes the launch key and then hands it to David. "For the eternal glory of God," Billy says.

David turns to Owens. "I believe it takes two to tango."

"No fucking way," Owens says. "Look, the keys won't do you any good. We can't decipher the Enable Code without an EAM. We can't enter the PLC, either. Even if you had them, it takes a matching command from another capsule. You can't do anything without..."

David silences him with a poisonous look. "Now, I could open that tin box with a rusty screwdriver, but destroying government property is a felony, and we wouldn't want to violate any laws, would we?"

Owens doesn't budge, but Billy goes to the second box and enters the combination, then hands David the second key. "I watched Owens and memorized the combination," Billy says proudly.

David cups his hands around Billy's head, drawing him close, then kissing him squarely on the mouth.

"What's with you guys?" Owens says, his voice rising. "Don't you understand? You can't fire the missile anyway."

"Simpleton!" David shouts at him. "Would I have come this far without having the ability to defeat your pathetic security?"

"Without the code, the keys won't do you any good."

David nods at Gabriel, who raises his gun.

"Only the President..." Owens continues, but he shuts up as he watches the gun barrel point at his head."

Gabriel shifts his aim slightly, and shoots Billy in the chest.

Billy's face is a mixture of disbelief and bewilderment as he slumps to the floor.

"Oh, shit!" Owens says, slouching back into his chair. "Oh, shit, piss, damn."

Startled, Susan puts a hand to her mouth. "Why? Why would you..."

"His work was done," David says evenly. Then, with an ironic snigger, "Besides, the boy was quite unstable."

-24-
Show Me a Hero

Deep in the sump, the three commandos follow the right-hand turn of the channel. The commando on point takes a step and snaps a piece of twine. A dead rat, its tail tied to an overhead pipe, swings down and smacks him in the face. He screams and squeezes off a wild burst of gunfire.

Farther down the channel, Jericho hears the shots behind him and picks up the pace. He comes to drainage pool where water pours into the sump from an overhead pipe and in the darkness, he slips and falls in the deeper water. Cold and grimy, the water pours down his back. The drainage pipe roars like a waterfall in his ears, and the channel becomes a flooded mine shaft. He squeezes his eyes shut, opens them again, and finds himself thinking of Susan Burns. *"Do you think you're the only one who has suffered a loss?"*

He blinks the water out of his eyes, forces himself back to reality, and reaches out for a handhold. He ends up grabbing an old string mop propped in the crotch of some piping. Carrying the mop like a rifle, he keeps moving.

The three commandos splash through the channel, pointing flashlights and rifles into the darkness. One raises his hand, and the other two stop. They listen to the sound of the launch generator and the pouring of water from the drainage pipe. Another few steps, and there he is!

A figure in the dark in a military t-shirt.

The commandos open fire, tearing the man apart, sending him tumbling into the water, his guts oozing out.

But it isn't a man.

It's a mop with a string head and a t-shirt stuffed with pink fiberglass insulation.

"He has more faces than the devil himself," the lead commando says, kicking at the fallen mop.

❧

A grate opens in the floor of the missile silo, and Jericho, bare-chested and sopping wet, crawls out of the sump. He looks up. The suspended missile hangs just above his head.

Moments later, the three commandos come up through the grate into the missile silo. One heads to the gantry and rides it up the length of the missile. The second heads into the tunnel toward the launch control capsule. The youngest commando, Daniel, stands under the rocket burners. He examines the wet footprints that seem to circle beneath the missile but don't lead away from it. He stares up into the darkness of the rocket burners themselves.

Then he looks down as a drop of water plops onto the polished steel floor. Then another. He lifts his rifle, when...

Jack Jericho dives from inside the cross-tubing of the rocket burners and crashes on top of Daniel, who drops his rifle. Jericho topples off him, landing hard. Daniel dives for the rifle, but Jericho kicks it away. The commando spins a roundhouse kick into Jericho's chest, knocking him down, then lifts a booted foot and drives it toward Jericho's head. Jericho grabs him by the ankle, flips him over, then scrambles to his feet and bounds for the rifle.

The commando leaps onto Jericho, who reaches back and slugs him with an elbow, knocking him off. Jericho dives for the rifle, but comes up short. Daniel tackles him, and they sprawl onto the concrete, rolling over each other. The commando is heavier, but Jericho is quicker and stronger. Like the high school wrestler he once was, Jericho slips behind the man, uses leverage to flip him over and ends up pinning him down by sitting on his chest. Jericho pulls his knife from its sheath and holds it to the commando's jugular.

&

In the launch control capsule, David sits at the console, watching a monitor that shows an overhead shot of the missile in the silo. He hits a button, and the monitor switches to a shot of the silo floor where Jack Jericho draws a knife at Daniel's neck.

"Looks like we missed one of the soldiers," he says calmly

Owens, his hands cuffed behind him, shouts, "All right!" Then he looks closer at the monitor, and his shoulders slump. "Oh shit, that's not a soldier. Not even an airman. That's Jericho, the janitor."

Turning to Gabriel, David says, "Would you please dispose of this fellow, whoever he might be?"

Gabriel nods and heads out the blast door at double time with three commandos.

David shoots a look at the monitor and then at Dr. Burns. He grabs a stack of personnel files piled up in front of her. Opening the first one, he says, "Oh, how I do love a bureaucracy." He thumbs through the folders, opening each one to look at the passport-sized photos of the airmen. "Ah, here's our janitor. Sergeant Jack Jericho, E-5, Sinkhole, West Virginia. My oh my, I do believe we've met before."

He turns to Dr. Burns. "Tell me about this Sergeant Jericho, doctor."

"My conversations with the airmen are privileged."

Which sets David to laughing. "I love the medical bureaucracy almost as much as the military bureaucracy." He drills her with a threatening glare and grabs her jaw, his thumb and index finger digging into her cheek, forcing her to open her mouth. "Now, doctor, tell me. Is Sergeant Jack Jericho, this Eagle Scout from the Appalachians, the kind of man to act heroically on behalf of duty and country?"

David lets go, revealing red splotches on her cheeks where his fingers dug in. "No," she says, her eyes moist. "Not based on past experiences."

"Good," David says. "Very good. Wasn't it Fitzgerald who wrote, 'show me a hero, and I'll show you a tragedy.'"

❧

Breathing hard, Jericho presses the knife into the young commando's neck until a pinprick of blood appears. "Who the hell are you guys?"

"I am called Daniel. We are Warriors of God," he says tentatively, his eyes darting around the missile silo, looking for his buddies.

"You don't sound too convinced."

"Brother David is the Lamb of Christ," the commando says, as if he memorized the words for such an occasion. "He will usher in the Apocalypse."

From the tunnel comes the sound of combat boots on concrete as Gabriel's commandos enter the silo.

"We follow the Word of God," the young commando says.

"You forget about, 'Thou shalt not kill?'"

Jericho heads toward the open grate as the footsteps pound closer. He climbs into the sump, realizing as he does that he's panicked. He could have grabbed the commando's rifle. Hearing voices above, it's too late to go back.

❧

Gabriel and his commandos troop into the silo to find the young commando standing in a daze under the missile. "Where is the heathen?" Gabriel demands.

Daniel's eyes flick to the grate over the sump. Gabriel glares at him suspiciously and motions his men toward the opening.

-25-
Rocky Mountain RAD

In the launch control capsule, Brother James sits in the deputy's flight chair, David in the commander's. Two armed commandos stand watch over Owens, who is hunched on the floor, his hands cuffed behind him. Dr. Susan Burns sits nearby, Rachel watching her.

James breathes on the lenses of his rimless glasses, then wipes them on his shirt. He flicks on the console-mounted teletype, brushes a lock of pale hair from his eyes and rubs the back of his fist against his acne-scarred face.

David clasps his shoulder. "Make some beautiful music, maestro."

James pounds out a message on the teletype keyboard: "Behold, I bring you the Morning Star." He hits a code and transmits the message, then turns to David and says, "Confusion to the enemy."

"And glory to God," David adds.

"Whatever you say, Davy."

David shoots him an exasperated look, and James laughs. Susan watches the two men interact, noting that James does give David the reverence that the other commandos do.

James slides his flight chair down the rail away from the teletype and toward the computer keyboard. "Okay, Brother David," he says, hitting the words with just a hint of sarcasm, "let's work on the codes." With that, his fingers dance across the keyboard, and six-digit alpha-numeric combinations begin scrolling down the monitor. David watches him work, his eyes never straying from the monitor.

The two men have known each other since elementary school and later, both were both expelled from a prep school outside

Colorado Springs. At the time, David's father was a consultant to the North American Aerospace Defense Command, commonly called NORAD, headquartered deep inside Cheyenne Mountain.

The mountain is a hundred million years old, but for the last thirty-five years, has housed a city, a complex of fifteen steel buildings constructed on steel springs to negate the earthquake effect of a nuclear blast. As a child, David accompanied his father to the nerve center of NORAD, the huge room known as the Air Defense Operations Center. David was thrilled to enter the long tunnel under the rock and wait for the huge steel blast doors – encased in concrete collars – to swing open. His father told him how Blast Door One is set flush with the tunnel's rock and designed to blow inward from a direct nuclear hit, guiding the fireball through the tunnel and out the south side of the mountain. A second blast door just fifty feet away is intended to withstand the blast and protect the 4.5 acre grid of buildings and personnel inside the rock.

In theory. In the event of near misses.

But if a massive Russian SS-18 penetrator/warhead package hit the mountain directly above the Op Center, it would be a different story. The hardened penetrator would hit the earth at seventeen thousand miles an hour, melting the granite and digging dig a shaft three hundred feet deep. The warhead would follow, setting off the largest manmade explosion in history. Other penetrators and warheads would follow, and if a cavity were opened inside the blast doors, the intruding warhead would shoot a flame of gases reaching ten thousand degrees down the tunnel and through the Op Center, incinerating everything and everyone inside. The expanding gases, moving in excess of three thousand miles and hour, would create a pressure wave that would blow off the blast doors, from the inside out, and the mountain would spew flames like an ancient volcano.

David was nine years old when his father told him these things, and for weeks, the boy awoke each night with dreams of nuclear explosions and firestorms sweeping through the mountain and the nearby town. They weren't nightmares, for David was not frightened by the visions of mushroom clouds and vaporized human beings. Instead, the visions fascinated him just as a bottle filled with fireflies might enchant other youngsters.

By the time he was eleven, no other child in the world knew as much about the strategic uses of nuclear fission. "The core is surrounded by U-235 and then a layer of U-238," David told his tow-headed friend James when they worked on a fifth grade science fair project.

"What if you can't get any U-235?" James asked.

"Plutonium will do," David says, confidently, as if he were substituting margarine for butter. "When the deuterium and tritium undergo fusion, high-energy neutrons cause the U-238 to undergo fusion."

Mrs. Scoggins, their teacher, had assumed the project would focus on the peaceful uses of nuclear energy. Mrs. Scoggins had assumed wrong.

David and James constructed a scale model illustrating the effects of a Russian missile's ten megaton air burst over downtown Denver. On the poster board, they headlined the project in red letters, "Rocky Mountain RAD." Mrs. Scoggins looked at the display, patted her grey bun of hair and wrinkled her forehead.

"Roentgen Absorbed Dose," David explained, happily, pointing to a chart on the poster board. "About 450,000 RAD within a mile of ground zero. A measly thousand will kill you, 'course you'd already be vaporized by the heat, so what's the big deal?"

"The big deal," she repeated, staring at the display, "is that I don't understand whatever possessed you to do this, this..." She couldn't finish because she was staring at the rest of the display. Besides statistical data showing atmospheric pressure and whole body doses of gamma rays, there were Ken and Barbie dolls with charred skin and melted eyeglasses, both courtesy of a backyard hibachi, plus some broken false teeth and a shattered pocket watch, its hands crumpled at 8:34.

"We figured an air burst in morning rush hour for maximum kill ratio," James explained.

Mrs. Scoggins blanched, looking at the boys as if they had just strangled her pet cat, but she gave them both A's, then sent them to the school psychologist for counseling.

While their classmates played ball or fished, these two sat in David's bedroom and talked for hours about optimum detonation altitudes, initial radiation yields, and the triggering devices for fission-fusion-fission bombs. James had an unquenchable thirst for knowledge, and David had most of the answers.

"The blast," James would ask, "do you see it or hear it first?"

"See it. A bluish-white flash, some ultraviolet, too."

"Cool."

"The temperature at ground zero is eighteen million degrees."

"Fahrenheit or centigrade?" James wanted to know.

"Fahrenheit. It creates a fireball that generates radiant heat traveling at the speed of light."

"A hundred eighty-six thousand miles a second," James added, knowingly.

"Then comes the blast. It's really a pressure wave moving at about eleven hundred feet a second. It hits the ground and bounces up, doubling the pressure into a mach wave. Then you get your negative pressure, and that's really neat, because it causes a firestorm, flaming winds at six hundred miles an hour."

James whistled. "Wow. Small craft should stay in port."

"Yeah. The fireball sucks debris into the air and all that vaporized crud forms the mushroom cloud."

"Way cool," James says, working on the idea of it. "You think you could score some U-235 so we could build one."

"Sure," David boasted.

He was right, though he never figured it would take this long.

-26-
STRATCOM

In the War Room at STRATCOM, technicians work at the unhurried pace of men and women used to the routine. In subdued light, a dozen hypnotic beams endlessly circle their radar screens while teletypes clack noisily. On the front wall, the huge screens occasionally flick with the movement of submarines or a satellite photo of a military installation in the Middle East. American and Canadian Air Force personnel roam among the computer consoles, as do some visiting NATO officers. Technicians sit at desks watching computer monitors that are recessed into desks, not visible only to foreign visitors.

Technical Sergeant Bill Ryder, U.S.A.F. E-6, a skinny thirty-year-old, tears a scroll of paper from a teletype and carries it to Colonel Frank Farris, who sips coffee while he watches the wall screens with little interest. "This just came in from 47-Q, sir."

"Good. They finally responding?"

"Not exactly, sir."

The colonel frowns and studies the teletype through his wire-rimmed bifocals. He is fifty-one, has a receding hairline and a soft belly. "What the hell is this 'Morning Star' gibberish?"

"Don't know, sir. It's not part of the code."

"You raise the base?"

"Tried, sir. No answer from Security Command, nothing from the capsule, except for the teletype. We thought their power was down until we got the message."

"Shit. Have Cryptography take a look at it. When will we have the satellite photos?"

"Any minute, sir."

Just then, the center wall screen on the Big Board blinks, and the map of North America is replaced by a photograph of Chugwater Mountain taken from Eyesat II. The dam and reservoir are visible, then farther down, the slope of the mountain, the dry river bed and a forest of pine and fir trees. A second photo replaces it, a shot of 318th Missile Squadron at the base of the mountain. The screen blinks, the photo is enhanced, and Colonel Farris stares at an overhead view of the blown front gate and the crumpled bodies of airmen outside the barracks and mess hall.

"Oh shit!" The colonel turns to the sergeant. "Is 47-Q still hot?"

"Yes, sir. Dismantling scheduled for next week."

"Oh, holy shitcakes!" Colonel Farris hurries to a computer console where a civilian technician sits, wearing a headset. "What's the target data for 47-Q?"

"Right now, just some icebergs in the Arctic Ocean," the technician replies. "Once the PLC is entered, of course, it'll revert to wherever they were targeted before the thaw with the Russians."

"Which is where? the colonel says, impatiently.

The technician punches some keys, and the wall screens blink again, this time with a map of the world as seen from above the arctic circle. Every few seconds, a dotted line tracks slowly from Wyoming over the North Pole to Moscow where it hits a cross-hatched bullseye. BLINK, the screen switches to a street grid of Moscow and its surroundings with pulsating crosses at the ten target sites for the multiple warheads. A sound comes from deep inside Colonel Farris, the moan of a sick cow. He hurries back to his desk and picks up a red phone. "General Corrigan," the colonel says, when the phone is answered. "We've got a problem here."

❧

In the launch control capsule, James merrily punches keys on the console's computer. "I'll bet we've got their attention."

David nods. "Do you have the target coordinates?"

"Right down to the last minute and second."

David is quiet a moment.

"What are you thinking?" James asks.

"My father. I want him to know."

James laughs. "Oh, he'll know. It'll be in all the papers."

"He has to know it was me."

James isn't looking at him. He is typing a series of six-digit codes very carefully, watching his fingers hit the keys. "Who the hell else could it be?" he asks his lifelong friend.

❧

In the STRATCOM War Room, the pace quickens. Technicians and crisis teams scurry around the cavernous facility, scrambling up and down metal ladders to a surrounding catwalk. The room is a three-story amphitheater with the computers and tracking stations on the first floor, offices and conferences rooms above. Dominating the room is the twenty-five foot high Big Board.

Air Force officers huddle around General Hugh Corrigan, his chest bedecked with medals, his silver hair cropped close. Colonel Farris stands off to one side as Clay Hurtgen, an FBI agent in a grey suit, briefs the general.

"For now, we're calling them, 'Morning Star,'" the FBI agent says.

"Who the hell are they?" the general demands.

"No one knows. The name doesn't cross reference with anything in our computers. CIA's come up blank. We're working on it."

Which does not seem to satisfy the general. "What do they want?"

"Nothing yet," Agent Hurtgen replies. "No demands, no threats. Just the one-sentence teletype message."

"'Behold, I bring you the Morning Star,'" the general says, as if repeating the phrase aloud will decipher it.

Colonel Farris clears his throat. "Maybe it has something to do with television, sir."

An army of heads swivel his way, tennis gallery style.

"I mean, like a morning television star, or something."

"Did the Pentagon notify the White House?" the general asks.

"Yes, sir. The President's Chief of Staff wants updates every fifteen minutes."

General Corrigan glances at his watch and starts to walk away from the circle of men. "Tell him at 14:30 hours, Rocky Mountain Time, the general took a piss."

"Yes, sir," the aide says. "He wanted you to know that they're notifying the Russians. I assured him that, other than political embarrassment, there's no chance of..."

A klaxon horn blares.

Lights flash.

The general stops short. His bladder can wait.

Heads turn toward the wall screens where a series of alphanumeric combinations flash by followed by computer directories and hundreds of pages of files, each page flicking into view for a fraction of a second. The general reads the directory titles aloud, "Silo blueprints, electrical grids, command data buffers, target coordinates, enable codes, prepatory launch commands, abort codes, warhead configurations. Who the hell's inputting that?"

Technical Sergeant Ryder, sitting at a computer console, watches his monitor, then answers. "Capsule 47-Q, sir. It's coming from Morning Star."

"Jesus H. Christ," the general says.

৵

In the launch control capsule, James works at the computer keyboard. On his monitor, the same data flashes by as in the STRATCOM War Room. He hits a key, and the words, "Target Coordinates," freeze on the monitor screen. He carefully punches in six sets of two-digit combinations.

৵

In the STRATCOM War Room, the screen comes to life with two sets of numbers: 32-28-15 and 35-01-13. Then, flickering below the numbers, the words, "Command Data Buffer Activated."

"I can't believe it," Colonel Farris cries out.

"Now what?" General Corrigan fumes.

"Morning Star's changed the target coordinates," the colonel replies.

"That's no surprise, Frank. If they know what they're doing, they're not going to try and launch into the ocean. They've got the PLC in the red box, so we expected them to enter it."

"But that would be Moscow," the colonel says. "This isn't Moscow. It's..."

The screen goes blank. Then, slowly, the words scroll down. "MK WARHEAD, MIRV 1: NORTH LATITUDE 32 DEGREES, 28 MINUTES, 15 SECONDS; EAST LONGITUDE 35 DEGREES, 1 MINUTE, 13 SECONDS."

"How's your geography?" the general asks Col. Farris.

"Somewhere north of the equator, east of..." He studies the numbers a moment, and just as a map of Africa comes on the screen, he says, "The Middle East."

The map is replaced by a smaller area, the eastern Mediterranean from Libya on the west to Iran on the East. The screen blinks, and now the map zooms in: Egypt, Israel and Saudi Arabia. Another blink, a closer look, and it's Israel alone. Finally, a flash, and a city street grid appears on the screen.

"Jerusalem," Col. Farris says, in disbelief.

-27-
Peace is Our Profession

In the launch control capsule, David watches James work at the computer. On the monitor, the number "6" appears, pulsing once a second.

"Ah, here she comes," David says. "A six." He turns to Susan Burns, who stares at the monitor in horror. "Six is the point. Who wants to lay their money on the pass line?"

Susan doesn't say a word.

"No crap shooters here, James my man. Roll 'em."

The number "8" flickers to life on the monitor, joining the "6."

David smiles at the sight of the two numbers. "Keep on rolling, James."

Next, the letter "B."

"There goes our craps game," David says. "Maybe we can play scrabble."

"Numbers or letters, it's all the same to me," James says. An "A" joins the alpha-numeric combination on the screen.

"It was Daddy's idea to complicate the code. Six spaces to be filled by one of nine numbers or twenty-six letters. What's the possible number of combinations?"

"About 1.8 billion," James says.

A "3" joins the pulsing numbers on the monitor

"Won't be long now."

"How?" Susan Burns asks, shaking her head. "How did you get the enable code?"

David gives her a small smile. "Between Billy's inside information, James' computer genius, and my familiarity with every missile from the Atlas to the Peacekeeper, how could we not?"

"Among," James says.

"What?"

"You gave three indicia. The word is 'among,' not 'between.'"

An "A" pops up on the screen.

"Among other things," David says, "we're just a lot smarter than the folks in Omaha, Cheyenne Mountain, and Washington."

As David gloats, James unfolds a laptop computer and inserts a cable coming out of its port into a plug on the deputy's console. James turns on the computer and begins entering a series of letters and numbers. "Time to fool the missile," he says.

❧

General Hugh Corrigan sits at a desk wondering why he turned down a chance to be commandant at the Air Force Academy. A graduate of the Academy, fighter pilot in Vietnam and later commander of the 21st Tactical Fighter Training Squadron, he was assigned to Air Force Space Command as a colonel when it was created in 1982. In typical military fashion, he paid his dues with a variety of other assignments, including a stint at the Pentagon, another at NORAD, and finally commanding the 379th Bomb Wing during the Persian Gulf War. From a Saudi Arabian airfield dubbed "Club Jed" by the Americans, Corrigan directed massive strikes by B-52 Stratofortresses against Iraq's Republican Guard in northwestern Kuwait. There were 523,000 American military personnel in the Persian Gulf, but none were more important than Corrigan's B-52 crews.

After the war, Corrigan had his choice, commandant of the Academy or commander of STRATCOM. Either way, he'd be flying a desk, so he chose the job that put him in charge of all ICBM operations. At this precise moment, he knows, there is an ICBM missile operation that is operating quite nicely, thank you, without any input from him whatsoever.

A flashing red light casts an eerie glow over the STRATCOM War Room. At a heartbeat pace, the light illuminates a sign on the back wall, "Peace is our Profession." The old slogan of the Strategic Air Command. There is no more SAC. With reorganization came U.S. Strategic Command and Air Force Space Command. Still, General Corrigan considers himself a SAC warrior.

"The intrusion is a nuisance," Colonel Farris says, "but that's all. It takes a second capsule to confirm the launch command, and without—"

"General, sir!" It's Technical Sergeant Ryder, angrily banging keys on his computer. "They're looping the enable code through a second computer and sending dual messages to the missile. The MGCS thinks the enable code's being confirmed by another capsule."

On the front screen, the code "6-8-B-A-3" pulses. The number "7" is added, and the code stops pulsing.

Beneath the six digits, a message flashes, "Enable Code Entered." A buzzer sounds.

A second message, "Enable Code Confirmed." Pandemonium.

The technicians bang away at their keyboards.

Air Force officers babble away on satellite hookups to Washington.

Digital launch information flashes by on the screen, the

numbers streaking too fast to comprehend. From somewhere in the equipment comes the soothing female voice of the computer: "Launch order confirmed. Confidence is high."

General Corrigan doesn't flinch. He figured it was coming. Turning to Sergeant Ryder, he says, "Activate command launch inhibitor."

"Yes, sir."

The sergeant frantically pounds his keyboard, grimaces when nothing happens, then tries it again. The wall screen flashes the message: "Launch inhibitor access denied."

"I can't get in," the sergeant says, his voice breaking. "The bastard's just stolen our missile."

General Corrigan is ashen, but his voice is steady. Turning to Colonel Farris, he says, "Get me the President."

-28-
Double Fail-Safe

Jack Jericho slogs through the shallow water of the sump, pauses and listens. No sounds other than the *thumpa-thumpa* of the pumps. He had taken a fork in the channel and lost them. Now confused and afraid, he thinks about these warriors of God. At first, he tells himself, it could just be a protest against nuclear weapons. Take a missile hostage, get some TV coverage, call it a day. Like the environmental groups that chain themselves to trees to stop the loggers. But these guys tried to kill him, and that's a step or two beyond paying your dues to Greenpeace.

He thinks about Jim Jones and David Koresh and that loon in Switzerland, what was his name? The guy with the Order of the Solar Temple, which sounded like a "Star Trek" episode. He knows that if armed men are in the silo, Security Command has been overrun, and he wonders if all the bases of the 318th are under attack. Wonders, too, if the invaders have laid siege to the launch control capsule.

He starts moving again, stopping only when he gets to a red box labeled, "Emergency Phone." He opens the box and grabs the phone. It rings immediately, an open line to the launch control capsule.

☙

David and James sit in the flight chairs at the console. Rachel leans over David, a hand on each shoulder.

"Time to sound the trumpets," David says.

"For His glory," Rachel says.

"Show time, baby!" James cries out.

A red telephone on the console rings.

"That's an internal line, isn't it?" David asks, turning toward Owens, who sits, handcuffed by the rear wall.

The phone rings again.

"Isn't it!" he demands.

"Yeah."

David gestures toward Gabriel who lifts Owens to his feet and drags him to the console. "Find out who he is and where he is," David says. "Be a good soldier, and you'll get an airmanship medal."

David hits a button, putting the phone on a speaker, and Owens answers. "Launch control, Lieutenant Owens."

"Lieutenant, thank God it's you."

"Identify yourself."

"It's Jericho. We're under attack! Get Air Cav in here, get Special Forces!"

Owens shoots a look toward Gabriel who pokes the barrel of his rifle at him.

"Five by five, Jericho. State your location."

"Lieutenant, are you listening? We're under attack. Keep the blast door sealed. Call in the fucking cavalry!"

"Affirmative. State your location, Sir."

In the sump, Jericho pulls the phone away from his ear, stares at it, then slams it down.

126

In the capsule, David furiously back-hands Owens across the face. "Sir! Sir?" He hits him again, and blood seeps from Owens' lip. "When did the Sergeant get a promotion?"

⌒

If ignorance is bliss, Captain Pete Pukowlski is the happiest man in the United States Air Force. Seated in the galley, just off the tunnel from the launch control capsule to the silo, he is drinking a beer and entertaining the U.N. Nuclear Non-Proliferation Commission. "I would have brought in some wine for you fellows if I thought of it," he says, nodding toward the French ambassador. "Not that I care for it myself. That red stuff gives me a headache and makes my piss smell like crankcase oil."

The French ambassador winces and sips at his beer. Pukowlski has set out a plate of pretzels and some onion dip in a metal container he picked up at a gas station/convenience store outside of town. None of the ambassadors seems anxious to try the dip, though the Englishman picks up the container to read the ingredients, most of which sound like experiments in a high-school chemistry class.

"Precisely when will this facility be closed?" the French ambassador asks.

"A week from today. Ain't that something? My bird's an endangered species. Soon, they'll be planting daisies right over our heads."

"And the warheads?" the Israeli ambassador asks.

"Dismantled, then shipped to a plant near Amarillo where they'll dilute the uranium and plutonium. All the technology and energy consumed to enrich the stuff in the first place, and then they just turn around and reverse it. Kinda seems like a waste, don't it?"

"And after it's diluted?" the Englishman asks, letting the question hang there.

"They ship it to nuclear power plants. In a few months, what had been the heart of the warhead will be powering some electric dildo."

The ambassadors snicker. "I believe those are battery operated," the Englishman says.

"You oughta know," Pukowlski says, draining his beer.

❧

Billy and James hold the two launch keys. The console is alive with flashing lights and digital displays. The computerized female voice is as calm as ever. "Launch mode yellow. Confidence is high."

"Let's take it from the top," David says. "Read'em out."

"Six, Eight, Beta, Alpha, Three, Seven," James says, nearly singing.

"I agree. Those are good values," David says, and James turns thumbwheels on his console, entering each number and letter.

"Down and lock," James says, hitting the switch labeled "initiate." Immediately, the computer begins printing out a continuous roll of paper covered with numerical codes.

"Plick switch," David says, referring to the Preparatory Launch Command.

"Foxtrot, Nine, Papa, Four," James calls back.

"Numbers good," David says, and James enters "F-9-P-4" on another set of thumbwheels.

"Flight switch on, launcher on, enable on," David says, checking his board, as new lights flash on. Time and target complete. Insert keys."

Simultaneously, David and James tear off plastic flaps covering key holes on the console. Behind them, Rachel stands, her dark eyes shining with excitement. Susan Burns and Owens sit, back to back, their hands cuffed together, their faces reflecting their fear.

"Key inserted," James says.

"Lock your board."

They both hit switches.

James nods, and says, "Board locked."

"Check your lights."

James scans the console. "Lights check."

"Launch mode green," the computerized voice says. "Strategic alert confirmed. All systems check and re-check. Launch is a go. Confidence is high."

☙

In the STRATCOM War Room, General Corrigan and his staff watch the Big Board where the latest message reads, "MIRV locked on primary targets."

"Launch is a go," the computerized voice says, but all the officers in the room know that.

The screen blinks with target information. A map of Jerusalem appears, with pulsating crosses on ten targets.

An aide approaches General Corrigan. "General, the President wants to know if we should advise the Israelis to evacuate Jerusalem."

"Not unless they can do it in thirty minutes. All we'll succeed in doing is having more people caught outdoors."

The aide disappears up a set of stairs, and the general studies the map with a rueful smile. "What do the Wailing Wall, the Church of the Holy Sepulchre, and the Mosque of Omar have in common?"

Colonel Farris shrugs. "They're all religious sites."

"One for each of the three great religions," FBI Agent Hurtgen adds.

"Right," General Corrigan says. "What we've got here is a non-discriminatory terrorist. He seems to loathe everybody." The general reads off the names of the other sites that are targets of the multiple warheads. "The Dome of the Rock, the Church of the Assumption, the First Station of the Cross, the Great Synagogue, the Chapel of Ascension, the Tomb of the Kings, and the Temple Mount. All of that and a million people. They'll be gone in the blink of an eye."

☙

BALLISTIC

David and James each have a hand on the inserted keys. Behind them, Susan's eyes desperately dart around the capsule, looking for help, an idea, anything. Owens mumbles a prayer, his lips cracked with dried blood.

"Clockwise on my count," David says.

"If you truly were a man of God," Susan blurts out, "you couldn't destroy the holiest city in the world. You couldn't kill all those innocent people."

"As it is written in Corinthians, 'Death is swallowed up in victory.'"

"This isn't about Resurrection."

David swivels in his chair and glowers at her. "Physician, heal thyself!"

He turns back to the console and nods to James. "Key turn on my mark." He closes his eyes and counts it down, "Three, two, one. Mark..."

David and James simultaneously turn their keys. "And hold," David commands."

A buzzer emits an insistent beep.

David silently counts to five. "And release."

Eyes closed, smiling mystically, David releases the key, and so does James.

☙

"One last look," Captain Pukowlski says, leading the ambassadors into the silo from the tunnel. "Kinda like a country-western song, I just wanna see my love one last time before she leaves me."

The group stands just a few feet from the missile, which hangs in its cables over their heads. "And what a shame, 'cause this baby's the most modern, most accurate missile in the most secure facility on the face of the—"

Ka-boom! The SQUIB explosives blow the concrete cap off the silo. The cap, made of solid concrete six feet thick, weighs more than two hundred thousand pounds, and is hurled off the top of the silo like a Brobdingnagian frisbee. It takes out a cyclone fence surrounding the silo and crumbles of its own weight when it hits the ground.Pukowlski looks up at the blue Wyoming sky. The ambassadors are terrified, turning to the captain for an explanation. Speechless, the captain stands beneath the missile, frozen in place.

Suddenly, *Whoosh!* The Launch Eject Gas Generator steams to life, pumping a mixture of water and pressurized gases through pulsating tubes into the missile canister. Hoses hiss menacingly and stiffen like angry snakes. The missile sways in its cables.

Though he is startled, at his core, Pukowlski is a trained officer who believes in duty, honor, and country. He lives by the book and would be willing to die by the book, and the only answer to what is going on must be found in the book.

"Gentlemen," Pukowlski says, not even trying to suppress a grin, "stiffen your spines and grab your cocks. We're at war!"

છ

General Corrigan presides over a War Room of apoplectic officers. The blinking red lights illuminate his face, which is locked into a grimace.

The computerized voice drowns out the buzz of the officers and technicians, "Countdown sequence initiated. LEGG activated. Confidence is high."

All eyes are on the Big Board where a dotted line tracks slowly from Wyoming across the arctic circle, across Greenland and the North Atlantic, across Europe southward toward Africa, finally touching down in Israel. The dotted line disappears, then re-tracks again and again.

છ

In the generator room beneath the silo, a horn sounds and thick hoses throb with heated propulsion gases. Shirtless and soaking wet, Jack Jericho hovers over the keyboard of the generator control panel, unsure what to do.

"Whoever's got his finger on the button ain't one of us," he says to himself.

The computerized voice from the speaker startles him. "All systems operational. Ninety seconds to propulsion launch. Confidence is high."

Jericho frantically scans the generator control panel. He tears a plastic shield off the keyboard and flicks the "on" switch. The monitor flashes to life with the message: "Launch Sequence in Progress. Generator Access Prohibited."

"Shit!" Then he remembers Dr. Burns' question as to whether he is a leader or follower. Neither one, he knows. And he isn't even sure what he's doing now, but he knows he must do something. Jericho hits the "stop" key, and an electrical shock jolts him. The monitor flashes: "Caution. Unauthorized Access Prohibited."

More gingerly this time, Jericho touches the same key. With a *ka-pow*, the shock knocks him down, blue smoke wafting above the control panel. Dazed, Jericho gets to his knees and looks up at the monitor, which mocks him. "Caution. Each shock increases in severity." Then, in smaller print, "OSHA WARNING: Repeated exposure to electrical shocks causes brain damage in rats."

Jericho gets to his feet, his hands dangling over the keyboard. As he tries again, he says, "I ain't a rat."

೧

In the launch control capsule, all the lights on the console are green except for one, which flashes amber. Brother David stares at it a moment, his brow furrowing. "What in the name of..."

"What is it?" James asks.

"Get over here."

James kicks his chair down the rail and studies the computer monitor in front of David where the message appears, "Input S.L.C. Now."

"What?" David stares blankly at the screen.

"Never heard of it," James says, shaking his head.

David wheels around in his flight chair, glaring at Owens, who sits uncomfortably on the floor. "Enlighten us!" David orders.

Owens hesitates, and Gabriel wags the barrel of a rifle in his face.

"The slick," Owens says. "Secondary Launch Code. The launch will abort unless it's entered. It's a double fail-safe mechanism entered after the Enable Code and the plick, the PLC, are activated."

"Since when!" David demands, growing furious. Why?"

"I don't know," Owens says, nervously. "Six, seven months ago."

"It was my recommendation," Susan Burns says. She is turned away from David, sitting back-to-back with Owens, their hands cuffed together.

"What!" David thunders.

She turns her neck uncomfortably to face him. "Preliminary tests showed that fifteen per cent of the missileers believed that any order to launch would be a mistake, a computer glitch. Of that number thirty per cent would refuse to turn the key. I recommended another level of security be added so that missile crews would have confidence that if the S.L.C. came down separately from the National Command Authority, we must surely be at war."

"Idiotic!" David thunders. "It complicates and delays the launch. That could be fatal if you're counter-attacking."

"But it thwarts terrorists," Susan says. "I was afraid you had it. You seemed to have everything else. But then, I guess you're not perfect."

"Input Secondary Launch Code," the computer orders in the same detached voice.

David screams at Owens, "The code, damn you!"

Owens is too terrified to answer.

"He doesn't have it," Susan Burns says, calmly. "It comes from the President after the Enable Code has been entered. That's what makes it double fail-safe."

David slams his fist into the console. "Damnation!" Turning to James, his voice breaks, "Do something! You're the cyberpunk genius. Do something, goddamit!"

"David," Rachel says from the back of the capsule. "Taking the Father's name in vain will not—"

"Shut up! Shut the fuck up!" He turns back to James, who already is hunched over the keyboard, banging away like Van Cliburn playing Tchaikovsky.

The voice of the computer is as calm as a warm breeze on a summer day. "Enter S.L.C." Launch will abort in thirty seconds."

⁊

Footsteps echo in the tunnel leading from the missile silo. Captain Pete Pukowlski leads the U.N. delegation at double time toward the launch control capsule.

"We go to DEFCON ONE, and nobody notifies me!" he fumes. "We're in launch mode, and I'm jerking off some diplomatic goofballs. Somebody's ass is grass, and I'm the lawn mower."

They pass the door to the Launch Equipment Room, which swings open. Gabriel and three other commandos come out and face the delegation.

"Who? What? Who the hell are you?" Pukowlski stammers, though it must be sinking in, because as the words come out, he is reaching for the .45 in a side holster. But Gabriel raises a pistol grip shotgun toward Pukowlski's bulging belly, which seems to flatten just a bit.

"We're the messengers of God," Gabriel says.

"I don't think so," Pukowlski says, raising his hands over his head. "God's on our side."

⁊

The officers watch the dotted line's trajectory on the Big Board as it soars from Wyoming toward Israel...then fades away. The computerized voice solemnly declares, "Launch Aborted. Launch Aborted."

Sighs of relief, backslapping, a couple of wolf whistles, and more than one, boy-was-that-close.

Colonel Frank Farris loosens his tie and turns to General Corrigan, who is not sharing in the celebration. "They didn't have the slick," the colonel says. "Jeez, we dodged a bullet, a big one."

"But they still have the base and the capsule, don't they?" the general asks. He knows it is not over yet.

On the board, the dotted line on the screen tracks from Wyoming across the arctic circle, stops, then disappears. "Yes, sir. They have the capsule," Colonel Farris says. "But there's no way they could get the S.L.C., is there? I mean, if they don't have it now, how could they get it before we roust them?"

General Corrigan gives the colonel a look an animal trainer might show to a slow chimpanzee. "They knew how to capture our missile base, how to re-target the missile and how to enter the plick and Enable Codes, didn't they?"

Colonel Farris nods.

"They hot wired our computer to simulate a message from another launch capsule in order to get dual confirmation, didn't they?"

Another nod.

"Then why in hell wouldn't they know how to get the Secondary Launch Code?"

"I have no idea, sir," the colonel says, straightening up. "I have no idea how they could take over a terrorist-proof nuclear facility."

"Neither do I," General Corrigan says. "But I'm going to find out. Get

me the son-of-a-bitch who built the damn thing."

BOOK FOUR

The Professor and the Prodigal Son

-29-
MAD

Professor Lionel Morton, seventy-one years old, wild mane of white hair flowing past his shoulders, sits on the lecture stage in a high-tech wheelchair equipped with a computer and monitor. In front of him, at desks on tiered rows, are fifty of the best and brightest of Stanford University's students. Behind the professor, the blackboard is filled with lengthy equations and diagrams of every missile in the U.S. arsenal from the old Atlas and Titans to the newest Minutemen III's and Peacekeepers, called in Air Force parlance, damage limitation weapons.

A plastic scale model of a rocket sits on a miniature launch pad on the stage. Holding a remote control device that resembles a garage door opener, Professor Morton throws back his head and in a voice that is part Olivier, part Brando, calls out dramatically, "I shot an arrow into the air..."

He pushes a button on the remote, and *whoosh...* The rocket blasts off.

"It fell to earth I know not where."

The rocket arcs above the students' heads, sailing up the tiers where it lands in the top row, squarely in the center of a cardboard bullseye.

"Horse feathers! Henry Wadsworth Longfellow didn't know a

damn thing about ballistics."

The students titter and exchange looks. They have witnessed Professor Morton's antics before. Part entertainer, part academician, he plays many roles. He knows the students call him Dr. Strangelove and doesn't discourage it.

"Why, we could hit Lenin's tomb or Quadafi's condominium with a nuclear warhead any time we like," the professor says with a touch of pride. "Pyongyang, Tehran, Baghdad, Beijing, Moscow... downtown Newark. We can nuke them all."

Nervous laughter from the students. They can never tell when the professor is joking.

"Of course, it wasn't always that way. On a cold March morning in 1926 on a farm in Massachusetts, Dr. Robert Goddard fired the world's first liquid-fuel rocket. It was ten feet long and traveled 61 yards before crashing into the snow. And that, I assure you, was an event as significant as Kitty Hawk."

Professor Morton pauses, wondering if he should explain the Kitty Hawk reference to these young knowledge seekers, then figures if he has to, it isn't worth the trouble. "In the following years, Goddard fired hundreds of rockets, always making improvements, gyroscopes for stabilization, movable exhaust vanes for steering, multi-stages to decrease weight and increase distance."

A hand goes up, and Professor Morton nods in the direction of an earnest young Asian woman in enormous round eyeglasses. "Professor, weren't rockets used in battle long before the 1920's? I mean what about the national anthem, 'in the rockets' red glare?'"

"Quite right," he says. "There were rockets at Fort Sumter. Hell, the British used Congreve rockets in the War of 1812, but they were little more than self-propelled artillery shells, and they couldn't hit the broad side of a barn. We're talking about something else here, the ability to launch a rocket with a substantial payload, and using the principles of ballistics, telemetry and inertial guidance, squarely hit a target. Now, after Dr. Goddard's experiments in the 1930's, you would think that the American government would pour money into rocketry research, wouldn't you?"

The students nod in unison.

"But you would be wrong!" the professor thunders. "Goddard's work was virtually ignored here. Not so in Germany, however, where the Nazis built a rocket station at Peenemunde on the Baltic Sea. By September 1944, Hitler was raining V-2's down on London. At the end of the war, Walter Dornberger, Wernher von Braun and 600 other German scientists came to the United States, and a damn good thing, because the Russians had their own advanced rocket program, even without the Germans they shanghaied."

Professor Morton pauses a moment and surveys his class. Some of the faculty complain about today's X-generation. To Morton, every class was the same. Ten per cent are brilliant and motivated; eighty per cent fall into the bulbous blob at the middle of the bell curve; and ten per cent who gained admission through family connections, computer error or downright bribery should be used for painful medical experiments. "The German scientists who came to the U.S. took the V-2 and modified and improved it into the MX-774, the forerunner of the Atlas and Titan missile systems that kept the Russians at bay before any of you scholars were born."

"But the Cold War is over," pipes up a studious young man in the front row. "What you're talking about is ancient history."

The professor smiles, admiring the lad's gumption, if not his perspicacity. To the students, ancient history is anything that occurred prior to MTV. "Yes, they say the Cold War is over. They say Mutual Assured Destruction, MAD, is obsolete. Hell, they say I'm obsolete. But they are idiots!"

The students roll their eyes and drop their pens. No use taking notes. It won't be on any tests. Besides, they've heard it before, a great soaring riff of a diatribe against the National Security Council, various presidential administrations, both Republican and Democratic, the C.I.A., the D.I.A., the Pentagon, Congress, and just about everyone else in Washington except the men's room attendant in the V.I.P. lounge at Dulles Airport.

Lionel Morton is at the juncture of tenure and academic freedom, an intersection where the driver has the unbridled right to preach, to rant, to defame and defile. It is, in fact, wondrous therapy for the professor, though it does little to teach theoretical physics to his students.

"If we let down our defenses, if we downsize and streamline and depend on Special Forces and quick-strike commando operations, we'll be a second-rate power. We must not only maintain our nuclear weaponry, we must constantly improve and refine it if we are to remain the greatest power the world has ever known."

"But nuclear weapons are just for defense," says a young woman in the back. "Without the threat of an attack from the Russians, why do we need—"

"Do you know why the Soviet Union crumbled?" the professor interrupts.

"'Cause they wanted Big Macs and Levis," says a long-haired guy in the first row.

Professor Morton hits a button, and the wheelchair buzzes closer to the front of the stage. "Because we bankrupted them with defense spending. They had to keep up with the Joneses...and the Reagans. Now, ask yourselves this. If the American nuclear arsenal was merely for defense, why would the Russians have to keep up? Why build the SS-17's, 18's, 19's, 24's and 25's? Why build a 25-megaton warhead, bigger than anything we've got, a digger that could penetrate Cheyenne Mountain and vaporize NORAD headquarters and obliterate any of our underground bunkers including ACC Command Post outside Omaha or the National Military Command Center underneath the Pentagon?"

No one answers at first, but a guy in the first row fiddles with his gold earring and seems to think about it, then says, "'Cause the Russians didn't trust us."

"Right! Because the Russians were afraid of preemptive deterrence."

Blank looks from the back rows.

"A first strike!" Professor Morton roars. "It was our first-strike potential that shriveled the commies' testicles, and don't ever forget it. From the last days on World War II right up through Reagan's second term, the bastards were afraid we'd hit 'em first. And they were right! The blockade of Berlin, the Cuban missile crisis, the Arab-Israeli wars of '67 and '73...hell, we came damn close a bunch of times." He pauses, maybe for effect, maybe to consider whether to say it at all. "And there were some of us who thought we made a mistake not doing it as soon as possible and as hard as possible."

No one is laughing. No one is moving. Few students even take a breath.

Professor Morton dabs his forehead with a handkerchief. He has worked up a sweat. "So ladies and gentlemen, never forget that we need that might, that ability to slick 'em with submarine launched missiles and glick 'em with land based missiles, the ability to make the rubble bounce with a clean fusion bomb, the ability to take out specific targets with a cookie cutter. Take away the missiles and you're castrating America."

The young woman in eyeglasses raises her hand. "You're not opposed to the START treaty, are you Professor? I mean, we have enough nuclear weapons now to—"

"To prevent World War III."

"But the threat's over," the earring guy jumps in. "I mean, the Russians are broly."

Professor Morton wheels the chair around to face the student, who likely will never make Dean's List, much less become another Oppenheimer. "Ah, the benefits of higher education. That broly bunch of guys at Glavkosmos sold rocket engines to India, missiles to China, submarines to Iran, and unless we stop them, ammonium perchlorate to Libyra."

"Ammon..." the guy stumbles.

"Rocket fuel! And another thing, uranium fuel rods are disappearing from Russian nuclear plants like trinkets shoplifted from Woolworth's. China is supplying reactors to every rogue country in the world. Even Algeria has a hot cell to make plutonium. The North Koreans have made enough nuclear material at Yongbyon to build five bombs and have a missile, the Rodong-1, that can hit Japan. The Ukraine has 1800 warheads.

Leonid Kravchuk may be okay, but what about its next leader? So, in short, ladies and gentlemen, the world is a far more dangerous place today than it was—"

A rumble interrupts him.

The lecture hall windows vibrate in their frames.

The walls shake.

Several students dive to the floor. "Earthquake!" one shouts.

"The big one!" another screams.

On the stage, Professor Morton calmly looks out the windows toward the quadrangle. He has heard the sound before, loves the growling roar, the sheer power of the engines.

A moment later, an Army UH-60 Black Hawk helicopter touches down in the grassy quadrangle. Four Airborne Rangers in battle dress jump from the helicopter. It is an impressive sight, even to the jaded Stanford students, who pause on their way between classes, to watch the rugged men whose faces are smeared with camouflage grease and who carry assault rifles at port arms.

Lieutenant Colonel Charlie Griggs, lean and graying, a triangular patch signifying Delta Force on his shoulder, follows the Rangers out of the chopper and leads them at double time toward the lecture hall. They burst through the door and pour into the hall, tromping down the steps to the stage.

Professor Morton hits a button, and his wheelchair spins ninety degrees to face the lieutenant colonel, a man in his late forties with a squinting eyes and thin, humorless lips. "Let's go, professor. It's happening."

Professor Morton doesn't even try to suppress a smile. He knows, of course. It's not End Game. No exchange of ICBM's across the polar ice cap. It would have been over in minutes, and there would have been no time to summon the man who built the systems, the genius who designed everything from the shape of the launch control capsule to the computer programs with the multiple codes. Designed them to be fail-safe. The system had checks, cross-checks and double cross-checks. It was flawless. But human beings were far from perfect, and this was a paradox that intrigued the professor. While humans passed on the same weaknesses from the days of the Garden of Eden, technology exploded exponentially and approached perfection.

That thought always made him smile. *Exploded.* For as a physicist, he loved the Big Bang of the creator, which he always imagined with a small "c," and he loved the little, big bangs he could create.

But human error was always the risk.

Incompetence or mendacity. Or both.

Whatever the crisis, he knew, that somewhere a nuclear weapon had been triggered, and he would walk – or more precisely, roll – right into the middle of it. Create the monster, slay the monster.

Professor Morton turns the wheelchair and faces the students. "Class dismissed. Next week, a quiz on deuterium fusion." He pauses and lets his eyes twinkle. "If there is a next week."

-30-
The Hot Breath of Lucifer

Jack Jericho slogs through the sump, stops, looks warily behind. Nothing but the throb of machinery. He is under the tunnel now, headed toward the Launch Equipment Room.

These fruitcakes have the launch control capsule, he now figures. Nobody ever calls him "sir," not even the ticket taker at the Laramie Cineplex. And certainly not Lieutenant Owens. Jericho is a non-com, and Owens knows it. He was sending a message, and Jericho hoped it hadn't gotten the missileer killed.

Okay, so the terrorists took over the capsule. Which means they've breached the perimeter and captured Security Command. And God knows what else.

But the bird didn't fly. Jericho didn't stop it, he knows. Hell, he nearly been turned into a fried mountaineer, working on the keyboard.

He had a weapon now. And they were on his territory. No,

check that. Outdoors, in the woods, along the banks of a stream, that would be his territory. Here, in the tunnel that resembled a mine shaft, even though he knew every twist and turn, it was not his territory. It was his purgatory.

ↄ

In the launch control capsule, Rachel watches over Susan and Owens while James works feverishly at the computer keyboard, his lank, pale hair drooping into his eyes. Brother David leans over his shoulder watching, growing angrier with every "Access Denied" message on the monitor.

"You're supposed to be the expert," David says, brusquely.

"Hey, it wasn't my job to get the codes, Brother Davy."

David kicks the railing that runs along the console. A petulant child. "Your blatant incompetence forestalls my destiny!"

James stops what he is doing and turns toward David, whose face is flushed. "You wanna cut the Messiah crap? This ain't like breaking into a switching station at Pacific Bell to make some long distance calls. It ain't changing grades at M.I.T."

"Who do you think you're talking to?" David demands.

"Back off, Davy. I know you. Hell, I'm the only one who knows you."

David angrily turns away from the console and faces Susan, who is staring at him. "What is it? Do you have something to say, Ms. Shrink? Do you have something to add to this fiasco?"

"I could help you."

"Really? Do you know how to acquire the Secondary Launch Code?"

"No, but with the proper therapy, we could exorcize your demons without a nuclear holocaust."

He glares at her. "You know nothing of my demons. You know nothing of me."

"But if I did, I could help you."

David considers telling her the story just to see her reaction. *"I shot my father, doctor? What do you make of that?"*

What an oedipal delight, a smorgasbord of delicacies for a psychiatrist. How they loved him at the hospital when he wasn't tormenting them. He spent eighteen months there, and it wasn't bad, not when you live inside your head. He used his free time – of which there was plenty – to read and to change and then to change again.

He had always been aware of his powers. He saw colors emanating from other persons and came to know that these were called auras. While still a child, he invented a parlor game he called, "I see." Wearing a black cape and a makeshift turban from a bathroom towel, he would squeeze his eyes shut, work up visions, and reveal all manner of data, some mundane and some astounding. He could conjure up the names of long-deceased relatives and he could tell a stranger whether his ailment was an ulcer or a boil. He didn't know how he saw these things; sometimes the visions came, sometimes they didn't. Sometimes he was right, sometimes wrong.

Family and friends often asked for predictions, but those were more difficult. David worked hard at making his prophesies come true, but nothing seemed to work, until he discovered a simple solution. Only predict those things over which you have control. If he told a neighborhood pal that his cat would soon die, and a few days later, the cat was found strangled, then David was a prophet, albeit a self-fulfilling one.

Years later, as a young man sitting in the sun in a white wicker chair on the sweeping lawn of the mental hospital, David studied a wide spectrum of metaphysical sciences. At various times, he dabbled in theosophy, I Ching, Mesmerism, kabalism, voodoo, santeria, and even a brief fling with Satanism. He re-read Robert Louis Stevenson's *Dr. Jekyll and Mr. Hyde* until the binding tore apart. The bookshelf in his tiny room was crammed with classic mystical literature including Marion Crawford's *Zoraster*, H. Rider Haggard's *King Solomon's Mines*, and Florence Marryat's *Daughter of the Tropics*.

Always possessed of self-awareness, David knew he was on

a quest for his own identity. He read Ammonius, Buddha, Pythagoras, Confucius, Orpheus, Socrates and Jesus. He invented and re-invented himself a dozen times. First believing in a divine wisdom and moral ideals, he adhered to the motto, "There is no religion higher than truth." Later he came to believe that he could define the truth.

He became fascinated with the early apocalypticists. He studied the teachings of Novatian and Donatus from the third and fourth centuries who prophesied the coming Armageddon. That took him to the millennialists, the Anabaptists, Waldensians, Albigenses, and Moravian Brethren. He listened to Jehovah's Witnesses and Seventh Day Adventists, and he consumed the Bible, focusing on the apocalyptic writings of Daniel, Ezekiel and finally, the Book of Revelations.

All the while, David practiced his psychic gifts. After he was released from the hospital, he lived in a commune in Idaho populated by a motley collection of New Age dropouts, time-warped hippies and lethargic lost souls. The others gravitated to him, drawn by his piercing eyes and uncanny mental abilities. He learned the art of hypnotism and sleight-of-hand and became a compelling speaker and performer. To earn money for food and books, he ventured into town and set up a tent, amazing the locals with his mind-reading demonstrations at ten bucks a pop.

When he had honed his gifts and perfected his performance, when he determined who he was, or at least who he wanted to be, David had but two choices: he could become a carnival act or he could start a religion.

No, David thinks now. He won't tell the psychiatrist his story. Not yet, anyway. But there is something within him, the showman, that cannot resist the center stage. It is the quality that makes him a seductive preacher. But even he knows it is built on the sin of pride. He turns to Doctor Susan Burns and says, "Do you believe that both God and Satan is within each of us?"

"Is that what you believe?"

"It is the Word. There is a constant struggle, the Lord our God against the fallen angel. Evil is such a powerful force."

Next to Susan, Rachel stirs from her chair. "David, don't. This isn't the time or—"

"I can lead the flock because I know sin," he goes on. "If I open the Seven Seals, it is because I was chosen to do so. If I am the Messiah, I am a sinful one. Even now, Lucifer's voice rings louder than pealing church bells."

"David!" Rachel knows what is happening, even if Susan does not. "This is between us, David. It is not to be spoken of."

"Still, I fear I feel his hot, sulfurous breath on my neck."

"David, please," Rachel implores him.

He closes his eyes and lets his voice rise and fall, the words like pounding waves breaking on the shore. "And I saw a mighty angel proclaiming in a loud voice, 'Who is worthy to break the seals and open the scroll? See, the Lion of the tribe of Judah, the Root of David, has triumphed. He is able to open the scroll and its seven seals.'"

"Ain't gonna open nothing," James says, "unless we get that code. I figure two hours before Special Forces gets here with a hard-on for the Root of David."

"But even as I follow my destiny," David goes on, ignoring his old friend, "even as I prepare to be martyred as the Lamb of Christ, Satan pulls at me."

David hits a button on the console and the blast door pops open with a *pflop* of its seals. He leans down behind Susan, opens her handcuffs, then roughly pulls her to her feet. As he drags her toward the open door, Rachel's voice takes on a scolding tone, "David, we have a higher purpose."

"Indeed, we do," he replies, "but all work and no play makes David an even naughtier boy."

❧

Captain Pete Pukowlski knows his rights. Which is just what he is telling this muscle-bound son-of-a-bitch who dispenses words as if they were silver dollars.

"I am intimately familiar with the provisions of the Geneva Convention as it pertains to prisoners of war," the captain says.

Gabriel says nothing, just gives Pukowlski a little shove as the group moves through the underground tunnel toward the missile silo.

"And under said provisions, I demand confinement in quarters commensurate with my rank."

Gabriel separates him from the ambassadors and shoves him through the door to a storage room. Using his shotgun to nudge Pukowlski along, they move to the rear of the room and stop in front of a steel vault with a wheeled door. "Open it," Gabriel commands.

"That's against the regs unless we're wearing—"

"Open it!" Gabriel pokes the shotgun barrel into the captain's rib cage.

The captain does as he is ordered.

"Inside! Now!"

Before he can protest, Pukowlski is shoved in the back and stumbles into the vault. Gabriel slams the steel door shut and turns the wheel, locking the door. Talking to himself, for the sound cannot penetrate to the other side. "Much more appropriate." Then he walks away, flicking off the lights. Even in the dark, the sign on the steel door is illuminated by a fluorescent orange border. Glowing ominously, it reads, "Danger—Radioactive Waste."

-31-
Nuclear Family

Brother David leads Dr. Susan Burns down the tunnel toward the silo, passing several commando sentries whose posture straightens as they pass. David nods to them but says nothing. His mind is elsewhere. He pushes open the door to the sleeping quarters/galley and shoves Susan inside. Shadowy, with a bare concrete floor and jammed with half-a-dozen bunks, the room is illuminated by a single yellow bulb. David does not turn on the overhead lights in the Spartan room.

"Now, doctor," he says, "before you get rid of my demons..." He pulls out two pairs of handcuffs, and fastens each of her wrists to an overhead pipe, arms spread wide. "I'm going to show you heaven."

He kneels down and removes her shoes. She is on tip-toes now, spread-eagle, exposed and vulnerable. David stands and places his face close to hers. She can feel his breath, warm and moist, coming faster now as he loosens her long, dark hair from a clip, then unties the bow-tie on her silk blouse.

"I thought you were a man of God," she says, struggling for control.

He unfastens the top button on her blouse. "The Lord works in mysterious ways."

"I didn't think you were a common rapist."

Another button. "Oh, but I was never common. Surely you are capable of a more sophisticated diagnosis."

"You're what the medical literature would call a middle-class psychopath."

"How bourgeois. I always imagined myself a bohemian." He grabs Susan by the chin and twists her head, forcing her to look him in the eyes. "Come now. Tell me my symptoms. What's bugging poor little Davy?"

Susan masks her fear, knowing part of his pleasure derives from her terror. She tries to control her breathing, aware that her face is flushed. Her arms are already growing heavy, and she feels the damp cold from the floor against her bare feet. "I'm sure you've heard it before."

"I have, but not from someone so lovely, so delicious." With fingers spread, he rakes both hands through her hair, which falls freely over her shoulders. "All the others just poked and prodded, tested and analyzed. There's never been anyone so perfectly suited to be the vessel of my wisdom, the repository of my seed."

"And if I refuse?"

"Oh, but you won't."

Susan fights to stay calm, wanting to draw him out, make him continue talking. She needs to probe his personality, find his weaknesses and attack them. At the same time, she knows that David is using his own psychological warfare against her, alternating doses of charm and terror. His flaw, she believes, is his ego, his overwhelming belief that his charisma will draw people to him, make them do his bidding. This leads her to a startling conclusion. David believes he can convert her, make her one of his followers and even more, make her worship him.

Susan Burns is well aware of the Stockholm syndrome, the intense relationship whereby a hostage forms an artificial emotional attachment to a terrorist, a dependence born of the lust for survival. He has traumatized her and weakened her. She is tired, alone and frightened. But she vows to fight.

"Tell me about your therapy," she says.

"Are you familiar with the Mach test, doctor?"

"It's named for Machiavelli and tests a person's willingness to manipulate, to dehumanize, to treat others as objects. At the high end, there is total lack of concern with conventional morality. Lying, cheating and deceit are considered the norm."

"And how do you think I scored?"

"A twenty."

"No, twenty-one."

"That's impossible. Twenty is the highest, or lowest, depending how you look at it."

"I got a bonus," he says, proudly, "for killing the psychiatrist's hamsters."

"You're trying to shock me," she says. "Why not just tell me about it?"

"The shrink was one of your sixties peaceniks who still drove a VW bus and listened to Joan Baez. Had a kitchenette in his office, used to make godawful fruit and veggie drinks. One day, I dropped the little fellow – the hamster, not the shrink – into the blender. Put some lumps in his smoothie."

Still fighting the pain in her arms, Susan struggles not to show her revulsion.

David smiles to himself and unfastens another button of her blouse. "So, doctor, any more thoughts on little Davy? And don't sugar coat it. If you lie to me, I'll cause you pain."

She takes a breath and says, "Primary narcissism with delusional episodes and bouts of sadistic sexual paraphilia."

"Mmm. You're getting warmer. And so am I." Suddenly, he rips the blouse open, popping the remaining buttons. Susan gasps with fear, then strains for control, even as her breasts heave under her bra.

David watches her intently, a smile playing at the corners of his mouth. "My mother wore white brassieres with little pink bows, just like you. Now there's grist for your mill, eh doctor?"

Susan is silent, afraid to venture more opinions. It is a struggle for control, she knows. She must wrest it away without enraging him.

"Come now, doctor," he says. Playful now. "Don't you want to know how a boy like me got to be a boy like me? Wouldn't you like to venture an expert medical opinion?"

"I would suspect that you had a successful, distant, authoritarian father and a frivolous, indulgent, highly seductive mother. Your parents were self-centered, and rather than being affectionate, merely indulged you. Instead of experiencing feelings, you became charming and manipulative and simply pretended to feel for others in order to obtain what you wished. It is possible that your parents, particularly your father, had criminal impulses which he never acted on, but which he unconsciously projected onto you, hoping you would actualize them, giving him the vicarious pleasure without the risk. In short, your nuclear family was sick, and they made you sick."

"Nuclear family," he muses. "An apt phrase, given our circumstances, don't you think? Still, you can do better than that. Be more specific. Your generalities may apply to bottom-feeding serial killers like Bundy and Dahmer, but I consider myself rather

151

special."

Susan feels the muscles in her calves beginning to cramp and her arms are growing numb. "From an early age, you engaged in fetishistic masturbatory fantasies. You daydreamed about killing, probably on a massive scale. You—

"You're getting off the track. My family, doctor. Tell me about my family, and do entertain me. If you're boring, I shall have to entertain myself, and you wouldn't like that, I assure you."

"As I said, your father was likely powerful and remote. He either pushed you—"

"Ah, more clichés."

"Or ignored you. The cliché would be that he never played ball with you."

"He played chess with me, taught me the game when I was four, my beloved father did. If I made a move he considered inferior..."

Wham. David slams his open palm into the overhead pipe. Startled, Susan instinctively raises her legs. The movement causes her to swing to and fro on the pipe. Her arms throb.

"He'd box my ears," David says.

Her voice quaking, a hot pain searing her shoulders, she says softly, "Your father didn't know how to express—"

"Shut up! It's my forty-five minutes, doctor. One day, when I was eight, we were playing chess, just like always. I tried a new maneuver, something he hadn't seen before, and it appeared that my queen was vulnerable..." *Wham.* David hits the pipe again, and Susan winces. "He hits me, screams at me for being stupid, but I don't cry. I just keep playing. Five moves later, checkmate. I win!"

"And he never hit you again."

"Wrong! He hit me harder. He just never played with me again."

Susan senses the opportunity and goes for it. "Don't you see? Surely, you do. You have the intelligence. You know precisely what shaped you. Armed with that knowledge, you can change. You can—"

"Doctor, doctor. What is the primary reason why therapy is almost always useless for true psychopaths?"

She considers lying, figures he would know, then simply speaks the truth. "Motivation. They don't want to change. They enjoy their aberrational behavior.

"Quite so," he says, as he unhooks her bra, and lets it fall to the floor.

ᘓ

The unmarked C-21A, a Lear jet in the military configuration, descends from twenty thousand feet over the flat Nebraska countryside. Professor Lionel Morton sits with his head pressed against the window, staring at the horizon. Lieutenant Colonel Charlie Griggs has silently studied the professor for the past ninety minutes. He knows that Lionel Morton was the boy genius of the missile program in the fifties and sixties. Now, he is considered an oddball, a dinosaur. Brilliant and combative, he's been fired and rehired by the Air Force a dozen times.

"Without the S.L.C., they can't launch the missile, can they?" Griggs asks. He has a well-trimmed mustache and his pale hair has gone gray at the temples.

"Correct. The professor still stares out the window.

"So there's no problem, is there? Special Forces can take back the silo in what, fifteen or twenty minutes. Hell, they would have done it already if we didn't have the bad luck to have half-a-dozen foreign ambassadors down the hole."

"Bad luck or clever planning?"

That makes the colonel think. "You mean the bastards knew about the U.N. delegation?"

"It was in the newspapers," the professor says, dismissing the notion of luck, good or bad. "It is consistent with a well-planned operation."

"Not so well-planned that they had the slick."

The jet begins its descent though a thin layer of clouds over Offutt Air Force Base just outside Omaha. Professor Morton turns to face the lieutenant colonel. "But they seemed to have everything else, didn't they? What makes you think they can't get the secondary code?"

"Well, how will they get it? The President's not going to give it to them. You don't mean to say they have access to it down in the hole."

Professor Morton closes his eyes and listens to the sound of the landing gear lower into place. "I mean we're going to find out just how clever they are."

"Damn." Griggs uses the knuckle of an index finger to scratch at his mustache. "Then we'd getter get ready to shoot down the missile."

"With what?" The professor seems oddly pleased by the suggestion even as he rejects it. "Tomahawks, Cruise, Sparrows? Lousy range, and none of them can do more than Mach 4. That bird flies at Mach 20, more than fifteen thousand miles an hour at burnout when it goes ballistic."

"We don't wait 'til it hits apogee, professor. We surround the silo with batteries of Patriots, kill the bird on liftoff."

"You think my missile is some rustbucket Scud from Baghdad?" He lets out a little laugh. The weapon's superiority is a source of pride and amusement. He lets his voice slip into its lecture mode. "The Air Force is just dandy at launching missiles, not at shooting them down. On liftoff you'd have no time to acquire the target. You'd either fire too soon or too late, or at the right time at the wrong angle. You might as well try shooting a lightning bolt with a pistol."

This quiets Griggs, and as the Lear's wheels touch down with a screech of rubber on pavement, he clicks open his seatbelt, as if that will hurry them on the way to STRATCOM. He stands before the small jet comes to a stop on the tarmac where a helicopter is waiting. Two Airborne Rangers help the professor off the plane and into a waiting military van. There is no time to lose.

༄

Susan hangs painfully from the overhead pipe, her breasts exposed. Brother David stands in front of her, his head cocked as if listening to a distant voice. His eyes are unfocused.

"Father and I always competed for mother's attention," he says softly.

A tear tracks slowly down Susan's cheek.

"Quite a wit, my father. Nicknamed me Oedipus." He waits for a response, doesn't get one, and continues. "Just for the record, doctor, I didn't really have an affair with my mother, then kill my father. But not for lack of trying."

David rests his head between Susan's breasts, and her shoulders tremble. "Did you know I had an appointment to West Point? Daddy arranged it. He was chummy with the chairman of the Armed Services Committee, and just about everyone at the Pentagon whose name started with 'General.' Loved the military, though he never served, of course. What hopes he had for me."

"Do you feel you failed him?" Susan asks, the numbness paralyzing her.

David nuzzles her breasts with his chin. "I'm sure he would think so. But he could hardly be the one to cast stones." He takes a nipple in his mouth, and sucks at it.

"What does that mean?" Susan asks, squeezing her eyes shut.

David releases her nipple and seems to appraise it. "I came home after plebe year at the Point and found my mother with three broken ribs." David reaches behind her and unzips her skirt and pulls it down over her hips. "And a black eye she pathetically tried to cover with makeup."

David drops to the floor on his knees, lifts up her feet, one at a time, gathers up the skirt and tosses it aside. Still on his knees, he presses his cheek into her abdomen and continues to talk. "He'd beaten her before, of course. For as long as I can remember. Accused her of adultery, of burning the lamb chops, of spending too much money. Such an angry man. And she always made excuses for him. As if it were her fault. But it wasn't."

David's arms are wrapped around her, squeezing her buttocks. "I always thought I should have done something when I was younger. I could have stopped him, but I didn't."

"But this time you did," she says.

"I found my father's gun. Bang! Bang! Then I found religion."

Susan begins to sob. David stands and studies her.

"Your nipples are erect, Dr. Burns. But alas, I am not."

He turns and walks from the room, leaving her suspended from the pipe, half naked and in tears. Without looking back, he says, "Pray tell, what would Freud say?"

-32-
Coward!

Jack Jericho splashes through the drainage sump, stopping to look up through the grates above his head. He knows he is directly under the tunnel leading from the launch control capsule to the silo, knows too that no one should be in the tunnel, but is not surprised to see the outline of two men through the shadowy grate.

"Are you ready, Ezekiel?" a voice asks.

"Always, Brother David. But will you open the seven seals?"

"In due time."

"The men believe in you, Brother David."

"Let them believe in the Word. It will lead them."

Weirdos of God, Jericho thinks. He moves directly under the grate, kicking a spray of water against some tubing. The conversation above him stops, and he freezes, a ray of light from the tunnel filtering through the grate and across his face. He imagines the two men peering down through the grate, spotting him. Brother David and Ezekiel. Even as he wonders what they look like, his heart pounds in his chest, so loud it seems, they must hear it, too. His imagination conjures up the sound of a rifle bolt *clicking* into place, the sight of a muzzle poking through an opening of the grate, even the sound of the gunshot that will end his life. But then, the conversation starts again.

"If you will forgive my sinful pride, Brother David, it would be a great honor to perform any tasks that would further the cause of righteousness."

"There is one thing," the other voice says. "I am teaching a lesson to a heathen. Give her another few minutes. Then take these keys, and..."

Using their voices as cover, Jericho carefully moves through the water down the tunnel, turning under what he knows is the galley-sleeping quarters. He looks up through the grate. Darkness. He takes a deep breath. He has two choices. He can stay in the sump, dashing around corners like a rat in a maze, or he can work his way up to the silo and the launch control capsule. He doesn't know what he'll do when he gets there, but he knows he's not doing anyone any good where he is.

Jericho removes the saw-toothed survival knife from a leg sheath and pries open the grate above his head. Then he pulls himself into the room, pauses a moment to let his eyes get accustomed to the dim light. He hears the unmistakable sound of strained breathing, senses the mixture of pain and fear, and as he turns and sees her in the yellowy light, his first thought is of a an animal caught in a trap.

೧

Susan Burns sees the figure pulling itself out of the grate. The man turns toward her, an apparition appearing through a blazing fire of pain. Her body stiffens. She begins to cry out, but Jericho covers her mouth with his hand.

"It's me, doctor, Sergeant Jericho," he whispers in her ear.

It takes a moment, but she recognizes him and calms. He releases his grip then lifts her at the waist to relieve the pressure on her arms.

"Thank God," she says, her head falling onto his shoulder. Please get me out of here. He was going to..."

Jericho reaches up toward the overhead pipe, finds the

handcuffs and curses. He was hoping she was bound with rope. The saw-toothed knife is in his hand. Wrapped cylindrical handle, a removable cap for storing matches, compass and fishing line. It can saw down trees, clean a fish, or gut a man. But it cannot open handcuffs.

Jericho digs at the lock with the tip of the knife, knowing it is useless. He is face-to-face with Susan, her legs wrapped around his hips instinctively, seeking shelter and protection. Her bare breasts are pressed against his chest, and he can hear her sobbing.

"I can't get it open," he says. "But there's a monkey wrench around here somewhere. Give me a minute. I'll separate the pipe at the t-joint, and get you out of here."

"Don't leave me," she pleads, tightening the scissors hold of her legs, letting all her weight fold into him. He puts his arms around her, tastes a salty tear that runs from her face to his.

Footsteps echo from the tunnel, interrupting them.

"The pipe, Jericho. Break it! Do what you have to. Please, hurry."

He releases her, looks for a wrench, but doesn't find it.

The footsteps grow louder.

He leaps up, grabs the pipe and swings on it like a gymnast on the horizontal bar. He tries to pull the pipe down, but it holds firm, doesn't even bend.

The door opens, a beam of light shooting across the floor past the cots and toward them in the rear of the sleeping quarters. Jericho turns his head toward the grate in the floor.

"Don't you dare leave me," Susan whispers, frantically.

Anguished, Jericho moves toward the grate. "There's nothing I can do." He swings his legs into the opening to the sump. "We're outnumbered and we're trapped. I don't even have a gun. I'll get us both killed."

"Don't go!"

"I'll come back for you."

"Jack!"

The sound of his name on her lips chills him.

"I promise. I'll be back."

"Damn you! You coward!"

The word cuts through him, and he drops into the sump as much to avoid her hateful glare as to escape. Pulling the grate back into place over his head, he sinks into the water, defeated and ashamed.

ᔰ

"I'll come back for you."

His father looks up from beneath the fallen beam, the pain etched into his face. He says nothing. Water pours into the shaft, and from overhead comes the angry growl of the earth. Rock moves against rock, timbers snap in two. The growl becomes a deafening roar. Jack Jericho reaches down and grasps his father's hand. His father latches onto Jericho's sleeve, holds him there for a moment, then lets go. Still, the older man doesn't say a word, doesn't protest as Jericho backs down the tunnel, toward the shouts of the crew boss.

"I'll come back for you," he says again, watching his father wince with pain. Jericho turns and scrambles toward the emergency egress ladder. He does not look back.

ᔰ

Ezekiel works his way to the rear of the sleeping quarters, sees Susan suspended from the pipe, and stops. He studies her, notes her exposed breasts, then looks her in the eyes. "Man is weak. Even the Messiah in human form knows sin."

He reaches for her, and she shrinks back, turning her head away. But Ezekiel merely pulls her torn blouse closed, trying to cover her breasts. Then he reaches up and unlocks her handcuffs. She falls to the floor and rubs her wrists, trying to work the blood back into her hands.

She puts her bra back on and tries to tuck in the blouse, but without the buttons, it's useless. Ezekiel moves to a metal shelving unit and pulls down a missileer's blue jumpsuit, which he tosses to her. "Put this on. Rachel sees you like that, there'll be hell to pay."

-33-
Death Waits in the Dark

The OH-58D Kiowa helicopter swings out of the shadows of Chugwater Mountain and descends from a position over the reservoir, following the path of the aqueduct down to the missile base on the plateau below. In Vietnam, the Kiowa led air cavalry assaults and located targets for attack helicopters. Today, the modified version is still a small, maneuverable chopper without much firepower, except when it's equipped with Hellfire and Stinger missiles. This one is in the scout mode with no armaments. Instead, it carries three men in its cramped compartment, an Army pilot and two passengers in full battle dress.

Colonel Henry Zwick, with twenty-five years experience in Armored Cavalry, slips on a helmet as they pass near the open missile silo, chunks of the blown concrete cap scattered in pieces on the ground. The colonel has salt and pepper hair and a jet black handlebar mustache that is more Salvador Dali than West Point.

Captain Kyle Clancy sits next to him, his camouflage pants bloused neatly into his combat boots. A jagged scar runs from the corner of his left eye down across the cheekbone and disappears under his pugnacious chin. The patch on his sleeve reads, "Death Waits in the Dark," the slogan of the Night Stalkers, the Army's cutthroat Special Forces unit.

The chopper dips lower and the two officers can see the bodies of airmen in front of the barracks, the shattered front gate, and the dead air policemen on the ground.

"What an unholy mess," Colonel Zwick says, shaking his head.

Captain Clancy makes a sound that reminds the colonel of a horse snorting. "Typical Air Force goat fuck," the captain says. "They couldn't defend an assault by a troop of Eagle scouts."

"Easy, Kyle. We're all on the same side."

160

"Shit, colonel, you know I'm right. The flyboys are trained monkeys. They're fine at pulling the trigger on some smart bomb at twenty thousand feet, just like playing a video game in an arcade. Put a bayonet at their throats, they piss their pants."

Overhead, a shadow crosses in front of the sun as a dozen CH-47 Chinook helicopters edge past the mountain and descend. The huge, two-rotor choppers carry troops toward a makeshift base camp just above the missile base on an elevated plateau. On the ground, tents are going up, men are digging in, and trees fall in the path of M1A2 Abrams battle tanks and M2/3 Bradley fighting vehicles with cannons, grenade and missile launchers.

Captain Clancy doesn't even try to suppress a sneer as he gestures toward the base camp. "No disrespect intended, colonel, but we don't need all that armor. And we don't need Rangers or Green Berets, either. Hell, my men could—"

"You'll have your chance, Kyle. But first, let's get an idea of what we're up against."

The Army pilot turns around and asks, "Another pass?"

Colonel Zwick points toward the ground. "Take it lower and see if we can get a rise out of them."

Captain Clancy smiles, stretching the scar at the corner of his mouth. The colonel might look like a pussy, but he's earned his eagle and arrows. Plus an oak leaf cluster and a couple of silver stars. After West Point, Zwick was commissioned a second lieutenant with the 11th Armored Cavalry Regiment in Vietnam and later Cambodia. It was the old Army, using outdated tactics of static warfare where the premium was on superior firepower alone. The Armored Cav had forgotten lessons first learned in the Bronze Age by Kazakh warriors who harnessed horses to chariots, all the better to hurl spears at their enemies.

In the recriminations that followed the Vietnam War, the Army changed. A mobile, fluid fighting force was created, and Colonel Zwick was in the forefront. After tours in Germany and studies at the Armed Forces Staff College and the Army's Training and Doctrine Command, Colonel Henry Zwick was part of the most

successful cavalry operation in history: Operation Saber of Desert
Storm. The new Army was high-tech. Soldiers carried cellular
phones and Global Positioning Receivers that gave their precise
location by satellite. Weaponry had reached new dimensions from
smart bombs to long-rod penetrators, officially known as high-
velocity, armor-piercing, fin-stabilized, discarding-sabot projectiles.
In layman's terms, it's a 120 mm. shell made of tungsten or depleted-
uranium alloys, and it exits the muzzle of a tank's smoothbore gun
at an astonishing Mach 4. It was used to pierce the armor of Iraqi
tanks at a distance of more than three miles.

Reconnaissance was handled by remote-controlled aircraft and
the sophisticated Fox recon vehicles that sense chemical warfare
devices. Zwick's tank corps was equipped with the M1A2 Abrams,
"Whispering Death," the world's best main battle tank manned by
the world's best tank crews. Multiple-launch rocket systems and
self-propelled 155 mm. howitzers added firepower.

Amazingly, the technology all worked.

Colonel Zwick commanded a unit of the 2nd Armored Cavalry
that engaged Iraq's Tawakalna Division in the Battle of 73 Easting,
annihilating the enemy. In one hundred hours of fighting, the
Armored Cav routed three Republican Guard divisions, destroyed
the Iraqi's 10th and 12th Armored Divisions and the 17th Infantry
Division. They destroyed 4,000 Iraqi combat vehicles and took
24,000 prisoners. Only 42 American soldiers were killed and 192
wounded.

So how difficult could it be, Colonel Zwick wondered, to take
back a missile silo from a bunch of half-baked terrorists? Not hard
at all. Unless the bastards could pull the trigger on the missile. That
changed the equation.

The Kiowa descends, hovering a moment over the security
building where the blown doors are clearly visible. The sound of
gunshots is drowned out by the chopper's engine, but tiny puffs
of smoke come from nearby trees, commandos firing at them.
Neither the colonel nor the captain flinches, and the pilot takes
evasive action, the chopper banking then cutting a figure-8 above

the missile base.

With a look of disdain, Captain Clancy watches the commandos take aim from positions in the trees and behind makeshift bunkers. "Dumb bastards are hiding, can't tell a recon mission from an assault." Unlike the colonel, Captain Clancy didn't have the benefit of higher education, unless you count El Salvador, Grenada, Panama, Iraq, Somalia, and Haiti. Years ago, he was a grunt who couldn't stay out of trouble in Basic Training at Fort Campbell, Kentucky. Though he regularly led his unit in the rugged physical tests and otherwise showed respect for his superiors, Clancy was an improviser on duty and a brawler off duty. The former troubled commanders who prefer followers, not independent thinkers. The latter caused concern in the New Army.

Clancy busted up bars, never backing down from an insult or a fight. Once in a tavern, he tore off a woman's red dress and wore it as an ascot. His defense to the M.P.'s was simple. In the war games, his unit was green. Red was the enemy. The woman turned out to be a lieutenant's wife, and Clancy was either going to end up in the stockade or on a bus home until a J.A.G. lawyer suggested the Special Forces. It was the perfect place for someone who could think on his feet and react with controlled fury when the coach called his number.

During the invasion of Panama, dressed in black and wearing night vision goggles, Clancy leapt out of a hovering MH-6 Little Bird helicopter onto the roof of the Càrcel Modelo prison. As Delta Force snipers picked off guards in front of the prison, Clancy blew open a steel door with plastique explosives, then with three other commandos, raced down the stairs. He shot three guards with a laser-scoped MP-5 Heckler & Koch machine gun, then used more explosives to blow open the cell of a CIA operative who would surely have been killed in retaliation for the invasion. Clancy led the operative up to the roof and the waiting chopper, which was shot down as it lifted off. A U.S. armored personnel carrier evacuated Clancy, the other commandos and the operative with no loss of American life. Just another day in the Special Forces.

Clancy loved all the action, but Desert Storm was his favorite. On G-minus-2, two days before the start of the ground war, he led a recon team across the border into Iraq. His job was to find a route through the mine fields and tank traps and also draw enemy fire so Colonel Zwick's 2nd Armored Cavalry could locate Iraqi positions. Clancy had the perfect temperament to be a human trip wire. He enjoyed being shot at nearly as much as he enjoyed shooting back.

On the Saudi-Iraq border, hundreds of thousands of Coalition troops were gathered: the British Desert Rats, French Foreign Legionnaires, the Arab Task Force, and of course, the might of the U.S. Army, the 82nd and 101st Airborne, the 1st and 24th Infantry, the 1st and 2nd Cavalry, the 1st and 3rd Armored Division. But across the border, inside Iraq, scuttling through mine fields and over trenches, were the Night Stalkers, some on foot, some in Light Armored Vehicles (LAV's), daring the enemy to shoot, then firing back with their 25-millimeter Bushmaster chain guns.

On G-minus-1, Clancy and his men did the job too well. Brazenly hurdling flaming tank traps, the Night Stalkers apparently convinced the Iraqis that the main invasion was underway. The Iraqis responded with heavy artillery, 122 mm. rockets, tanks and FROG missiles. Which, of course, was what Clancy wanted all along, because it gave him a chance to stand and fight instead of just "flashing our petticoats and running home to Mama," which was what he called decoy missions.

Clancy stood atop his unarmored HUMVEE, firing TOW missiles at the Iraqis T-62 tanks, taking out three with direct hits, while his men pinpointed artillery positions and picked off Iraqi infantry with machine gun fire.

Now, as the Kiowa dips to five hundred feet, Clancy can imagine the crackle of small-arms fire from the ground, though he cannot hear it. He and the colonel peer down and see commandos running haphazardly from the security building, firing rifles at them. A lone bullet *pings* off a landing skid.

"Amateurs," Clancy says. "We'll go through them like a knife through an eyeball."

"I think the expression is, 'a knife through butter,'" the colonel says.

The captain smiles, and the scar at the corner of his mouth stretches and whitens. "Not where I come from, colonel."

-34-
Run Jericho, Run

Jack Jericho carefully slides the grate from its grooves and pulls himself out of the sump and onto the floor of the missile silo. He is directly below the suspended Peacekeeper missile. As he gets to his feet, he is shocked to find himself ten feet behind a man in a dark suit. The man, whose long hair is tied back in a ponytail, is staring straight up into the burners of the rocket. Jericho drops into a stalking crouch, takes a step and comes down on the outside ball of his foot, rolls to the inside ball, then lowers his heel. He's practiced in the woods, so that the stalking crouch could bring him close enough to a deer to hear its breathing. Now, deliberate as a heron stalking a frog, he approaches the man from behind.

There is a sense that is part sight and part sound, and yet it does not depend on the eyes or ears. A warning reflex, an electrical synapse more finely tuned in prehistoric man where the rustle of leaves or the breaking of a twig could mean danger or death. Sensing movement he can neither see nor hear, the man whirls around. Jericho leaps out of his crouch and grabs him by his ponytail, yanking his head back, and sliding the saw-toothed knife under his neck. "Who are you!" Jericho demands.

Startled, Brother David peers over his shoulder at Jericho, but it only takes a moment to regain his composure. "*Bitte tue mir nichts!*"

"What! What the hell are you saying?"

David trembles. His look is pure terror. He is a good enough actor to fool Jericho, who releases the pressure on David's ponytail, then gets a look at his profile. There is something familiar about the man. "Who are you?"

No answer, just the same terrified look.

"Where are you from?"

"*Deutschland.*"

"Oh." Jericho spots the dried blood on the man's shirt and suit coat. "Jeez, are you hurt?" He lets go and sheaths his knife. "You're with the U.N., aren't you? I think I must have seen you yesterday in the silo."

David nods at him.

"Have you been shot?"

"*Nein.* One of the others," David says, affecting a German accent. "The Englishmen. He died in my arms."

"Oh, God. You get separated from the group?"

"*Ya.*"

"Look, all hell's broken loose, but I guess you know that. We've got to do something or more people will be killed. Maybe a lot more people."

David fixes him with a look of wordless astonishment.

"You guys should have shut this place down yesterday," Jericho says.

"*Ya, gestern.*"

"You better stick with me." Thinking this guy isn't going to be much help, Jericho just wants to get him out of the silo. He speaks slowly, hoping the man understands. "I'll get us out of here, and we can call in the Marines."

"*Ya, waffen,*" David says, smiling obligingly.

They walk to the gantry and get on, David trailing slightly behind. Jericho pulls a lever, and the gantry begins to ascend the silo wall against the backdrop of the black PK missile. "Their leader's some kind of religious psycho. Had a woman psychiatrist strung up like a gutted deer. We've got to get her out of here and bring in some help, pronto."

"This woman," David says, slowly, as if trying out the words for the first time. "Is she your *geliebte*, your sweetheart?"

"Fat chance. A woman like that. What would she see in me?"

Jericho pulls back the lever, and the gantry stops one hundred feet above the silo floor. He points toward the wall where a screen covers an exhaust tube. "We'll get out through that tube. It runs up to a river bed."

"We will be wet," David says deliberately.

"No. We'd be under water now if the river was still there. The water's dammed at a reservoir on top the mountain. Just a little trickle in an aqueduct now, and the river bed's as dry as Army pot roast."

David does not appear to understand.

"C'mon," Jericho urges him. "You're not afraid of tight spaces, are you?"

"*Nein.*"

"Good, 'cause I am."

Jericho removes two screws from the top of the screen and pulls it open. Suddenly, a voice crackles, and David reaches into his suit pocket for a walkie-talkie. "Angel, this is Eden," a man's voice says through the static. "Do you read me?"

"What the hell is that?" Jericho asks.

David smiles placidly, pivots and hooks a sucker punch into his gut. Jericho doubles over, gasping for breath, and David smashes the walkie-talkie across his skull. A blaze of fireworks ignites Jericho's eyes, and he struggles not to black out. David locks his hands together and brings them down hard on the back of Jericho's neck, knocking him to the floor of the gantry. Jericho gets to one knee, but David kicks him in the chest, knocking him back down.

"A patient," David says.

The world spinning around him, Jericho isn't sure what he heard. "What?"

"Your lady friend, the shrink. You asked what she would see in you. She'd see you as a patient, Sergeant Jericho, a pathetic loser, a wanderer who has lost his way and who turns to secular healing for answers that will not come."

"What the hell are you talking about?"

"I've read your file, sergeant."

Jericho is on all fours, trying to clear the cobwebs from his brain. He looks up at David, and now it comes to him. "I remember. You're the preacher on the horse. You kept the sun at your back so I never made out your face."

"You are blind, Jericho. Even with the sun at your back, you would not see."

"And you're going to show me the light, right preacher?"

"Oh, but I shall. Jericho, you carry the name of a city ten thousand years old. Are you a believer?"

"Not in politicians or preachers."

David kicks him again, this time in the ribs. He's flat on the floor of the gantry now, gasping as David kicks him again, pushing him toward the ledge. Then a downward swing with the walkie-talkie smashes an ankle hard on the bone, and Jericho yelps and tries to scramble to his knees but the movement takes him closer to the ledge.

"You've got to be saved, sergeant."

Another kick digs into Jericho's abdomen, and a moment later, the acrid taste of bile fills his mouth. He tries to get to his knees, but his hand slips over the ledge. He looks down, dizzily. The silo floor swirls around him.

"You can die saved or die damned," David says. "It makes no difference to me."

"Is there a third choice?" Jericho asks, spitting blood.

"You're a heathen and a fool!" David prods Jericho with a foot, and one leg slides off the ledge. Jericho tries to grab at the smooth metal flooring, but he can't get a grip. With a final, vicious kick, David sends Jericho over the ledge.

Plunging into space.

The smooth black missile just feet away, seeming to launch as he plummets.

Reaching out, windmilling his arms, grabbing for something, anything.

Just above the polished steel floor, his arm hooks the thick umbilical cord that runs from the silo wall to the warhead.

The impact pops his shoulder out of its joint, but Jericho still holds on, swinging on the cord, first away from the PK then back where he bashes into the missile canister. He cries out in pain, then falls ten feet to the floor, where he lies in a heap.

On the gantry, David peers over the ledge and looks at the motionless body one hundred feet below. He pulls hits a button on the dented walkie-talkie, and says, "Gabriel, would you be kind enough to join me in the silo? I'd like you to scrape up the janitor."

David rides the gantry down to the silo floor. He gets off, walks a few paces beneath the missile, and finds...

Nothing.

Jericho is gone.

From the tunnel comes the *clack* of combat boots on concrete. Gabriel and four young commandos rush from the tunnel into the silo. David kneels at the spot where Jericho fell from the umbilical cord. Drops of blood lead to the grate, which lies outside its track. "Bring him to me!" David shouts.

Gabriel climbs through the opening, followed by three of the commandos. David grabs the fourth commando and points at the dangling screen over exhaust tube high on the silo wall. "Get up there and fix that. And stay there. Keep a lookout until Gabriel reports that he has captured the heathen."

The commando mumbles his acquiescence, hops onto the gantry, and rides up the wall. As the gantry slows to a stop at the exhaust tube opening, the commando fails to notice a drop of blood on the floor.

Suddenly, Jericho swings down from the roof of the gantry and crashes into the commando. They both fall to the floor, then scramble to their feet. With one arm dangling uselessly, Jericho takes a swipe with his knife, but the commando knocks it away with his Uzi, then levels to fire. Jericho barrels into him like a middle linebacker on a blitz. The Uzi flies out of the man's hands and slides to the ledge of the gantry. Both men dive for it, wrestling at the edge, Jericho howling in pain when he lands on his shoulder.

On the floor of the silo, David watches the struggle above him on the gantry, then angrily punches a button on the walkie-talkie. "Gabriel! Get back here."

David watches angrily from the silo floor. This janitor was proving to be more trouble than he had expected.

On the gantry ledge, Jericho's head is over the edge, the commando trying to shove him off. Jericho rolls over, pinning the commando beneath him. The commando kicks at Jericho, toppling him backwards into the silo wall, which is studded with hoses and gauges. The commando dives for the Uzi.

Jericho spins the wheel of a valve just below a sign emblazoned, "Warning: LOX." He grabs a hose and aims it at the commando. A blast of liquid oxygen shoots out and hits the man commando squarely in the face, blinding him and searing him with a freezing pain. He staggers backwards, squeezing the trigger of the Uzi, firing wildly, the shots *pinging* off the silo wall. He pirouettes, claws at his eyes, takes a step backward, then another, then a final one. But his foot doesn't come down. He has stepped off the ledge, seems to hang there a moment, then plummets toward the floor, screaming, falling, falling...and landing with a *thunk* at David's feet, the Uzi skittering a few feet away.

Jericho makes his way to the edge, looks down at David, and for a long moment, the two men just glare at each other. "I'll be back!" Jericho shouts. "I'm coming back for the woman, but I'm coming back for you, too."

"No you won't! It's not in your nature. Run, Jericho, Run. It's what you're good at."

There is nothing Jericho can say. He backs away from the ledge, painfully pops his dislocated shoulder back into place and retrieves his knife from the gantry floor. He moves back to the silo wall, climbs into the exhaust tube, and disappears from view.

He wriggles slowly through the tube, climbing toward the surface. If the commandos cannot find the tube's outlet pipe which is obscured in the old river bed by underbrush, safety waits above.

But safety can be a hell all its own.

So Jericho is not thinking about escape.

He is already planning how he will join the battle.

-35-
Ask the Missile

Base Camp Alpha is a scene of controlled chaos at the foot of Chugwater Mountain eleven hundred meters from the blown front gate of the 318th Missile Squadron. The sights, sounds and smells are pure military as Quonset huts are erected, tents are pitched, and men and materiél pour in.

Loaded with equipment, olive green deuce-and-a-half trucks pull up the gravel road. Moving slower in the procession, massive trucks called HEMETTS carry tons of ammunition and building supplies. CH-47 Chinook helicopters off-load troops of the Armored Cavalry, and CH-46 Sea Knight copters lower Light Armored Vehicles on cargo hooks.

Forklifts move pallets loaded with wooden crates and bladders of fuel. Bulldozers clear trees and push topsoil spiked with twisted limbs into makeshift fortifications. A dozen M2/3 Bradley Fighting Vehicles equipped with grenade launchers, TOW missile launchers and 25 mm. cannon take a forward position alongside six M109A6 Paladin self-propelled howitzers. Poking through the pine trees, a 120 mm cannon appears. It is attached to an MA1A2 Abrams main battle tank, a seventy-ton fighting machine that is the most sophisticated piece of rolling armor in the history of warfare. Four of the tanks, encased in armor plate tougher than the eighteen inches of solid steel protecting a battleship's control tower, crunch through trees and underbrush and take their positions.

MLRS rocket launchers on tracked vehicles pull into place at the perimeter. Called "steel rain" by the Iraqis whose parade they rained on. the rocket launchers fire TGW smart missiles. As the vehicles come to a halt, struts extend, elevating the rocket tubes to fire at an thirty-degree angle over the missile silo. It is a strategy that might be called, "if all else fails..." for no one believes they can shoot down a Peacekeeper missile.

The PK is cold launched, ejected from the canister by pressure created by a mixture of water and gases in a generator. The missile literally pops up out of the silo when the pressure in the sealed canister reaches three hundred twenty pounds per square inch, and something's got to give. What gives is the missile, all one hundred ninety thousand pounds of it.

There is that moment, less than one second, when the PK hangs there, one hundred feet above the ground. If a ground-to-air rocket launcher could acquire the target, if the gunners knew precisely the moment the Peacekeeper would be there, maybe it could be shot down. But there is no time. In that next second, the rockets ignite with the roar of an angry god, and in the next sixty seconds, they catapult the missile to eighty-six thousand feet.

The first stage peels off, and the second stage fires up, again burning brightly for just a minute, but carrying the missile to a height of three hundred seventy-thousand feet. The third stage is not much longer lived, giving its all in less than ninety seconds, but by this time, the missile is in space traveling at an incredible fifteen thousand miles an hour. It has gone ballistic.

Everywhere at Base Camp Alpha, there are the sounds of chugging diesel engines and spinning rotors, the shouts of men hard at work building and digging. The fragrance of the trees and rich brown earth is mixed now with the pungent smell of diesel fuel and wet canvas and lubricated metal.

By nightfall, there will be enough firepower here to overthrow a healthy number of third-world countries. Whether it is sufficient to take over a missile silo without killing half-a-dozen foreign ambassadors or causing what the Atomic Energy Commission would blithely refer to as a nuclear incident is another matter.

Half a mile above Base Camp Alpha, on an old logging road whose ruts are now overgrown with sunflowers and bright red Indian paintbrush, a lone rider in buckskins sits astride a golden Palomino. Motionless, Kenosha watches as the elaborate war machine is assembled. Then, with a tug of the reins, man and horse turn and make their way higher up the slope, through strands of white birch trees, across a plateau of sagebrush, then higher still through a stand of fir trees. Kenosha works the horse farther away until he can no longer see or hear the grinding engines below him, until he is swallowed by the ancient forest itself.

∽

In the launch control capsule, James works doggedly at the computer as Rachel watches over his shoulder. Brother David enters the capsule from the tunnel, and Rachel glares at him.

"How was your proselytizing? Did you convert her?" Rachel's tone is sarcastic, and she shoots an angry look at Susan Burns, who is handcuffed and sitting on the floor against the rear wall of the capsule. The psychiatrist wears a blue flightsuit, her hair flowing over her shoulders.

"The woman is not important," David says, "but something else is. We seem to have a stray airman who refuses to either die or see the light."

Susan looks toward him, and then away, trying not to reveal her interest. Still, David catches the look in her eyes. "Yes, doctor, I refer to your favorite patient, the cowardly coal miner from Shitkicker, West Virginia." He turns toward Rachel. "Have Matthew's men above ground scour the river bed. He'll be there presently."

"Armed?" Rachel asks.

"Only with a knife. Matthew will dispose of him." He looks back to Susan who gives no reaction. "Other than the vexatious sergeant, everything is under control. The ambassadors are confined in the equipment room, and the loud-mouthed sergeant has his own quarters." He walks down the rail toward the launch commander's console. "James, how goes it?"

"Damn slow."

"What can I do to help you?"

James lets out a mirthless laugh. "Bring me the President."

"Why, looking for an appointment to the cabinet? Secretary of geekdom, maybe."

"No. I want to ask him the Secondary Launch Code."

"I doubt he'd tell you."

James laughs but there is little humor in it. "Yeah, but he told the missile, didn't he?"

"What do you mean?"

"The PK's computer has been programmed to recognize the slick, so in a sense, the President told the missile the code."

"Right." The shadow of an idea crosses David's face. "Forget the President. You've got it. The missile will tell you."

David turns and bolts out through the blast door, leaving James and Rachel to exchange puzzled looks.

ల

Jack Jericho has worked his way up to the final turn in the exhaust tube. Around the bend, he can see light coming through the screen where the outlet pipe empties into the dry river bed. He wriggles ahead and brings a knee up toward his chest.

And gets stuck.

His knee is lodged against his sternum, his combat boot propped against the side of the tube. His head and back are pressed against the opposite side, so that he cannot move.

He tries wriggling backward. No dice.

He tries wriggling forward. Nothing.

He tries working his knee free from his chest but cannot. He fears getting a cramp in his calf and begins to massage it. Sweat drips from his forehead and *plops* off the metal tube.

Then he hears a voice and freezes. At first, he can't make out the words. Then, louder, "Over here!"

The voice comes from the river bed. Jericho doesn't know if he's been discovered, but there it is again, even louder. "Jeptha, over here!"

Jericho squeezes his eyes shut and hears another voice. His father's.

"Over here, Jack! Help me, son."

In the collapsed mine shaft, Jericho squirms on his stomach through a nightmarish web of fallen timbers. Water pours through a crevice over his head, dousing him.

His father's voice is desperate, pleading. "Jack! Where are you?"

Jericho opens his eyes and wipes the sweat away by brushing his face against his shoulder. He sucks in a deep breath, exhales, and lets his body go limp, willing himself into a state of relaxation. Closing his eyes again, he fights off the visions and lets his mind see the exhaust tube expanding while his own body shrinks. He continues to exhale until he has no breath left.

Suddenly, his foot slides free, and he straightens his leg, then crawls a few feet to the screen.

He looks outside. The exhaust tube ends in a clump of underbrush. Jericho can see the shapes of two men moving slowly across the dry river bed, poking at the brush with their rifles. They are doubtless looking for the exhaust tube's outlet pipe. If he kicks out the screen and jumps into the river bed, they will see him. If he stays put and they find the tube, he'll be trapped. Courage is so often the choice between equally unappealing risks. He cannot decide, which is a decision in itself. Jack Jericho stays right where he is.

❧

The gantry moves up the silo wall, then stops level with the fourth stage of the Peacekeeper. David hits a button, and the work cage extends horizontally until it is just inches from the missile. Wearing thin white gloves and a headset, David carefully loosens the first of four bolts from a metal plate in the deployment module, just below the titanium shroud of the nose cone.

In the launch control capsule, James watches David on a TV monitor. Rachel sits in the second launch chair. Behind them, Gabriel keeps watch over Susan Burns and Lieutenant Owens.

James speaks into a microphone. "Once you break the seal,

you've only got ten seconds before auto-lockdown."

His feet planted firmly on the gantry, David removes the second bolt from the metal plate. "Be still, Brother James. We've been over this."

"Godspeed, David."

"Precisely."

David knows they are watching. Enjoys it. He is the center of their universe, and indeed, the center of everyone's universe at this moment. If he fails and the system shuts down, they will be locked out of the command data buffers and the launch control computers. If he succeeds, they will have broken the system, will have the Secondary Launch Code, and nothing can stop him.

If he can freeze the lockdown, he will extract the computer containing the Multiple Guidance Control System. The computer is the brains of the missile. It arms the warheads, measures inertial flight distances and performs a host of other functions. For David's purpose, the most important is that it reads the S.L.C. to determine whether to accept a launch command. To recognize the code, David reasoned, the computer must know the code. If it does, James can work his wizardry and find the damn thing. Once they have the code, they will enter it on the console and the re-installed MGCS will happily confirm the S.L.C. is correct.

David removes the third bolt and gently places it on the floor of the work cage. He crouches down and opens what looks like a laptop computer, punches a few keys, then stands up again, holding a multi-pinned plug attached to the computer by a ten-foot cord. He holds the plug between his teeth, then uses both hands to remove the last bolt from the metal plate. He slides off the plate and looks inside the computer box. An LCD display on an interior gauge flashes the countdown as David searches for the female receptacle.

10-9-8...He jams the plug into a hole, but it doesn't fit...*7-6*... Another try, and the plug catches, but the clock keeps clicking away...*5-4*...David drops down to his laptop again, punches in a dizzying combination of letters and numbers...*3-2-1*...The LCD display freezes at 1. He's done it.

David exhales a deep sigh, then reaches into the deployment module and pulls out the computer.

Watching on the monitor in the launch control capsule, James excitedly pounds out a drum role on the console. "Awright! That man has the touch!

"He will never fail us," Rachel says. "He is truly the chosen one."

Behind them, Susan Burns feels a chill. Who will stop this maniac? Not Jack Jericho. Not Captain Pukowlski. Special Forces? The only means of access is to rappel down the silo wall or the elevator shaft. The men would be sitting ducks for the well armed commandos.

Halting the greatest tragedy in the history of civilization, Susan Burns thinks, will be entirely up to her.

 confused

In the river bed, one of the commandos pushes away the pungent leaves of a sagebrush plant. Hidden behind the plant is the U-shaped outlet pipe of the exhaust tube. "Jeptha! Over here."

In the exhaust tube, Jericho is startled by the commando's voice. So close. He removes the knife from the sheath on his leg. If one of the commandos ventures inside, Jericho will gut him. Then be shot to ribbons by the other, he knows.

Now, two voices from outside. "Use your bayonet to pry off the screen."

Jericho can hear the scraping of the bayonet blade against the metal of the screen. He inches backward just enough to be in the shadows of the bend in the tube. If they come into the outlet pipe, he'll have to crawl back down toward the silo. The screen clatters to the ground, and the men's voices are louder. Jericho knows they are poking their heads into the outlet pipe.

"Dark as Hades down there."

"You're smaller, Jeptha. You crawl inside, and I'll stand watch here."

"Stand watch? For what?"

"For other infidels."

"Isn't that just like you, handing off the dirty work?"

"What's the matter. You afraid of some spiders?"

To Jericho, it seems, there is no clean line of command beneath Brother David. For a moment, he wonders if maybe the military has the right idea about discipline and command control. These bozos wouldn't know Reveille from Rachmaninoff. Suddenly, there is a sound behind Jericho, farther down the tube.

Trapped.

He freezes and listens.

A squeak, then a scraping sound, then another squeak, only louder.

"Jeptha, did you hear that? In heaven's name, what—"

"Rats! Satan's own pets. I'm not going in there."

Jericho stiffens but as the sound gets closer, he recognizes it. A moment later, Ike the ferret is nuzzling his leg. "Here boy," he whispers, grabbing the animal and placing him in the deep pocket of his fatigues.

Above him, the two commandos continue to argue. "Brother David ordered us to find the infidel. He won't care if rats or elephants are in that—"

A noise overhead interrupts them. The two commandos look up to see

a Kiowa reconnaissance helicopter dipping low over the base. Two video cameras are attached to the chopper's skids. "Brother David promised extra rations for the man who shoots it down!" one yells.

They both whoop and run off through the river bed, firing wildly in the air, fruitlessly chasing the copter as it banks and runs through a series of well-practiced evasive maneuvers.

Jericho crawls the short distance to the opening, tumbles from the outlet pipe onto the ground, then scuttles across the river bed toward a stand of pine trees. His shoulder is swollen and throbs at the joint. He is grimy and sweaty and nearing exhaustion. He is just yards away from cover when he stops short.

Must be dreaming.

Hallucinating.

First the mine shaft. Then this.

In front of him, above him actually, as he is on all fours, is a girl of about ten. She wears a yellow sun dress with blue polka dots. Her blonde hair is in pigtails. She waves a small plastic wand over Jericho's head, leaving a trail of bubbles that float in the soft breeze.

"Do you love the Lord?" the girl asks.

"What?"

"Do you love the Lord and accept the Word?"

Jericho is speechless.

"'Cause if you don't," the little girl tells him, dipping the wand into a blue plastic bottle, "you'll get boils, your teeth will rot, and vultures will eat your liver."

"Is that all?"

"No, then you'll croak, and the fires of hell will melt your eyeballs."

As the bubbles float above him, Jericho turns over and flops onto his back, breathing hard. "Just now," he says, "that would be an improvement."

-36-
Threatening the General

The Big Board at STRATCOM shows live video of the 318th Missile Squadron, taken as the Kiowa recon helicopter sweeps over the base. General Corrigan, Colonel Farris, F.B.I. Agent Hurtgen and a circle of military aides watch as the commandos race helter-skelter below the chopper, blasting away with automatic weapons.

"Small arms fire only," Colonel Farris sniffs. "No organization, no interlocking fire patterns."

"We lost a nuclear missile to the military equivalent of a drive-by shooting," F.B.I. Agent Hurtgen says.

"They were good enough to take over the base, weren't they?" the general asks. No one answers the question, which was addressed mostly to himself anyway. "Their training was fine for what they had to do."

"But they planned to launch the missile before we could respond," Agent Hurtgen says. "Now we can respond, and they likely didn't train for that."

"Right," the general agrees.

"But either way, they'd still have to defend themselves," Colonel Farris says, puzzled. "They'd have to fight their way out whether they launched or not."

"Not if they never intended to get out of the hole," General Corrigan says. The assemblage seems to think it over. Kamikaze warriors of God. Not much difference between them and fundamentalist Shiites in the Middle East, except these guys aren't fooling around with car bombs or plastiques.

On the Big Board, a live aerial shot shows a commando standing in the open on the gravel road that runs from the front gate to the security building. The Air Force officers cannot make out Matthew's face, wouldn't know him if they could. But there is something about this one. He stands motionless, his feet spread to shoulder width, as he raises a tube to his shoulder.

"Shit!" Colonel Farris blurts out. "He's got a Stinger."

There is a puff of smoke and an animated blur of yellow. The video from the chopper is up-linked to a satellite, then down-linked to a ground station, where it is fed through underground lines to Offut Air Force Base. Fast motion, such as a race horse or a heat-seeking Stinger missile appears as a streaking blur of color.

The ground tilts away at a sudden angle as the chopper banks in an evasive maneuver, but a second later, there is an explosion of orange flame and the Big Board goes blank.

For a long moment, none of the officers says a word. Finally, the general speaks. "We'll need to assess enemy numbers and weaponry before there's an assault." He turns to Colonel Farris. "Has Intelligence analyzed the satellite photos?"

The colonel nods to an aide who hits a button on his console, and the Big Board flashes with a black-and-white still shot of the missile base shot from a low-orbiting satellite. Enemy commandos have been electronically enhanced and numbered. "Fifty to sixty men above ground. We don't know what they've got in the hole."

The Big Board flashes to a second shot, a close-up of the open missile silo. The shiny titanium shroud of the PK missile can be seen, but the rest is in shadows.

"Any demands yet?" the general asks.

"Nothing. And no word on the ambassadors."

"They could be dead."

The colonel shrugs. "Would make our decisions easier, wouldn't it?"

General Corrigan gives the colonel a sharp look as a satellite photo of Base Camp Alpha flashes onto the Big Board. "When one of your staff takes early retirement and sells his story to television, you'll probably be sorry you said that."

Colonel Farris flinches. He now regrets loosening his tie, treating the general with excessive familiarity. General Corrigan still has his fresh, crisply laundered look, his silver hair neatly in place. The general wasn't finished chastising Farris, but an aide interrupts and hands him a red telephone. "It's Morning Star, sir. He's asked for you by name."

General Corrigan's glance shoots the aide a question.

"Voice analysis confirms Morning Star is a white male," the aide says, "probable age mid-thirties, most likely raised west of the Mississippi."

"That narrows it down," Agent Hurtgen says derisively, as the general takes the phone.

"General Corrigan here. Who is this?"

"Hello Hugh," the voice says. "Congratulations on getting that second star. Lord knows, you deserve it."

"Who the hell is this?"

"I understand Cliff has an appointment to the Academy. You must be so proud. And how is Edna?"

General Corrigan stands looking into the phone as if trying to divine the identity of the caller. Colonel Farris whispers to an aide. "I'll bet the bastard even knows about the barmaid in Stuttgart."

Finally, the general says, "What is it you want?"

"Salvation for all eternity."

Eternity is not on General Hugh Corrigan's mind just now. Making it to retirement without presiding over a nuclear holocaust is a higher priority. "What do you want from me?" he asks.

In the launch control capsule at the 318th Missile Squadron, David sits in the commander's red-cushioned flight chair, his feet propped up on the console. Speaking into the headset, he says, "A word of caution. Don't do anything foolish, Hugh. I imagine Delta is on its way from Bragg, and a contingent of SEAL's from San Diego, maybe the black hat Red Cell team, too. Then There's the F.B.I. Hostage Response Unit, Army Night Stalkers, Green Berets, the 82nd Airborne, and probably the A.T.F. just for good measure. I'll bet some bright boy in D.C. wants to send in the flame throwers. I have women and children here, Hugh, just like Waco. You want another Texas barbecue?"

"Is that what you are?" the general asks, "another David Koresh?"

"You insult me, Hugh, comparing me to that low-rent charlatan who founded a religion in order to have sex with little girls. A bit tawdry, don't you think? Do you know his real name was Vernon Howell? Now, doesn't that have Texas trailer park written all over it?"

"What's your real name, Morning Star?"

"In due time," David says. "I'm sure you'll figure it out without any help from me. In the meantime, I'd caution against using the same tactics the F.B.I. used in Waco. This time, you'll fry a delegation of U.N. ambassadors."

"How do I know they're still alive?"

David's tone is teasing. "If you like, I'll send out one's ear. It'll still be warm. Let's see, who should we start with? There's a rather fussy Englishman who is getting on all our nerves. But in the spirit of the European Community, perhaps the French and

German ambassadors should join him. Or, how about the Israeli? How fitting, given our circumstances. He's already told me that his country's response to our little plan will be most enlightening."

"What does that mean?"

"Oh, I'm sure the President knows and you'll be told in due time if you're in that loop, Hugh."

"Look, why not just let the ambassadors go and we'll talk about resolving this?"

"Actually, I'm reluctant to do that. It could be dangerous. Your boys tend to fire first and ask questions later, don't they? I always thought the term 'friendly fire' was an even juicier oxymoron than 'military intelligence.'"

"Look, you..."

"Morning Star, Hugh. But let's not kid each other. Sure, you'd like to have the ambassadors safe and sound, but if I offered to return your big, beautiful missile in return for their blood, you'd take the deal in an instant."

The general doesn't respond. For a moment, there's the fleeting hope that maybe the terrorists are after the ambassadors, but no, they had tried to launch. "Morning Star, I don't know what you're getting at. I can't help you if you don't tell—"

"Hugh, you've got it all wrong. I'm helping you. I'm giving you advice that will save your career, maybe even get you that third star, make Edna so proud, to say nothing of all the bar girls in western Europe."

Behind Corrigan, Colonel Farris winks at an aide.

"I'm listening," the general says.

"Hugh, you have all these killing machines at your disposal, and soon you'll be under enormous pressure to do something, anything. Am I right?"

"Go on. What's your point?"

David's tone changes, his voice taking on a steely edge. "My point, old man, is simply this. If a Ranger, Seal or Boy Scout sets foot in this silo, I'll start sacrificing U.N. ambassadors. Your so-called Allies will be pissed. And then..." He lets his voice go up an octave in a child's sing-song, "I'll launch your pretty back birdie."

"You're bluffing," Corrigan shoots back. "If you had the S.L.C., you'd have launched already."

"When you've got only one wad to shoot, you don't want to fire prematurely, do you? Let's wait for dawn. Don't you just love the sight of an ICBM lifting off into the rising sun?"

"You still haven't convinced me you can do it."

"But you're not sure, and you can't take the chance. Besides, Hugh, even without the code, you know I could create a hell of a nuke flash right in the hole."

"I don't know that at all. You'd have to arm the warheads. You'd have to detonate. It's not as simple as you may—"

"Would I come all this way and not know how to do a little fission-fusion-fission? Oh, can't you just envision two deuterium atoms colliding and fusing into Helium-3?" Suddenly, David laughs and begins singing, "Oh, the lithium's connected to the deuterium, and the deuterium's connected to the tritium, and the tritium's connected to the plutonium, and the plutonium's connected to the uranium, and the uranium's connected to...me!"

At STRATCOM, there is worried mumbling and the exchange of astonished looks. "That fellow's toothpick don't go all the way through the olive," Colonel Farris says.

"What a big bang," David says, "all ten warheads detonating at once in the same location. You'd lose all your ground forces, which serves them right." He laughs and lets his voice fill with sarcasm. "They're making so much noise digging in, my men can hardly read their Bibles. And the Sierra Club will be all over your back what with all the dead fish and deer in these bucolic parts."

"You'll be killed, too," the general says flatly.

"No, I will live forever, and even my ashes will have a half-life of 700 million years. What a way to achieve immortality, eh Hugh?"

General Corrigan stares at the Big Board. The map of the world has replaced the satellite shots of the missile base. A dotted line tracks across the continents from Wyoming to Israel. In a corner of the map, the target coordinates appear in a black-lined box: NORTH LATITUDE 32 DEGREES, 28 MINUTES, 15 SECONDS; EAST LONGITUDE 35 DEGREES, 1 MINUTE, 13 SECONDS.

"Why Jerusalem?" the general asks.

"Oh, come now, Hugh. Where should we hit? The boring old Kartaly Missile Field, or Khabarovsk, or the Kremlin. That wouldn't take any imagination, would it? Russia pales in comparison to the ancient walled city, to Assyria and Babylon, to Mesopotamia where the Tigris meets the Euphrates, and our cup runneth over with prophets and infidels alike."

At STRATCOM, the officers exchanged puzzled looks. "The fuck is this maniac talking about?" Agent Hurtgen whispers.

"Do you want to kill millions of innocent people?" the general asks.

"You're ignoring the concept of original sin," David says.

"You know goddam well what I mean!" The strain is showing on Corrigan's face and in his voice.

"I wouldn't be so self-righteous, if I were you, Hugh. I know how you got your second star. Your 379th Bomb Wing baked a hundred thousand Iraqi boys in their bunkers. Scared kids, conscripts from the countryside. Now you tell me, what is the moral difference between dropping ten thousand bombs from the belly of your B-52's and launching one missile from its silo? Aren't the deaths just as real?"

"We were at war!" Corrigan thunders.

"Aren't we always," David says, not making it a question. "Good-bye, Hugh."

"Wait! You still haven't answered my question. Why Jerusalem?"

"It's really quite simple," David says. "I must destroy Jerusalem in order to save it."

-37-
Until the Bitter End

185

Jack Jericho breathes in deeply, inhaling the fragrance of the pines, sensing the moistness of the earth in the shade of the great trees. The little girl in pigtails sits next to him. They are playing tic-tac-toe by drawing in the dirt with sticks.

It is mid-afternoon. In the silo and the sump below, there is never a sense of time or weather. There is only the blandness of re-circulated air, the synthetic smells of fuels and polymers and metals. Here it is cool as the sun slants through the pine needles to their hiding place beneath the umbrella of trees.

"What's your name, honey?" Jericho asks.

"Elizabeth, but you can call me Betsy." She reaches down and pets Ike, the ferret, who arches his back, enjoying the attention.

Within minutes, Jericho learns that Betsy's mother was a member of the Holy Church of Revelations. She had been a Seventh Day Adventist in San Diego but left the church, telling Betsy its teachings had been watered down. The end is coming, and it will be glorious, her mother repeatedly told her. About a year ago, the woman left her husband, a non-believer, and drove with Betsy from southern California to Wyoming.

Now, Jericho scratches an "X" in the wrong place, letting Betsy win the game. She laughs, runs her hand over the dirt, erasing the game, then draws the lines for a new round. Ike grows bored and wanders off, sniffing at fallen pine cones. "Mommy is one of Brother David's favorites, though not as favorite as Rachel. Mommy cooks. Do you like rice?"

"Not particularly."

Betsy wrinkles her nose. "Me neither. We eat a lot of rice. Do you think there's rice in heaven?"

"Why do you ask?"

"'Cause that's where we're going, silly."

Jericho considers his reply before saying, "Of course you are, but not for a long time."

"No, we're going soon. We'll be lifted through the clouds and *poof*, we're there. I just hope we don't have to eat rice or bean sprouts there."

"In heaven, there's pizza and cheeseburgers and cherry Cokes," Jericho says. "But no rice and no bean sprouts."

That makes her smile. "I haven't had a cheeseburger since we left California."

"Does Rachel cook, too?"

"No, Rachel is David's Mary Magdalene."

"Who tells you that?"

Betsy uses the twig to scratch at a mosquito bite on her ankle. "Mommy says Rachel was a coke whore."

Ike stops his sniffing and looks at Jericho. From his expression, he seems to be listening.

"She sold her flesh," Betsy says innocently. "David saved her, just like he saved all of us, but Rachel needed it more. Now, she's David's best friend. Mommy says she believes even more than David."

"Believes what?"

"In the Word. The Word will save us."

"Betsy, listen to me. It takes more than the Bible to save people. Unless we get some help, a lot of very nice people are going to get hurt. Will you help me?"

She seems to think about it as the breeze rattles the tree limbs. A soft shower of pine needles floats over them. "But Brother David will protect us. He loves all the people."

"Maybe he doesn't love himself, and that makes him confused."

Her forehead is wrinkled in thought, but she remains quiet. Ike slinks back and rubs against Jericho's boot. Jericho picks up the animal and places him in a pocket on his fatigue pants.

"Sometimes, something happens to a man," Jericho says, "something in his past that affects him forever. Makes him somebody he didn't think he was and doesn't want to be. Ruins him, really."

Betsy's appraising look is so knowing and mature that Jericho is chilled. "Who are you?" she asks.

"Your friend. Your secret friend. You shouldn't tell anyone about me."

She stands and brushes dirt from her knees. "I can't have any secrets from Brother David, and you're saying bad things about him. Whenever anybody says anything bad about him, we have to tell Brother David right away, even if it's our friend or our very own mother."

"No, no, I was talking about myself," Jericho says, believing it to be at least partially true.

"You say Brother David is confused, but you're wrong. Brother David has seen the light." Agitated now, backing away from Jericho. "Brother David gives us the Word. Only bad people will get hurt. Brother David said so." She is near tears. "And you're a big old liar, and besides that, you smell stinky."

Jericho reaches out to take her arm, but she backs away, turns and runs down the embankment and into the dry river bed. She will tell the commandos about him, he knows. Jericho crouches low and, staying in the shadows, heads toward the barracks on the east side of the missile base.

He weaves through the pine trees, then crawls through the underbrush, listening and watching. He sees commandos working in pairs, fanning out from the river bed over the missile grounds. They could be on routine patrol, but he assumes they are searching for him. Search and destroy.

Jericho has the ability to stalk game without breaking a twig underfoot or snapping a tree branch. Camping out in the mountains of West Virginia, he has made flour from the bark of a spruce tree and brewed tea from its green needles. He has made arrows from a fire-killed sapling and boiled tamarack pine shoots to eat as vegetables. But those skills will do him little good here. This is survival of a different kind. Here, the enemy is man. Another difference, too. Others depend on him, now. Susan Burns, for one. Maybe the whole damn world. For a man who ran away the first time he was needed, it is a frightening proposition. He will have to go back into the hole, into the man-made hell he hates so much.

Jericho comes upon the shredded barracks. There is no sign of life. Bodies of airmen lie where they fell. He circles the barracks, then slithers on his stomach to a rear wall. He hoists himself up and tumbles through a blown-out window, landing squarely on the back of a dead airman, through-and-through wounds puncturing his chest. The barracks is a shambles, the aftermath of a massacre. Nine bodies are strewn on and between bunks. All show multiple gunshot wounds. The walls are peppered with bullet holes, and the barracks have been ransacked. Jericho makes his way to the weapons locker. If he can lay his hands on an M-16...

The locker door has been jimmied.

Empty.

Jericho makes his way to the sleeping compartment at the end of the barracks – the security officer's quarters. The room has been tossed. Jericho picks up the phone. Dead. He opens a desk drawer, roots around inside and finds a cellular phone and a palm-sized Newton Messagepad Wireless Fax. He puts both devices in his pockets.

Back in the interior of the barracks, he uses his knife to pry open several footlockers, rifling their contents like a burglar. Through the broken windows, he can hear the shouts of the commandos but cannot make out their words. At the locker marked "Sayers," he pulls out three long bungee cords and stuffs them into a rucksack. He moves to the locker marked "Jericho." The lock has been broken, and the contents are scattered on the floor, but nothing appears to be missing. What would be? He finds a telescoping fishing rod which has rolled halfway under his bunk and puts it in his rucksack. As he closes the lid on the locker, an old black and white photo slips out and skids across the floor.

He picks it up and looks into the faces of three smiling men, their faces stained with dirt, helmets on their heads at jaunty angles. Two of the men – his father and brother – are ghosts, and the third man, Jack himself, has often wished he were dead. In the background is a long, dark bar in a dingy saloon. He stares at the photo for a long moment, remembers the salute they always gave each other after work on Fridays. This day, he knows, was special. That morning, the Appalachian Anthracite Company had opened two new shafts.

There would be work through the winter and spring. He looks at his father's wide grin, the eyes red dots from the flash and a little glazed from the beer. He looks at his brother, two years older, Jack had idolized him as a child.

Mike Jericho never asked for much, never needed much. Married a girl he had dated since seventh grade and only wanted to live in the mountains, raise a lot of kids and a little hell. Jericho looks at his own picture, barely recognizing himself. Not because he was younger then, but that he was so much more innocent. He looks at his own guileless smile, knows he will never recapture that moment. He remembers the words they spoke just before the photo was taken. Always the same, their arms intertwined, their glasses raised.

"All for one," Jack Jericho said.

"And one for all," his brother replied.

Then they both looked at their father who unfailingly said, "Until the bitter end, my boys."

-38-
A Man Who Loves the Bomb

An unmarked van with bulletproof glass, armor-plated doors, and run-flat tires approaches the sentry post at STRATCOM headquarters, Offutt Air Force Base, Omaha, Nebraska. A helmeted sentry checks the papers of the driver, makes a quick call on his phone, and waves the van through. Two minutes later, the van speeds past an imposing windowless concrete building and squeals to a stop in front of a titanium blast door cut into a hill. The side door of the van opens, and a motorized ledge lowers Professor Lionel Morton in his wheelchair to the ground.

Lieutenant Colonel Charlie Griggs leads a procession of four Army Rangers, their pants bloused neatly into their combat boots, and the professor, who aims his wheelchair for the open blast door. As he motors into the bunker, Morton smiles at the STRATCOM insignia cut into the wall: an iron fist gripping three lightning bolts, wrapped by an olive branch.

He stops the whirring wheelchair for a moment, sighs, and says, "Home sweet home." Then with his military escort, Professor Morton proceeds into the bunker, and the huge door closes behind him with a pneumatic *whoosh* and a metallic *clang*.

❧

A four-door green Chrysler with black wall tires and tinted windows pulls up to a two-story house on a leafy street in Palo Alto, California. Four men in dark suits get out and walk briskly to the front door. Across the street, an elderly man waters his lawn and looks suspiciously at the strangers.

Once on the porch, one of the men rings the doorbell.

No answer.

Another opens the mailbox and pulls out a wad of third-class mail. The first man stops ringing the bell and tapes to the door a document with an impressive blue cover and the signature of a federal judge. The other two men hit the door with sledge hammers, shattering it. Across the street, the fellow with the hose is suddenly watering his own feet.

"My name is deputy United States Marshal Brian Healey, and I am serving an emergency search warrant on these premises," the first man shouts as he enters the house. No one answers, and the four men pile inside.

They will painstakingly go over the entire house, but they start in the cluttered study of the owner: Professor Lionel Morton. They pull down photographs from the walls, looking for compartments hidden underneath. While the others search the desk and file cabinets, deputy Marshal Healey takes inventory. He is about forty with close-cropped gray hair and a gut that is just starting to bulge over the 34-inch waistband he has proudly worn since his sophomore year at San Jose State. Healey studies the photos starting with a grainy black-and-white shot of a mustachioed man in an overcoat and galoshes standing in the snow with a rocket that looks like an oversized Roman candle. Underneath, a caption, "Dr. Robert Goddard, March 16, 1926."

Nearby, a framed shot of the "Enola Gay" crew taken on the island of Tinian on August 2, 1945, just days before they took off for their rendezvous with history. Then, a group shot of the Manhattan Project scientists, a photo of a young Lionel Morton standing beneath the rockets of a first generation Thor missile, and finally, a series of mushroom cloud explosions captioned "Bikini Island 1956" and Eniwetok 1952."

On a credenza, a scale model of an MX-774 experimental missile sits on a plaque with a brass plate inscribed, "White Sands Proving Grounds, 1948." Other models, like children's toys, are lined up alongside: an Atlas Missile with a plaque reading "Cape Canaveral, 1958," and a Titan II with the notation, "McConnell Air Force Base, Kansas, 1962."

Like a room frozen in time. other black-and-white photos memorialize a slice of history. Healey picks up a signed photo of Defense Secretary Robert McNamara standing next to an Atlas missile. He reads the inscription aloud, "To Lionel. You made it happen. Bob."

Healey is mesmerized by the nuclear weapons memorabilia. "What kind of man would create a shrine to nuclear weaponry?" he wonders aloud.

"A man who loves the bomb," another marshal replies.

"Or worships it," a third marshal says.

They empty the desk drawers and search the filing cabinets, but do not find what they are looking for. Healey approaches a large globe of the earth, propped on a floor stand. He spins the globe, letting his finger drag across the continents. He finger feels an imperfection in the globe, and he uses his other hand to stop the spinning. He slips his fingers into a groove at the equator and swings the northern hemisphere open like a lid. He pulls out a metal briefcase from inside and opens the latch. Inside is a foam indentation, the perfect size for a computer disk. Only there is no disk. The case is empty.

ᘓ

A courier in civilian clothes dashes across the catwalk in the amphitheater above the STRATCOM War Room. He clatters down the ladder to the main floor and hands a sealed envelope to F.B.I. Agent Hurtgen. General Corrigan, Colonel Farris and their aides turn away from the Big Board and watch as Hurtgen unties the cord and breaks the seal.

"What are you looking at?" he says, moving back a step.

"What the hell is that?" Colonel Farris demands, sneaking a peek at the "Top Secret" seal on the envelope.

"Behavioral Science Unit report. Level Six clearance required. What's your security rating?"

"Security rating!" General Corrigan booms. "Do you know where you are? Are you out of your mind, you, you..." The pressure is getting to the general, and all he can say, his voice trailing off, is, "you civilian."

Chagrined, Agent Hurtgen opens the envelope and pulls out the King James version of the New Testament.

"Top secret," Colonel Farris says, sneering.

"Might as well be," Hurtgen says. "It's not like anybody inside the Beltway's ever read it."

Agent Hurtgen opens the Bible where it has been book-marked and reads aloud from a yellowed passage, "'The first earth had passed away, and the Holy City, the new Jerusalem, came down from Heaven.'"

General Corrigan's look asks for an explanation.

"Revelations," Hurtgen says. He unfolds a report on F.B.I. stationery, spends a moment reading it, another moment milking the situation for its drama, then says, "Paraphrasing now. To get a new Jerusalem, a place where all believers live forever, first you gotta blow up the old one."

"Says who?" the general demands.

"Peter."

"Peter who?" Colonel Farris asks.

"The Bible guy," Hurtgen says, thumbing to another marked page. "Peter, chapter three, verse ten. 'The Lord will come as a thief in the night, and the heavens will open with a great noise and fervent heat, and the earth shall be burned up.'"

"The Morning Star," General Corrigan says, grimly.

"Jesus Christ," Colonel Farris mumbles under his breath.

"Exactly," Hurtgen says, closing the book.

The courier whispers something in Hurtgen's ear and on the Big Board, the map of the world is replaced by a photo showing the aftermath of the New York porn shop bombing. Again, Hurtgen consults his memo and says, "They call themselves the Holy Church of Revelations. They're led by a fellow who calls himself Brother David, a charismatic fanatic. The Behavioral Science Unit's working on a psych profile."

The Big Board blinks with what looks like a high school yearbook photo of a younger, short-haired David. It blinks again, and a slightly older David is carrying a sign at a protest rally: "Abortion is Murder."

"He's an only child, a loner as a kid," Hurtgen continues. "Grew up on different military bases, even had an appointment to West Point."

That draws a murmur from the brass. The Big Board blinks again. Another protest rally. This time David carries a hand-painted sign: "No More Nukes."

"But he got bounced out after his plebe year," Hurtgen says.

"It's no damn wonder, if he was one of those anti-war kooks."

"No, he could have weathered that flack," Hurtgen says. "But his father made some calls that got him tossed."

There is a buzzing behind the group as Professor Lionel Morton zips into the semi-circle of officers in his wheelchair.

"I don't understand," General Corrigan says. "You saying his father didn't try to keep him in the Academy?"

"Just the opposite," Hurtgen says. "He called—"

"The President!" Professor Morton thunders, and heads turn his way. "The Secretary of the Army, the Chairman of the Joint Chiefs, the heads of the C.I.A., the D.I.A., the Secret Service, and Jesus H. Christ himself if I had his 800 number, because David Morton is a goddam lunatic who should have been locked up years ago."

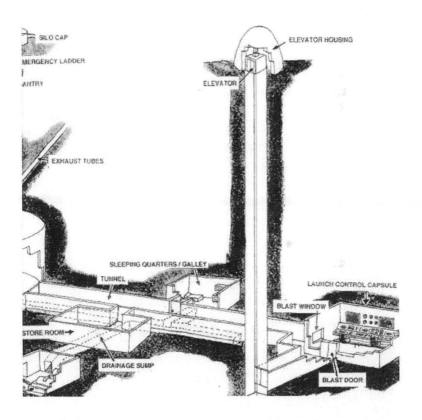

BOOK FIVE

Worst Case Scenario

-39-
West Virginny Rules

Jack Jericho is still searching for weapons in the security officers' quarters when he hears the noise from outside.

Voices.

Too close.

The barracks door squeaks open and bangs shut. Footsteps make the floorboards sing.

"How long we supposed to search for this infidel?" one voice says.

"Until we find him."

A laugh. "I'll bet he's halfway to Canada by now. For soldiers, they did not put up much of a fight."

The voices grow louder. The two commandos are approaching the security officer's quarters. "Brother David wants to make an example of this one."

"What, crucifixion?"

"He has spoken of it. He told Gabriel to build a cross near the silo cap."

There is a pause, as if both men are thinking about it, visualizing the sight.

"Brother David says he would love to see the general's face when they bring him a satellite photo with a crucified airman next to a launching missile. Says it should be the new Air Force logo."

"Dramatics," one man says. "Always the dramatics."

Jericho slides the window up and crawls out, dropping six feet to the ground. He flexes his knees and lands gently, keeping his balance. Then he scuttles along the building and through some light underbrush to the nearby mess hall. On his stomach, he does the infantryman's crawl underneath the temporary wooden building – made permanent by budget cuts – which is raised on concrete blocks.

Once under the building, Jericho lifts a grimy grate from the floor above him. Removing the grate, he hoists himself into the galley, emerging from a dripping grease pit next to an old gas stove.

If filth were a virtue, Jack Jericho would be a saint. He is covered with grime from the exhaust tube, brambles and leaves from the underbrush, and a thick layer of gunk from the grease pit.

Trays of bologna sandwiches sit on a counter. A sizzling vat of oil bubbles away in a French fry cooker. Figuring he's not going to be alone for long, Jericho stuffs several sandwiches into his pockets and begins searching for weapons. The kitchen knives aren't sharp enough to cut the bologna, and besides, he still has his Jimmy Lile survival knife. He could use matches, however, already thinking about building a homemade bomb out of a milk carton, Joy liquid soap and cigarette lighter fluid. He's looking through some drawers when he hears the sweet, soft voice of a little girl.

"There he is, Brother Matthew," Betsy says.

Jericho wheels around to see Betsy in the doorway. Next to her, a muscular, bearded man wearing a green military t-shirt and camouflage fatigue pants holds a Remington 870 pistol grip, short-barreled shotgun. The barrel is pointed squarely at Jericho's solar plexus. The sight tightens his gut into a knot.

Betsy is pointing at him. "He said he was my friend, and that Brother David was confused."

Matthew pats her on the head. "Thank you, child."

She gives Jericho a sweet smile and skips out the door.

The shotgun still leveled at Jericho, Matthew clicks on a walkie-talkie and says, "We have the infidel." After a garbled reply, he speaks to Jericho, "I'm supposed to keep you alive, but it doesn't matter to me one way or the other."

Jericho shrugs. For a long time, it wouldn't have mattered that much to him, either. But now, for a reason he does not completely understand, staying alive – saving Susan and the others – has become paramount. "Do what you have to do. I know I will."

Matthew takes a step closer. "What's that in your pockets?"

"Supper. I was getting hungry."

"Hands behind your head. One move and your guts will be sprayed all over the wall."

Jericho does as he's told. "The death penalty for stealing sandwiches? That's even worse than what they did to Jean Valjean."

"Who is this John, one of your comrades?"

Jericho allows himself a scornful smile. "You've read one book too much and the others too little."

"Turn around! Face the wall." Angry now.

Again, Jericho does as he's told,

"Spread 'em," Matthew orders, kicking Jericho's legs apart. He begins frisking Jericho, opening the snap pockets on his fatigues. He finds a sandwich, pulls it out and tosses it across the room. Another pocket, another sandwich. In a moment, he'll come across the cellular phone, then the knife, strapped to Jericho's leg. "What's this?"

Patting the long pocket on the pantleg, Matthew reaches in and pulls out something, not quite sure what it is. In the split second it takes for him to realize that it's alive and that it's head is turning, he has no time to react. The ferret sinks its teeth into the webbing between his thumb and forefinger. "Ow!" he screams, jumping back. "Satan incarnate!"

Matthew is off balance as Jericho spins to his left, grabs an iron skillet from the stove, and swings a forehand with a slight uppercut. Matthew sees it coming, brings up the shotgun, but too late. The skillet *clanks* the barrel, knocking it skyward. A blast tears a hole in the ceiling. Matthew swings the shotgun back toward Jericho who grabs the barrel and yanks hard across his body. The gun flies out of Matthew's hands and across the room.

Jericho drops to the floor and uses a single leg takedown to bring Matthew to the floor "You wanna wrassle?" Matthew taunts him, slipping out of Jericho's grasp and spinning into a reverse. He grabs one of Jericho's elbows, the other hand slips around his waist in the classic referee's position. A two-point reverse. "I was state champion at 180 pounds," he boasts. He breaks Jericho down to the floor, banging his head into the floorboards and scraping his ear along the wooden planks, picking up splinters. "You want to go Greco-Roman or freestyle rules?"

Jericho works his left arm free and sends his elbow backwards, bashing it into Matthew's mouth. The commando spits out blood and a chipped tooth. "West Virginny rules," Jericho says.

Still sprawled on the floor, they tussle, exchanging punches. Jericho clobbers Matthew with a fist, but the punch glances off his skull. Then, Matthew kicks Jericho away, and both men get to their feet, locking up, again. Wrasslin' style. They push and shove, trying to get leverage, banging each other against the galley wall, a rack of heavy spoons and spatulas crashing to the floor.

Suddenly, Jericho lifts one leg and slams his combat boot down on Matthew's instep. The man howls in pain, and Jericho clotheslines him with a forearm to the Adam's apple.

Jericho slips behind Matthew, works both hands up under his arms and locks them behind his head in a full nelson. An illegal maneuver in both Greco-Roman and Olympic freestyle, but not in West Virginny. Arms straining, the veins standing out on his neck, Jericho pushes forward, bending Matthew's head close to the old stove and the french fry vat. Matthew's eyes are wide open, and he sees the boiling oil grow larger until it fills his range of vision, the same view Icarus must have had on his way to the sun.

Matthew tries to pitch to the right, but Jericho braces his leg and won't allow himself to be thrown off. Matthew tries to buck his head backward and smash Jericho in the face, but the grip on his neck is too strong.

"Say your prayers," Jericho says through gritted teeth, pushing Matthew's head closer to the scalding oil.

"I'm not afraid to die," Matthew rasps.

"If you help me," Jericho says, "I'll let you go."

"You son-of-a-bitch," Matthew hisses, his voice weakening.

"C'mon! Help me stop Brother David. He's a madman. You must know that."

"He's the savior," Matthew says through clenched teeth.

"Good, 'cause you're going to need him." Jericho pushes harder, and Matthew's face is close enough to the vat to feel the sizzle of the boiling oil.

"Go to hell," Matthew rasps.

"After you!" Jericho gives a last lunge, dunking Matthew's head into the bubbling oil, holding him under. "If I were you, I'd cut back on the fried foods," he says, helpfully.

Ker-click. The unmistakable cocking of a shotgun.

Jericho looks around, sees another commando in the doorway pointing the Remington 870 at him. He pushes Matthew toward the man, takes two steps and dives into the well of the grease pit just as a shotgun blast tears a chunk out the wall above his head.

-40-
The Father and the Son

In the STRATCOM War Room, the Big Board blinks with blueprints of the missile silo and schematic cross-sections of the launch control capsule, the sump, and the sleeping quarters/galley. General Corrigan and Colonel Farris are joined by Army Lieutenant Colonel Charlie Griggs. The officers plus FBI Agent Hurtgen stand over a sprawling diorama of the 318th Missile Squadron base.

Colonel Farris uses an elbow to put himself between Griggs and General Corrigan. Farris would like to keep this an Air Force operation and the last thing he wants is Army Special Ops coming in and saving his ass. "Sir, we could zip a smart bomb right down that silo. Bingo! No more missile."

"Bingo," General Corrigan says softly, "no more hostages."

"Yep," Griggs says, using a sidestep to get back in the general's field of vision. "When the rocket fuel blows, count on a hundred per cent kill ratio in a thousand meter radius. And that's if there's no nuclear reaction. If they can arm the missile and you get yourself a nuke flash, well..."

"So, our smart bomb isn't so smart after all," the general says.

"Sir," Griggs says, "if I could make a suggestion. We could drop Delta Force down the elevator shaft with a simultaneous descent into the open silo and secure the area in less than five minutes."

"Casualties?" the general asks.

Agent Hurtgen clears his throat. "The Psych Pro leaves no doubt that Morning Star, that is, David Morton, will execute the hostages at the first shot."

Lieutenant Colonel Griggs nods in agreement. "That's a given cost of the operation."

General Corrigan takes it in. "So the President tells the world, 'Sorry, we just killed the U.N.'s non-proliferation team to take back an ICBM we don't need from a nut who probably couldn't launch it or detonate its warheads.'"

"But that's not the worst case scenario, sir," Agent Hurtgen says.

"No, it isn't," the general agrees. "Worst case scenario, he can launch the damn thing."

"And if he has the ability, the experts say he'll do it," Hurtgen adds. "The middle ground is that, failing the ability to launch, he can still arm and detonate the ten warheads."

"What are the projections on reasonable probability?"

"Fifty per cent on the ability to launch, fifty percent on the ability to detonate without a launch," Hurtgen says.

"The D.I.A. concurs, sir," Colonel Farris says.

"Fifty per cent. "You pick'em. General Corrigan shows a sad smile. "You know, I've been in the Air Force thirty-six years."

"Yes, sir," chorus Farris, Griggs and Hurtgen.

"All of them with distinction," Colonel Farris adds, polishing the general's apple.

"Including half-a-dozen years in that five-sided building where there are more asswipes than toilets," General Corrigan adds, eying all three men.

"Yes, sir," Griggs responds.

Colonel Farris, who spent two years in the Pentagon as an aide in U.S. Space Command, keeps quiet, not knowing where this is going.

"So cutting through the bullshit, gentlemen," the general says, "what you're telling me is that we don't have the slightest idea what Mr. Morton can do."

No one disagrees.

"And what you're also telling me is that the bastard's got Uncle Sam by the balls."

Again, no dissent is heard.

As the general ponders the situation, a thin man of fifty with a close-cropped gray beard works his way through the semi-circle of officers. Colonel Farris sees the newcomer and waves him toward Hugh Corrigan. "General, I don't think you've met Dr. Rosen. He's the expert on eschatology."

Blank looks greet that announcement.

"End times study," Dr. Rosen explains. "Doomsday cults, the apocalypticists."

The general gives him the once over. Dr. Stuart Rosen wears rumpled gray trousers and a navy blue sport coat. He's balding on top and tries to conceal it with back-to-front brushstrokes that look like a wheat field plowed by a drunken farmer.

"I've also handled hostage negotiations for the Bureau," Dr. Rosen adds, "which is serendipitous, is it not?"

General Corrigan hates rhetorical questions and has little use for psychiatrists so he ignores the question and instead, asks one of his own. "Who the hell are these nuts, anyway?"

"Just the latest in a long line, I'm afraid," Dr. Rosen says. "Cults in this country go back to the Shakers and the Hutterites. They're mostly benign, but once in a while, you'll get a Jim Jones or David Koresh. There is an interesting twist in this case. According to some of his dropouts, Brother David has psychic powers."

"You mean he claims to have..."

"They gave concrete examples of his ability to 'see' things in their past, things no one else could know. Apparently, it was quite convincing."

The general is incredulous. "That's how this crackpot got his followers to attack a missile base, with an Amazing Kreskin routine?"

Dr. Rosen scratches at his beard and says, "Oh, I'm sure that helped. But cults have been seducing followers for hundreds of years with far more basic techniques. The indoctrination methods are amazingly similar, whether you're dealing with Moonies, Hare Krishnas, or apocalyptic groups. They prey on what they call 'sheepy' people, depressed, borderline antisocial, lonely rejected types in search of a family. Folks with low self esteem, impressionable and malleable, some truly schizophrenic. They're looking to a leader to solve all their problems, and indeed, all the world's problems. They have a sense of incompleteness, maybe even self hatred."

"Not the makings of a good army," Colonel Farris chimes in.

"No, not at first. The conversion process begins with isolation from all past life and friends. They strip the newcomer of all possessions, even his or her name. Humiliation and guilt are used to dismember the former self. They indoctrinate and brainwash. They use sleeplessness and food deprivation combined with drug-induced hallucinations. I'd be surprised if our Brother David didn't keep a healthy supply of LSD, mescaline, or psilocybin in the compound. Anyway, after they destroy the person that was, the convert gets a new identity, a new purpose in life."

"To die?" the general asks, in wonderment.

"To die in a blaze of glory, and maybe to live forever," Dr. Rosen says. That's how they achieve the ultimate in sanctity. In a way, they're similar to the Nazis in the 1930's, who would be considered a cult by today's standards. Hitler's genius was that he saw that he could build a charismatic cult, not by promising creature comforts, but rather by promising struggle, danger and glorious death."

The general shakes his head. "What about the specifics of dealing with our nut case?"

"Well, you've got the combination of two forces, end-time prophesy and millenarism, the predicted thousand-year reign of Christ. Many cults have been preparing for Judgment Day, engaging in ecstatic behavior through prayer, trances, hysteria, even paranoia. The Cargo Cults in Melanesia thought they could turn back colonization that way. So did the Paiute Indians not far from here."

"What's that got to do with Brother David."

"Same *modus operandi*," Dr. Rosen says. "All these cults traditionally regard contemporary morals and laws as irrelevant. The only thing that matters is the impending catastrophe, which to them is a glorious event. Before leading his cult to mass suicide, Jim Jones predicted a nuclear war in which only his followers would survive. David Koresh considered himself the Messiah, and an angry one at that."

Dr. Rosen pulls out a notepad and reads from it. "'I am your God and you will bow under my feet.'"

"I beg your pardon," General Corrigan says.

"These were from Koresh's final writings recovered after the conflagration in Waco. 'I am your life and your death. Do you think you have power to stop My will? My seven thunders are to be revealed. Do you want me to laugh at your pending torments?' Et cetera, et cetera. Anyway, you get the same drift from the Holy Church of Revelations. They have a charismatic leader, totally committed followers, and apparently no fear of death."

"Oh, there is one difference," the general says.

Dr. Rosen raises an eyebrow. "What's that?"

"These bastards have ten nuclear warheads."

There's a commotion at the back of the group. An aide approaches and nods toward a phone. "It's Morning Star again, sir."

"Speak of the devil," the general says with a mournful smile.

The aide hits the button on a speaker phone and General Corrigan leans close to the microphone. "How are you, Mr. Morton?"

"Mr. Morton?" Amused and playful now. "You're showing off, Hugh. Letting me know how clever you can be with a budget of just a few hundred billion. So you know who you're up against. Only child of the famous Lionel Morton, but now just a poor country preacher with a handful of disciples. Taking on you and your minions must seem as foolish as challenging Pontius Pilate and the Legions of Rome."

Behind the general, Dr. Rosen whispers, "Talk about delusions of grandeur."

"I think it helps us both, Mr. Morton, to know who we're dealing with," the general says.

"I know what the Behavioral Science Unit must have told you. 'Deny him his identity. Don't feed his delusions. Make him play on our field.'"

General Corrigan kneads his knuckles into his forehead. The beginning of a four-aspirin headache. This David Morton is smart, cocky and dangerous, and he enjoys all three. Hugh Corrigan is pure military. He has covered his ass on funding, training, and deployment with the best of the Pentagon bullshitters and congressional budget cutters. He has eaten steaks and guzzled whiskey with the Armed Services Committee and remembers the names of their wives and mistresses – and never confuses them – even after a fifth round of drinks. But he doesn't have the slightest idea how to deal with David Morton.

The general gestures toward Professor Lionel Morton, who motors over to the speaker phone, a gleam in his eye. "Why don't you give it a try, professor?"

Morton leans close to the microphone. "Okay, Davy," he says, his tone defiant and challenging. "Your childish dramatics have gotten my attention. So let's get on with it."

"Ah, the famous Professor Morton, scourge of academia, apologist for the Pentagon, unrepentant symbol of the military-industrial complex, and primary piglet sucking at the pork-barrel tit of the Air Force." He lets his voice become childlike. "Hello Daddy."

"Hello yourself, you self-centered, egomaniacal son-of-a-bitch."

"Staring into a mirror can be so painfully revealing, eh Daddy?"

"This is all about me, isn't it Davy?"

"It is ironic, *Paterfamilias*, that the world will remember you for what *I* shall do."

"I've already made my mark, you little snot. You think you were reborn? Hell, I was reborn on July 13, 1948 when I saw the launch of an MX-774 at White Sands."

"Sorry, Pops, but no one wants to hear of your past glories, not even your toady military friends."

"What do you want, Davy?"

"I wanna be just like my Daddy," David croons.

"You're trying to be sarcastic, but you're really telling the truth and don't even know it. You didn't think you could measure up, Davy. That's why you became a nihilist or whatever the hell you are. I did things. I made things. I was there from the beginning, the Matador, the Snark, the Rascal and the Navaho. The Jupiter and the Thor. I built the Atlas and Titan, built them from the ground up! Damn you, do you know what that means?"

"No one cares, Daddy. No one even remembers their names. Or yours."

The professor's tone is mocking. "And what have you done?"

"I've seen the light," David says. "And now I'll act."

"You'll fail! Just like you failed at the Point. Just like you did at the Seminary. Maybe a bunch of losers and dead-head misfits think you're the Second Coming. But I know you. I know what excites you and what frightens you. You're the same little shit you always were, only your toys are more dangerous."

"They're *your* toys, daddy. I'm just borrowing them."

"You always wanted what was mine. Well you couldn't have your mother, and you can't have my bomb! Not then, not now, not ever!"

Dr. Stuart Rosen tugs at General Corrigan's sleeve and whispers, "I strongly advise against confrontation until the first four steps of persuasive reasoning have been attempted."

The general ignores him, letting Professor Morton go on.

"You were a fuck-up then," the professor says, "and you're a fuck-up now...Oedipus!"

"Ah, there you go again, Daddy dearest. But let's explore the analogy. I suppose I'm destined to kill you."

"Then gouge your own eyes out," the professor says. "Why not try that first?"

"No, Daddy, I won't kill you, either. You must witness God's work, his power as embodied in the missile and unleashed by me."

"It's *my* missile, Davy. You don't have the slick code, and you can't get it."

"If you thought that, if you really knew that, dear old Dad, you would have told your buddy Hugh, and he'd have dropped Special Forces down the hole quicker than you can say, 'ICBM.' Good-bye for now, Daddy. See you at dawn."

-41-
Water Ride

Exhausted and dripping with grease, Jack Jericho crawls through the scrub brush on the banks of the dry river bed. A commando sentry patrols nearby. Waiting for the chance to get by him, Jericho hears what sounds like a man's heavy breathing somewhere behind him. Then the *cr-ack* of a twig snapping. Jericho flattens himself to the ground.

Another *cr-ack*.

The bushes move beside him.

A snort.

Then a plug-ugly boar scuttles over, sniffing and licking his ugly chops. Jericho doesn't move.

"Who's there?" A commando's voice, perhaps 10 meters away.

The man is obscured by the heavy underbrush.

The boar gets a whiff of Jericho's filthy pants, seems to like the rank odor, and begins licking. "Good, eh boy?" Jericho whispers. "Bacon grease, probably one of your cousins."

The boar slowly moves up Jericho's body, its mouth drooling, its tusks jabbing him. Finally, the boar begins licking Jericho's face.

"Identify yourself!" the commando demands, his voice louder. "I hear you in there."

Jericho listens to the sound of a magazine being clicked into place, the commando nervously checking and re-checking his rifle.

The boar lets out a grunt, then trundles off in the direction of the voice. It sniffs the air, getting the man's scent. Jericho reaches into his rucksack and pulls out one of the bungee cords. Making a loop out of a small piece of the cord, he fashions a homemade slingshot. He picks up a small round stone and wedges it into the loop. "Sorry, boy," he says, and lets fly.

Thwap! He nails the boar in the ass.

It emits a beastly roar and charges toward the commando.

"Last chance!" the commando yells. "Come out with your hands up." He storms through the bushes toward Jericho. The boar bursts out of the bushes in an explosion of tusks and teeth and barrels into the man, eviscerating him with its razor-sharp tusks. The man's shrieks cut through the woods.

Jericho gets to his feet and takes off across the dry river bed. In a few moments, he is trudging up a trail above the missile base toward Chugwater Dam. The sun has set, and the base is lit by sweeping searchlights from the Army's base camp, plus the work lights at the ever-expanding front line of tanks, trucks and other military vehicles. He pauses, realizes how hungry and thirsty he is. The bologna sandwiches are gone from his pockets.

He knows that a river used to flow down the mountain, but the Army Corps of Engineers took care of that with Chugwater Dam. Now, the mountainside is inhospitable, unless you're good at foraging. Jericho quickly locates some thistle plants, peels off the thorns and chews on the tender stems. It's a watery snack he called "survival celery" back in West Virginia. He peels another and hands it to Ike, who stays at his feet. Ike chews the stem, keeping his eyes on Jericho.

After a moment, he continues up the trail in the dim light. Along the path are fir and birch trees. He finds a wild blackberry bush just off the trail and pauses to pick a handful. Sour but not bad. A few more paces, and Jericho comes across the fern called fiddleheads. Pulling out some young ones, he chews the leathery fronds that taste a bit like raw asparagus.

Looking up the mountainside, Jericho sees the night lights at the Chugwater Dam control building. He pulls out the cellular phone he had found in the security officer's office.

⚮

The command tent at Base Camp Alpha is jammed with maps, charts and communications gear. Outside, the sound of heavy vehicles has faded, and the shouts of soldiers have quieted. It is dusk, and the Army is in place. Puffing a pipe, Colonel Henry Zwick fills the tent with cherry blend smoke, a trick the Armored Cavalry officer discovered years earlier to avoid the stench of diesel fuel, metallic lubricants, and too many men with too few showers. The colonel stands inside a semi-circle of Special Forces officers, using a wooden pointer to highlight sections of a scale model of the missile base.

"In conclusion, gentlemen," the colonel says, "if every last one of you does exactly as ordered, and if every one of your men performs exactly as they've been trained, maybe – just maybe – we can end this without a nuclear catastrophe or the loss of the hostages."

There is some mumbling among the officers, interrupted when an aide signals the colonel to pick up a red telephone. Zwick punches a button, activating the speaker and a tape recorder. After listening a moment, the colonel says, "What's your name again, son?"

"Jack Jericho, United States Air Force, E-5." For once, Jericho sounds like an airman. In the tent, the officers stop talking among themselves and listen. The voice is distant, and there is a sound of rushing water.

Colonel Zwick fiddles with his handlebar mustache. "You in the latrine, sergeant?"

Jack Jericho sits on a steel catwalk above a spillway at Chugwater Dam. Twenty feet below, water tumbles into an aqueduct which runs from the dam down the mountain and around the missile base. From his perch, Jericho can see the lights from the open missile silo. Every few seconds, searchlights sweep over the missile base from the Army base camp nearby.

"I'm on the dam, sir, above the aqueduct," Jericho says. "I've got a cellular phone." The Green Beret officers exchange looks. Base Camp Alpha is equipped with five military radio systems: UHF secure, HF secure, FM secure, SATCOM and VHF, and this dipshit is calling on a cellular, like some orthodontist in his BMW. A goofball kid with a scanner could pick up the call.

The colonel gestures to the miniature dam on top the scale-model mountain, then drags the pointer down the slope toward the missile silo. "How'd you get up there? Were you in the silo?"

Jericho hesitates. A faint notion of guilt clings to him, as if the colonel asked why he hadn't died fighting the terrorists. "Yes, sir."

At that moment, in the security building of the 318th Missile squadron, a commando wearing earphones sits with his hand on the dial of a radio frequency scanner. He listens to the scratchy voice of Jack Jericho. "I was there. I met the enemy, sir, and he ain't us."

"Sounds like you're going to be of considerable help to your Uncle Sam, airman. We need you to brief us on Morning Star."

"Sir, I know that hole better than anybody," Jericho blurts out. "Every nook and cranny. I can help your men launch an assault. I'd like to go with the first wave."

In the command tent, Colonel Zwick puffs at his pipe. Behind him, an Army Ranger captain whispers, "The first wave. Thinks he's at Omaha Beach."

"You're not Air Force Special Ops, are you son?" Colonel Zwick asks.

"No, sir."

"Have you ever seen death up close?"

Jericho's eyes flicker, but he doesn't answer. It is a question that defies an answer.

"Son, what is it you do for the 318th?"

"Maintenance, sir. I clean the sump, maintain the perimeter fence and keep the launch generator running."

In the command tent, some of the officers – Delta Force, Rangers, and Night Stalkers – exchange crooked grins.

"That's an important job, and I've got another important job for you," the colonel says. "I want you to brief us on everything you saw and heard down there. I've got diagrams of the tunnel and the sump, but diagrams only get you so far. I want you to look my officers in the eye and tell 'em what the hell's going on down there. Then you'll get out of the way, and we'll do whatever we're ordered to do."

"Sir, I don't think there's time for all that. There are innocent hostages down there. There's a woman they're torturing. They're trying to launch the missile, and maybe they can do it and maybe they—"

"Son," the colonel interrupts. "If it were up to me, we'd have been down that hole faster than shit through a goose, but I follow orders. You get my drift?"

"Yes, sir."

"Good. Because I'm ordering you to get the hell off that mountain and make your way to the base camp. You'll do us no good if you get killed. I'll alert our perimeter. Give me your E.T.A."

"It's going to be a while, sir."

"What does that mean, Sergeant?" The colonel has abandoned his avuncular tone. Now, it's all business.

"I have a detour to make."

"Sergeant! I want you off that mountain. I want you off the missile base. Do you read me?"

"Five by five, sir."

"Good. Now, get over here where you'll be of some use."

"I'm afraid not, sir."

"What!"

"I've got to go back into the silo."

"Sergeant!"

"I promised someone," Jack Jericho says. "One of the hostages."

Jericho stares across the pouring water of the spillway, pondering what he has just done. Refused a direct order, for one thing. The only comforting thought is that he can't be court-martialed if he's killed by Brother David's maniacs. For a moment, he listens to the colonel yammering at him, then looks down at his filthy t-shirt and brushes at a pink spot, absent-mindedly trying to wipe it off.

The spot moves.

Jericho brushes at it again.

It moves again, centering on his sternum.

Jericho looks up. At the end of the catwalk, a commando aims a laser-sighted Mauser 66 at him. *Ping!* A bullet ricochets off the steel railing. The phone is still locked in Jericho's grip. He can hear the colonel screaming, "Sergeant! You'll be court-martialed."

Jericho tucks and rolls across the catwalk. *Ping! Ping!* Two more misses. Jericho scrambles to his feet and begins running to the far side of the catwalk, zig-zagging away from the rifleman.

"I'll lock the cell at Leavenworth myself!" comes the colonel's muffled voice.

Jericho stops short. A second commando lies in the prone shooting position on this end of the catwalk, too. A shot misses. Then another. Jericho jams the phone into his rucksack and vaults over the railing. Kicking at the air, he tumbles into the spillway twenty feet below where he sinks into the cascading water. The force carries him under, smashes him against the bottom of the concrete spillway, then carries him to the surface and into the narrow aqueduct that curls down the slope. He sucks in a greedy breath of air and is swept under again. In seconds, he has traveled hundreds of feet down the aqueduct, and he can no longer hear the gunshots.

-42-
Let It Blow

Reams of paper spill out of the console computer in the launch control capsule. Eyes bleary, James works at the keyboard, occasionally lifting the pages to examine the scrolling numbers.

"Can you get the code or not?" David asks, his tone querulous.

"I th-ink I can, Bro-ther Davy," James says, playing dumb, dragging out the words, having some fun.

"What's taking so long?"

James takes off his glasses, rubs his eyes, then turns toward David. "It doesn't help if you keep pestering me every fifteen minutes. Aren't you supposed to have the patience of Job?"

"Right now, I have the wrath of Zeus!"

James turns back to his work. "Pagan. I knew it would come to this."

David slides his flight chair down the railing. He knows when it's best to let James alone. Behind him, Rachel keeps a watch over Susan, whose hands are cuffed behind her. Owens, also cuffed, sleeps on the floor, his head slumped against the capsule wall. "Let's play, 'Imagine,'" David says to Susan.

She looks at him through sullen eyes. "I'm tired of your games."

"No, no, no. You must play with me. What do you imagine they're doing at STRATCOM right now? And at Cheyenne Mountain and at the Military Command Center?"

"They're talking about you," Susan says. "You're the center of attention. Does that make you happy?"

"Of course. But what are they saying? What are they doing?"

"Deciding how to kill you without killing us. Figuring out if you can launch the missile or detonate it if you can't launch." Her tone takes on an angry edge. "Trying to figure what makes a schizo like you tick."

"Changing your diagnosis, eh doctor?"

"No. Just adding paranoid schizophrenia with delusions of grandeur."

That brings a smile of mock disbelief. "Paranoid? My dear, doctor, as you have just acknowledged, the entire United States military *is* trying to kill me."

☙

Naked, soaking wet and shivering, Jack Jericho peers out of the underbrush near a concrete pillar of the aqueduct. The temperature has plunged as the sun settles below Rattlesnake Hills to the west. Over his head, water roars down the elevated aqueduct and around the missile facility.

"Guess I needed a bath, anyway," Jack Jericho says to himself. Except for the survival knife strapped to his ankle, he could be Adam in the Garden of Eden. He wrings out his clothes and tests the cellular phone. The little green light clicks on, but he doesn't feel like talking to Colonel Zwick and having his prison sentence increased.

Jericho hears a rustling in the underbrush, turns and looks straight into a glaring flashlight.

The man's voice is urgent, perhaps a little afraid. "Who are you? Identify yourself."

Jericho shields his eyes and sees a commando holding a flashlight in one hand, an Uzi in the other. The flashlight is pointed at Jericho's face, the Uzi at his gut. "They call me Brother John," he calmly tells the man.

The flashlight works its way down Jericho's body. "You're out of uniform," the commando says.

"Occupational hazard, but I'm clad in God's own garment."

The commando regards him suspiciously. "I don't recognize you, Brother John."

"I am a recent convert, but I believe I have seen you at evening vespers." Holding his breath, hoping to hell there are evening vespers.

The commando moves closer, studying Jericho. "Then you should have no trouble telling me the hidden meaning of the sixth seal of Revelations."

"The sixth seal," Jericho repeats, nodding appreciatively. Buying time now. "One of my favorite passages."

"Mine, too."

"Do you know it by heart?" Jericho asks.

"Who does not?"

"Indeed," Jericho says.

"'I watched as he broke the sixth seal,'" the commando recites with appropriate fervor. "'The sun turned black as a funeral pall and the moon all red as blood, and the stars fell to earth, like figs shaken down by a gale. The sky vanished and every mountain and island was moved from its place.'"

"Sounds like a hell of a storm."

"Do you joke about such things?" The commando moves even closer.

"No, I just thought the meaning was obvious."

"Of course. But the *hidden* meaning. What does Brother David teach us?"

"Oh, that," Jericho says. Their faces are just inches apart. "That's easy. Do unto others..."

Jericho viciously head-butts the commando, breaking the man's nose with an explosion of cartilage and blood. "*Before* they do unto you!"

The man falls backward and writhes on the ground, spitting foamy blood. Jericho picks up the Uzi and points it at him. "I want your clothes. We'll finish the Sunday school class later."

"My clothes?" the man says, the words barely audible. Disoriented from the pain, confused by the demand. "Do you wish to join us?"

"No, I want to join the circus. Now, c'mon. Give me your clothes."

The commando strips out of his fatigues, and Jericho tears his own wet clothing into strips that he uses to gag the man, then ties him to a tree with another of Sayers' bungee cords. Newly dressed, with the Uzi in hand, Jericho picks up his rucksack and heads through the dry river bed toward the exhaust tube. Peering through the underbrush, he sees a commando sentry standing at the outlet pipe. So they found it. Too late to trap him inside, but just in time to keep him out. Fifty yards away, three sentries patrol the circumference of the open missile silo.

"They don't want me around for the party," Jericho says to himself. He sits back on his haunches and thinks.

What would Special Forces do?

Call in an air strike.

But what can I do?

Diversion.

He grabs the cellular phone and calls a number he knows by heart.

⁊

General Corrigan, his cheeks flushed, is on the phone with Colonel Zwick. "A sergeant?"

"An E-5," Colonel Zwick says from the command tent at the base camp. "He's the maintenance man for the launch generator."

"What the hell can he do?"

"Nothing but get in the way," the colonel tells him. "Special Ops is ready, sir, and awaiting your orders."

"Thank you, Henry. You sit tight for now." The general clicks off the phone and turns to his staff. "There's one airman still roaming around the missile base, and naturally, it's some swab jockey, second class."

Professor Morton sits off to one side in his wheelchair. "Wasn't it Clemenceau who said that war was too important to be left to the generals?"

"It was, Lionel, but do you think he wanted it left to the janitor?"

"Oh, I'm sure he can't muck it up any worse than Special Ops."

"Enough!" Corrigan says. He wags a finger in Professor Morton's face. "Lionel, what the hell was that disk doing in your house?"

"I designed it," the professor says, petulantly, turning his wheelchair away. "It's mine."

"Yours! ICBM Enable Codes and P.L.C.'s are yours? They're U.S. government property. They're classified! They're Top Secret! What the hell's wrong with you, Lionel?"

"I like to have my work close at hand."

That brings a snort of disbelief from Colonel Farris, who has been observing from the circle of military brass surrounding the two men. "Did Eisenhower leave the plans for D-Day laying around the house?" he asks. "Did Westmoreland misplace maps of Cambodian air raids at the convenience store? Did Meade discuss plans for Gettysburg at the saloon?"

"There were no plans for Gettysburg, you ninny," Morton responds. "Gettysburg was an accident of history, a mistake, like your commission." He turns to General Corrigan. "Hugh, why do you surround yourself with these imbeciles?"

"Don't change the subject," the general says. "You're a goddam security risk."

"But you keep calling me back to upgrade your toys, don't you?"

The general sighs. What's done is done. "Is there any chance that lunatic son of yours can get the Secondary Launch Code?"

"It's not on the disk."

"We know that. Had it been, ten nuclear warheads would already have detonated over Jerusalem."

"Can little Davy get the code?" Professor Morton muses, a wry smile on his face. "No, because he refuses to see himself for what he is."

General Corrigan shakes his head at the enigmatic statement. "What the hell does that mean?"

"Perhaps in time, you shall know. Meanwhile, let's consider the benefits of a first strike."

"A what?" General Corrigan isn't sure he heard correctly.

"The benefits to the United States of America of allowing the

PK to fly its coop."

"What the hell are you talking about?" The general is incredulous.

"Well, obviously there'd be a wealth of in-field research, material we just couldn't duplicate in the lab. Temperature and dynamic pressure of the blast, firestorm, base surge, afterwind speeds, hard data we could gather by satellite, but only from a real detonation, not computer models. Plus medical information, statistical analysis of fatalities and casualties such as blindness, radiation poisoning, internal injuries. Psychological studies of survivors, that sort of thing. All invaluable and simply not able to be duplicated in the virtual world."

"You're not serious," General Corrigan says. "You want to kill hundreds of thousands of people as a lab experiment."

"Not for that alone. The political consequences might be even more compelling, so bear with me. For now, call it an academic inquiry. Or contingency planning, Hugh. Isn't that what you do all the time?"

"Go on. I'm listening."

"Let's assume that my only child, bless his dastardly heart, acquires the S.L.C. and that you are unable to stop the launch by either technological or strategic means. What happens?"

"A holocaust. A one-hundred per cent kill ratio for a radius of twelve miles from ground zero of each warhead. Lingering death by radiation poisoning, burns and internal injuries to several hundred thousand others. Complete destruction of the holiest city in the world, home to three religions. The greatest single catastrophe in the history of the world."

"Of course, of course," the professor says, a bit impatiently. "But politically, what are the consequences? Surely, you have discussed this with the National Security Advisor."

"I have, and that's classified. Frankly, Lionel, you're the last person I would share—"

"Oh, stow it, Hugh! I can figure it out. The State Department has already alerted the Israelis as to the silo takeover and the reconfiguration of the command data buffer. If the slick is entered into the capsule computer, the damage will be catastrophic, the psychological injury unprecedented in history." A smile plays at the corner of Morton's mouth. "Which raises a question. If little Israel is laid waste by ten nuclear warheads, what would Iraq, Iran and Libya do? Maybe Syria, too."

"You tell me, Lionel."

"They'd finish the job," Colonel Farris breaks in. "They'd attack. It'd be their one and only chance to defeat a stronger, better organized military power. They've waited fifty years, and it's like all those prayers to Allah will have been answered."

"Right!" the professor proclaims. "Colonel, you are not the complete idiot I always took you for."

Colonel Farris nods a thank you.

Nobody says anything for a moment. Then in a low voice, General Corrigan speaks. "It's a possible scenario that's been discussed."

That brings a laugh from the professor, who hits a button, and moves his wheelchair closer to the general. "Damn right it's been discussed. That's what would happen, and everyone in Washington knows it. What those short-sighted, pension-loving, pencil-pushers haven't thought about is the potential benefit of letting it all happen."

No one asks the question, but Professor Lionel Morton answers it anyway. "The benefit, gentleman, is that with one fortuitous stroke, we will have neutralized the world's hot spot. Between the militant Arab fundamentalists, those pesky Palestinians and the hard-line Israelis, the Middle East is the world's powder keg. We can just let it blow."

"Let it blow?" General Corrigan shakes his head.

"Boom! Boom!" the professor whoops. "Let the Arabs and Israelis engage in a final, all-out war. A pox on both their houses. They will expend themselves, destroy each other, and end World War III before it begins."

The officers exchange looks and mumble to themselves. Finally, Agent Hurtgen says, "What asylum did this maniac escape from?"

"Ours," General Corrigan replies.

-43-
The Diversion

The old Volkswagen Beetle chugs past the sign reading, "Rattlesnake Hills Sewage Plant," grinds its gears and chugs up the mountain road at a clunky fifteen miles an hour. Inside, Jimmy Westoff inhales the tangy aroma of charred meat and sizzling grease. The tiny back seat is loaded with Styrofoam cartons of cheeseburgers, chili and french fries.

Unbeknownst to Jimmy, eight M-16 rifles are trained on him. Camouflaged in the gully at the side of the road, a squad of Army Rangers watches Jimmy drive by. A lieutenant with a darkened face and a helmet disguised as a mulberry bush speaks into his radio. "Possible enemy vehicle on Access Road One."

A scratchy voice comes through his headset. "How many men, what sort of weaponry."

Through an infrared night scope, the lieutenant sees the placard attached to the VW's roof: "Old Wrangler Tavern—We Deliver." Maybe it's his imagination, but he thinks he gets a whiff of burgers as the car passes. "One man in a VW Beetle," he says. "No known weapons."

"One man?"

"Unless it's one of those clown cars where they just keep piling out."

Jimmy stomps on the accelerator, the little car bucks and rounds the last curve, sputtering to a stop in front of the sentry post of the 318th Missile Squadron. Jimmy gets out of the car, feels a tickle in his nose from the dust the VW has kicked up, and sneezes loudly. A kilometer away, at Base Camp Alpha, watching through a telescopic night scope and listening through bionic earpieces, Colonel Henry Zwick says, "Gesundheit."

The road had been purposely left open in the hopes that

reinforcements the Holy Church of Revelations would arrive. Colonel Zwick wanted to capture several commandos and interrogate them, but so far, the road has been quiet except for the asthmatic Volkswagen.

The colonel watches Jimmy pull out several grease-stained cartons filled with Styrofoam boxes. "We're about to see if Napoleon was correct," Zwick says.

"About what?" Captain Kyle Clancy asks, raising his own night scope. His face is covered with a thick layer of camouflage grease which seems to overflow the deep scar that runs from his cheekbone to his chin.

"About an army marching on its stomach. These fellows are into fast food."

The captain lets out a little laugh. "Shit, colonel, it can't be any worse than our M.R.E.'s."

His arms loaded, Jimmy Westoff walks up to the guard house. He doesn't recognize the commando in combat fatigues with no military insignia. "Who ordered forty buffalo burgers, twenty fries, and ten sides of chili?"

The commando points an M-16 at Jimmy's head. "Outta here. This is restricted property."

"No shit, like I really thought it was a sewage plant. You new or somethin'? And what's with the uniform?"

From his view in the underbrush, Jack Jericho can see the sentry post in the flickering headlights of the Volkswagen. He had called the tavern an hour earlier on the cellular phone, and now he waits for his chance. A commando still guards the exhaust tube's outlet pipe, but with any luck, he'll be fetching dinner soon.

At the guard house, the commando is becoming annoyed. "No one told me anything about burgers."

"Like what else is new? You wanna call the Pentagon and get authorization, 'cause I'm telling you, my arms are getting tired, and in a minute, you're gonna have chili all over your boots."

"Okay, okay. Leave it all here."

Jimmy puts the boxes on the ground, goes back to the car

and brings over some more. "That's two hundred twelve fifty, not including tip."

The sentry pats his empty pockets. "Do you believe, as it is written in Ecclesiastes, that 'money answereth all things'?"

"I believe that if I don't get paid, Uncle Buck will kicketh my ass from here to Hell's Half Acre."

"Sorry," the sentry says, inhaling the aroma of the burgers, and dragging one of the boxes inside the guard house. "I'm requisitioning the food in the name of the Lord." He is salivating. Other commandos begin to drift over to the guard house, eager to eat. Their mission should have been over by now. They should be ascending to heaven. Death they could take; hunger bothered the hell out of them.

Jericho waits and watches, but the commando near the outlet pipe doesn't move.

At the guard house, Jimmy is throwing a tantrum. "You shittin' me? I drive all the way up here and now you're jerking my chain." Jimmy's voice is cranked up a few notches. "Where's Dempsey anyway? Sleeping one off."

"Dempsey?"

"The security dude who's usually here. He never stiffs me."

From inside the gate, a broad-shouldered commando carrying a shotgun pushes his way past the others. His harsh voice carries all the way to the underbrush where Jericho watches. "What's going on here?" Gabriel demands.

"Supper," the sentry says, a little unsure.

"Back to your posts! All of you, now!"

Jimmy Westoff, with the blissful ignorance of the young, yells at Gabriel. "Hey, cowboy! Whether you want the grub or not, you still gotta pay. C'mon, or I'm gonna complain to the captain how you're jerking me around out here."

Gabriel wheels around, the shotgun pointed at Jimmy Westoff's Adam's apple.

"On the other hand," Jimmy says, "if you're a little short, maybe Uncle Buck would take a check."

The shotgun drops toward the ground, and a second later, the *blam* echoes through the trees and across the missile base. Jimmy Westoff's pant legs are warm and wet. At first he thinks he's been shot. Then, he realizes he's peed his pants. The rest of him is covered with cheeseburger shrapnel.

Reacting to the shotgun blast, the commando near the outlet pipe clicks off the safety on his rifle and heads toward the sentry post. Taking advantage of the diversion, Jericho darts toward the flared end of the pipe.

At the perimeter of Base Camp Alpha, a sharpshooter with a tripod-mounted Israeli Galil sniper rifle has Gabriel in the crosshairs of his infrared scope. "I can take him," he says, keeping his finger on the trigger, his breathing soft and slow. He moves the rifle slightly up and to the right, taking into account wind speed and the gravitational fall of the bullet over eleven hundred meters.

"I'm sure you can," Colonel Zwick says. "But we don't fire a shot until our orders change."

"Yes, sir," he says, releasing the pressure on the trigger, and muttering an inaudible "shit" under his breath.

At the guard house, the commandos begin to disperse and resume their positions. One comes back to the exhaust tube's outlet pipe. He does not notice that the screen has been replaced just a tad cockeyed, it being hard to pull into place from inside the pipe.

Now, in the darkness and gloom of the exhaust tube, Jack Jericho works his way back toward hell. That's the way he thinks of it. But Jericho knows there are all kinds of purgatory. He's been doing a slow death in one of his own making. How much worse can this one be?

❧

Sweating heavily, Jack Jericho works his way down the exhaust tube toward the missile silo. He is halfway there, the Uzi slung over one shoulder, the rucksack on the other, when he is startled by a sudden, discordant sound. It takes him a moment to realize that the cellular phone is ringing. He digs it out of a pocket and answers, "Yeah."

"Sergeant, you surprise me," a male voice says with a hint of amusement.

At first, he thinks it's Colonel Zwick, calling to give him hell. But it's Brother David. He knows where I am, Jericho thinks, feeling trapped, a rat in a maze. Scanning equipment picked up his earlier call to the Colonel.

"Are you there, Sergeant Jack Jericho from Sinkhole, West Virginia? Why haven't you high-tailed it like some scared rabbit? Flight would be so much more consistent with your profile."

"Fuck you and the horse you rode in on," Jericho fires back. He had wanted to stay quiet and now curses himself for letting the bastard get to him. Over the phone, he hears David's laughter.

In the launch control capsule, David hits the speaker button and nods to Rachel, who uses an Uzi to prod Captain Pete Pukowlski toward the microphone. "Someone wants to talk to you," David says.

Pukowlski shuffles to the console, his feet shackled by leg irons, his hands cuffed behind him. "Jericho, give yourself up."

"Puke, that you?" an astonished Jericho replies. "I thought you were dead."

Captain Pukowlski reddens. "You will address me as 'sir.' I am still your captain, Jericho."

"Not any more. I am the master of my fate. I am the captain of my soul."

"The fuck are you talking about? That's insubordination."

David pushes Pukowlski away from the microphone. "Actually, it's 'Invictus.' It was intended for me, the sergeant's way of rejecting determinism. But he is wrong. His fate, like yours and mine, is sealed."

"We make our own fate," Jericho says. "We have free will."

"Sergeant, you are so much more interesting than these uniformed eunuchs like Pukowlski, who couldn't captain the H.M.S. Pinafore. I'd like to know more about you, Jericho."

"Go screw yourself."

"Did you sit on some mountaintop in the Appalachians reading poetry while your countless cousins picked lice from their scalps?"

"Let the hostages go and I'll answer all your questions."

"Do you really believe all that whimsical claptrap about free will?"

"I don't believe it's all preordained."

"Oh, but it is. An Apocalypse followed by the thousand year reign of the Savior."

"With you his right-hand man."

"I am the vessel chosen to set in motion the forces that cannot be restrained. I can no more resist my fate than a wave can resist being driven against the shore."

"That's a cop out. We're all captains of our own destiny."

"As I suspected, the son of miners and moonshiners is a poet at heart. Look at your life, Jericho. If you are right, if your fate has not been sealed, look how abysmally you have exercised your free will."

"I'm about to change that."

"Yes, you are. You're about to die. Oh, I wish I had time to spar with you. We could go a few rounds of dueling bards. Reason versus belief, rationality versus spirituality. But duty calls."

"Meaning what?"

"Simply this, Sergeant. If you don't surrender at once, I shall have to kill the captain."

Jericho continues crawling through the tube. "Promises, promises," he says into the phone.

"Jericho!" Pukowlski screams.

"Ah, perhaps I've chosen the wrong hostage," David says. He moves to the capsule's back wall and roughly grabs Dr. Susan Burns, yanking her out of the chair. Her hands are cuffed behind her, and she still wears the missileer's blue jumpsuit. "Sergeant, there's someone else who wants to say hello."

"Jericho, just take care of yourself," Susan says, her voice breaking. "Don't worry about me."

David pulls the microphone away. "Sorry, sergeant, she's the next to die."

Jericho strains not to lose it, not to show emotion, but he fails. "Hear *my* word, dirtbag! You hurt that woman, and I'm going to gut you like a barnyard pig. I'm going to skin you and nail your hide to the barn door, and I'm going to sip rye whiskey while I watch you rot."

"How quaint, how country," David mocks him. "I'd be scared to death if I didn't know all about Sergeant Jack Jericho, the sniveling coward. You can make all the threats you want, Sergeant. Problem is, it takes balls to go ballistic!"

"Let's go at it, just you and me," Jericho shoots back. "Or are you afraid without your zonked-out warriors?"

"You dare call me, 'afraid?' You, whose life is circumscribed by fear. Like the Sioux warrior who is hung from a line of rawhide strung through his back, I fear no pain. I fear no man. And most of all, I fear not you, Jack Jericho."

David cackles spitefully and hangs up. Jericho angrily bangs his fist against the wall of the tube, and even the metallic echo sounds like a scornful laugh.

☙

Ten minutes later, Jericho is at the screen separating the exhaust tube from the interior of the missile silo. He peers through it, sees two commandos on the floor of the silo ninety feet below. Carefully, Jericho removes the screen, then swings out of the tube onto the orange steel ladder that is bolted into the silo wall. He slides down the ladder several feet to the gantry and flattens himself against its floor. He is staring directly at the fourth stage of the missile, just below the nose cone, and something is wrong.

A hole.

Like a cavity in a tooth.

The computer box is missing.

"Son-of-a-bitch," he says to himself. He remembers the palm-sized Newton Messagepad Fax he lifted from the security officers' barracks and pulls it out of the rucksack. Hitting the power, he uses the electronic stylus to draw a picture, then punches out a number and hits the SEND button.

༄

Colonel Henry Zwick stands in front of the command tent, admiring the spruce and fir trees silhouetted by a half-moon. It is just after nine p.m. His men and machines are primed, and it's quiet at Base Camp Alpha. As he puffs on his pipe, the only sound is of the wind through the trees, the chirping of night birds, and the belly-aching of Captain Kyle Clancy, who has been pleading his case for the Night Stalkers.

"My men are ready, colonel. Damn, this is a cakewalk, if you'd just let us go."

"It's not up to me, Kyle. You know that."

"This can't be any harder than breaking a hostage out of Cárcel Modelo prison in Panama or getting back Napoleón Duarte's daughter in El Salvador."

"Be patient, Kyle. You know, the best Viet Cong snipers could sit in a tree for two weeks without moving just to get a good shot at an American officer."

"Before my time. All I know is, my men got real hard-ons for some action."

"Tell 'em to keep it in their pants for now, Kyle."

An aide emerges from the tent and hands Colonel Zwick a sheet of paper. The colonel examines Jericho's FAX, a crude drawing of the missile with an opening in the nose cone. Scowling, the colonel says to the aide, "Get me General Corrigan." Then he turns back to Captain Clancy. "Kyle, your men may get to unzip after all."

The colonel turns to head back into the command tent. He takes one last puff on his pipe and disappears inside. In his wake, wisps of cherry-flavored smoke curl into the breeze and disappear into the night air.

෨

Lying prone on the floor of the gantry, Jericho peers down at the silo floor. White steam hisses from the idling launch generators, and in the reflection of the red silo lights, billows up like blood-stained fog.

Two commandos patrol the floor of the silo. One opens the grate to the drainage sump while the other holds a flashlight and looks inside. "It's wet down there, Jacob," says the one with the flashlight.

"You won't melt."

On the gantry, Jericho opens the rucksack and pulls out the last of Sayers' bungee cords and the telescoping fishing rod he retrieved from the barracks. He secures one end of the cord to the gantry railing and ties the other end around his waist. It's the only way he figures he can get to the silo floor without using the gantry, which makes too much noise, or the ladder which is too slow and in plain view. He slides the fishing rod open to its full length, then roots around in the rucksack until he finds a whipperwhill skeeter fly and a long-shanked hook. Then he lets loose with a long, graceful cast toward the floor one hundred feet below.

The fly dangles near the ear of the commando named Jacob. Absentmindedly watching his buddy, who is halfway down the grate into the sump, Jacob swats at the skeeter and misses. Jericho reels in and casts again. This time the fly buzzes just off the man's earlobe. He slaps at it and plants the razor-sharp triple barbed hook in his ear. "Yee! Ouch! Holy..."

Jericho reels in as the commando yelps and begins a crazy dance across the silo floor, pulled along by the hook that is embedded firmly in his ear. The other commando crawls out of the grate. Unable to see the thin fishing line, he stares in disbelief at his comrade. "Jacob, are you possessed?"

Two other commandos hear Jacob's yelping and race in from the tunnel. They behold the weird sight of their comrade jitterbugging across the silo, his head cocked to one side. "Brother David says

Satan's minions can make themselves invisible," one commando says.

"If we don't find this infidel, Brother David will make us invisible," the other replies.

One looks up and spots Jericho on the gantry ledge, preoccupied with his fishing. The two commandos begin climbing the metal ladder that runs up the silo wall. On the gantry, Jericho keeps reeling line in and letting it out, as if he were fighting a marlin. All the time, he is leading Jacob just where he wants him, until splash, Jacob falls into the open sump. His buddy jumps in to rescue him. Jericho watches a moment, waiting for more commandos to come to the aid of their brethren. He cannot see the two commandos ascending the ladder, and by the time he realizes they are no longer on the silo floor, it is too late. He hears a noise behind him and whirls around to see the men climbing onto the gantry from the ladder.

"What have we here?" one commando says, triumphantly, pointing an Italian Beretta —12 at Jericho's chest.

"The infidel," his friend answers. "Brother David will reward us."

"Sure he will," Jericho says. "You'll get an extra ration of librium with your rice pudding."

"Don't move, heathen!"

The Uzi is on the floor of the gantry. If Jericho goes for it, he'll be cut in two. "Brother David and I have an appointment," he says. "You best take me to him."

"Any tricks, and we're to send you straight to hell."

Sizing up the situation...

"Already been there," Jericho says, "and all things considered, I'd rather be in Wyoming."

Nowhere to go...

"Now, put your hands on the back of your head," the commando says.

But down!

Jericho obeys, then flexes his knees and leaps backward off the ledge of the gantry. He plunges toward the silo floor, and above him, the startled commandos hear his cry, "Sh-i-i-i-i-i-t!"

But there is no *splat* of bone and tissue against steel.

Exchanging startled looks, the commandos cautiously approach the

edge and look down toward the silo floor. Suddenly, Jericho bounces back up, grabs an ankle of each commando and yanks them off the gantry. Now, three bodies plummet toward the floor.

Two sounds.

The simultaneous, sickening *crunch* of the two commandos splattered on the polished steel floor.

And the *bo-ing* of the bungee cord as it reaches its full length just five feet above the floor and springs Jericho back up toward the gantry a second time. Down he goes again, and *bo-ing*, back up again, finally coming to rest five feet above the bodies. Jericho unhooks the bungee cord and drops to the floor. He races to a closed grate at the entrance to the tunnel, opens it and climbs into the sump, just as Jacob, holding a bloody ear, and his buddy crawl out of the grate beneath the missile. As Jericho slides the grate back into place over his head, he hears the thunder of footsteps and the shouts of commandos in the tunnel. He pauses a moment to let his eyes become adjusted to the darkness, then works his way through the maze of pipes and equipment, listening to the rhythmic *thumpa thumpa* of the generators.

"Welcome back to hell," Jericho says to himself.

-44-
Humans Never Win

Despite the clamor all around him – huddled conferences of military officers, F.B.I. and D.I.A. agents – Professor Lionel Morton plays a quiet game of chess on his wheelchair computer. He is as placid as a white-haired retiree on a park bench, oblivious to the commotion. He appears, in fact, just the same as he has been his entire adult life, completely indifferent to those around him. To Lionel Morton, with Pd.D.'s in both physics and aeronautical engineering, with a complete understanding of both theoretical and applied uses of nuclear energy, the world is merely his test tube. If other people have any use, it is as guinea pigs, laboratory rats. They are neither hated nor loved but are to be used for the advancement of knowledge and science.

The professor hits a key and moves a pawn, sacrificing it to the computer's next move.

Certain people are more valuable than others, he knows. A runny-nosed child who wants to play baseball – even one's own son – is no use whatsoever. This is so clear that Lionel Morton does not even try to understand why many so fathers waste their Saturdays at ball games, bowling alleys, or beaches. They could be productive, but instead choose to fritter away their time with wives and children. Children, for chrissakes, are of even less use than women.

Morton moves a black pawn to f-4, and the computer moves a white pawn to f-5.

Shortly after World War II, Morton read of the numerous experiments conducted on concentration camp prisoners by Nazi scientists. Young men were forced into vats of ice water while technicians timed how long it took them to die of hypothermia. The world was revolted by these and other medical experiments performed by supposedly reputable physicians. But to Lionel Morton, then a graduate student, it all made sense. The Germans wanted to know how long their own pilots could survive in the frigid waters of the North Atlantic. No use wasting precious airplane fuel searching for airmen already dead. As for the concentration camp prisoners, well, they were dead men, sooner or later, anyway.

The problem with most people, Lionel Morton concluded long ago, was that they could not be objective. Emotion clouded judgment, so he banished it from his life. He prided himself on his ability to place rational thought above all else. Romantic love was a psychotic state to be avoided, so he never suffered a broken heart, never even cried. Sports, movies, music and TV were mindless excursions from reality, wastes of time. On vacation, he would visit the Stone Age nuclear reactors at Oak Ridge, Tennessee, or stay home and fool with mathematical formulas that would disprove cold fusion. On his desk in his university office, instead of family mementos, Lionel Morton placed gruesome photos of burn victims from Hiroshima. He neither mourned for these victims nor gloated over their pain. To him, they were simply scientific exhibits, proof of the ultimate power of man's genius.

Lionel Morton hits a key and moves a pawn to d-4, where it stares the white pawn in the eye at d-5. He takes a moment to admire the board. With his black knight at f-3 and his two pawns facing two opposing pawns on row four, he has created an unbreakable bind on e-5 and has frozen the white pawn at e-6. The computer *clicks* for a moment before a mechanical voice says, "Congratulations, Professor Morton. Your successful deployment of the Sicilian defense results in a Maroczy Bind. We could continue to play, but it will result in a draw. Thank you for a most interesting game."

Morton angrily pounds the keys on his typewriter, writing, "But I want to win."

The computer's voice responds almost immediately, "Humans never win."

With Colonel Farris at his side, General Corrigan leaves a cluster of officers and approaches the wheelchair. He watches over the professor's shoulder as the computer sets up another game. Without looking up, Morton says, "William the Conqueror was once so enraged at losing a game that he broke his chess board over his opponent's head. Then there was the French knight, Renaud de Montauban, who succeeded in killing an opponent with a heavy wooden chess board."

The general doesn't respond, and Morton looks up. "Hugh, could we speak privately a moment?"

The general nods, and Colonel Farris slips off to one side. Morton hits a button and clears the chess game from his computer screen. "It's amazing how closely chess resembles war, isn't it Hugh?"

"It's been said before, but personally, I prefer poker."

Morton goes on, "Even the terminology of chess sounds like a session at National Military Command. Attacks and double attacks, blockades and decoys, strategic defenses and escapes and, of course, my favorite, the end game."

"War's not a game, Lionel, just because we make it sound like one."

"Humor me a moment, Hugh, and let's play out the analogy. The pawns are the infantry, slogging it out in the trenches, even more valuable if they breach the other's line. The knights are the airborne, vaulting over the enemy. The bishops are powerful artillery, but clumsy in closed positions, while the rooks combine might and mobility like the armored cavalry. In both war and chess, you must out-think the enemy, always planning two steps ahead. You must box in the enemy, limit his choices until you have achieved what the Germans call *zugzwang*, where any move worsens his position. You want to force him to either surrender or die."

"What's your point, Lionel?"

"They think I'm crazy," he says, gesturing toward the ensemble of officers, "but you know I'm not. I'm the last of the objectivists. I can separate all elements of external cognition from internal feelings."

"Then I feel sorry for you."

"Don't. I meant it before when I said you should let the bird fly for purely strategic reasons."

"I'm sure you did."

"No one can make the hard choices anymore. In the last fifty years, we've become a nation of weaklings. Not since Hiroshima and Nagasaki has an American president shown any real guts. They're too worried about the polls and the Sunday morning interview shows. We wimped out in Korea and Cuba and Vietnam and everywhere else where we've been seriously challenged. A couple of nuclear payloads over Hanoi, and Ho Chi Minh would have surrendered in a week."

"Would he, or would the Russians have responded in kind

against Saigon, and then would we hit the missile fields at Yedrovo, Kartala and Kostroma, and then would they hit Cheyenne Mountain? Where would it end?"

"Those are precisely the chances you have to take," Morton says, looking off into space. "It's ironic, Hugh. You're a general who never believed in military solutions, and I'm a scientist who always did."

"You put too much faith in your machines," the general replies.

"The weak link is man, not the machine. All my creations work just the way I designed them."

General Corrigan turns away. "That's the damned scary truth."

၁၃

James continues to work at the computer while Brother David watches over his shoulder. "Davy, I can see your reflection in the monitor."

"So?"

"So, it bothers me."

"Would it be better if I gave off no reflection, like a ghost in one of those horror films."

"It would be better if you just let me alone."

David turns away, seemingly bored. Behind him, Susan Burns has been dozing. Slowly, her eyes open, and she stifles a yawn.

"Ah, the doctor is in," David says. "Shall we resume our discussion?"

"You want to talk more about yourself?"

"It is a subject of which I never tire. Tell me more about my charming personality."

"It's true that psychopaths often have a certain beguiling charm. It's used to manipulate others. Underneath the veneer, they are unsocialized. You, for example, are grossly selfish, callous, irresponsible, and unable to feel guilt or to learn from experience and punishment. Your frustration tolerance is low. You blame others or offer seemingly rational reasons for your anti-social behavior. You manifest aggressive-sadistic tendencies and exhibit what used to be called a 'moral insanity.'"

"Is that all?"

"And you probably have a very small penis."

That gets a chuckle from James, who doesn't look up from the computer. If the remark wounded David, he doesn't show it. "I have a new job for you, doctor."

That causes Rachel to stir. "David..."

"I believe Dr. Burns would make an excellent deputy at the console. When Brother James has retrieved the S.L.C., the good doctor's job will be to turn the second key."

"Not a chance," Susan says.

"Not even to save your own life."

"I couldn't live with myself."

"You can live with me. Forever."

Furious, Rachel stands and stomps to the rear of the capsule.

"Do you think you can convert me to your cause?" Susan asks, eyes wide in disbelief.

"Yes, and to me," David says, confidently. "But that can wait, at least for a while." A small smile plays on his lips. "But enough about you. Now, tell me about my father."

"You hate him," she says, "but you admire him, too. The contradiction, the cognitive dissonance, makes you loathe yourself."

David barks out a laugh and moves closer to Susan, leaning over her. She doesn't flinch. "I think you understand what makes you tick, and you know the mechanism is broken. But your revel in your own knowing insanity."

"I'm just doing Daddy's work, like any loving son. As it is written in John, 'Ye are of your father the devil, and the lusts of your father ye will do.'"

"Only because you want to. You willed yourself to become your father, only more so. He built the bomb but couldn't use it. You took the bomb and—"

"And will light the fuse to it," he says with a grin.

༄

Lieutenant Colonel Charlie Griggs despises Commander Elwood (Woody) Waller.

Always has. Always will.

Friggin' Navy Seals.

Sure, they're tough. Hell, all the Special Ops are tough. Green Berets, Night Stalkers, Air Force Commandos, and the friggin' SEALs with their Trident insignia that always looked like the Budweiser logo to Griggs.

He never doubted his own personal toughness. He led operations in Central America that never made the newspapers or the Congressional Record. Tougher than he looked, they said about Charlie Griggs. He didn't have the brahma bull neck and rocky ledge jaw of the recruiting posters. With the thin mustache and pale hair going gray, with the slightly receding chin, Charlie Griggs looked like an accountant. If you noticed the size of his pole-ax wrists, though, if you watched the way he walked, bouncing slightly on the balls of his feet, aware of all movement around him, you might have a clue.

These days, Charlie Griggs was driving a desk at Fort Bragg. It was his bad luck to get the job baby-sitting this maniac professor for reasons of geography. At the time the 318th Missile Squadron was being overrun by a bunch of Bible-spouting crazies, Charlie Griggs was a special guest visiting Hell Week at the Naval Special Warfare Center, the SEALs training base outside San Diego. He had just walked into the "grinder," the forlorn asphalt exercise yard, passing under the sign, "The Only Easy Day Was Yesterday," when he was ordered to fly up the coast to Palo Alto and snag the professor. At least the surprise assignment got him away from Woody Waller's constant bragging.

God, they were a tiresome bunch, and Griggs had seen enough push-ups in the mud and screaming drill instructors to last a lifetime. As for the macho saloon antics – pouring rum on a bar and lighting it in memory of a dead colleague – well, melodrama never played well for Griggs. These days, his specialty was hostage rescue. He was an expert in demolitions and small arms fire and could tell you just how large a charge of plastique to attach to a door to blow it without killing the hostages inside. He was equally adept at "instinctive firing" and "rapid-aim fire," and to this day, would not mind being the first one through a blown door where the first decision is whether to shoot and whom.

But Griggs' days of rappelling down buildings are over. Lately, he's been drawing up contingency plans for Delta Force's counter terrorist unit, coordinating with Woody Waller's SEAL-Team 6 and the F.B.I.'s Hostage Response Unit. Griggs hates the parochial rivalries, hates playing the role of the eager cutthroat commando, but it has to be done, or Woody Waller would gobble up ever blood-and-guts assignment. Now, the two of them have General Hugh Corrigan surrounded and are pleading their respective cases.

"General, my men deserve to be first to go down that hole," Griggs says.

"With all due respect, Charlie, SEAL Team-6 is faster and better than any team Delta can muster," Waller responds.

"Easy, Woody. You too, Charlie," the general says. "You'll both get your chance."

"I hope so, sir." Griggs knows he is expected to beat the drums a little harder so he sucks it up and lets loose with the macho bullshit. "My men haven't tasted blood since Desert Storm."

Commander Woody Waller laughs in mock disbelief. He is a square-jawed, crew-cut Hollywood version of a Navy SEAL. "That was a real ballbuster, huh Charlie? Rounding up some starving ragheads."

"My men were human trip-wires behind enemy lines while your Malibu lifeguards were playing with boogie boards in the Gulf."

"Individual experimental landing craft," Waller corrects him, though in fact, they were black boogie boards sent from California for a nighttime beach landing that never occurred.

"Delta Force was eating the Republican Guard for lunch, not riding around Kuwait City in dune buggies."

"Fast Attack Vehicles. Charlie, why are you so jealous of the

SEALs, anyway?"

"Enough, already!" General Corrigan holds up his arms. "Colonel Zwick reports that Morning Star has removed the MGCS computer. There's the distinct possibility that they already have the Secondary Launch Code or are about to get it." The general pushes past the two rivals. "So I suggest you save your animosity for the enemy, gentlemen."

-45-
Operation Masada

A grate opens in the floor and Jack Jericho pulls himself into the Launch Equipment Room. He moves to the door and peeks cautiously into the tunnel. Three commandos are headed his way. Jericho ducks back inside, dashes through a row of supply shelves and climbs to the top shelf. Just then, the door opens, and the commandos come in, high-low, M-16's wheeling in every direction.

One of the commandos flicks on the light switch. Each takes a row and begins searching. In the middle row, a commando stops and listens. Maybe he's heard something, but it could have been the footsteps of his comrades. He listens again, seems to sense something, then hears a metallic rattle above him. He looks up just as a Jeep's heavy snow chain drops around his neck. He reaches up to toss of the chain, but above him on the shelf, Jack Jericho yanks it tight.

A gurgling sound comes from the commando who struggles against the pressure on his neck. Muscles straining, Jericho lifts the commando off his feet and ties both ends of the chain around the shelf's support pole.

"Samuel!" one of the other commandos yells. "Samuel, where are you?"

Jericho leaps off the shelf and scurries down the row toward the light equipment pen at the end of the room.

The other two commandos race into the middle row where

they find Samuel hanging by his neck, feet swaying two feet above the floor. The first commando yells to his unseen foe, "I'll kill you myself!"

Jericho hears the threat as he opens the gate to the equipment pen.

"Come," the second commando tells his comrade. "Let's call for the others."

"No! He's in here, and we'll find him."

A sound stops them.

A whirring.

A blinding headlight turns into their row. Something moves toward them. They shield their eyes and see it.

A forklift!

Jack Jericho pulls back a lever, and the lift blade rises. The forklift is barely narrower than the row between the shelves. The commandos can turn and run, or they can stand and fight. Both raise their weapons and unleash a barrage of gunfire that ricochets with metallic *clangs* off the approaching forklift. Then, they turn and run. At the first opening, they duck into the next row, Jericho turns the corner and chases them through the maze of shelves. Finally, they come to a dead end against a concrete wall. The commandos turn and fire. Jericho hunches down into the seat of the forklift. Sparks fly as bullets *ping* off the steel shelf that supports the blades.

The forklift plows ahead, Jericho leaning hard on the throttle.

The commandos stand their ground.

The two-pronged forks bear down on them, gut-high.

Whomp! Whomp! The commandos are impaled like olives on toothpicks.

The forklift stops with a *thud* as the blades crunch into the wall, blood spurting. Jericho throws the machine into reverse, and with the commandos still attached, he wheels out of the Equipment Room and into the tunnel. He turns toward the launch control capsule and opens up the throttle. Fifty yards down the tunnel, he passes under a panning video camera.

At that moment, in the launch control capsule, Brother David looks up into the panel of security monitors. Flashing by, he sees the forklift with the two bodies aloft. "Damnation!"

David stands and looks out the small blast window overlooking the tunnel. The forklift is aimed straight for the side of the capsule. "Stop him!" Two commandos storm out of the capsule and into the tunnel. They open fire just as Jericho locks the throttle down and dives off the forklift, rolling over twice and coming to a stop within five feet of a floor grate.

The forklift rolls on, each skewered commando still hoisted there. The two commandos on the floor duck out of the way just as the forklift crashes into the capsule, plastering the bodies to its wall and streaking the blast window with blood.

Inside the capsule, David paces like a caged tiger. Turning toward Dr. Susan Burns, he fumes, "The fool dares to taunt me. He has shed the blood of saints and prophets." David picks up a microphone and hits a button. His voice can be heard all throughout the missile facility, even in the sump under the tunnel, where Jericho now makes his way through the maze of piping. "Now, heathen, hear the Word. As it is written, 'I will make Mine arrows drunk with blood, and My sword shall devour your flesh.'"

❧

Brother David sits in the deputy's flight chair, barely noticing James, who continues to work at the computer. "I may have misjudged the sergeant," David says, perhaps to himself.

Overhearing him, Susan Burns says, "So you admit fallibility."

"Don't play your shrink games with me, doctor. I know all the tricks of the trade. I never claimed infallibility. If I am the Messiah, it is in sinful form."

"Or are you just a charlatan? Didn't Jesus warn of false prophets, wolves in sheep's clothing?"

"Then you should be afraid of my bite."

"There's still time to back down. You can make a statement on television, get your message across."

"My message will be delivered with the heat of a thousand suns."

"Unless the sergeant stops you."

"The sergeant," he repeats. Thinking about him now. Not admitting, even to himself, the concern, but summoning up a vision. Just a color at first, a grayish white. He concentrates and sees it clearer, a flowing grayish sheet, and he peers deep into his mind but can only think of a banner waving in the wind. It does not compute. Not getting a handle on the vision, he lets it go.

He opens Jericho's personnel file and thumbs through the pages. "I thought the sergeant would run and hide at the sound of a shaken leaf. What do you suppose has gotten into this cowardly coal miner?"

Susan Burns does not answer immediately, and David shoots a lethal glance at her. When she remains silent, he approaches her and places his face close to hers. "Your diagnosis, doctor, or would you prefer to stretch your arms again?"

"Jack Jericho has a purpose," she says, finally. "A reason for living, at least for a while."

"And what would that be?"

"To kill you, of course," she answers, "or to die trying."

⁂

Jack Jericho moves deeper into the sump, takes a fork in the channel and pauses to listen. Just the familiar *thumpa* heartbeat of the pumps. He is alone. He wonders when the Army's assault will come, wants to be part of it, his mind's eye painting wondrous pictures as he leads a contingent of Delta Force soldiers into the capsule. Rescuing the damsel, saving the world. Stupid, he thinks. Special Ops won't let him near the place, and he'd probably screw it up if they did.

Suddenly, the cellular phone rings.

Jericho clicks a button. "Yeah."

"You're making a mess of things, maintenance man," David says.

"Just doing my job."

"I think not. I think it's become personal. But your heroics are futile."

"I never wanted to be a hero."

"And you've succeeded." He laughs. "But where do you go from here?"

"Wherever you are, pal. You want to get rid of me, let the woman go."

"Oh, how gallant, how chivalrous. And here, I thought you were protecting the interests of your government. It turns out you're just pursuing an unrequited love." He turns toward Susan Burns. "It is unrequited, isn't it, doctor? I'd hate to think you were mixing business with dubious pleasure of fornicating with the janitor."

"You're wrong," Susan says. "The pleasures were exquisite. Jack Jericho is all man." Mocking the preacher. Letting him know who measures up and who doesn't.

Through the phone, Jack hears her, and for a moment, wonders if he has missed something. No, even drunk, he would have remembered that.

"Liar!" David fumes, but his voice betrays doubt, the beginning of weakness.

Jericho keeps quiet. In the capsule, David punches a button, muting his microphone, then gestures toward Captain Pukowlski, who is shackled against the wall. "That noise on the phone," David says, "what is it?"

The captain doesn't answer, and Rachel presses a rifle barrel into his fleshy jowls.

"What is it!" David demands. The *thumpa* can clearly be heard on the speaker.

"The drainage pump," the captain says, grimacing. "In the sump."

"But where?" The rifle barrel presses harder.

"Channel B, maybe sixty meters west of the missile."

"Thank you, captain," David says. He gestures to a commando guard. "Now take him back to the storage room with the ambassadors. Keep him out of my sight, or I'll kill him." David turns his mike back on and says into the phone, "Sergeant, you seem to be all alone in the world."

In the sump, Jericho slogs through the dirty water. A rat scurries across a pipe above his head. He listens to David's voice on the phone. "Perhaps we could make room for you in our family."

"No thanks," Jericho says. "Your family is seriously dysfunctional."

He hangs up.

ↄ

Two uniforms and a suit surround General Corrigan. F.B.I. Agent Hurtgen, Lieutenant Colonel Charlie Griggs and Commander Woody Waller, the three hostage response team leaders, jockey for position and plead their cases as the general examines the sophisticated diorama of the missile facility, complete with miniature commandos and toy soldiers.

"I'd run a diversion toward the elevator," Griggs says, gesturing to the model, "then run a full rappel strike down the silo wall."

The general nods, then using a wooden pointer, slides a platoon of toy soldiers and tiny Armored Personnel Carriers toward silo.

Agent Hurtgen shakes his head. "It'd be ninety seconds quicker straight down the elevator shaft, based on our Hostage Response Unit computer simulation."

"Simulation, masturbation," sneers Waller. "Fuck 'em in both holes at once."

"I agree with Woody," Griggs says.

Waller beams at the support from his Army rival. "And let the F.B.I. sit this one out. When it comes to rappelling under fire, you have to go with SEAL TEAM-6."

"SEALS, schmeals," Hurtgen responds. "This isn't a beach landing."

Woody Waller bristles. "One contingency was an amphibious assault. The map showed a river running next to the silo."

"The river's been dry for five years!" Hurtgen yells. "Shit, even the Triple-A maps have that right. What's the matter, can't the Jedi Warriors read?"

Mocking the nickname of SEAL TEAM-6 was too much. Waller wouldn't mind taking this guy on an underwater demolition job and shoving the explosives up his ass. Just as he's about to suggest that, General Corrigan sweeps the pointer across the diorama, scattering the toy soldiers over the miniature countryside. "Men, let's work together, okay?"

Colonel Griggs clears his throat and says, "General, if we don't kick off soon, Delta Force and the SEALS are going to start killing each other."

❧

Bells ring and chimes sound in the computer, and James sits ramrod straight, watching a blizzard of numbers flash across the monitor. "*Voila*," he says, triumphantly.

David slides his flight chair down the railing next to James. "Do you have it?"

"Got my foot in the back door." James' eyes are red and he is fatigued, but his voice reflects the excitement of a new discovery. A message scrolls across the monitor, "SECONDARY LAUNCH CODE MATRIX."

"Yes!" James shouts. He hits several more keys, sweat plastering his pale hair to his forehead. "Just one more little..."

Another message appears on the monitor, "ENTER PASSWORD TO ACCESS CODE."

"Shit!" James bangs several more keys, but the same message repeats itself.

David wheels around and faces Owens. "Don't look at me," the lieutenant says. "The password is transmitted with the E.A.M. launch order. I've never seen it, never heard it."

Rachel jams the barrel of a rifle against Owens' temple. "Might as well shoot me," he says, "'cause I don't know shit."

David bangs his fist against the console, then turns to James.

"Can you extract it from the M.G.C.S. computer?"

"It's not there," James says, still working away. "All I've got is this."

David swings back to the monitor. On the screen, seven cursors pulsate.

"Fill in the blanks," James says. "It's a seven-digit password, letters or numbers or both. You want to know the possible number of combinations?"

"No! I just want to launch the missile."

ತಿ

In the STRATCOM War Room, the klaxon horn is blaring. On the Big Board, two messages appear, "SECONDARY LAUNCH CODE MATRIX." and "ENTER PASSWORD TO ACCESS CODE." A technician pulls off his headset and turns to General Corrigan, "They got in, sir. If they enter the password, all they have to do is re-enter the Enable Code, turn the keys, and the bird is gone."

General Corrigan turns to Professor Morton. "What about it, Lionel? You said he couldn't—"

"Quite creative," Morton says with grudging admiration. "I didn't think he'd get this far, but now who knows? The little momma's boy may surprise us after all."

"Percentages, Lionel. Give me some numbers." There is the sense of urgency in the general's voice.

"No way to tell. But remember one thing. David Morton is flesh of my flesh, blood of my blood. He's not stupid, Hugh."

The general ponders that for a moment, agreeing with the professor. Crazy yes, stupid no. He turns to Colonel Farris. "Tell Colonel Zwick to prepare for kickoff, but not to move until he receives my direct order."

An aide works his way through the crowd of officers and brings General Corrigan a telephone, then whispers in his ear. The general straightens his shoulders and speaks into the headset. "Yes, Mr.

President."

A pause.

"Yes, Mr. President."

Another pause.

"Yes, I understand, Mr. President."

General Hugh Corrigan's jaw muscles clench with each tight nod of his head. He hangs up the phone and turns to the circle of brass. His face is gray, and he looks ten years older than just a few hours earlier. "Tel Aviv has just informed the Commander-in-Chief what its response will be to a nuclear strike."

"Jesus, General, they're not going to do something stupid like counter-attack us, are they?" Colonel Farris asks.

"Not us. But they've got something called Operation Masada in the event one of the Arab countries hits them with a nuclear weapon."

"Masada. A fight to the finish," Dr. Stuart Rosen says, and the military men turn toward him. "After the fall of Jerusalem to the Romans in the first century, the last of the Jewish zealots occupied a mountaintop fortress at Masada. There were only a few hundred zealots, but they were vicious fighters, and it took fifteen thousand Roman troops two years to defeat them. As the fortress fell, the remaining Jews took their own lives, rather than be enslaved by the Romans."

"I don't get it," Farris says, a puzzled look on his face. "The Arabs have nothing to do with—"

"Doesn't matter," Professor Morton breaks in. "'Never again,' and all that Holocaust melodrama. I hadn't thought of it before, Hugh, but it makes perfect sense. The Israelis must strike first just like they did in '67. When they waited, when they let the Arabs hit them in the Yom Kippur War, they were nearly pushed into the Red Sea. This time, if they wait, they'll be annihilated. Maybe they will be anyway, maybe it's as suicidal as the zealots on the mountaintop, but at least, they'll take a good portion of their enemies with them."

"All of them," Corrigan says. "Their response will be nuclear. Baghdad, Tripoli, Tehran, the oil fields of Saudi Arabia and Kuwait."

"A flamboyant acting out on a grand scale," Dr. Rosen says, disapprovingly.

"Can't we talk the Israelis into just taking the hit?" Farris asks. "Hell, we'll help them rebuild."

"Apparently, they feel their people have taken one hit this century, and that was quite enough," General Corrigan says.

"Jesus," the Farris mutters. "Looks like the professor's going to get his wish."

General Corrigan turns toward Lionel Morton, who is making a series of mathematical calculations on his wheelchair computer. "Lionel, why don't you tell everyone what would happen if the Israelis make good on their threat."

"Assuming they use all their warheads, and there's no reason not to, radioactive clouds of sand and oil will reach the stratosphere," he says, still studying his computer monitor. "Fires in the fields will be too hot – in every sense of the word – to put out. They'll burn for fifty years to seventy-five years. The clouds will superheat the atmosphere, changing the climate. It will be warm at first, but then, the sun will be blocked for several decades. It will snow in Miami, and the polar ice cap will extend as far south as say, Virginia."

"Nuclear winter," Colonel Farris says, shaking his head.

"I always thought that was an overly dramatic term," the professor says, "but you've got the idea."

"Lionel," the general says, "if there's any chance that you still can influence your son, you've got an obligation to your country to try."

The professor seems to think about it, and Dr. Rosen, the shrink, pipes up, "General, I must advise against another session of paternal brow-beating. Overt hostility will only provoke the young man. This rivalry between father and son can only exacerbate—"

"Shut up, you fleabag Freudian," the professor snarls. He turns to the general. "Okay, Hugh. Get the son-of-a-bitch on the phone."

-46-
Postponing the Inevitable

"I knew you'd call again, *pater*," David says, when they get him on the line. He speaks into the old black, rotary telephone and smiles at Susan. Proud they're coming to him.

"Mistakes were made, I'll admit that," Lionel Morton says, softly.

David smiles again and hits a button, turning on the speaker. Letting his audience enjoy his handiwork, admire his repartee. "Is that an apology, that *sotto voce*, passive *voce*, mealy-mouthed evasion?"

"Yes, goddamit! I'm sorry. I'm sorry I wasn't the father you wanted."

"Apology not accepted," David says, gleefully. "And for the record, I'm not a bit sorry I wasn't the son you wanted, assuming you wanted a son at all."

"I did the best I could."

David barks out a bitter laugh. "What do you think of that, Dr. Burns? Dear old Dad did the best he could."

"It's a shopworn cliché," she answers. "It's what virtually every parent in a dysfunctional family says."

"Did you hear that, Daddy? You're just a worn out cliché. Come on, Dr. Burns, tell us more. Daddy never had the benefit of therapy and doesn't know what he's missing."

"Your father was remote and demanding. Nothing you did was ever good enough for him."

"No, no, no. Nothing I ever did was bad enough."

"Godammit, David," the professor's voice rumbles through the speaker. "What do you want? Do you want to kill me?"

"Heavens, no. I already tried that. I prefer you alive and crippled. But that isn't politically correct, is it? Alive and ambulatorily disadvantaged, that's my Daddy. Do you still need medication for the pain? I'll bet the dosage has increased over the years. I'll bet you're so strung out most every night, you wouldn't know if someone broke into your house and rifled through your study."

"David, I swear to Christ I never knew what made you tick. You were always a weird kid, and now...and now..."

"I had powers! I had visions!"

"Yes, you did. In another age, you would have been burned at the stake. Righteous folk would have considered you the devil."

"Or his misbegotten son."

"Go ahead," the professor says. "Have your fun. Crucify me."

"What a delicious thought."

"Look, I admit it. I didn't know how to be a father. I was in love with my work."

David's tone is mocking as he mimics his father's voice, "Not that I loved my son less, but that I loved the bomb more."

"Damn you, David. What do you want?"

"Salvation, Daddy. Salvation for all eternity." He clicks off the phone, then dials another number.

❧

Jack Jericho is deep in the sump when the cellular phone rings. "Yeah, asshole. Talk to me."

"Sergeant, in the game of chess, do you know what it's called when you sacrifice your queen to save the king?" David asks him.

From his perch on a web of pipes in the drainage sump, Jericho speaks into the cellular phone. "I dunno, the Heimlich Maneuver?"

"It's called postponing the inevitable."

"Yeah, but I can wait."

"Unfortunately, I cannot."

"I understand," Jericho says. "So many psychoses, so little time."

"We're going to launch the missile, sergeant. You can't stop it. All the king's horses and all the king's men can't stop it."

"So why are you concerned with me?"

"I want you here in the capsule. I want you here with me, Jack."

249

The sound of his name runs a shiver through Jericho. He checks the clip on the Uzi, snaps it into place. "Why? Aren't your half-wit apostles interesting company?"

"Jack, don't you know our fates are intertwined?"

"Then I want a new fortune teller."

"I can give you the peace you've never known. I can give you the power of which you've dreamed."

"You don't know anything of my dreams."

"You have nightmares, don't you Jack? I knew it the moment I saw your muddied aura. But I didn't know then what haunted your nights. You dream of the mine, the deep, dark, scary mine."

Jericho slumps against an electrical conduit. He doesn't want to listen, but he does not click off. For the briefest second, Jericho wonders if he enjoys the pain, wonders if he might not deserve it.

"Jack, your ran from your destiny while I pursued mine...with a vengeance."

Jericho's voice is weak, his eyes hollow. "If I'd gone back in, I would have slowed the evacuation of men coming out."

"Fate gave you one chance for glory, and you ran the other way. I'm offering you a second chance."

"I did the right thing. I would have caused others to die."

"You could have saved your father and your brother!"

"I followed orders, dammit!"

"And look where it got you." David turns to Susan Burns. "Tell him. Tell him who he is, for the fool does not know."

Susan remains silent. David slaps her hard across the cheek, then drags her to the phone. His face is red, his mood swinging wildly into rage. "Tell him, mindfucker! Tell him, you mother of harlots, you Jezebel!"

Blinking back tears, Susan says, "Survivor's guilt. You want to be killed, Jack. You want to die now to repent for living then."

David's voice drops into a whisper. "That makes you a very dangerous man, and I want the dangerous men on my side."

Jericho's grief turns to anger. Images of his wasted years flash by. Thoughts of his family collide with fury at this madman who would destroy so much. "You're right, I'm dangerous. I'm *your* nightmare because I'm just as damaged as you are. You want to die, and I just don't give a shit. But if I die, I'm going to take you with me."

"Words! Empty words! So long, sergeant."

David clicks off the phone and smiles with cruel satisfaction. Susan Burns turns away so that David will not see her tears.

ᗛ

In the drainage sump, Jack Jericho stares into space. He is numb, detached, unfocused. The channel is lit only by dim yellow bulbs, and Jericho sits deep in the shadows. He is in a nook in the wall of the channel, a location that offers the illusion of protection. A closet in a haunted house. The phone rings again, and Jericho angrily punches a button and yells, "Go fuck yourself!"

The voice on the other end of the line seems genuinely startled. "Sergeant Jericho, must I remind you of the proper method of addressing an officer?"

"Sir, I'm sorry sir. I thought—"

"You thought nothing," Colonel Zwick says. "Now, did I order you off the missile base?"

"Yes, sir."

"Then get the hell out of there. I swear, if Morning Star doesn't kill you..."

A noise startles Jericho.

"...I will!"

Jericho pulls the phone away from his ear and listens. Nothing but the thumping pumps. What was that noise, like the *clank* of a rifle barrel against a pipe? The colonel's distant voice grows angrier. "Sergeant, are you there? Dammit, sergeant!" There is a soft splash in the water, and Jericho hangs up.

ᗛ

Thirty yards from Jericho, around a bend in the channel, four commandos with weapons drawn are on the prowl, hunched over in the low sump. They use hand signals to communicate and slow their steps to prevent splashing. A low-hanging conduit pipe from a generator blocks their path. The commando on point reaches up to brace himself. He does not see that the insulated rubber covering has been sliced open, a clean incision from a Jimmy Lile survival knife, and his hand slips into a mass of exposed wires as the insulation slides off.

Sparks explode from the opening. High voltage surges through the commando's body, which convulses wildly, the electricity amplified by the knee-deep water, which seems to boil at his feet. Smoke billows from the open collar of his field jacket, and the channel is filled with the sickly sweet smell of burning flesh. As he sinks to the floor of the sump, floating face down in the grimy water, a second commando races to him.

"Judd! Judd!"

But poor Judd is dead. The other three commandos splash past him, rifles raised, looking for someone to shoot.

Ahead of them in the channel, hidden in the womb of the generator piping, Jericho closes his eyes and listens. Judging from the noise, he knows there are at least two more commandos, perhaps a third. He hits a switch in the nook, killing the yellow lights and plunging the sump into total darkness.

The commandos slip on infrared goggles and keep coming. They are within ten yards of Jericho's hiding place when he grabs a handful of steel bolts from a tool tray and tosses them down the sump away from the approaching men. He ducks back into his nook, and the bolts rattle off the piping. A second later, the noise of the automatic weapons is deafening. Before the echoes have completely died out, Jericho tosses another handful of bolts in the other direction, behind the oncoming commandos. He can hear the men splashing in the water as they turn to shoot. Another volley of gunfire reverberates through the channel. Then, a scream, "Adam! You shot me! Adam..."

The commando named Adam slogs through the water toward

his friend, crying out, "No! No! No!"

Then, in the darkness, Jericho says. "Nice shooting, Adam."

Adam whirls and fires. The bullets ricochet off metal and reverberate in the narrow channel.

"You killed him," Jack Jericho says, "but you missed me. I'm behind you."

Adam turns the other way and fires on full automatic, letting a burst go until, *click*, he's out of ammo. He fumbles with another clip.

Jericho hits the switch again, and the yellow lights flicker on. Another switch, and stronger spotlights fill the sump with a white glare. Blinded, Adam tears off his night goggles and through squinting eyes sees a figure six feet in front of him. A man holding something. An Uzi! The three-shot burst to the chest is mercifully on target. Adam is dead before he splashes to the floor.

Jericho turns to head the other way, wanting to duck back into cover, still not knowing if there is a fourth commando in the sump. He never sees the rifle butt swinging at his head, and it catches him squarely on the chin.

Jericho's world explodes into a galaxy of shooting stars.

He hears himself grunt, feels a jolt that rockets from his spine down through his fingertips and his toes.

The pain lasts just a second, because a moment later, he is tumbling backward, unconscious, never feeling the cold, dark water that envelops him.

BOOK SIX

Fire and Water

-47-
Overkill

Green sodium vapor lights cast an eerie glow over Base Camp Alpha as the Army prepares for battle. The base is a symphony of competing sounds, the crunch of M60A3 tanks with bulldozer blades and the diesel roar of M1A2 Abrams battle tanks moving to front-line positions. On the flanks, M2/3 Bradley fighting vehicles with cannons and missile launchers pound over the rough terrain. HUMVEES grind their gears, and Armored Personnel Carriers rev their engines. Orders are shouted over loudspeakers. The tracked equipment kicks up clouds of dust that float in the breeze. On the horizon, the half-moon provides a sliver of light on the cloudless night.

Delta Force soldiers darken their faces with camouflage grease. Army Night Stalkers and Navy Seal Team-6 clean their weapons and load their rucksacks with flash-bang grenades, bolt cutters, harnesses, nylon ropes and rappelling gear. The FBI's Hostage Response unit studies maps and the latest satellite photos. In a compromise that satisfies no one, virtually all the Special Ops Forces will play some role in the assault.

In front of the command tent, Kimberly Crawford, the media's pool reporter, tags along after Colonel Henry Zwick, whose cold pipe is clamped in his teeth. A short, husky cameraman walks backward in front of them, keeping the colonel in focus. Nearby, a CNN truck festooned with antennae and dishes, up-links the signal to a satellite. "Colonel, colonel," Kimberly Crawford implores him, jamming a microphone into his face. "Can you verify reports that the missile base has been overrun by Palestinian terrorists?"

"I'm not at liberty to comment on the identity of the enemy," he says.

"Can you tell us where the missile is targeted?"

"No comment."

"Has the Army been in contact with the terrorists?"

"I'm not at liberty to say."

"What about the report that the terrorists have the ability to launch the missile?"

Zwick has held her off as long as he can. Looking straight into the camera, he says, "Absolutely untrue. The launch system is fail-safe."

"Then what's all this?" she asks, sweeping an arm over toward a pair of Bradley Fighting Vehicles, with their 25 mm cannon and TOW missile launchers pointed toward the missile base. "Isn't this overkill?"

Colonel Zwick studies her a moment. Not a day over thirty, a blonde with gold-green eyes, she's wearing a khaki jumpsuit with epaulets and a sky-blue silk scarf. Some sort of journalists' war couture, he supposes. The colonel would like to tell her that 'overkill' is the best kind of kill there is, that he'd like to outnumber, out-weigh, and out-caliber every enemy he's supposed to destroy. He wants better training, better food, and warmer boots than the opposition. He wants more iron, more ammo, and a bigger dick than the guy on the other side. But he doesn't say these things because the media types would probably make him sound like a cross between Ivan the Terrible and General Jack Ripper. Nothing on television ever comes out right. "Precautions. Just precautions," he says, after a moment.

At that moment, in the launch control capsule, David watches a television set where an attractive young woman chases after a colonel whose jaw muscles are working overtime on a cold pipe. In the corner of the screen is the logo, "CNN LIVE."

"So, Colonel Zwick," the woman says, "are you denying that an assault on the missile silo is imminent?"

"That's correct. It's unnecessary. There is no risk of the missile being launched, and our primary concern is the safety of the foreign ambassadors as well as the American airmen who are being held hostage. As I said before, these are just precautions. We expect reason to prevail and the incident to end without further violence."

The message, David knows, is for him. "They must think I'm an idiot," he says aloud. He punches a button on the console and speaks into a microphone. "Full alert! No one sleeps! And find that maintenance man!"

ço

The world is dark and shadowy.

And spinning. Jack Jericho is the center of a universe that revolves out of control around him.

There is no color except black, which dissolves into an ashen gray. Then, in the corner of his eye, there comes a sick, pale yellowy light. Somewhere in his head, there is a roar. A freight train rumbles over the tracks, toots its horn, and keeps going. Around and around in his skull.

Jack Jericho rubs his aching jaw. Which tells him he is conscious. Then the throbbing pain comes, and he would prefer to be unconscious. He rotates his neck. His head is a bucket of sand, but nothing seems to be broken. He opens his eyes one at a time. It would be easier with tire jacks. A figure stands above him, saying something, but what?

"You have..." and then the words are swallowed into the black hole.

"What? Who are you?" Jericho hears himself say, the words echoing from a tunnel.

"Don't you remember me?"

Jericho squints into the yellowy light. The universe slows. The young man is familiar. So is the M-16 pointed at Jericho's head. "Yeah. Your name is Daniel. Daniel Boone, for all I know. About a million years ago, you tried to shoot me in the L.E.R., but your rifle jammed."

"The safety was on," Daniel says. Towheaded, a peach-fuzzy round face, he cannot be more than twenty.

"Then you were poking around in the silo. You figured I was hanging on the struts in the rocket burners, and you were right, so I jumped you."

"You could have killed me," Daniel says, "but you did not."

A jungle animal roars inside Jericho's skull. "I made a mistake. It won't happen again."

"Why didn't you kill me?"

Jericho thinks about it, at least he tries to think above the metallic clanging in his brain. In the silo, he could have killed this man but did not. Until that moment in his life, he had never intentionally hurt anyone. But in the day and endless night that followed, the world had changed. "I didn't know what you maniacs were up to, and you looked so young that..." He just leaves it hanging there.

"No, that is not it. God's psalms sang in your heart, filling you with compassion and mercy. God protected you and then me. He sent us a message. 'The sun shall not smite thee by day, nor the moon by night.'"

"I haven't heard too much about compassion and mercy from your pals, Daniel."

"I am sorry about that. I thought David had seen the light. But—" A splashing sound down the channel interrupts them. "You have very little time."

"Time for what? To welcome the Apocalypse?"

"No. To get the hell out of here." Daniel swings the rifle away and uses his free hand to help Jericho to his feet. The splashes are drawing closer, and a flashlight beam dances down the channel in the distance.

Jericho takes a few wobbly steps down the sump the other way, then looks back over his shoulder. "Why are you doing this? Aren't you a believer?"

"Oh, I believe, all right. I believe in a forgiving God. I believe in love and goodwill toward our brothers and sisters. I just don't believe in Brother David."

❧

Moments later, Jericho stops at the intersection of two channels in the sump. He hears the splashing and occasional *clanging* behind him as the commando team hunts him down.

He can outrun them.

He can hide from them.

But it won't do any good. It won't stop David and his band of crazies.

He tears a strip of cloth from his fatigues and wedges it into a piece of piping directly over the channel. Then he goes down the intersecting channel. Bolted into the wall is an orange steel ladder leading into a vertical metal chute. A sign bolted to the chute reads, "Personnel Evacuation Shaft."

It will take him all the way to the river bed above the missile silo. He will have to find another way back in, but he's already thinking about it, and it may just work.

He remembers something Kenosha told him, something about the missile raping the earth. Sooner or later, Kenosha said, the earth would reclaim the land. He pictures Kenosha, hears his words. *"In the end, my friend, the earth will prevail."*

"That's right, you smart old coot," Jericho says to himself. "But maybe I can give Mother Earth a helping hand."

❧

Colonel Henry Zwick and Kenosha stand over a table, intently studying reconnaissance photos of the missile facility. "What we're trying to do," the colonel says, "is achieve simultaneous entry into as many access corridors as possible with maximum firepower. Our problem is that the only sure way to get down there is the elevator shaft, and it's—"

"Sir!" Captain Kyle Clancy, his face coated with camouflage grease, interrupts. "With all due respect, sir, strategy and tactics should not be discussed with..."

For a moment, the colonel thinks Clancy is going to say, "Indians." For the same moment, the colonel is ready to throttle the younger man. But finally, Clancy says, "civilians."

"If you don't shut up, captain," the colonel fires back, "that's what you're going to be. Now, you can listen if you want, but the man I want to hear from is Kenosha. He knows the territory, Kyle, and he's too modest to tell you, but he earned a Silver Star when you were still in knickers."

Clancy shoots a look at Kenosha, but doesn't get a rise out of him.

"Eleventh Armored Cavalry in 'Nam," the colonel says.

"The Blackhorse," Clancy says, beginning to connect the dots. "That was your regiment, wasn't it, colonel?"

"Damn straight!"

Then simultaneously, Zwick and Kenosha loudly declare, "If you ain't Cav, you ain't!"

To Clancy, the cavalry trooper's slogan sounds strange coming from the pony-tailed man in buckskins, but what the hell. "Okay, I'm outnumbered by the guys who believe in firepower and armor."

"Mobile firepower," Kenosha corrects him.

Pointing to a satellite photo on the table, Zwick says, "We need a second access corridor. We have to divide the enemy's fire and have a second route to the capsule."

"The open silo," Kenosha says.

"Right. But it's farther up the mountain, and the terrain's too rugged for APC's. Choppers are too loud for a surprise attack, and infantry will be exposed crossing the river bed."

Kenosha points to a map showing the mountain and the valley to the north. "There is a natural drainage ditch on the back side of

259

the mountain. It is steep and rocky, but you could climb it without being discovered, then approach the silo from the rear, coming down from the dam."

The colonel looks from the maps to the photos, then back again. Finally, Clancy says, "How the hell would we get up there without being seen or heard?"

"The old fashioned way," Kenosha says. Both officers look at him, waiting. "Horses."

Zwick and Clancy exchange surprised glances. Then Zwick breaks into a grin. "Sure, why not? We are the cavalry."

"Horses," Clancy ponders. He pictures himself atop a galloping steed, blasting away with pistols in each hand. "My men can shoot from damn near any position. Standing, prone, kneeling supported, kneeling unsupported, forward slope, bunker windows, sitting on the can taking a dump, if we have to. No damn reason in hell we can't shoot from horseback."

⁊

The ladder ends at metal shelf just below ground level. A sign on the shelf reads, "Emergency Egress Only." Jericho reaches over his head and pulls a metal chain, and the shelf folds in two, dumping three feet of sand onto his head. Blast insulation. In the event of a strike by enemy warheads, the sand would be fused into glass and the missile crew – if they survived the hit – would have to chip through it to get out of the hole and discover what was left of their world. Jericho shakes the crud out of his hair and reaches up to open the hatch.

The cool night air hits his face, and he sucks in a long breath. It is nearly three a.m. It's only been hours, but it seems like days since the nightmare began. He climbs into the dry river bed and looks around. Searchlights sweep across the missile base. He turns away from the silo and heads toward a rocky trail that leads up the mountain.

In launch control capsule, a bell rings, and a message flashes across a monitor: "Security Breach." David hits a button, and a three-dimensional grid of the missile facility appears on the screen. A blinking red arrow appears over the words, "Personnel Evacuation Shaft."

David picks up a walkie-talkie and clicks it on. "My brother, he is in the river bed. Bring me his head!"

-48-
Sibling Rivalry

At just after 3 a.m., David turns to Susan Burns and says, "I was hoping to convert you."

"How? With your so-called psychic powers? Do you expect me to swoon because you see my aura?"

"You have been wounded. My flock is made up of the lame."

"Lame brains," she says. "Look, nothing is going to bring me to you. Not force. Not the Stockholm Syndrome. I don't identify with you. I pity you."

David is silent a moment, and then he says flatly, "I should kill you now and get it over with."

Susan Burns shrugs. "Would that make you happy?"

"Deliriously."

"Then do it. I prefer my patients to enjoy life."

"Or should I tie you to the blast door, spreadeagled and naked, a sacrificial offering for the Special Ops boys? They won't know whether to shoot you or fuck you."

"But you can't do either one, can you?"

"You mock me!" he thunders. "You, the symbol of a profession of frauds and quacks! You, who follows a false science instead of the Word."

"Show me the light. Shoot me. Kill me now."

David grabs Rachel's rifle and swings the barrel toward Susan's head. Then, just as suddenly, he lets the rifle fall to the floor. He laughs, throws his head back and cackles until tears flow. "You are so clever, Dr. Susan Burns. You think that if I kill you, I'll be so revolted, so changed in some fundamental way by the utter cruelty of the act that I'll stop. I'll surrender, repent, and give them back their missile. Isn't that it?"

She stays quiet and he goes on, "You're willing to sacrifice yourself for all mankind. A gesture brimming with Freudian *noblesse oblige.*"

Still, Susan is silent.

The phone buzzes. "What does old Hugh want now?" David says. Enjoying himself again, occupying center stage. He hits a speaker button and puts a tune to his voice. "Be all that you can be, in the Ar-my."

"Mr. Morton, we'd like to engage you in a discussion." General Corrigan's voice is calm, polite.

"Or a distraction. You're looking for a few good men, eh Hugh?"

"We know you're searching for the password. We don't think you'll get it, and we prefer to end this without bloodshed. We're prepared to discuss amnesty."

"Off we go into the wild blue yon-der," David sings out, "higher still, into the sun." He laughs, then says, "You're lying Hugh. Besides, only the Lord can offer forgiveness. Your amnesty is a purely secular concept of no interest to me."

"What is it you want, Mr. Morton? Death and devastation?"

"The few, the proud, the Marines!" David calls out.

"We're not going to make progress this way."

"Progress, Hugh? Like the progress my dear Daddy made for you. *Semper Fi.*"

"Mr. Morton, I know you're a very intelligent young man, but I'm not sure you comprehend just what those ten nuclear warheads can do."

"*Au contraire.* Do you know what the first injury will be to a person standing at ground zero?"

"Injury?" General Corrigan lets out a humorless laugh. "Injury hardly begins to describe—"

"A broken ankle, perhaps a broken leg, and certainly burst eardrums."

"Are you out of your mind? A person at ground zero will be vaporized."

"Not at first, not until after thirty seconds or so of quite unimaginable horror. At the moment of the air burst, there is a flash that will blind anyone whose eyes are open. The shock wave from the ionized atoms then causes a pressure wave that will buckle the ground with such force that it will break the bones of anyone standing there, hence our broken ankles. Then an atmospheric blast wave will surge out horizontally and flatten every manmade structure at ground zero, be it the Wailing Wall, the Church of the Holy Sepulchre, or the Mosque of Omar. The dynamic pressure of the blast will set loose winds of six hundred miles an hour. Anyone unfortunate enough to be in the vicinity will be picked up and swirled about in the firestorm. The radiant heat of the fireball will turn glass, metal and wood into ash, and a person's internal organs will simply burst into flame. You use the word, 'vaporized.' I prefer to think that a person is ultimately reduced to one's essential elements."

"What does that mean?"

"It really isn't 'ashes to ashes, dust to dust,' Hugh. More like ashes to nitrogen and hydrogen."

In the STRATCOM War Room, General Hugh Corrigan stares into space. "If you're attempting to be utterly repulsive, Mr. Morton, you're succeeding. If you want to shock us with your inhumanity, fine, we're shocked."

"Why, Hugh? It's *your* weapon. I'm just using it before you have the chance."

"It's not intended to be used," Corrigan says, angrily. "It's intended to deter war."

"How quaint a concept. But if you ask me, it's use it or lose it. And guess what, Hugh? You lose it, and I use it."

General Corrigan's shoulders slump. He is willing to try just about anything, so he signals Dr. Rosen to come to the phone. The balding psychiatrist looks like he slept in his sport coat, and in fact, he's been cat-napping most of the long night. Behind Dr. Rosen, three nervous middle-aged men in suits – one polyester, two brown plaid – look on.

"Mr. Morton, there's someone I'd like you to hear from," the general says.

"Pray tell, who could it be? Not Daddy, again. Hopefully, you've locked him up. He's quite insane, you know. What now, an expert hostage negotiator dyspeptic shrink?"

"David, this is Dr. Stuart Rosen," the FBI psychiatrist says in an unctuous tone. "Think of me as a master of ceremonies."

"Or masturbator," David adds, helpfully.

"David, we have three theological experts here representing a wide spectrum of views on the Book of Revelations."

In the launch control capsule, David listens listlessly while scanning the security monitors. On the screens, Army searchlights sweep the darkened perimeter of the missile base. Next to him, James still works at the computer, trying out a variety of seven-letter words in the blinking cursors. "Missile" doesn't work. Neither do "Goddard," "Nuclear," "Liberty," "Kennedy" or a hundred more improbable ones including "Sputnik" and "Hussein." James tries to imagine the technicians who programmed this sucker. It's a No Lone Zone with the codes, too. One technician could have the Enable Code, but another would possess the S.L.C. James conjures up a nerdy guy working for defense contractor, a guy who goes to the grocery store himself because he doesn't have a girlfriend or a wife. "Grocery" doesn't work. Neither does "forlorn."

The shrink goes on for a while about what he calls the "panorama" of interpretations of the Book of Revelations. "Our experts believe your view of the prophesied Apocalypse is, shall we say, premature."

"No doubt, like your ejaculations," David says.

"David, we need to discuss your current plans," Dr. Rosen says, ignoring the remark. "Let's put them in perspective with your overall goals, how you see yourself in the universe, your relation to people around you, what we might call your personal context, your—"

"Hugh!" David interrupts. "Why do you insult me with this

thumb-sucking bed-wetter?"

General Hugh Corrigan grimaces and doesn't respond. Next to him, Colonel Farris whispers, "First thing the fucker's said all night that makes any sense."

"Goodbye, doctor," David says. "Goodbye, Hugh."

The phone clicks off. Dr. Rosen wrinkles his forehead. "I'm not sure I liked the sound of those 'goodbye.' They had an air of finality about them."

General Corrigan would like to lend an air of finality to the F.B.I. psychiatrist, but an aide signals that he's wanted on another line. "If it's the President again, tell him to go to sleep. We'll wake him if—"

"It's the Pope," the aide says.

"What does he want?" Stunned.

"He wants to know if he can help."

"Sure. Ask if he can rappel two hundred feet down an elevator shaft with automatic weapons pointed up his skirts?"

Taking the telephone, the aide's tone is formal and respectful. "Your Holiness, the General asks for your prayers."

❧

Jack Jericho is on all fours, scrambling up the steep trail toward Chugwater Dam. Below him, the lights from the open silo cut into the night sky like signals to heaven. From this height he can see the war machinery in place on the perimeter of Base Camp Alpha. Searchlights from the camp sweep the mountainside, intermittently passing over him.

He thinks of Susan Burns and how he left her and what will happen to her if there is an all-out assault on the capsule. He quickens his pace, hoisting himself on reedy branches that grow out of the parched soil.

❧

The back side of the mountain is lit only by the half moon. Riding easily on a golden palomino, Kenosha leads a company of Night Stalkers up a boulder-strewn drainage ditch. Some of the soldiers appear unsteady on their horses, awkwardly clutching their saddle horns, cursing as their asses bounce in the saddle. A corporal's horse veers out of the ditch and into the trees. He kicks it in the ribs but doesn't pull hard enough on the reins, and the horse carries him straight into a tangle of low branches which knock him to the ground.

Kenosha looks at the soldiers and wonders if mules might have been a better idea. For a moment he ponders how his ancestors ever lost their land to the white man. Numbers, he knows. Too many men, too much firepower.

Adrenalized by the impending action, Captain Kyle Clancy slaps his horse's rump with a cowboy hat and catches up with Kenosha at the point. Clancy has ridden before and he is comfortable in the saddle, holding the reins loosely in one hand, letting the other hand dangle at his side. "Whoopee! On a night like this, there's only one thing better than a good fuck, and that's a good fight."

"What is a good fight, captain?"

"One you win, of course. Cutting off the other guy's nuts before he cuts off yours." Captain Clancy notes the pistol in Kenosha's holster. "Lord, what's that? The barrel must be a foot long."

"Exactly. The Colt .45 Peacemaker."

"Peacemaker," the captain muses. "Just like the Peacekeeper missile."

"Only this one was made in 1873, the single action army model. It's signed and numbered, the third one ever made."

"How the hell did you ever get it?"

Kenosha whispers something to his palomino, then says, "It was bestowed on a member of my family by General Custer."

"What?"

"At Little Bighorn. To my great-great grandfather. Of course, the general was dead at the time."

The captain finally gets it. "Why you sly fox! One of your

ancestors was in the greatest Indian battle of all time. You son-of-bitches sure kicked Custer's ass."

"It was a disastrous victory," Kenosha says.

"Whadaya mean?"

"It was the humiliation at Little Bighorn that forced Washington to set about a serious war. It was a success for my people only as Pearl Harbor was a success for the Japanese."

Clancy chews this over for a while. There is more to this Kenosha than he recognized at first. Vietnam. The Silver Star. His past with the colonel. The Indian is not a bad companion for battle, he decides.

က

David intently scans the security monitors, but there is no movement. He uses the walkie-talkie to check on his sentries, then turns back to James, who still works at the computer. A rifle slung over a shoulder, Rachel keeps a watch on Susan.

James angrily bangs his fist on the console. "It's no use. I've tried every trick in the book. Without the slick password, we're locked out."

"Have you prayed for divine guidance?" David asks.

"Hey, Davy, cut the shit. I remember when we were breaking into mainframes and mail-ordering dildoes for our French teacher."

"Just deliver me the password, James." David closes his eyes and attempts to conjure up a vision. Only colors come, a bright, runny red that he takes for blood and that same flowing gray that reminds him of a banner blowing in the wind. The images make no sense to him, and he tries to let them go. Still, the notion of the blood stays with him."

"They will attack soon," David says, "and blood will flow like a river that has flooded its banks. Unless you come up with the code, we will die without bringing about the New Jerusalem."

"But we will live forever," Rachel says. "It is prophesied. You have seen it yourself."

"I have seen many things," David says, enigmatically.

"And you cannot separate the visions, can you?" Susan Burns asks, a note of derision in her voice.

"Be still!" David commands.

But she will not. Susan Burns believes she is going to die at David's hand. To fight him, to stop him from killing so many others, she probes for the weak spot. "You cannot tell the delusions from the visions, the warped dreams from psychic phenomena."

"Shut up!"

Rachel stands and moves menacingly in front of Susan. "Don't listen to her, David."

"You are plagued by doubts, David Morton," Susan says, taunting him. "Just as you were as a child. Your father built something, something awesome and powerful, and what have you done? You sneak into your father's house like a vandal spray painting graffiti in a church. Your greatest fears are about to be realized. You are about to fail in the eyes of your father."

David roars like a wounded beast and yanks the rifle away from Rachel. "Enough! Damn you, I have had enough of your mockery!" He jams the barrel into Susan's forehead, pushing her back against the wall. She refuses to close her eyes, and instead, glares back at David whose own eyes blaze with maddened fury. "I will not fail! And you will not live to see my glory!"

"Shoot me!" she yells at him. "It won't change a thing. You're still not the half man your father was. You're not half the man he is. He's beaten you again."

"My father has nothing to do with this."

"He made you. He made the missile. You're both his children. Your brother is the bomb, David. You said it yourself. Your father always loved the bomb more than he loved you. Sibling rivalry, and you came in second."

"Psychological claptrap!" He switches the safety off and eases his finger onto the trigger. "Sometimes, doctor, a cigar is only a cigar, and a missile is only a missile."

"When you were a pacifist, you wanted to destroy the bomb to get even with your father. Now you're trying to destroy it another way, a way that will destroy him. This has nothing to do with Jerusalem or the Bible or anything else."

"Don't listen to her!" Rachel screams.

"It's even your father's code that baffles you," Susan says. "It's his handiwork that has stymied you again."

"Wrong! My father retired before they added the code," David says, lowering the rifle. The shadow of a thought crosses his face, and Susan fears she has made a mistake. Realizing now she gave David information he did not have. She wanted him out of control, wanted him raging, turning the gun on her, and then on himself. Instead, he is pondering something, and Susan's terror is greater than if the gun were still jammed against her head.

David looks at Lieutenant Owens and says, "Wasn't the S.L.C. added in the last year?"

"Yeah, less than a year ago."

"James, what about it?"

"Your Pop may have been retired, Davy, but his fingerprints are all over this program, everything from terminology to digital access routes. They must have called him back in as a consultant. I double-damn guarantee you, this is his baby."

David has forgotten all about Susan. He rushes to James. "Why didn't you tell me?"

"I don't know. It didn't seem—"

"Hush! Let me think. My father came up with the code. I can do this." He squeezes his eyes shut. Tries to conjure something up, but there's interference, something kicking around in his brain, something...

"James! What did you say?"

"Huh? Nothing. I'm letting you think or whatever the hell it is you do."

"No, a moment ago. What did you say?"

James licks his lips and tries to remember. "I said it didn't seem relevant who designed—"

"No! Before that. You guarantee me..."

"'This is his baby.' That's all I said. 'This is his baby.' Why? Do you see something, Davy? Do you have a vision?"

David Morton smiles to himself. He has no vision. Psychic phenomena are fine when they come, but the bitchy doctor is right. He cannot separate the wheat from the chaff. But this time, he does not need paranormal powers. He needs only memory and logic, and he is thinking very clearly, indeed.

-49-
A Seven-Letter Word

Kenosha and Captain Clancy lead the Night Stalkers up the steep slope, near the top of the mountain. Suddenly, a gunshot from the darkness rings above their heads. Other gunshots, and two soldiers topple from their horses. Clancy tries to find the source of the gunfire, but seeing no flash, and with the sound echoing off the rocks, he cannot. Kenosha points higher on the slope, and Clancy signals his men to take cover. More fire, and one of the horses spooks, throwing its rider. The other soldiers dismount and dive for cover. Kenosha calmly walks his horse out of the ditch and joins the captain behind a boulder.

In Army parlance, the soldiers establish a "hasty fighting position," then unleash a volley of automatic weapons fire, killing a number of rocks, but no commandos. Return gunfire keeps them pinned down.

Clancy looks through infrared binoculars, scanning the mountainside above them. He sees the flash of gunshots in the darkness. "Only four of them, but the bastards have the high ground. Never expected they'd post sentries on this side of the mountain."

"It is not the first time the Army has underestimated an enemy's prowess," Kenosha says.

Clancy shoots him a look.

"Little Big Horn is not far from here, just over the Montana border."

"Yeah, well you're on the other side now, chief, and if you've got any bright ideas, let me hear them."

"As a matter of fact," Kenosha says, "I do."

∾

Jack Jericho climbs a jagged cliff above the trail on the front side of Chugwater Mountain, pale moonbeams reflecting off massive boulders over his head. He claws at a crease in the rocks, slips, catches himself and keeps going. He can see the lights of the dam and its control buildings above him. Again, he slips and nearly falls, his boots digging into the cliff, seeking a hold, dislodging loose pebbles, which trickle down the slope. He regains his footing and pauses at the sound of gunfire from the backside of the mountain.

It's begun, he thinks, and quickens his pace.

Below the cliff, farther down the trail, the pebbles come to rest alongside a combat boot. The man wearing the boots looks down and then up at the cliff, then resumes following his prey.

∾

James sits with his hands poised like a pianist above the keyboard of the computer. "It's a seven digit password. We're talking eight billion possible combinations if it's alphabetical only. If it's mixed, alpha-numeric, there'd be—"

"No," David says, "there's only one."

"You're sure, aren't you?"

"I'm sure it's one of just a few choices. All I have to do is climb inside my father's warped brain and find them."

"Okay," James says. "Let it rip."

"I'll do it," David says, motioning for the flight chair.

James shrugs and gets up. David sits, takes a breath and hits a key. On the monitor, the letter "M" replaces the first cursor. David fills in the rest of the word, "M-A-T-A-D-O-R."

"What is it?" James asks.

"The nickname for the XB-61 missile my dear Daddy worked on in the fifties."

The computer makes a whirring sound. Then a discordant beep, and the screen flashes, "Password Rejected. Enter Secondary Launch Code Password."

David types, "A-E-R-O-B-E-E."

""Another missile?" James asks.

"The X-8," David tells him.

"Who would even remember the name?"

"I think that's the idea."

Again, the computer rejects the word. "One more try," David says, punching in, "P-O-L-A-R-I-S."

They wait in silence, and after a moment, another rejection message. David sits staring into the monitor, then says, "My father's baby."

"That'd be you. But 'David' has only five letters."

"The son-of-a-bitch could have been making a joke. A perverted private joke that only he would get."

"What are you talking about?"

David quickly taps out, "O-E-D..."

"No," James says. "It couldn't be."

David smiles, watching his own reflection in the monitor, and hits another key. "We'll soon find out."

At that moment, in the STRATCOM War Room, the Big Board shows four letters and three pulsating cursors:

O E D I _ _ _

Colonel Farris wrinkles his forehead and says, "Ed-dy...Oh-dee? Now what's he doing?"

Professor Lionel Morton motors over in his wheelchair and blurts out a bitter laugh just as a "P" is added to the screen.

"Goddamit! He's got the password. He's got the code."

In the launch control capsule, David Morton's eyes burn with hate. In the reflection of the monitor, he resembles a younger Lionel Morton. On the screen, 'OEDIPUS' stares back at him like a vicious taunt. Five seconds after the "S" appears, the computer's mechanical voice intones, "Secondary Launch Code Password Confirmed. Re-Enter Enable Code. Launch Sequence in Progress."

James slaps David on the back. Rachel bursts into tears of joy. Susan slumps against the back wall in anguish.

At STRATCOM, the mechanical voice delivers the same message: "Launch Sequence in Progress." The uniformed officers are frozen in place. Professor Morton hits a button on the wheelchair and moves past the contingent of brass. "Checkmate, gentlemen."

-50-
Flood Gates

Four commandos with automatic weapons are hunkered down behind boulders, firing straight down the drainage ditch at the dug-in Night Stalkers.

The Night Stalkers load 40 mm. grenades into M203 launchers and let them fly. The launcher has a range of 350 meters and is accurate to about half that distance. The commandos are 150 meters away, but the angle of the slope throws off the targeting. Grenades land twenty feet behind the commandos and rain dirt on them, but they keep shooting.

Other soldiers unleash soaring tracer shots, incandescent threads illuminating the night. Still, they are pinned down by the commandos above them. Captain Clancy speaks to Colonel Zwick on the radio. "Colonel, we need air support. Gimme some Cobra gunships."

Kenosha grabs the colonel's arm. "There is another way."

છે

The gantry moves vertically up the silo wall, stopping at the level of the PK's fourth stage. Wearing white gloves, David holds the computer box as if it were a newborn babe. He uses an elbow to hit a button, and the gantry extends horizontally to the missile. Slowly, carefully, he fits the box back into its compartment, reattaches several plugs and hits a switch. The computer springs to life. He replaces the metal plate and inserts the four bolts.

For a moment, David just looks at the missile. Then he lays a hand on the titanium shroud, the silvery cap of the nose cone. Finally, he places his cheek against the smooth metal and spreads his arms around it. He stands there, listening to the heartbeat of the beast. At peace.

❦

Looking down the slope, the four commandos of the Holy Church of Revelations see a horse without a rider bolt from the drainage ditch and race into the woods. They do not see the man hanging onto the horse's neck, his body tucked away on the far side. In a moment, the horse disappears.

Lying prone at the front of the Night Stalkers's position, a soldier opens up with an M-60 machine gun, spraying 200 rounds per minute up the slope. With their assault rifles, other soldiers lay down a blistering barrage, providing cover, as Kenosha rides out of the woods and up the rocky incline around the right flank. The slope is impossibly steep and covered with a loose, slippery gravel. Kenosha navigates by memory and by the light of the tracer rounds. The horse slips backward in the gravel and raises up its head in fear, and Kenosha whispers soothing endearments.

Higher up the mountain, the four commandos dig deep into their hiding places, burying their heads, bullets ricocheting around them.

In the drainage ditch, Captain Clancy looks at his stopwatch. Four minutes. Kenosha said he could get up there in four minutes. "That old bastard better be in place," he says to himself, "because we can't help him now." He raises his right hand in front of his forehead, palm to the front and swings his hand up and down several times in front of his face. Though it looks like a drunken salute, it is the cease fire signal, and the men obey. In a moment, there is no sound coming from the ditch. "Now!" Clancy orders.

A soldier with an M203 launcher pulls the trigger, and a grenade sails high over the commandos' position. "Eyes closed! Everybody!" Clancy yells.

Flash-bang! The burst of a million candlepower isotropic grenade ignites the sky.

Then, from the top of the mountain comes a blood-curdling war whoop.

The soldiers hold their fire. Kenosha is behind the commandos. Any gunfire from below would be as likely to hit him as the enemy. He is on his own.

Kenosha rides down the ditch, the blazing light behind him. He attacks the exposed commandos from the rear. They turn and look up, blinded by the bright flash, their eyes spotted with thousands of pinpricks in dazzling colors. What they see reflected off their corneas freezes them.

Indians on horseback!

Screaming at the night in a language they have never heard.

An avalanche of attacking warriors waving long-barreled pistols in the electrified air.

Kenosha holds the palomino's reins with one hand and aims the heavy revolver with the other. Shooting a target from a moving horse is akin to surfing and playing the violin at the same time. But Kenosha takes down the first commando where he stands. The second tries to hide between two boulders, squeezing into a crevice, but gets stuck. Unable to move, he aims his rifle in the general vicinity of the moon, and Kenosha drops him with two shots to the chest. The third commando flattens to a prone position and gets off a quick burst that sails over the Indian's head. Kenosha pulls the palomino into a zig-zag gallop, misses with the first shot, then gut shoots the commando with the next. The fourth commando runs from behind the rocks, scurrying over a boulder, trying to get the hell out of Dodge.

Cr-ack. Captain Clancy drops him with a hundred-fifty yard scoped shot to the head.

"Damn good shooting!" he yells up the slope to Kenosha. "We make a damn fine team."

એ

Jack Jericho climbs over the railing of the observation deck that juts out from the dam control building and overlooks the missile facility far below. He crosses the deck and peers through a window where illuminated gauges and meters glow in the darkened control room. The controls are run by computer and monitored twenty-four hours a day at the central water district headquarters outside Laramie. The building itself is deserted. Jericho tries a door leading from the deck to the control room.

Locked.

He knows he has very little time. A few moments ago, the sky lit up like the Fourth of July. Now, the gunfire from the backside of the mountain has stopped, but he figures it was just a prelude.

A table and three redwood chairs sit on the observation deck. Jericho picks up one of the chairs. Heavier than it looks. He struggles with it and approaches the window.

એ

Kenosha and Captain Clancy ride side-by-side on horseback, approaching the dam control building from the back side of the mountain. The rest of Clancy's men follow. They are chattering happily, adrenaline pumping. They've had a taste of battle. Now they want the main course.

They pull up behind the control building and Clancy speak into his radio. "Jackal reporting. Objective one achieved, sir. Delta team..." He winks at Kenosha, "plus one tough Indian, ready for kickoff."

Colonel Zwick says something, but Clancy can't hear it over a discordant crash, the sound of glass breaking.

"Now what the hell was that?" Clancy says.

✍

It is 4:35 a.m. when Jericho steps through the broken window into the control room. He navigates in the dark through a maze of overhead piping, meters, valves and gauges, listening to the steady hum of machinery. A window on the far side of the room looks out over the dam itself. Sodium-vapor lights illuminate the water far below, an artificial lake created by closing off Chugwater River and diverting it to a trickle that runs down the front of the mountain through the aqueduct.

Jericho finds a switch and flicks on a set of overhead lights. He wanders around, examining the massive control panels, not knowing exactly what he's looking for, and not knowing if his plan will work. He's good with machinery, but the names on the panels speak a foreign language: Riprap Sensors; Filtration Governor; Spillway Intake. Then, Sluice Gate.

Which had to be the one. A chrome wheel four feet in diameter is attached to the Sluice Gate panel. Jericho tries to turn it counter-clockwise, opening the gate, but it doesn't budge. He tries to turn it clockwise. Still, nothing. He braces both feet against a floor panel and gives it everything he's got, but nothing moves except a disk in his lumbar spine that threatens to explode.

Okay, the wheel is locked.

Which makes sense.

You don't want some boozed-up technician stumbling into the controls and opening the flood gates.

He looks at the panel and finds rows of numbered green and red lights and switches. Somewhere, there's a release for the Sluice Gate valve. How much harm can he do, he wonders, by hitting a few switches. Probably less than he's going to by finding the right switch. Just as he's about to find out, he there comes a sharp and angry voice: "Infidel!"

Jericho whirls around. He barely notices the shotgun pointed at his chest. Instead he is drawn to the face of the ugliest man he has ever seen. The man's skin is a mass of raw, festering blisters. Blood mixes with pus on open sores. "Do you know who I am?" The voice slurs from a mouth hidden under swollen, purple lips.

"Your voice is familiar, and you sort of look like Elvis if they just dug him up."

Ker-click. The man pumps the shotgun. Jericho's Uzi is slung across a shoulder. It might as well be at Fort Bragg.

"They call me Matthew."

"Oh," Jericho says, remembering their encounter in the kitchen. "You're the guy who can't stay away from the french fries."

Matthew's lips twist like fat worms into a grotesque smile. "I want to see your pain when I shoot you. I want you to die slowly."

"You don't have to shoot," Jericho says, not giving in to the fear. "Just looking at your face ought to do it."

"I'll cut your legs off at the knees!" Matthew drops the barrel low, aiming for Jericho's lower legs.

Jericho leaps up, grabs an overhead pipe and swings his legs as high as he can. The blast caroms off the floor beneath him, and he can feel ricocheting pellets stinging his rump. Matthew pumps again, and Jericho dives from the pipe, shoulder rolls under a counter and out the other side. A second blast shatters a row of gauges and monitors.

Jericho scurries on all fours along the floor. *Ka-boom.* A third shot pelts him with shards of shattered glass from the light fixtures. Once behind a table, Jericho comes up and fires a short burst from the Uzi, inflicting serious wounds on a bank of computer consoles but nothing else. Though he can't see Matthew, he hears the shotgun pump, and the next blast blows up an electrical panel, which sizzles with orange sparks. Jericho fires a burst at the opposite wall, then scrambles around the eight-foot high control panel, peers out, and spots Matthew turned the other way. Jericho pulls the trigger, and *click.*

Empty!

Matthew spins and faces him.

Jericho dives for cover behind a green, ceiling-high control panel. Matthew follows, shotgun held at gut level. He wheels around a corner, but Jericho is not there. He spins three hundred sixty degrees, looking for his game.

"Come out. Show your cowardly face."

Suddenly, Jericho dives from the top of the control panel, knocking Matthew over. They tumble to the floor, entangled, and the shotgun skitters away. Matthew shoves Jericho off and gets to his feet. Jericho is on one knee when a thunderous kick to the chest sits him down again. He expects Matthew to come at him, but instead, the commando pulls a 9 mm. pistol from under a bloused pantleg and backs up, putting distance between them. He raises the pistol and says, "I have fifteen bullets, and I will use every one of them. You won't die until the last one enters your brain."

Jericho's hand flashes from behind his neck, and a blade glints in the air. The soft *pffffut* sounds like a melon being sliced in two. The handle of the Jimmy Lile protrudes from Matthew's throat. He staggers backward and falls into the control panel, bracing himself with a hand that hits a red switch.

Lights flash and a buzzer sounds.

Matthew bounces off the panel and pulls the knife out of his throat. As he does, the blood erupts, a geyser spraying the ceiling. He crumples to the floor, next to the Sluice Gate wheel. Jericho looks at the wheel and the flashing lights. Why not? He gives the wheel a counter-clockwise turn, and it spins free.

Jericho can hear the movement of machinery, can feel the vibrations beneath his feet. Deep inside the steel and concrete wall of the dam, the huge sluice gates open and water surges from the spillway into the aqueducts.

Jericho checks on Matthew. Dead. He returns to the wheel and spins it wide open. A roar can be heard in the control room, and outside, water cascades from the spillway, overflows the narrow aqueduct and pours toward the missile facility far below.

Jericho picks up his knife, wipes off the blood, and walks to the window overlooking the observation deck. He sees a waterfall tumbling down the mountain.

"Freeze!"

Ignoring the suggestion, Jericho dives to the floor and scrambles under a counter. Across the control room, Captain Clancy stands, legs spread, his M-16 at hip level. "Son-of-a-bitch." He peppers the wall with gunfire, and motions to three of his men to flare out across the room. "Corporal, cover the exit!"

Corporal? Jericho hears the captain. From beneath a desk, he calls out, "Army? If you're Army, identify yourselves."

A rapid burst of gunfire tears up equipment on top of the desk. "How's that for identification, scuzzbag?"

"Hold you fire!" Jericho yells. "I'm Air Force."

"Whose?"

The question throws Jericho for a moment. "Ours. The U.S. of A."

"Are you that dickhead who wouldn't get off the base?"

Jericho briefly considers whether there might be a second dickhead to whom the question might apply. "That's me."

"Hands behind head. Come out slowly."

Jericho does as he's told. "Jack Jericho, Airman E-5, United States Air Force, 318th Missile Squadron."

The captain gives a once over to the commando fatigues. "You're out of uniform, sergeant."

"Occupational hazard, sir."

"Lemme see your tags."

"Threw 'em out, didn't match the apparel."

Clancy appraises him suspiciously. Just then, a lieutenant dashes in from the observation deck. "Captain, quick! We gotta close the valves or something. The whole damn valley is flooding. We'll never get down the mountain."

Clancy surveys the room. The dead commando, the blown out control panels. "What the hell's going on in here?"

Gesturing toward the wheel, Jericho says, "I opened the sluice gates."

"Why?" The captain doesn't wait for an answer. He goes over to the wheel and tries to close it, but it won't budge. "Shit!"

"It's open all the way," Jericho says. "The water pressure's so great, there's no way to close it manually."

"Then how—" Clancy interrupts himself. He's looking at a gauge labeled, "Emergency Sluice Gate Closure." The switch dangles uselessly on its wires, the glass facing on the gauge shattered by a shotgun blast. Furious, the captain bangs his fist into the control panel, shaking loose more broken glass. He turns toward the window, watching the water pour down the mountain. Then he raises his M-16 toward Jericho's chest. "Sergeant, give me one good reason I shouldn't splatter your guts from here to Hanoi."

Jericho is trying futilely to think of an answer when Kenosha strides into the control room with the bearing of a great warrior. "Because Jack Jericho is a good man," he says.

-51-
Hello Darkness

"Flight switch on," David says.

"Check," Rachel responds.

"Launcher on."

"Check."

"Enable on."

"Check."

"Enter Enable Code, now," David orders.

"Six," Rachel says.

"I agree," David responds.

David's hand is steady as he turns over a red flap on the console and spins a thumbwheel. He stops at the number, "6."

"B," Rachel says.

"I agree." David flips the second flap and spins its thumbwheel, this time stopping on the letter, "B." He pauses and listens to an old song that swirls around in his consciousness. The song has a special meaning for him, he always believed. "'Hello darkness, my old friend,'" he sings aloud. "'I've come to talk with you again.'"

281

Susan Burns watches as David and Rachel work at the console, re-entering the Enable Code. Going through the familiar protocol, David adds an "8" on the third thumbwheel.

"6-B-8-A-3..." appears on the monitor.

"Seven," Rachel says.

"I agree," David responds, thumbing the wheel to number seven, then hitting the Initiate switch. He leans back in his flight chair as three chimes ring a tune of their own.

☙

Pandemonium in the STRATCOM War Room.

"Kickoff now!" General Corrigan orders. "Kickoff now!"

"Go, go, go!" Colonel Farris yells in the phone to Colonel Zwick at Base Camp Alpha.

Officers and aides dash everywhere. Coded telexes are sent and received from the National Command Center in the Pentagon. It is five a.m. in Wyoming, and seven a.m. in Washington, and the President is already awake when the direct line from the Pentagon rings on his bedroom phone. In a moment, he will be on the phone with the president of Israel. The president cannot believe that a nuclear holocaust is about to happen on his watch. He will plead. He will promise aid. He will even cry. But the Israelis vow to set Operation Masada in motion. Once the PK hits apogee, Israeli planes will take off with their nuclear payloads that are being readied even now.

General Corrigan stands motionless, a rock in the midst of the turbulent sea. Colonel Farris stands behind the general, awaiting further orders, trying to appear calm. Watching from his wheelchair, not even attempting to hide his mocking smile, Professor Lionel Morton gestures toward the Big Board. "You must admit, Hugh, that the PK is a thing of beauty."

"Lionel, if you don't wipe that smirk off your face, I'll have you arrested."

On the Big Board, there is a schematic diagram of the PK missile and the flashing message: "LF 47-Q LAUNCH ENABLED." The computer's female mechanical voice intones, "Enable Code confirmed. Secondary Launch Code confirmed. Confidence is high."

"I want continuous progress reports on the assault," the general tells Colonel Farris. He has approved Colonel Zwick's the two-pronged attack plan: the direct assault to get Special Forces to the elevator shaft and the surprise descent down the mountain to give the Night Stalkers the chance to rappel down the silo walls.

The colonel has the phone to his ear. Putting a hand over the mouthpiece, he says, "Something strange, general. You better take a look."

A technician punches a button, and the Big Board is filled with an aerial video shot from a helicopter. A spotlight illuminates a raging torrent of water surging down the mountain.

General Corrigan says, "What the hell is that?"

"We thought the bastards had blown the dam, but it seems one of our men opened the sluice gates," Colonel Farris says.

"One of our men!"

"Well, not exactly, sir. That Air Force E-5, the maintenance man. He's stranded Delta on top the mountain, and the water's headed toward the silo."

The general grinds his teeth. In his younger days, as a fighter pilot, he wore a plastic mouthpiece at night sleep to keep from crushing his molars into dust while he slept. "What the hell was he thinking?"

"Thinking? He's just a sergeant."

Professor Morton sits nearby in his wheelchair, listening. He coughs out a laugh and says, "Your erstwhile sergeant thought he could stop my missile with a squirt gun."

❧

The men and machines of Base Camp Alpha are massed on the perimeter. Wooden ammunition crates have been cracked open and emptied. For the tenth time, men check their weapons, clicking magazines into place again and again. Faces and hands are covered with camouflage grease. Engines rev on the great pieces of mobile armor, fouling the early morning air with diesel fumes.

Standing in the command tent, Colonel Zwick yells into his radio transmitter to Captain Clancy, still stranded atop the mountain. "Jackal, I'm sorry, but you're on your own. We gotta kickoff without you."

The battle begins with two gunshots.

Two expert Army marksmen – snipers by any other name – each with a night-scoped spotter and M24 rifle are ensconced in a camouflaged bunker dug into a raised bluff. They are two hundred meters in front of the base camp perimeter, nine hundred meters from the missile base sentry post.

Well within range.

In Desert Storm, each had confirmed kills at the magical thousand yard distance. Superbly conditioned in both body and mind, they can kill without their pulse rates topping fifty-five. Keeping it under the speed limit, they call it. Now, at a signal, they fire simultaneously. It takes nearly three seconds for the *cra-ack* of the rifles to reach the sentry post. By which point, both commando sentries are dead.

A moment later, four Abrams main battle tanks lurch down the gentle slope from base camp, cross a open field, then the access road, and finally tear through the perimeter fence of the missile base. Bradley Fighting Vehicles are close behind, fanning out toward the security building and the barracks. A mounted machine gun rakes the buildings, and commandos return the fire from dug-in positions.

Soldiers swarm through the woods, tearing apart commandos on the way to the elevator housing. The soldiers are well trained and well equipped. Some carry the new lightweight machine guns called SAWs. Others fire grenades from M-203 launchers attached below the barrels of their M-16 battle rifles. Some of the Special Forces platoons – Green Berets and Rangers – also carry Beretta

9 mm. pistols and combat knives. Their ammunition is virtually limitless. Reinforcements are ready if needed. It is not a question of whether the Army will take back the base, but how long it will take and how many – hostages, soldiers, enemy – will die.

The commandos are outnumbered and outgunned, but they gamely fight back, welcoming their own Armageddon. They are not stupid men. There was always an awareness that it would be easier to attack the sleepy missile base than to defend it. They are prepared to die, and that always makes for good fighting men. But still, they are not prepared for the ferocity of the onslaught. How could they be? Their training – mock battles, target practice and obstacle courses – was a fantasy camp for would-be soldiers. The men facing them now are hardened Special Op soldiers plus the armored cavalry, gritty professionals whose job is simply to make other men die.

It is one thing to lie comfortably in the prone shooting position on a range, adjusting the battlesight aperture on the M-16A2, rotating the windage knob just a tad, taking your time, exhaling, then zeroing in on a stationery target. One that doesn't shoot back. It is quite another thing to have a horde of trained killers swarming at you from three directions, wanting nothing so much as to kill you and all your friends.

During the day and night of occupation of the missile base, the commandos have buried several dozen US MI 14 anti-personnel mines in the woods. They were stolen from the Denver Armory, surplus munitions dating from the 1950's. Half don't explode at all. The others explode harmlessly as the tanks crunch over them. Randomly placed "dragon's teeth," concrete blocks intended to break the tank's tracks, slow the huge death machines, but do not stop them. Once past the obstacles, the tanks open up with their 120 mm. main guns, blasting holes in the fortifications constructed by the commandos. With each shell, dirt and debris splatters the men behind the barricades. As Special Op troops advance on foot, Bradley Fighting Vehicles spray the commando position with machine gun fire and occasional bursts from their Bushmaster 25 mm. cannons.

Still, the commandos fight like men possessed. Which, of course, they are. Possessed by the passion of their leader, possessed by a wishful belief in the Apocalypse, possessed by the desire to be more than the faceless nobodies they always have been.

And it all comes true. Just as Brother David said it would. They stand their ground, battle valiantly. They recklessly toss grenades in close quarters, for if you plan to die anyway, it is best to take the enemy with you. Some are decent shots, at least at close range, and they take down the occasional soldier.

And when the end is near, when they are outnumbered and nearly overrun, some charge forward with bayonets mounted, like ancient Biblical warriors. They die glorious deaths. The Hereafter, they know with all their hearts, will be nothing short of eternal bliss.

-52-
Rotate and Hold

Water overflows the spillway and pours down the mountain. Captain Clancy stands on the dam's observation deck, listening to gunfire from the missile facility below.

Caged.

Crazed.

Missing the fight, the kind of fight he lives for. And would die for.

He stalks back and forth, pounding his fist against the deck's railing. Knowing his mood, Clancy's men give him distance. Oblivious, Jack Jericho works his survival knife into the latch of a storage locker at one end of the deck. Clancy stomps toward him.

"You stupid son-of-a-bitch! You horse's ass worthless scum-sucking, shit-eating son-of-a-bitch."

Jericho ignores the captain and cracks open the locker.

Which only makes the captain angrier. "Didn't you know that

big cock is cold launched?"

"Yeah, I know. I run the generator that compresses the propulsion gases."

"Then what did you think? That you could drown the missile?"

Jericho digs a coil of heavy rope and a tool belt out of the shed. He tosses a couple of screwdrivers out of the belt, leaves two wrenches and a gas-powered stud driver in, then fastens the belt around his waist. "I thought I could foul them up, make that lunatic think it was a Biblical flood, Noah or somebody. I don't know, I just thought I should try to stop them."

"You stopped *us*, you pathetic excuse for a soldier, you worthless piece of whale shit."

"I need a gun."

"What!"

"Or just some clips for the Uzi."

"Are you out of the mind? You're under arrest! You'll be court-martialed."

With the rope coiled around his shoulder, Jericho crawls over the deck railing onto the jagged rocks. A few feet away, a vicious torrent of water surges down the mountainside.

Clancy yells over the noise of the rushing water. "Where do you think you're going?"

"I've got an appointment with my psychiatrist."

"The hell you do!" Clancy menacingly gestures with his M-16. You think you can surf the mountain? If you didn't drown, you'd find a way to fuck up the rest of the operation. You're staying put, sergeant."

Jericho takes a first step on the rocks, then drops to all fours. He reaches out toward a fallen tree trunk as thick as a man's waist. "Can't do that, sir."

"What!"

"I promised."

"Yeah, well here's another promise. You take one more step, I'll shoot you. I'll blow your kneecaps off."

"That's pretty much what he said," Jericho says.

"Who?"

"His name was Matthew. Everybody wants to kill me. You, him, Brother David, and all of you seem to prefer the most painful method possible. I guess I bring out the worst in people."

Clancy is livid. He wants to shoot somebody, and if it can't be the terrorists, it might as well be Jack Jericho, who deserves it just as much. Maybe he *is* a terrorist. Maybe he's one of the crazies, and this was just a cover. The Indian could have been wrong about his old fishing buddy. Clancy clicks off the safety on the rifle. "I'm ordering you to stand down, sergeant. Disregard the order at your own peril."

Jericho has his hands on the tree trunk and is tying the rope around a gnarled branch. "I've followed orders before, captain. I've done the right thing, and the safe thing, and it didn't work out. I'm through following orders. I'm doing what I think is right. You do what you have to do." Jericho leans down over the tree trunk and ties an end of the rope around his waist.

"Halt!" The rifle is at Clancy's shoulder, and he squeezes his left eye shut. "Last warning. Halt!"

Clancy knows his men are watching him. He's never backed down from anyone. He also has never shot an American before, not even a worthless airman.

Jericho shoves the heavy trunk toward the rushing water. It catches on a rock.

Clancy has a clear shot at the back of Jericho's skull. He drops the rifle lower until he can put a bullet through the meaty part of Jericho's hamstrings. Cripple but not kill.

Jericho braces his legs and pushes against the trunk, clearing the rock.

Clancy tightens his finger on the trigger. Then eases off.

The tree trunk slips over the side of the rocks, and Jericho with it. In a second, they are swallowed by the raging torrent.

Clancy lets the rifle fall to his side. "Go get 'em, Noah," he says with resignation.

❦

David and Rachel sit in the flight chairs. James stands behind them, excitedly pacing. Susan, her hands cuffed behind her, nervously watches from her position on the floor.

"Time and target complete," David says.

"I have good lights," Rachel responds.

The console printer unleashes a blizzard of paper as the launch commands are confirmed and recorded on printouts.

"Lock your board," David says.

Rachel hits a switch. "Board locked."

David pushes down the Enable switch. "Insert your key," he orders.

Simultaneously, David and Rachel slide their keys into the slots twelve feet apart on the console.

"Key inserted," Rachel says.

David scans a security monitor showing his men falling back toward the elevator shaft as the Army troops advance. Calmly, he says, "Key turn clockwise...on my mark."

From behind them, James watches the console as if hypnotized. He does not see Susan roll to her feet, drop into a crouch, then bring her arms underneath her, stepping through her clasped hands. She is still handcuffed, but now, her arms are in front of her chest.

David counts slowly, "Three two, one..."

Suddenly, Susan dives forward, loops her cuffed hands around Rachel's neck. Rachel's right hand reflexively releases the key and claws at Susan's arms. Susan roughly pulls Rachel sideways out of her chair.

"Rotate and hold," David says, as if nothing has happened. "James, take over the deputy's chair and be kind enough to rotate and hold."

James reaches for the key, but Susan kicks him in the groin, doubling him over. Rachel is on the floor, holding her neck, gasping. The key remains in the slot, unturned.

"Susan, please turn the key," David says. "And hold on my

count." His voice is confident, the voice of a man whose orders are obeyed without question.

She stops, thunderstruck at his words. "What!"

"End your pain. End your anger. It can all be over. Let us welcome the Apocalypse together."

James gets to one knee and is ready to tackle Susan. "No!" David commands. "She is one of us. Only now does she realize it. My will has triumphed over her secular pseudo science."

Susan looks deeply into David's penetrating stare. She reaches for the key, her hand resting on it without moving. Their eyes are locked on each other for a long moment.

"Rotate key on my command," he says softly.

She breaks his hypnotic gaze. "Like hell!" She yanks the key from the slot and dashes toward the open blast door. David scowls and hits a red button. The door begins to slowly close. Susan sees it, thinks she can make it.

Rachel gets to her feet, grabs for Susan but misses her. James comes from behind and dives at Susan, taking her down at the ankles, a desperate cornerback tripping up the receiver who has broken free. As she falls, Susan whips her cuffed hands forward. The key sails out the narrowing opening of the door and skitters across the concrete floor of the tunnel, sliding ...sliding...sliding until it comes to rest at the edge of a metal grate where it balances for a precious second, then plops into the black water of the sump.

David glares at James. "Get it! Now!"

Her face flushed, Rachel stomps toward David. "And you thought she was under your spell," she says, bitterly. "Vanity of vanities. Even with you, David, all is vanity."

-53-
Fire in the Hole

The Army troops work their way across the grounds. In minutes, they have taken the security building. No commandos surrender;

no one survives.

The troops head across the bridge toward the elevator housing where the himself Ezekiel and four of his comrades have retreated. One-by-one, the commandos fall under the ferocious attack. Propping up a bulky M-60 machine gun, Ezekiel stands with his back to the elevator housing door, spraying lethal 7.62 mm. shells across the bridge. He cuts down half-a-dozen soldiers and pins down the rest.

ᴄ⁄ᴐ

Driven by the fierce current, a tree trunk rushes down the flooded river bed toward the open missile silo, bouncing over rapids and banging into boulders. The trunk spins in the water, collides with more flotsam, then turns over, exposing a man's hand.

Then an arm.

Then a head.

Jack Jericho appears lifeless as the heavy tree trunk continues to twirl, helpless against the forces of nature unleashed. Finally, it comes to rest against a wedge of concrete, a six-feet thick chunk of the silo cap which was blown off during the first countdown. Jericho stirs from semi-consciousness, opens his eyes, coughs and sputters, then returns a few jiggers of muddy water to the river. He unties the rope that binds him to the trunk, coils it over a shoulder, climbs over the concrete slab, and splashes into the water. Still wearing the tool belt, he paddles along. Battered and bruised from the ride down the mountain, he half swims, half body surfs in the current. In a few moments, he is at the edge of the open silo. A lip five feet high has kept the first surge of water out, but now, the swelling river laps over the top and pours down the walls.

Slivers of light appear on the horizon as the sun peeks over the mountains to the east. In a moment, the dark water takes on a pink glow. Jericho rigs his rope around a metal stanchion barely visible under the rising water and climbs over the lip and into the silo. As the water cascades over him, he lowers himself into the opening.

Looking down, he sees the nose cone of the Peacekeeper directly below him. He remembers dangling from a line, much like this, scrubbing the walls of the silo. He remembers many other things, too, the beauty of a fall day in the mountains, the fallen leaves crunching underfoot, his mother's sour apple pie, a white-tailed buck drinking from a cool stream. He remembers his father and brother and their endless card games on the front porch. And now, with his butt hanging over the nose cone that contains ten nuclear warheads, he says a brief prayer aloud, "Lord, I've always believed in you, though sometimes, it may seem like I forgot. I've believed you made the mountains and the rivers and the yellow tulips in the Spring. I know you've got a lot to worry about, but if it isn't too much trouble, I'd surely appreciate it if you didn't let them launch that missile just now."

❧

In the launch control capsule, David watches the security monitors. One camera at the elevator housing catches Ezekiel's heroics, holding off the first of the forces of Satan. David knows he has little time. The troops will be down the elevator shaft in minutes. There are still commandos in the tunnel and outside the capsule. He yells into a mike. "Everyone with a weapon to the elevator shaft!"

His men tromp from the silo through the underground tunnel and take up positions on the catwalk outside the elevator door. The first of the Special Forces will be cut down when they emerge from the elevator. There will be more, though, David knows. Too many. On another security monitor, he sees a waterfall surging into the silo. He hits a button and speaks again into the mike, "Make haste, James."

In the drainage sump just outside the capsule, James shines a flashlight into the water. He speaks into his headset, "The Bible advises us to 'run with patience the race before us.'"

"Screw the Bible! Find the key!"

There is nothing David can do. He looks at the key still in his slot, then shoots a look at the deputy's slot, as if miraculously the other key might appear there. No miracles today. Frustrated and angry, he gets out of the flight chair, turns around and approaches Susan. Rachel watches over her with a rifle. David leans down and grabs Susan's cheek, pinching her jaw muscles hard. "And you, Dr. Burns, are the biggest fool of all. Bigger even than the sergeant who cares so much for you."

He releases his grip and she just stares at him defiantly, not saying a word.

"Thou could have shared my throne," he says to her.

Glaring back. Unafraid. "I wouldn't even drinketh from the same cup."

༄

Ezekiel's —60 jams, just for a moment. Which is long enough.

The troops pour onto the security bridge, firing M-16's from their hips. Ezekiel is struck more than thirty times in the chest, a cluster of wounds opening a gaping hole the size of a basketball. Another burst of direct hits to the head and neck nearly decapitate him. His body does a macabre dance backward into the elevator door, a red smear left behind as he crumples to the metal floor.

The troops rush across the bridge, and a mustachioed lieutenant wearing a sidearm and carrying a briefcase approaches the keyboard at the elevator housing. He pulls a card from the briefcase, studies it a moment, then enters the PAL code. The heavy door slowly opens, and the lieutenant jams a detonator into a wad of Semtex, tosses it into the empty elevator, hits the down button and steps back. "Fire in the hole!" he yells at his men.

As the soldiers back away from the opening, sporadic gunfire comes from the surrounding woods, the remaining commandos gamely fighting on. The Army, though, now controls the bridge, the security building, the barracks, and the elevator housing.

In the capsule, David watches a monitor as a mechanical voice intones, "Elevator Access Granted." David yells into a mike: "They're coming! Send them straight to hell!"

At the foot of the elevator shaft, Gabriel commands half a dozen commandos. They know their friends above ground have been annihilated. They know they will die, too. First, though, they will dispense punishment to the minions of Satan's army. "Hold your fire until my order!" Gabriel commands, listening to the elevator descend.

The elevator clunks to a stop, and the door slowly opens. Gabriel's men obey, peering suspiciously into the compartment which appears empty...until Gabriel sees something on the floor. The Semtex.

Oh shit.

Oh holy shit.

The sound of the explosion is magnified by the close quarters, and the reverberations from the rocky cavern produce an ear-shattering, disorienting echo. Blood streams from both of Gabriel's ears, and a soaring cloud of dust fills his nostrils. His men stagger backward into the twisted railing of the catwalk. Knowing they cannot hear him, Gabriel simply motions for them to get into kneeling position, rifles pointed at the gaping opening of what had been the elevator car.

At the top of the elevator shaft, the soldiers push a prisoner to the lieutenant. The commando, wearing a black hood, stumbles and is held up by a sergeant who is bleeding from a bayonet wound to the shoulder. "He's the only one who surrendered, sir," the sergeant says.

"What's your name, jerkoff?" the lieutenant says, yanking off the black hood.

"Danny Price, but they call me Daniel." It is the pudgy, peach fuzzy commando who let Jericho escape.

"How would you like to help your Uncle Sam, Danny boy?"

"Do I have a choice?"

"Yeah, you can help dead or help alive." The lieutenant nods, and his men begin stripping off Daniel's camouflage garb. Quickly, they re-dress him in Army Ranger combat fatigues. "Do you know the Rangers' creed, Danny boy?"

A nervous shake of the head, no.

"'Never shall I fail my comrades.'"

"You're a Ranger now, Danny. And I'm sure you won't let us down." They slip him into a metal harness, thread a black rope through the a metal clip and gag him. "Of course, we're going to let you down." The lieutenant nods, and two soldiers push Daniel into the shaft. The soldiers let out the rope, and Daniel disappears into the darkness below.

"Let's see if this baby's still hot," the lieutenant says.

The descent takes only thirty seconds, the soldiers not particularly concerned about their bait bouncing off the walls or being cut up as he's lowered through the blown roof of the elevator. A moment later, Daniel is dangling in the opening of what had been the elevator door.

Gunfire from Gabriel's men virtually cuts him in two.

At the top of the shaft, the lieutenant grimaces. "Yep, the baby's still hot." He speaks into a radio transmitter. "This is Beta. Come in Alpha. We got a problem here."

BOOK SEVEN

END GAME

-54-
Die a Hero

Jack Jericho is drenched.

And exhausted.

And bloodied from bouncing off rocks and trees on the way down what used to be – and once again is – Chugwater River.

Rappelling down the silo wall, the adrenaline ebbs, and he feels his arms give out. He hangs there a moment, then kicks off the wall, letting yards of rope escape. Without gloves and a harness, the rope burns a trail around his waist and tears skin from the palms of his hands. He swings lower, strikes the wall with his boots and kicks off again, teetering into space.

Clang, he bangs into the missile, rebounds like a pinball back into the silo wall and off again. This time he desperately reaches out and grabs the nose cone. Hugging the missile. Struggling to hang onto the top of the titanium shroud with one hand, he uses the other to dip into his tool belt where he comes out with one of the wrenches. Too big. He tries the second wrench, adjusts it, and goes to work.

A moment later, in the launch control capsule, David is looking at a monitor showing water pouring into the silo. He hits a button, and a different camera shows the missile. The shot pans from the floor of the silo, where the water is now three feet deep, up to the burners, suspended another seven feet higher. The camera moves higher, showing the shaft of the missile to the fourth stage where David sees a sight that freezes him.

Dangling on a rope, a man has a wrench attached to the nose cone computer box.

The sergeant!

The maintenance man.

Like the beggar Lazarus, rising from the dead.

"I knew he'd come back," Susan Burns says from her position at the back wall.

"You knew nothing!" David yells.

"He wanted to change. You gave him the chance."

"I gave him the chance to die. Now I will have to help him." David grabs a headset and an Uzi and turns to Rachel. "Launch the instant you have the second key."

"But what if you are in the silo?"

"Launch!"

Watching him go, Rachel has tears in her eyes.

ço

In black watch caps and darkened faces, the Green Berets and Rangers are slipping into their harnesses, which fit uneasily over their Kevlar armored vests. Each man is responsible for his own rope, assault rifle, gas mask and saw-toothed knife. They are thirsting for the chance to go down that hole.

It's what they've trained for. To save their country. And the world.

The Rangers are famed as assault troops. The product of intense, dangerous training, they are among the world's best fighting men and truly believe the mystique that goes with the Ranger creed: "I accept the fact that as a Ranger my country expects me to move further, faster and fight harder than any other soldier. Never shall I fail my comrades."

The Green Berets trace their history to the early 1950's when eight-man "A-Teams" were trained to fight the Russians behind enemy lines in the event of World War III. Today, they undergo grueling training and are experts in raids, reconnaissance, ambushes and sabotage.

The lieutenant knows it's a death trap. Bodies will be stacked like cord wood at the bottom of the shaft. They'll be the only cover for the men who come after them. He hears Colonel Zwick's raspy voice through the headphones. "Son, you gotta get your men down that shaft. Jackal's stuck on top the mountain."

"I could divert half my men to the silo," the lieutenant says. "Divide the enemy force in the hole."

"Too late. That's low ground, under water now, and not passable. Not even the SEALs could get down there."

❧

Jack Jericho is not a Navy SEAL, Army Ranger or Green Beret. At this moment, he could be a window washer on a high-rise skyscraper. Except his rope is looped through a clip on his tool belt and wrapped twice around his waist – wrapped so tightly he thinks a boa constrictor has chosen him for a mate – and a waterfall pours over him from above. But he's not washing windows. He's performing a lobotomy on a nuclear missile.

Jericho has two of the recessed bolts out of the computer box. It is not easy work. The wrench does not fit perfectly and keeps slipping off. His hands are wet, and his arms are dead. He tugs hard on the third bolt. Tighter than the first two. He places both hands at the end of the wrench handle for additional purchase and puts all his weight behind it. The wrench slips, Jericho loses his balance and dangles precariously over the silo floor. He reaches up, steadies himself on the rope, then swings back to the nose cone.

He's back at work on the third bolt when he thinks he hears a familiar sound. He stops and listens. The roar of rushing water. His own breathing. Nothing more.

But there it is again, an electrical hum that grows louder, and

Jericho watches as the gantry's work cage heads up the silo wall. He can't see through the roof of the gantry, and Jack Jericho has never been blessed with even modest extrasensory powers. But he knows who's there, knows it in his heart, feels it in his bones. Brother David has come to kill him.

Jericho regains his balance, gets a decent grip on the wrench, and urgently works at the third bolt. The wrench catches and the bolt comes free, Jericho dropping it into the water far below. The gantry has not even come to a stop when David fires a burst of 9 mm. shells from the Uzi. He aims for Jericho's back, the widest target, but the movement of the gantry throws him off. The Uzi shoots high, and the shells *plunk* into the concrete wall of the far side of the silo.

Jericho spins in his rope, a fly caught in a spider's dangling web. Pushing off the nose cone, he spins to the other side, using the missile itself for cover.

Another burst from the Uzi, several shots *pinging* off the titanium shroud of the nose cone. Jericho winces as sparks fly.

The gunshots stop.

Stalemate.

David can't shoot him, and Jericho can't reach the computer box.

David yells over the roar of the waterfall. "You're finally going to get your wish, maintenance man."

Jericho stays hidden behind the nose cone, but David sprays a half-dozen shots over him anyway. "You're going to die a hero," David says.

-55-
Nailing It

Water pours through the grates in the floor of the silo. Not enough to keep the water level from rising under the missile, but enough to flood the sump. At an incline in the sump near the launch control capsule, the water is just below James' waist and still rising.

James takes a deep breath and dives under the surface, holding a flashlight. Cheeks blown out like a tropical fish, he sweeps the floor with his hand, desperately reaching for the key.

Hitting it.

Knocking it farther away. Damn. Damn. Damn.

He comes up for air. Gasping. He's in lousy shape, a condition he blames on the lack of protein in the Eden Ranch diet. Funny, thinking about food at a time like this. But that's what is going through his mind. Things he'll miss when he's dead. Which won't be long, he is sure. Steaks and crossword puzzles and jazz quartets, and the computers, of course. But not much more. James always knew what it would be like, joining Davy on this gig. The final riff. A long way from taking yokels' money for ten minutes of mind reading.

More than any of David's followers, James knew. Not that he considered himself a follower. Buddies, pals, best friends. Okay, so Davy was the leader, as between the two of them, but James was no born-again groupie. Since the time they were kids, he knew Davy had a gift, could see things, and that was cool. It was long ago that James attached himself to Davy like a pilot fish to a shark, and it paid off for both of them. James had no life, he'd be the first to admit. Never did. No other friends as a kid, unsure with girls, then hopeless with women.

If he had to sum it up in a bumper sticker, "Life sucks, then you die" wouldn't be a bad slogan for his life. Might as well go up in a ball of flame. If Davy makes the cover of TIME, James figures he'll be good enough for a sidebar around page twenty.

He takes a deep breath, goes under again, opens his eyes and sees the key. Cautiously this time, he extends a hand and grabs it. He comes up, bursting out of the water, both arms raised above his head as if he's just won an Olympic medal. He spits out a mouthful of water that tastes of slick metal. "Read my mind, Davy. I got the key into heaven!"

Or put another way, James thinks, the key out of hell.

ↂ

Gabriel watches as two commandos cautiously approach the shredded body, the top half still hanging in the dangling rope. The carcass is bloody and torn like a side of beef, but his face is still recognizable. "It's Daniel!" one commando shouts, shrinking back in horror, both at the thought he killed his comrade and at the fate that awaits them all.

There is a *plunk-plunk* as two fragmentation grenades land in the blown-out elevator. The two commandos are five meters away and turn to run. But it is too late. The grenades explode, and shrapnel tears through them. The echoes of the explosion reverberate off the underground rock shelf. Another two grenades land, but these hiss and release smoke instead of hot metal. Like a rock band, the Green Berets and Rangers will make an entrance through a smoky haze.

The soldiers begin their descent down the shaft, their ropes whistling in the harnesses. They open fire with their assault rifles even before touching down, but the return barrage cuts down the first five men. Other brave men follow. One is able to toss a grenade that bounces on the steel catwalk and rolls toward Gabriel's feet. Jeptha, a young commando, dives onto it, and its explosion kills him instantly in a muffled roar. Gabriel's men have donned gas masks and stand their ground. He turns to then, "For the glory of God! Die like men and live again as angels."

The fire now is heavier from the Green Berets and Rangers. Using the debris as cover, several have leapt out of the blown elevator car. They return fire as more soldiers rappel down the shaft, futuristic warriors in their masks, harnesses and vests.

Fifty meters away, James rushes from the sump back toward the capsule. He hunches his shoulders and lowers his head, tortoise-like, as shells from the battle whiz past him and bury themselves in the walls. The air is thick with cordite and dust and he coughs, then winces at the deafening roar. James is just steps away from the open capsule door when a stray bullet from a soldier's rifle catches him in the thigh. It is a clean, through-and-through shot, and it drops him to his knees. He gets up scrambles, half crawling, trying to reach the capsule. But he's gotten turned around, and in the smoke and din from the gunfire, in the pain and shock from the wound, James is headed down the catwalk toward the battle. He looks up to see his compatriots dying as the soldiers pick them off, one-by-one. In moments, it will be over. He is disoriented, in pain, and nearly paralyzed with fear.

From somewhere, he hears his name called. Or is he imagining it? He cocks his head. There it is. Rachel's scream, "James! James!" But so faint. He turns around, sees the light from the capsule's open blast door. He scuttles toward it, fighting off the urge to look behind him. He has the sensation of being chased, being hunted. He staggers inside the capsule, and Rachel hits the button, closing the eight-ton door.

&

David leans far over the edge of the gantry, trying to get the angle. Jericho is still hidden on the far side of the nose cone. David fires off a burst, but it's no good. If he can't see Jericho, he can't shoot him. "Stay where you are, sergeant!" he yells. "You're going to get a helluva ride."

Three bolts gone, one to go, Jericho thinks.

And time running out.

He wonders why they haven't already launched. He knows he will be shot removing the last bolt, but wonders if he can still do it and pull out the computer before he dies.

Suddenly, Jericho swings out from behind the missile, one hand on the rope, the other hand pulling the stud driver from his tool belt. David is off balance at the gantry ledge. He raises the Uzi, but Jericho fires first with the stud driver from his tool belt. *Whomp.* A four-inch carbon steel nail strikes David in the abdomen.

David lurches forward, and his Uzi drops over the edge of the gantry, plunging into the water far below. Grimacing, he pulls the nail from his gut and jams it through his left palm. He glares derisively at Jack. Showing no pain. Watching the blood drip from his palm, then turning his hand over and studying the pool of blood that forms around the protruding point of the nail. "I forgive you, Jericho, for you know not what you do."

"You've got a serious identity crisis, pal," Jericho says, then swings to the front of the computer panel and goes back to work on the fourth and last bolt.

❦

The remaining commandos fall back along the catwalk, making a last stand as they retreat to the launch control capsule. Half-a-dozen Green Berets advance, spraying 5.56 mm. fire from their lightweight Squad Automatic Weapons.

Gabriel screams at his men to fight back, and they do, even with those with multiple wounds. Gabriel is out of ammo for the assault rifle but still has a Mossberg shotgun, and the first soldier to get within twelve feet of him takes a full load in the chest.

Finally, a Ranger with a laser-sighted assault rifle lines up a pink dot squarely in the center of Gabriel's chest. He tattoos Gabriel with four shots to the sternum and two more above the heart for good measure. Gabriel sinks to the catwalk, and the remaining commandos fight to their own deaths, except for one who puts the barrel of a rifle in his own mouth, strains to reach the trigger, then ends the pain forever.

The lieutenant with the mustache advances across the catwalk. His men are peppering the titanium blast door with small arms fire. They do no damage and run the risk of hitting themselves with ricochets. The cylindrical capsule is designed to withstand hits above ground from Russian SS-18 missiles. The idea never was to guard against terrorist takeovers, but the door is doing just fine. The lieutenant takes a quick look and signals his men to stop firing.

"Okay, where the hell's the plastique?"

&

Through his headset, David hears Rachel's voice screaming. "James has been shot. Where are you David?"

"Did he get the key?"

"Yes, but the soldiers are..." Her voice trails off, and though David cannot hear the sound of gunshots from outside the soundproof capsule, he can see the Special Forces in his mind's eye. This vision, he knows, is real. He shoots a look at Jericho, who cannot loosen the last bolt.

"Launch!" David commands her. "Launch for a new Jerusalem."

"Not with you in there, David! Please!"

"Heed my Word."

She clicks off and David looks back at Jericho. Then he screams, "Praise the Lord," dashes toward the edge of the gantry and leaps into space.

&

Two Rangers with expertise in demolitions are stacking wads of C-4 plastique against the blast door. When the stack is waist high, one of them lets out a whistle and says, "Might cause an earthquake, but don't know if we can peel the top of that can." He embeds a tiny antenna into the putty-like plastique and turns to the lieutenant. "Sir, you might not want to get up close and personal with this."

The lieutenant agrees and motions his men to take cover. As they head down the ramp toward the tunnel, they notice the rising water coming from the silo.

&

Jericho still works on the last bolt when he hears David's wailing praise to the Lord and turns his head in time to see the man flying through the air, legs churning.

A second later, David slams hard into Jericho, banging his head into the nose cone. Fireworks explode behind Jericho's eyes. David is screaming something, but Jericho cannot make out the words as a thunderstorm rages in his brain. Two hands are around his neck, choking him. One hand is impaled with the nail, and it slashes Jericho's neck.

Jericho feels the warmth of his own blood but as his head clears, he hits David with a backward elbow strike. The elbow cracks two ribs. David winces, then cries out, "Pain, Jericho! Pain means nothing!"

"Good, 'cause I owe you some."

The two men exchange punches while clinging to each other. Only the rope around Jericho keeps them from plunging to the rising water below. David's voice comes in short, pained breaths, "As written in Job, 'The eyes of the wicked shall not escape.'"

Jericho hits him with two short rights to the gut, working on the broken ribs. David jams the heel of his hand into Jericho's Adam's apple, and Jericho hoarsely rasps, "As said by John, 'I won't be wronged. I won't be insulted. I won't be laid a hand on.'"

"John never said such things."

"John Wayne, dipshit." Jericho kicks away from the missile and they swing into space, water pouring over them from above. They trade punches and swing back to the missile. David gets a hand around Jericho's neck and slams his head backward into the nose cone. The *thud* echoes inside Jericho's brain.

Now, they are wrestling, becoming entangled in the rope, twisted twice around the nose cone and themselves. Instead of one or the other falling, they are tightly bound to the missile.

David's headset, long since torn from his head, is tangled in the rope. It crackles with static, but then a faint voice is heard by them both.

"Key turn clockwise...on my mark," Rachel says.

-56-
Underwater

The keys are in their slots when the C-4 explodes. A concussion wave roars down the tunnel and knocks half-a-dozen Green Berets to the floor, shattering their eardrums. It cracks a hundred-ton sheet of rock in the roof of the cavern, fills the tunnel with dust and sets loose a landslide of pebbles.

But it does not open the blast door.

Inside the capsule, James sits in the commander's chair, a belt tied around his upper thigh as a makeshift tourniquet. Rachel sits in the deputy's chair. They each hold a key in the slots twelve feet apart.

The explosion jars the capsule, which noses down at the concussion, then pops up again, its four shock absorbers, each thick as an oil drum and eight feet high, absorbing the impact. Lights flicker for an instant, then come back on.

"Key turn clockwise...on my mark," Rachel says.

James nods. Behind them, Susan sits, shackled, watching in terror.

In the tunnel, the lieutenant angrily shouts into his radio transmitter. "Get me more Semtex, now!" He clicks off the radio. "Logistics," he says to himself. "All war is logistics and supply."

"Three, two, one," Rachel counts aloud. "Rotate and hold."

They both turn their keys.

Five seconds pass. An eternity.

"And release," she says.

They both allow the keys to turn back. A klaxon horn honks. Lights flash.

"Kingdom come," James says.

"Thy will be done," Rachel adds.

Susan is out of ideas and deathly afraid. So she turns to the only resource she has left. Prayer.

ↄ

In stunned silence, the brass watches the Big Board flash with the words, "LAUNCH SEQUENCE IN PROGRESS." The computerized voice is calm as ever, a housewife reciting her grocery list. "Generators activated. Launch in ninety seconds. Confidence is high."

"Lionel, if you have any bright ideas, you might pass them on just now," General Corrigan says.

In his wheelchair, the professor stares vacantly at the board. He gives no sign of having heard the general but begins speaking softly. "I was there, Hugh."

"What? Where?"

"I was there at Eniwetok in '52 when we detonated the first hydrogen fusion bomb. I was there with the Teapot Committee and I was there when we needed to reduce the weight of the payloads just to get the birds to fly. I was there when the Army still thought missiles were fancy artillery shells and couldn't imagine why we needed an ICBM program. I did it, you know. I did it all for thirty-eight years."

"And now it's come to this," the general says.

"It's not the way I planned it," Lionel Morton says. "You know, back in the fifties and sixties, I always hoped we'd use the missiles. Hell, I prayed that we'd use them when we had clear nuclear superiority. I know that sounds..." He pauses. "Inhumane."

"Insane is more like it, Lionel."

"I didn't want an all-out war. No attacks on their cities. Preventive deterrence. A limited strike on the Russian missile fields plus simultaneous hits on their bomber bases. Then a demand for total unilateral nuclear disarmament or we'd finish them off."

"We'd have to," Corrigan says, "because they'd have come at us with everything they had left."

"We could debate that all day, Hugh, but you're missing my point."

"Which is?"

"Now that's it happening, I can see that I was wrong. I can see it all now. God forgive me, I was wrong."

☙

In the waterlogged sump, the pumps are throbbing. Generators drive heated gases through thick, insulated tubes into the missile canister. Rising water in the silo roils like a stormy sea.

On the missile's nose cone, both Jericho and David – tangled in the rope – can hear the driving force of the pumps. It seems to vitalize David, and he unleashes a series of punches. Jericho fights back, but the endless night has taken its toll.

David gets a grip on the rope and pulls, spinning Jericho hard into the nose cone. Then he yanks the rope the other direction, and it gets stuck in the clip attached to Jericho's tool belt. "Jack be nimble!" David cries out, yanking again on the rope, bending the clip, then breaking it. The rope spins free of the tool belt. "Jack be quick!" One more tug, the rope comes loose from Jericho's waist. He tries to grab the end but misses and plummets toward the water. "Jack fell off the candlestick!" David shouts triumphantly.

The surging water is fifteen feet deep, lapping at the rocket burners, suspended off the silo floor. In the confined space of the silo, the water sloshes against the walls like breaking waves on a pier.

Jericho hits the surface and goes under. He touches bottom, bounces back up to the surface, takes a breath, and is swept under again by the tug of a whirlpool. Like an underwater tornado, the water swirls downward into an open drain. Jericho tries to swim against the surge, but it's useless. He is sucked into the drain and driven by the force of the water into the flooded sump.

He kicks and paddles but mostly is just propelled by the force of the water, deeper into the channel. The walls seem to press in on him. His shoulder strikes a duct, and he bounces into a web of piping where he becomes stuck. He struggles in the dark, cold water, but cannot free himself.

Underwater.
Lungs ready to burst.
A miner in a flooded shaft.
Crushed by a timber.
Waiting to die.
Jack Jericho has become his father.

-57-
The Morning Star

The second explosion rocks the underground cavern and sets loose a choking cloud of dust. The powerful Semtex jars the blast door, and a burly N.C.O. pries it open with a crowbar. The lieutenant leads six Green Berets into the launch control capsule. The first two inside roughly yank James and Rachel from their flight chairs.

"It's too late!" Susan Burns cries out. "The launch is activated. When the gases reach full pressure, the missile will go."

"How do we abort?" the lieutenant demands.

James looks up from his position on the floor. "You don't. Once the key is turned, it's too late." James gives him a sickly smile and sings out, "Sor-ry."

The lieutenant kicks him in the ribs with a hard-toed combat boot. The computer's voice says, "Launch in sixty seconds."

The lieutenant looks up at a security monitor. A camera halfway up the silo wall is panning from the floor where the gases beat the gushing water into a seething foam. The camera pivots skyward, up the length of the missile. There at the top, a man is tangled in a rope. He seems to struggle, and at first the lieutenant thinks the man is trying to get free so he can leap from the nose cone to the gantry. But then it becomes clear.

The man is tying the rope tighter. He wraps it around his legs and loops it over the nose of the missile, pulling it taut, then knotting it.

"Who the fuck is that?" the lieutenant asks.

With tears in her eyes, Rachel answers, "The Messiah."

"Yeah? Well, he looks like hood ornament to me."

❦

A torrent of water that began its journey in Chugwater Dam, then spilled down the mountain and cascaded into the silo, now surges through the drainage sump. Compressed into the channel, it picks up speed, tearing at ductwork, breaking Jericho out of the web of piping, and carrying him farther away from the silo. There is nowhere to go but where the water will take him. The channel reaches an incline where the water slows and becomes more shallow. Out of breath and barely conscious, Jericho reaches up, grabs an overhanging pipe and pulls his head above the water.

He drinks in a series of short breaths and hangs there, gasping.

And thinking.

He can let the slowing water carry him farther into the sump, away from the silo. Which is what he should do. Get out of harm's way before the missile blows.

He tried to stop it. There's nothing more he can do.

He thought he was going to die, but now he knows, he can survive this. No one could blame him for running now.

No one.

Except himself. He's run before. He was frightened then. Afraid to die. If heroism is acting courageously in the face of fear, what he is about to do isn't heroic at all. He is a man without fear, something he has not been for a long time. Unafraid to die, he is nonetheless a man with a purpose for living. And that, too, is something he has not been for a long time.

Jericho turns back toward the silo, fighting the current, which tears at him and tumbles him backward into the water. He gets up and struggles on, desperately pulling ahead on pipes and conduits. The water deepens as he gets closer to the silo, filling the channel, and his head bangs against the ceiling. He has no choice but to go under. He takes a breath and exhales, sucks in another breath, and dives under, kicking hard, swimming against the current, pulling himself along on scaffolding and floor-mounted equipment. He blows out some dead air, feels the ache in his lungs, kicks harder, and keeps going. He swims up through the open drain and into the silo where he bobs to the surface and takes in a long breath.

The water is twenty feet deep now, extending ten feet up the suspended missile, which bobs in its cables. The steaming gases continue to fill the canister. The propulsion launch can only be seconds away, he knows. He kicks out of a swirling whirlpool, swims alongside the missile, reaches up and grabs the umbilical cord that hangs from the fourth stage. He pulls on the umbilical and steadies himself, then hangs there, half in the water, half out. Does he even have time to climb up the cord to get to the computer box? If he makes it, how will he get the box open?

He sees David above him, lashed to the nose cone. Jericho looks at his own hands. He holds the umbilical, the spinal cord of the missile, where even now, final digital instructions are being fed to the MGCS from the launch control capsule's computer. On the gantry, he couldn't reach it. On the floor of the silo, same thing. But now, lifted by the water, here it is. If only there is enough time.

Jericho grabs the saw-toothed survival knife from the sheath on his leg and begins frantically cutting through the thick rubber casing to a mass of colorful wires underneath.

જી

In the STRATCOM War Room, no one speaks as the computerized voice calmly announces, "Propulsion steady. Pressure three hundred pounds per square inch. Launch in fifteen seconds. Systems go. Confidence is high. Ten seconds, nine, eight, seven..."

જી

Jericho saws away at the umbilical, cutting deeper through the web of wires, down to the last, thin filaments, which he severs just as...

Whoosh! The rocket erupts skyward, bursting from the water and out of the silo with incredible speed.

The roiling water propels Jericho to the bottom, sweeps him into the vortex of an underwater maelstrom. He smashes against the silo floor, spins a dizzying circle under water and is driven to the surface, then hard into the steel ladder on the silo wall, where he desperately clings to a rung as the water surges over him.

ↄ

From the perimeter of Base Camp Alpha, Colonel Henry Zwick watches through binoculars, and what a sight. Against the first light of dawn, the sleek black missile soars above the waterfall pouring into the silo. "Mother of mercy," he whispers to himself.

Trailed by a blast of steam, the missile seems to hang in the air for a moment.

Motionless, as if deciding on its own, whether to fly or...

The missile pitches over and drops back to earth, splashing down into the river that once again flows through the missile base and onward into the valley. The missile picks up speed in the current, bouncing down a series of rapids in the shallow water, now tinted red by the rising sun.

ↄ

The Big Board shows a computer simulation of the PK lifting off, and then, the impotent missile simply drops back to earth. A technician in a headset stands at his console, "No first stage ignition! No flame! The bird is down! The bird is down!"

A second of quiet relief. Then jubilation. The officers slap each other on the back as if their genius resulted in the triumph. General Corrigan walks around, thanking his staff. Nervous laughter. Locker room congratulations. *"We had'em all the way."*

The celebration is still going when the technician sits back down at his console. Watching the monitor, he hits a few keys. His brow is furrowed. "General," he calls out. "You'd better have a look at this."

∽

Dazed and bleeding, Jack Jericho climbs the steel ladder toward the lip of the silo. He can see the contrails in the sky above him, but he knows it is merely a steam trail. He would have heard the rockets explode to life if there had been ignition. He would have seen the burst of orange flame from the first stage of the rocket, would have been scorched by its heat.

He knows the missile is down, and reason tells him, it is dead. The warheads would not have armed until the missile was on its ballistic descent. Reason tells him that David is dead, too. But a feeling of utter dread tells him something else. Other than the nightmares that peered into his own past, Jack Jericho never had a vision. Now, he does not so much *see* as *feel*. He feels the malefic presence of David Morton and can nearly sense his derisive laughter. A wave of fear sweeps over Jericho. For he knows, without knowing how, that David is alive.

∽

The missile spins lazily in the water. As it completes a revolution, David becomes visible, still lashed to the nose cone. Blood flows from his mouth and ears. His arms are spread wide, his feet are together – a watery crucifixion. He appears dead, but slowly his eyes open and his lips move. The missile bounces off a shallow rock, then lodges between two boulders.

He sees the vision again, the flow of grayish white. Sees it more clearly than before. It is not a banner blowing in the wind, as he had thought. It is a great river, moving slowly at first, still and shallow, then surging forward, faster and rougher, until it plunges over a great waterfall.

"The bomb leadeth me beside the still waters," he recites. "It restoreth my soul."

❧

General Corrigan stands behind the technician at the console. Professor Morton motors over and wedges the wheelchair between two officers at the general's side. The female mechanical voice intones, "Air burst programmed at five thousand feet. Detonation in seven minutes."

"What the hell's going on!" the general demands.

The technician bangs his keyboard in frustration. "The computer thinks the missile's in flight, and it's armed the warheads."

"That's impossible!" Professor Morton yells. "I designed the accelerometers myself. They're interfaced with the Environmental Sensing Devices. Unless they detect that the missile has left the earth's atmosphere, then re-entered, there can be no detonation. I designed it to prevent us from blowing up Denver or Salt Lake City."

"You might have designed it that way, professor," the technician says, "but there must have been a defect. The missile thinks it's on ballistic descent to the target. The fusing system already sent a test signal to the firing system, which relayed the signal to the firing circuits. The MIRV's are armed. When they think they're at five thousand feet, they're going to detonate, all ten of them."

Professor Morton looks at the general, seeking support. "Hugh, I'm telling you, it's not possible."

"Air burst in six minutes," the computer's voice says, blandly.

General Corrigan clasps the professor by the shoulder. It is a gesture both of long friendship and sadness. "You always said that the machines worked, Lionel. Only the men were defective. Have you forgotten who made the machines?"

❧

Jack Jericho is nearly swept off the ladder by the waterfall that gushes over him. Climbing the last few rungs through the downpour, he does not see the man standing on the lip of the silo, bracing himself on a stanchion.

Jericho pulls himself over the last rung and finds himself staring straight into the savage face of Gabriel. The commando, who should have died a dozen deaths, is badly injured. Blood oozes from several wounds. Two bandoliers of shells criss-cross his chest. Under a torn shirt, a dented forty millimeter grenadier vest is visible. It took the brunt of the kill shots to the sternum and over the heart. Gabriel aims a bulky M-60 machine gun at Jericho's midsection. "Prepare to meet your Maker, son of Satan."

Jericho is oddly calm, though he knows the massive gun will cut him in two. "My father's name was William, and he was the best man I ever knew."

"Then join him in hell!"

Blam! Shot between the eyes, Gabriel topples sideways into the silo, disappearing in the foam and mist of the waterfall.

Standing eighty yards away on the river bank, Captain Kyle Clancy lowers his scoped M-16.

"Stay there!" he yells at Jericho. "We'll come get you."

"No time!" Jericho yells back. "Gotta go!"

Go where, Clancy wonders. The sergeant looks like one of those victims of a Midwestern flood, stranded in the middle of a river that shouldn't be there at all. Now what the hell is he up to?

Jericho dives into the swift-flowing current. The captain stares incredulously. "Oh, shit!" The current takes Jericho closer to the shore, and Clancy tosses a rope to him. It falls short, but it wouldn't matter anyway because Jericho makes no attempt to grab it. Clancy watches Jericho body surf down the rapids, slamming into rocks, bouncing off fallen trees. Clancy winces with each jolt.

⌘

Jericho can see the missile lodged between two boulders. In

the distance, he hears the roar of tumbling water. He kicks and paddles, doing the West Virginia version of the Australian crawl, something learned long ago in water-filled limestone quarries. Just as he grabs the trailing umbilical cord, the missile works itself free of the boulders and continues down river. As the missile picks up speed, Jericho crawls up the cord, hand-over-hand.

Once aboard, he works his way up toward the nose cone where David lies sprawled on his back, entangled in the ropes. His face is a deathly gray, his eyes closed. Blood is caked in his ears, his nose, and in the corners of his eyes. His face a battered mess. Suddenly, in a rasping voice that reminds Jericho of a rattlesnake, David says, "Sergeant Jericho, my favorite janitor."

Scrambling on all fours up the rubberized fuselage, Jericho approaches him.

"I knew you would come, sergeant. I saw it. But *why* did you come?"

"To make sure you were dead. To kill you, if you weren't."

David's hacking gurgle of a laugh brings a pink bubble of blood to his lips. "Can you hear the heart of the beast, Jericho?"

The missile rotates slowly in the water, and Jericho has to grab the ropes to hang on. The roar of rushing water grows louder. "What are you talking about?"

"The bomb lives!" David proclaims. "Hear its Word."

Stunned, Jericho slides over to the computer box and puts an ear to the cold metal. He hears the unmistakable *clickety-click* of the computer.

"As the sound picks up tempo, we approach detonation, Jericho. Surely you know that. I would say we have less than three minutes. But have no fear. You can live forever at the foot of my throne."

"Your throne will be a pyre in hell," Jericho says, taking the knife from the sheath on his leg. He begins working on the one remaining bolt in the computer box but can't get enough purchase and the knife slips off.

David, eyes closed, begins chanting. "I am Alpha and Omega, the beginning and the end. Who is and who was. And I bring you the Morning Star."

-58-
Friendly Fire

A blizzard of information flashes across the Big Board: air speed, altitude, fusing and firing system checks, and detonation time. It is the same readout the Board would show if the MIRV's were on ballistic descent to their targets. The computer's voice calmly recites, "Initial air burst in two minutes."

General Corrigan and Colonel Farris watch the display in silence until the colonel speaks, "The good news, sir, is that if we were going to have a nuclear incident anywhere in this country, Wyoming's about the best place."

"What?"

"I've been on the horn to the Pentagon," the colonel says, "and it's generally agreed we can handle this. National Guard and Red Cross are being alerted, of course, but official policy will be to downplay the nuclear incident."

"Downplay ten nuclear explosions, each one seventeen times more powerful than the Hiroshima bomb?"

"Well, you gotta look at the bright side." The colonel stops and lets out a little laugh. "No pun intended. There aren't half a million people in the whole state. The official spin is to regard the incident as an unfortunate military accident, sort of like friendly fire."

"Jesus H. Christ."

"Maybe we'll vaporize some trees, and you're not going to eat the trout for a hundred years, but in terms of what could have happened, it's not that bad. That's our stance with the press, so the anti-nuke crowd doesn't use this as an excuse to plant flowers in the silos we still have left. I mean, sir, we don't want..."

Colonel Farris looks up and notices that the general has walked away, leaving him alone.

❧

The bolt will not move, so Jericho uses the knife to pry open the plate covering the computer box. There is a moment when he thinks the blade will break, but it does not. He gets leverage, then slides the plate around the fulcrum created by the remaining bolt. Inside Jericho sees a tangle of wires and electronic gizmos. The *clickety-click* seems louder, faster. He has no idea what to do.

The missile collides with a boulder, and Jericho nearly falls off. Regaining his balance, he looks downstream. He hears the rush of cascading water, and just ahead, the river seems to stop well in advance of the horizon.

"It must be a glorious sight," David says. "Can you see it, Jericho? Can you see the falls?"

"The what?"

But then he knows. Jericho had climbed Chugwater Cliffs. Three hundred feet nearly straight up. Rock climbing in summer, ice climbing in winter. Before the Corps of Engineers built the dam, it was a towering waterfalls. And it is again. What was it Kenosha said? *"In the end, the earth will prevail."*

Jericho takes a breath and jams his hand inside the computer box, ripping out a trail of wires, chips and plugs. A series of *pops* and *sizzles*. He reaches in with both hands and struggles to pull the computer out of its compartment. Getting to his feet, Jericho raises the computer high above his head. Standing there, the missile revolving in the water like a giant tree trunk, Jericho is struck by notion buried deep in his unconscious, an image from his childhood. He remembers a picture on the wall of the First Lutheran Church back home, Moses with the tablets of the Law held high over his head. Moses had come down from the mountain with the Lord's commandments and found the Hebrews worshiping the golden calf. They had broken their covenant with God, and Moses was pissed.

But the computer is not the voice of God, Jericho thinks, hurling it into the river where it floats for a moment before disappearing from view.

&

General Corrigan and his staff watch the Big Board as the seconds tick down. The computer speaks in that irritating, calm voice, "Altitude thirty thousand feet. Air burst in..."

The voice goes silent.

A message flashes on the board. "Firing system disabled. Warheads disarmed."

The officers have been on a roller coaster too long. They cannot celebrate. Some are dubious. General Corrigan turns to a technician. "Can you confirm—"

As if to reassure the brass, the computerized voice says, "Detonation aborted. Detonation aborted."

The technician simply says, "Yes. Yes. Yes."

Finally convinced the crisis is over, the officers slap each other's shoulders and whoop it up. A football team after a win. Someone passes out cigars as if a baby has been born.

In the center of the celebration a somber General Corrigan turns to Professor Morton.

"Thank God," Corrigan says.

"Amen," Morton adds.

&

The waterfalls rumble like an angry god. The missile spins one hundred eighty degrees in a whirlpool, heads backward toward the precipice, then straightens itself and continues at even greater speed. David lies on his back, barely conscious, barely alive.

"It's all over," Jericho tells him. "The bomb is dead."

David's voice is barely audible. "Then I shall carry it unto the Lord."

"He doesn't want you. Either damn one of you."

David's lifeless eyes close and his head drops to the side. Jericho gives him one last look, then dives into the river. He tries to swim to shore, fifty yards away, but the current is too strong. Losing strength, he's swept toward the waterfalls alongside the missile. Dangerously close to the edge, Jericho struggles futilely against the raging current. He tries to grab onto a boulder rising out of the water but is swept past it. A large tree limb comes by. He grabs at it and misses. No matter. It would only carry him over the falls. The water pushes him under and brings him back up again.

He is past fatigue, beyond exhaustion. He is at the point of giving up, of accepting the pain that is brief, the darkness that is forever. Or is it? In these last seconds, he thinks about his own beliefs. He has tried to be a decent man, to do as much good and inflict as little damage along the path of life as possible. He believes in God and in a hereafter. God who made this stream and the men who drink from it. He remembers the incredible beauty of the sun rising over Devil's Tower and knows now that it is misnamed. God made the Black Hills and the Belle Fourche Valley and the volcano that became the stark, unearthly tower. God made the prairie dogs and porcupines, the golden eagles and mountain bluebirds. God made me, too, Jericho thinks. And he is ready to go home.

He stops kicking and his arms, heavy as pine logs, drop to his side. He turns over on his back, squints against the morning sun, and lets the raging water carry him on.

A shadow passes over him, and he opens his eyes.

A strong hand reaches down and grabs him under one shoulder. Jericho does not have the strength to either help or resist. He lets himself be picked up and hauled over the side of a dugout canoe where he coughs water out of his lungs, then deeply inhales the sweet air. He looks up to see Kenosha, bare-chested, paddling with powerful strokes, propelling the canoe toward the river bank.

Jericho hauls himself up and looks toward the falls. He catches a last glimpse of the grotesque manmade beast of metal, fuel, and cataclysmic power as it sails over the falls and disappears in a sea of foam, swallowed up by the eternal forces of nature, by the Earth itself.

-59-
One Final Ghost

The sun is high in the blue Wyoming sky, and Base Camp Alpha swarms with suits.

State Department flunkies sip bottled water and tend to the freed ambassadors, toting food from a catering truck commandeered from a movie set in the Black Hills. No M.R.E.'s for the diplomats.

Gleaming trucks with huge satellite dishes are in place, network news crews dropping in by helicopter. Reporters jockey for position in front of the command tent, waiting for a glimpse of Colonel Zwick and Captain Clancy, already anointed as the brains and brawn of Operation Peacekeeper.

The armor is moving out, raising a racket, to the consternation of the TV reporters who are doing their stand-ups in front of Abrams tanks that won't stand still or be quiet. Medics patch up wounded soldiers, and the F.B.I. hauls off Rachel, James and the few surviving commandos in shackles.

Jack Jericho stands alone, a blanket wrapped around his shoulders. He sips coffee and seems at peace with the world, if a bit removed from it. There are too many thoughts to sort out just now. He thinks of his father and his brother, and for once, the thoughts do not bring anguish. Strange, random memories come to him. He remembers catching his first trout, his father helping him clean the fish, then cooking it over an open fire. Has anything ever tasted so good? He remembers wrestling with his brother in a field of freshly mowed hay. He remembers the coal mine, too, but the feeling is different, now. There is a sadness, but it is a sadness without pain. He thinks of the memorial outside the collapsed shaft that was erected by the union. Twenty-seven names are inscribed on a bronze plaque.

Jericho has never seen the memorial. He never went back to the mine after that day. Now, he is swept by a desire to lay his hands on the plaque, to run his fingers over the letters of his father's name, his brother's name. Now, he can do it. He must do it.

Suddenly, Elizabeth, the little girl in pigtails, skips away from a pack of soldiers and rushes toward Jericho. She waves her plastic wand, and a trail of crystalline bubbles floats above her in the breeze. "Will you still be my friend?" she asks.

"Always," Jericho answers, smiling. A female lieutenant comes over and takes Elizabeth by the hand. Jericho waves good-bye.

Though he does not hear the footsteps behind him, Jericho senses movement. Turning, he sees Kenosha approach. The two men stand there a moment without speaking. Their understanding and care for each other transcends language. "You have changed, Jack," Kenosha finally says.

Jericho nods. "You have helped me learn."

"It wasn't me. It was you. You listened to the voices of the spirits."

"And now it's time to go home, Kenosha. I can do it now."

"Then go, my friend."

"Not without words of wisdom from your ancestors."

Kenosha seems to think about it. "Be cautious, my friend."

"Cautious?"

"Speed traps on Interstate 80. The troopers in Nebraska are the worst."

Jericho laughs. He hugs his friend. "Now that you've saved my life, aren't you responsible for me forever? I've seen that in the Westerns. Isn't it an old Indian custom that—"

"You were swimming, and I gave you a lift to shore," Kenosha says. He turns to leave. Several yards away, his golden palomino waits in front of the command tent. "Besides," Kenosha says, turning back, "you'd be too damn much trouble." He mounts the palomino and rides off.

Colonel Henry Zwick and Captain Kyle Clancy come walking out of the tent, a cluster of reporters in tow. Zwick stops and jabs his pipe in Jericho's direction. "Now, there's the airman you should interview," the colonel says. "Sergeant Jack Jericho is either going to get court-martialed or win the Medal of Honor." He turns to

Clancy. "Isn't that right Captain?"

Clancy looks Jericho up and down. "He's doesn't follow orders, but he's got brass balls."

"Captain, I didn't get a chance to thank you," Jericho says. "You saved my life."

Clancy cracks a crooked grin. "What makes you think I was aiming at him?"

Jericho smiles back and snaps off a salute. Reporters bombard the colonel and the captain with more questions as they walk away. Alone now, Jericho walks slowly toward the flowing river.

"Ser-geant!"

He knows that insistent, bellowing voice. Turning, Jericho sees Captain Pete Pukowlski.

"Sergeant, you're out of uniform."

"Yes, sir. It won't happen again, sir." Jericho salutes again, a new record, two in one day.

"The hell it won't. You'll probably be on CNN wearing one of those Eye-talian suits, telling everybody how you saved the world." For once, Pukowlski's tone is laced with humor.

"I'll tell them I owe everything to my captain's rigorous training."

"Damn right you do." Pukowlski returns the salute. "You're a shitty airman, Jericho."

"Yes, sir. I know."

"But you're a helluva man."

Without another word, Pukowlski turns and leaves.

It takes Jericho several minutes to work his way from the camp to the shore of the river. Coming down the embankment, he sees Dr. Susan Burns, standing alone, looking across the water that flows through what had been the 318th Missile Squadron. She is pale, and her face is bruised where David struck her. For an awkward moment, they stand wordlessly, watching the river, now flowing peacefully through the rugged landscape. On the other shore, an elk cautiously approaches the water, eying them. They don't move, and the elk begins drinking from an eddy at the shoreline.

"I came back for you," Jericho says. "I mean, I tried to come back. I wasn't going to leave you there."

"I know. Everyone knows."

"It's not that I'm a hero or anything. I had to do it. Even if I wanted to run, I..."

Susan Burns steps close to him and touches a finger to his lips, hushing him. "Thank you, Jack. Thank you for everything." She puts a hand around his neck and pulls him down. She is waiting with parted lips.

He holds her in his arms, and they kiss until he feels warm tears tracking from her face to his. At last Jericho pulls back and says, "If it hadn't been for you, I never would..."

She silences him again with another kiss. When they separate this time, she says, "Where will you go now?"

"Back to West Virginia. Lay one final ghost to rest."

Across the river, the elk feeds at a clump of berries.

Susan gives Jericho a hug, then one last lingering kiss, the best of the three. "Washington's just down the road. Maybe you'll visit."

He tenderly wipes a tear from her eye. "I will. I promise."

He wraps an arm around her and they turn toward the resurrected river, just as a trout leaps from the water, glinting silver in the sun.

ALSO AVAILABLE

TO SPEAK FOR THE DEAD: Linebacker-turned-lawyer Jake Lassiter begins to believe that his surgeon client is innocent of malpractice...but guilty of murder.

NIGHT VISION: Jake is appointed a special prosecutor to hunt down a serial killer who preys on women in an Internet sex chat site.

FALSE DAWN: After his client confesses to a murder he didn't commit, Jake follows a bloody trail from Miami to Havana to discover the truth.

MORTAL SIN: Talk about conflicts of interest. Jake is sleeping with Gina Florio and defending her mob-connected husband in court.

RIPTIDE: Jake Lassiter chases a beautiful woman and stolen bonds from Miami to Maui.

FOOL ME TWICE: To clear his name in a murder investigation, Jake follows a trail of evidence that leads from Miami to buried treasure in the abandoned silver mines of Aspen, Colorado.

FLESH & BONES: Jake falls for his beautiful client even though he doubts her story. She claims to have recovered "repressed memories" of abuse...just before gunning down her father

LASSITER: Jake retraces the steps of a model who went missing 18 years earlier...after his one-night stand with her.

Visit the author's website at www.paul-levine.com for more information. While there, sign up for Paul Levine's newsletter and the chance to win free books, DVD's and other prizes.

About the Author

The author of 14 novels, Paul Levine won the John D. MacDonald fiction award and was nominated for the Edgar, Macavity, International Thriller, and James Thurber prizes. A former trial lawyer, he also wrote more than 20 episodes of the CBS military drama "JAG" and co-created the Supreme Court drama "First Monday" starring James Garner and Joe Mantegna. The critically acclaimed international bestseller "To Speak for the Dead" was his first novel. He is also the author of the "Solomon vs. Lord" series and the thriller "Illegal." His newest novels are "Lassiter," published in hardcover by Bantam, and "Paydirt," an e-book original crime thriller. Visit Paul Levine on the Web at http://www.paul-levine. com.

Made in the USA
Lexington, KY
09 October 2012